Please return/renew this item by the last date shown. Books may also be renewed by phone or internet.

💻 www.rbwm.gov.uk/home/leisure-and-culture/libraries

☎ 01628 796969 (library hours)

☎ 0303 123 0035 (24 hours)

ANATOMY OF A HERETIC

David Mark

An Aries Book

First published in the UK in 2022 by Head of Zeus Ltd
This paperback edition first published in 2022 by Head of Zeus Ltd,
part of Bloomsbury Publishing Plc

9 7 5 3 1 2 4 6 8

A CIP catalogue record for this book is available
from the British Library.

ISBN (E): 9781800244009
ISBN (PB): 9781801105316

Typeset by Siliconchips Services Ltd UK

Printed and bound in Great Britain by
CPI Group (UK) Ltd, Croydon CR0 4YY

Head of Zeus
First Floor East
5–8 Hardwick Street
London EC1R 4RG

WWW.HEADOFZEUS.COM

For Elora... (also known as Cory, Nico, Cinnamon, Lucy the Police Dog, Bad Kitty and Panther). With love and wonder.

'Make my breast transparent as pure crystal, that the world, jealous of me, may see the foulest thought my heart does hold.'

George Villiers, 1st Duke of Buckingham
(28 August 1592 – 23 August 1628)

PROLOGUE

Haarlem, Holland

March 4, anno 1628

She comes together like liquid metal; puddling into a quicksilver slick of jumbled senses. For a moment she is nothing and all. She hears with her flesh; sees with her tongue – tastes darkness in her every tingling pore.

That *smell*, suddenly. Burning meat and spilled blood: mildew and onions and ulcerated skin.

There is a fluttering in her chest, as if her ribs were full of caged, frightened birds.

'*...and thus, we commence God's work...*'

She feels something uncoiling in her guts. Thinks of butcher's shops and the meat market. Hears metal upon stone; offal upon earth: the slice and bubble and drip and suck of cleaver disconnecting muscle, fat and bone.

Applause, now. Palms slapping damply upon palms.

The swish and rustle of a sheet caught by the breeze.

Mannered, scholarly intonations at her ear.

A tugging at her wrists, as if a too-tight glove were being yanked free.

'...*apologise for the unseemly appearance of our specimen. The grime upon the skin was so unyielding that there were fears she may come apart were we to subject her repugnant flesh to our usual preparations, though as you can see, the eyes have been removed ahead of our commencement. You will remember from past lessons the disagreeableness of sightless eyes, and the unsettling effect those specimens have had upon some of the good burghers of this fair city...*'

Low, muttered utterances. The riverbed gurgle of genteel laughter. Soft exclamations and that dry, bat's-wing rustle of hushed conversation.

Dampness, now. Something wet and warm and sticky upon her flesh. The sensation of being touched, of being made and unmade; created and dismantled.

The drip of hot wax onto a polished, hardwood floor.

'...*and you shall see, as if by some heretical magic, that the action of clenching and unclenching the fist can be continued even after death, by the application of simple pressure here, and I may ask the good* Mijnheer *Klaasen to loan me his timepiece, you will see how the subject's finger and thumb can be manipulated to grip and release, grip and release...*'

A dream, she tells herself. A sickness dream. A punishment for the strong Rhenish wine and the spoiled oysters and the sleeping in damp clothes.

'...*our specimen clearly bears the mark of that most shameful of diseases. You will know that we have been the beneficiaries of numerous criminals whose unworthy lives have been surpassed by the gifts they have lent our Guild in death. Though this poor wretch is unknown to me, a man of science cannot help but note numerous scars beneath the dirt upon her skin – scars that date to childhood, ill-set bones, brandings, the mark of the whip... It would be a cold-hearted man who did not say a silent prayer that the horrors endured in life are now at their end...'*

She tries to wake. Tries to push through into consciousness.

'...a sharp blade, making the incision along the ridge of the hairline, ensuring to cut through the epidermis as if separating chicken from the bone...'

She cannot quite recall herself. Cannot quite fathom whether this is dream, or the presage to wakefulness. Had she taken drink? There is the memory of something sweet upon her tongue. The ghost of flavour, treacly, earthy: sugar and skin and fresh-dug mushrooms.

A sensation in her scalp, now. The feeling of being dragged like a sack of grain.

'...we have sweet-smelling candles above but you will no doubt wish to cover your nostrils lest this odour offend...'

And now, at last, there is fear. She cannot move. She feels pinioned, trapped, as if beneath the weight of so many stones.

'...and here, you will see a section of skull that has built up into a ridge, covering a lattice of fractures, their sharpened edges perhaps grazing the tissue of the brain... we will endeavour to open the skull in tomorrow's lecture, for the edification of those who are considering joining our number and embarking upon a career in anatomy...'

A memory now. A soap bubble, popping on a scrubbed

step. She had celebrated, had she not? Drunk deep and well on Loth Vogel's money. There had been a tumble or two. She had bedded the old widower while wearing only her new astrakhan cape, soft as fresh-fallen snow. Had there been cross words? Some accusation that she had tarnished the reputation of a goodly, grieving woman? She knows herself to be vicious in drink, and there are few moments when she could place her hand on the Bible and swear herself sober.

She had stumbled from his bed and out into the warren of tumbledown alleyways, the honeycomb of tiny, crowded streets. Out into the Bleacheries: women stooped and wrinkled beyond their years, coughing and fitting in two-room hovels, reeking of the poisons in which they dye their linens. She had staggered on, into the centre of Haarlem, seeking company, seeking drink. Her footsteps had worked their way past the splendid *Grote Kerk of Sint Bavo*, yelling her drunken greetings to the men of the fish market and meat hall, unsure if they were rising early or retiring late. Then south, onto the quiet grandeur of Grote Houtstraat.

She sees herself. *Heyltgen Jansdr*. Sees this slight, filth-rimmed woman: clumps of hair missing from her weeping, patchy scalp; ridiculous in her fine cape and her new, ill-fitting boots; her lace collar dangling from her hand. Sees herself standing before the apothecary's shop, just as she had on many nights. She had planted her feet at the doorstep and summoned a crowd of smirking gawpers, cursing the apothecary and his grieving wife, beating her fists, hurling stones, screeching profanities about the master and mistress of the fine property. She had done all that Loth Vogel had paid her to do.

A wave of regret, now: rising like bile. The child had been a happy little thing. Golden-haired, bright-eyed – little meaty fingers probing everywhere, twisting at her curls, reaching under her ragged smock for her dugs, pink gums fastening onto her chewy, still-sweet nipples. She had been a good nurse, had she not? Cared for him, sung to him, stroked his little cheek with her grimy knuckles and held his gaze while he fed. When he took ill, she did all she could to soothe his agonies. She bathed the lesions upon his skin, applied cool cloths to his burning brow, placed her hands over his eyes so he could not see the apparitions that burst forth from the empty air and sent him into great paroxysms of terror. She had done more for him than his father, whose bitter potions and glistening unguents only served to make his pain increase.

His death, when it came, was a mercy. It was the will of the Lord – of that there could be no doubt. And yet the surgeon had declared the child to be a victim of that most repulsive of afflictions. Even as his precious body was lowered into the earth at the Church of St Anna, word had spread. The boy had succumbed to syphilis.

And now her mind is full of him.

Jeronimus Cornelisz.

The apothecary.

The very devil.

She sees him now. Sees the slight man with the pinched face and the painful, fish-scaled skin. Sees his delicate, willowy figure: pursed mouth and bow legs and those pale, watchful, mismatched eyes. She had never thought to fear him. There may have been an eeriness about the way he lingered in dark spaces to watch her at her work, but she had never known a man without a repulsive habit or two. She certainly never feared his wrath.

He had emerged from the darkness as if made of shadows, smiling that crooked smile and wrapped in the coal-dark cloak of his trade. He held a bottle in his hand – black gloves obscuring the whiteness of his skin. And for the first time, she saw a glimpse of that malignancy that he so expertly concealed. As she stood in his presence, she had felt the nearness of something powerful – something that seemed to flow out of him, adding a crackle of light to the air around him. She had thought of the way river slime can emit a greenish light on pitch-dark nights. He seemed somehow emboldened; somehow *more*.

'I commend you,' he had said, his voice seeming to arrive in the centre of her head. It had spread out like fire, warming her, the edges of her vision tinged with a corona of gentle, red-gold flame. 'Drink with me, Heyltgen. Toast your victory. Marvel at the desecration of your fallen master.'

And she had drunk. Drunk deep. Sobbed and wailed and fallen against his bony shoulder as she spilled out every detail of the cruel plot to which she had been party. She remembers the way he had swaddled her in his cloak. Remembers falling into darkness to the sound of that low, insidious voice. Nothing she told him had come as a surprise. He had always known that it was Vogel, his business rival, who had engineered the campaign of slander. But he had taken satisfaction in her confession.

The words come back to her, causing her every nerve to stiffen.

'You have taken everything from me, Heyltgen. You and Vogel. And you shall receive your reward. You shall experience suffering of which the devil himself could barely conceive. The drink that addles your mind is a brew of which I am most proud. You will know of nightshade, but mixed with a little seed of bulrush and leopard's bane, and stirred with the shinbone of a drowned sailor, and it is a potion that imitates death so perfectly, even the good men of the Surgeon's Guild will not know the difference until they have you open, and your insides in their clammy palms. I trust you will take comfort in the knowledge that what you endure will be for the advancement of science. As they unfold you, dismantle you, yank at the tendons beneath your flesh and make merry with the crevices in your skull – they will be learning much about the human form.

'You will have heard of the anatomy lessons, which have proven so popular in Amsterdam? Here in Haarlem, they are not such grand affairs, but there will still be many goodly men to witness your dissection. They have paid handsomely for the opportunity to look upon your vile flesh. That coin shall be put to good use. I am to depart the Provinces. I tire of the sanctimony and hypocrisy of our land. I shall begin again; begin anew. I am bound for the New World – bound for a destiny that was foretold.'

And now the pain comes. Fire burns beneath her flesh: her bones white-hot as if cut out and thrown upon the fire. She understands. Remembers. Recalls those final words, and knows why she cannot see: why she feels cold and damp, unclothed, exposed.

'...there will now be opportunity to handle these organs, and though we shall endeavour to clean them, I trust you have a handkerchief with which to wipe the gore from your fingers. The temptation for keepsakes is strong, but there *is a six guilder fine for anybody caught absconding with one of this good lady's organs, and I must also warn you all from my own experience that the black bile of the liver has a tendency to stain the lining of even the finest cloak...'*

And she feels fingers in her guts. Feels herself being unravelled like rope. Feels the soft, warm parts of herself being removed like fish from a barrel.

The sharp, ice-bright agony of sharp steel against her brow.

Firm, unyielding fingers gripping the flesh of her scalp.

The gruesome, burning agony of flesh tearing as her skin is unpeeled, inch by inch, drawn like curtains – unrolled across the bloody whiteness of her skull and furled down across her features, eyeless sockets exposed in tiny increments as the physician pares her down to muscle and tendons and bone.

There is a moment, as her heart is plucked from her ribs and held aloft for inspection, that she fancies she hears a clear voice: a gasp of alarm. '...it beats... she's alive, her mouth... she gasps, oh merciful God... she's alive!'

And then there is nothing but flame and pain, and darkness.

PART ONE

I

Marshalsea Prison, London

July 29, 1628

A darkened cell: the air thick and murky as bog water. The stink of captive men. Of spoiled food and weeping flesh; of open wounds and human waste.

A single candle gutters high up one sodden, crumbling wall, softly illuminating the green slime that dangles from the roof joists like the hair of drowned sailors.

A mulch of sodden rushes carpets the damp stone floor, saturated with sweat and puke and piss.

And here, squatting barefoot, the remnants of a fine-featured gentleman. He is wiry, still strong. His hair tumbles in ringlets, framing high cheekbones and playful, intelligent eyes. He seems out of place, here. He has the air of a bird of paradise chained in a privy.

His name, for now, is Nicolaes de Pelgrom. He has been prisoner in this reeking clink for the past six weeks and has still not had opportunity to present his case to a judge. He hopes fate intervenes before such a day comes. He is not entirely innocent of the charges against him. He did, indeed, inflict a mortal wound upon a member of the City Watch and found opportunity to draw his dagger across the throat of a Limehouse lawyer. But in both cases, he feels entirely justified in his actions. In the first instance, he was defending himself. In the second, the victim was a swindling bastard who fully deserved to have his fat neck split to the bone. More importantly, in both cases he was following orders. That those orders were whispered in his ear by a man he would sooner die than identify, remains a problem to which he has yet to fathom a solution.

'Drink, Pelgrom. Drink good and deep. You know the game, sir. Ink and parchment can be yours if you just guess right...'

Nicolaes considers the two pewter tankards he holds in his hands. Both contain roughly the same level of frothy brown liquid. Both reek of earth and hops and ammonia. He sucks on his lower lip, thoughtfully. He attempts to remain aloof and unruffled: a gentleman cherishing the honeyed scents of a finely aged Armagnac.

A voice from behind the locked door, the words arriving in a spray.

'Choose, you bastard lubberwort.'

Nicolaes smiles, sweetly. Ignores the piggish grunts of the jailer. Swills the tankards. Hears the sudden bout of coughing from the assemblage of rags and bones that huddles, half-dead, in the shadows.

At length, the coughing subsides. Becomes a weak, rasping voice.

'Have you ever thought of trusting in Providence, Nicolaes?'

Nicolaes smiles at the Papist. Feels a surge of pity for the dying man and hides it behind a smile. 'Providence, Jacob?' he asks, his air flamboyant. He gestures at their surroundings, stirring the air with a grimy hand. 'The temptress seduced me when I was but a boy. I consider myself poxed by Her affections.'

'Heresy...' whispers Jacob, instantly.

Nicolaes blows him a kiss, putting the tankards down upon the reeds. 'So says the man who goes to the rope for killing a soldier with a crucifix.'

Jacob gives a twitch of a grin, showing off rotting gums. He settles back into the straw, looking with glossy yellow eyes at the cell where he shall spend his final day. The dank space is as long as two men and half as wide.

'Drink, you limp-wristed fop!'

Nicolaes looks to the doorway. Runs his finger around the lips of both tankards. He smiles, as if remembering some jest made at a gathering of gentlemen: some flirtatious comment spoken by a maiden from behind a silk fan. He raises his fist to his face. Inside, crushed to his palm, is the little nosegay he has crafted from the assorted twigs and berries that have blown into the cell from the small, solitary window. The perfume is almost gone. Soon he will have no barrier against the stench that assails him. Each breath pulls the miasma further inside him: a green-brown stew of saltwater, mud, unwashed flesh and the high, iron reek of bad blood. He will grow sick soon. He will lose the ability to pretend. And then, they will come for him.

'How do you see her, Nicolaes?' asks Jacob, quietly. 'This Goddess Providence in whose name you damn your soul.'

Nicolaes steeples his long fingers, 'Golden-haired,' he says, an exaggerated whimsy to his voice. 'Green-eyed. Perhaps an elegant neck. That sparkle of wit and devilment in her eyes. Inquisitive, certainly – the sort who makes for a dangerous lover, nipping at your earlobe, scratching at your back, telling you of the other lovers who have pleased her better. Ah yes, Jacob, Providence is a beauty who has bedded me well.'

Jacob manages a laugh. Spits, foully, onto the rushes. 'The Lord hears all,' he says. 'He hears your heresies. Hears our prayers.'

'If he hears you, Jacob, could he not intervene? You, who has done nothing but worship in the way you were taught. You who has endured so much in His name?'

Jacob tries to talk but his tongue is too swollen. He begins to cough. Hacks up something vile and spits into his hand: jewels of clotted red speckling his beard. Nicolaes puts down the tankards and moves to his side, palm upon his shoulder, afraid to hold him close in case he crushes his fragile bones. There is barely any meat upon him.

Jacob manages a smile, wheezing: red seaming his eyes. 'You mock me with your prettiness, Nicolaes,' he croaks, wiping his hands upon his bare chest. 'Look at you. I've only seen your like in the glass of our church. I know you to be a gentleman and yet you carry yourself with the bearing of a common soldier. You can philosophise and quote scripture, and yet when you strip and scrub yourself with the rushes I see the scars of a fighting man. You have delicate fingers and broken knuckles and you watch that window as if awaiting the return of a ship. I die today, Nicolaes. You have nothing to fear should you confide in me.'

'Truth, Jacob?' he asks, ebullient and animated – the perfect English gentleman. 'Why that is a currency worth more than gold! More than the bulbs that make men insultingly rich at the markets in Amsterdam! Should I impoverish myself for no more than sentiment?'

'Please, Nicolaes...'

Nicolaes looks at the pitiful figure in the damp straw and drops the pretence.

'Dr Lambe,' he says, in a new voice. 'It was my honour to protect him from those who misunderstood his gifts.' He suddenly sounds like a common soldier: his accent a soft Dutch. Every "s" becomes a soft exhalation. 'Yes, I have seen battle. Yes, I have had some schooling. I am, as you would say, a Hollander, but have considered myself an Englishman these past years. I perform the tasks required by my retainer – my skills and my loyalty purchased with gold.'

Jacob looks at him, his breathing shallow. 'Please, Nicolaes.' He coughs. 'To distract me, in my final hours. I have spent these days with a spectre, a doll. Please, be true. Tell me of yourself. Your age, perhaps.'

Nicolaes shrugs. 'I believe I am twenty-three, though my mother kept no record. I doubt it was a date she wished to remember.'

Jacob wrinkles his face, tasting the words for truth. 'Thank you,' he whispers. 'Thank you for all you have done to fill my final days with colour.'

Nicolaes squeezes his friend's arm. Stands and gazes up to the small barred window. For a moment his thoughts drift outside, down to the river and the tangle of crowded streets where he failed the man it was his duty to protect. He has a sudden vision of Dr Lambe, splendid in his great cape and velvet hat, whirling and cursing at the mob who struck at him with stones and sticks, boots and fists, stamping him bloodily into the ground and bludgeoning him until that clever, avuncular face was nothing but tenderised meat. Nicolaes had fought as many as he could. He had broken skulls and struck out with sword and pistol, roaring at the crowd to stay back, beseeching his companion to run. But his voice was lost amid the great crashing wave of hatred. Lambe was a witch, they said. Lambe was a monster. Lambe slurped the blood of little girls. Lambe had enchanted the king and his courtiers. Lambe was the Duke of Buckingham's creature, and as everybody knew, Buckingham was the devil himself.

When the bricks began to fly, skill with sword counted for nothing. Nicolaes had been crushed by the tide of hate-filled men: beaten down then trampled into the sticky brown earth. He had woken in Marshalsea Prison. His sword was gone; his purse, hat and pistols, all swallowed up by the mud of the Thames. Munce, the fat, hog-jowled turnkey, had taken real pleasure in telling him that Lambe was dead, and that he was facing the rope for his part in the melee. He had not known that the man who coshed him was a watchman until he had stuck his blade into his belly. But he had been entirely sure of the identity of the lawyer. The bastard had refused the doctor sanctuary as he fled the mob, denying him shelter within unless he gave him a fortune in coin and trinkets. When Lambe handed over what little he had, the lawyer had closed the door on him.

Nicolaes had been attending to his master when the city apprentices gathered their reinforcements and descended. The fight had been bloody and short. Munce has regaled him with descriptions of the state of the dead man's corpse – mounted for public enjoyment on the city walls. Told him how the eighty-year-old alchemist had been beaten so badly by the mob that his eyes were rent from their sockets. Through the window, Nicolaes has heard the songs of celebration. There are men out there praising themselves for having done a Christian thing in the murder of an old man.

Nicolaes gives his attention back to Jacob. His ragged jerkin hangs open to reveal the ugly criss-cross of weeping, half-scabbed scars upon his pale, hairless chest. He has been relieved of his crucifix, but the guards, eager to provide him comfort in his final days, have taken the time to carve a replacement into his wicked flesh.

Nicolaes turns away and retreats to his place by the wall. Looks, again, at the two brimming tankards. 'That one,' he announces, firmly, pointing to the beaker on the left. He lifts it and takes a swig. He turns to face the door. 'Munce, my friend. I believe you now owe me two pencils and a sheaf of parchment.'

Munce spits a string of peaty saliva through the opening. 'You'll have that taste on your tongue all day. Small price to pay.' He presses his face to the bars, his flabby, sweaty skin oozing through the gaps like rising cake. 'Won't be long now,' he leers, looking down. 'You still have that dandified swagger to you but it won't last. Weeks, months, years – they do things to the skin. You'll lose your bloom. And I mean to find occasion to smash those teeth; I give you my oath upon it.'

Nicolaes spreads his hands. 'Munce, my diary is clear. Please, if you have no pressing engagements of your own, I implore you, do try and make good on your threats. I tire of empty promises.'

Munce spits again. Turns away from the hole.

Nicolaes waits for the sound of the key in the lock, hoping that the big, meaty grotesque will choose today to finally deliver upon his threats of violence.

'He won't come, Nicolaes,' says Jacob, his throat dry. 'Still too much life in you. He'll wait until you're broken. Until you're no threat. Then the pain will begin.'

Nicolaes rubs at his lips. Spits, and scours his tongue upon the stained sleeve of his shirt. Picks up the other tankard and drains it.

'You chose wrong?'

'No.' Nicolaes sighs. 'There was no choice to be made. He takes his pleasures in seeing me drink. Pisses in both tankards.'

'And how do you know he will honour the terms of the lost bet?'

Nicolaes shrugs. 'Everybody has their own code, Jacob. And Munce is, in his own grotesque way, a man who respects the rules of the game.'

They sit in silence. After a time, Jacob's head lolls onto Nicolaes's shoulder. He presses his cheek against the other man's gritty, filth-streaked hair. Closes his eyes and listens to the muffled sounds that bleed in through the great stone walls of the prison. He fancies he can hear horses: big, dinner-plate hooves clattering down upon the dry earth and loose stone that leads to the big portcullis and the wooden doors of the jail. From nearby comes the muttering of the faceless, nameless imbecile who occupies an adjacent cell. He talks to himself throughout the day, conducting lengthy conversations with an entire company of second-selves.

Nicolaes turns his attention back to his cellmate. The execution is scheduled for today: another Papist lost to the rope. Nicolaes is half tempted to spare the executioner his work. It would take no more than a moment to snap Jacob's neck or to press a hand to his mouth and nose and hold him fast. It is only his own tenderness for the man that stops him from acting. He has grown fond of Jacob. Nicolaes has never killed in anger, nor stopped the heart of a good man. He fancies that to add Jacob's name to the tally of dead men would be to invite a decent soul to join the horde of villains, ghouls and liars who linger within him.

He shakes his head, gathering his wits. Pulls himself upright and gently lays Jacob down upon the soggy, lice-infested straw. Walks silently to the darkest recess of the cell. He reaches down and removes his good leather boots. Unrolls the silk stockings and pushes his hand down to the toe. His fingers find the silver chain and he deftly pulls the necklace and pendant free. It is too dark to see the picture within but it does Nicolaes some good to sit and hold the humble silver chain and press the pendant to his lips.

He thinks of the orphanage. Of the almshouse. The teachers at the Latin school in Leiden, telling him he had been chosen for a great honour. He was to be apprenticed to a scholar in London; a great man eager to give back to a foundling some portion of the good fortune he had lately enjoyed. Nicolaes hadn't given a damn about the apprenticeship but he had delighted in the chance to visit England. There, he intended to find his father: the pitiless young gentleman who had bought his mother's virginity at an inn on the Amsterdam road.

Footsteps, suddenly. The thud of heavy feet hitting stone.

Munce is running, thinks Nicolaes, looking around for something with which to defend himself. *Munce has never run.*

Nicolaes drops the locket back into his sock and yanks on his boot. He glances at Jacob. *There's still time*, he thinks. *End him now. Spare him the block. Spare them all the satisfaction…*

Munce's face, at the hatch, grooves and sweat in his bulbous forehead, eyes roving madly. His gaze alights upon Nicolaes.

The sound of keys. More footsteps. Raised voices.

The door opens and Munce tumbles in. Fat, toothless Munce, with his big, hairy pig-trotter fists and a face like rancid pork.

'Pelgrom… Pelgrom… I've been good to you, have I not? We jest, of course, but it was all sport, as any friends are wont to do… I am a humble man, a father, a good man…'

Nicolaes rubs at his chin. He has been days without shaving but there is little growth upon his smooth, young flesh. His moustache and pointed beard are a little unkempt but after a month of sleeping upon a wooden board and sipping on piss and ale, he forgives himself the aberration. He pushes his hands through his long, dark hair and pinches some colour into his cheeks. Slowly, he lets himself smile.

'We have visitors, I assume?'

'He spoke of you with fondness,' stammers Munce. 'Demanded to be brought straight here – how could I know? I knew you a gentleman, but the company you kept, the circumstances... the sins of your master... the devil himself...'

'You mean the good doctor?' asks Nicolaes, sweetly. 'An aged man killed by a mob of empty-skulled arseworms?'

'He summoned demons! Could see the future in a water glass. Could create storms that whipped the dead from their graves and filled the air with bones and gore!'

'He was a man of science,' says Nicolaes. 'He was a man of learning. He was my friend.'

'Please, Pelgrom, please...' Munce falls to his knees. Tugs at Nicolaes's shirt front. Tries to grab his hand to slobber fawning kisses upon the knuckles. Nicolaes shakes him off. Looks up as a figure appears in the doorway.

'Good God, Nic, I knew you for a charming man but to have the jailer upon his knees before you...'

The man in the doorframe was once considered the handsomest in all creation. Vulpine features, piercing eyes, athletic build and with lips that promise the taste of honey, he has been favourite to two kings. He shared King James' bed and held his hand as he died. He is George Villiers: a politician of vision, trickery and endless ambition. He is the Duke of Buckingham, chief adviser to King Charles, and among the most powerful men in England. And Nicolaes de Pelgrom is his most valuable agent.

Nicolaes looks past the scabby, lice-jewelled head of the turnkey who has denied him food and pissed in his morning ale.

Allows himself a moment's satisfaction as he greets his benefactor.

'Hello, Uncle.'

2

Nieuwmarkt, Amsterdam

July 29, 1628

A heavy grey sky: all coiled rope and dirty stone. Greasy, close, the summer air pushes down hard upon this fan-shaped tangle of tall brown buildings and greenish canals.

Men and women clad in earthy tones: a collage of damp autumn shades. Coffee brown, tobacco-brown, dun and cocoa: capes and mantles and cloaks all stained the shade of freshly dug graves.

The air, a miasma of warring odours: offal and blood, fresh herring and crushed fruit; the high delicate tang of cut stems and spilled petals; horses and sweaty leather, burning wood and smouldering sea coal.

A place of chatter and shouts; of barter and disagreement.

A place where one may succeed in losing oneself.

And *here*. A stick figure. Insubstantial. Not much more than a series of slashes made with a lump of charcoal.

This is Jeronimus Cornelisz.

He moves through the market at a leisurely pace, his manner untroubled: a gentleman taking the air. He carries himself as a man of significance: of some success and no little ambition. Anybody witnessing his progress might remark upon his curiously linear progress. He does not alter his path – the merchants, the traders, the stall-keepers and servants, all drifting out of his way as if some higher power were softly blowing them in the direction that best suits his passage. That same observer might note the curious absence of second glances. Cornelisz is disfigured, his countenance misshapen and twisted: his lumpen head topping a high-shouldered, bony frame. He wears his black cape as if wrapped up against the cold, even as a varnish of sweat, thick as ointment, greases his ridged cheekbones and wrinkled brow. And yet he attracts no attention. Nobody nudges their fellows to nod in the direction of the small, red-haired man whose face is scaled with the silver and pink of unhealed burns. His jawline is a shimmer of raised, bubbling skin: a great boot print stamped from the brim of his hat down to the point of his neat beard. His eyelashes and eyebrows are entirely absent. The eyes themselves are mismatched, as if spooned from the sockets of two different dead men. One is a haunting, livid blue; the other an absolute black.

But nobody truly looks at Cornelisz. Nobody sees. He passes through the marketplace like a small, intimate pestilence, insinuating himself into mouths and nostrils: manifesting as a moment's foulness upon the tongue, or the sensation of spider legs, scuttling upon necks and wrists and hips. He is a sensation of icy breath upon the neck, a whiff of brimstone and something gone bad. People turn moments after he has passed by, momentarily unsettled, as if they have come upon a headstone that carries their own name.

Cornelisz, in return, sees *them*. Every single detail of every little thing he has ever witnessed is stored in the great gallery of his mind. Cornelisz can retreat into the cool of his memory and gaze at scenes from any moment of his thirty-plus years of life. He can consider inconsequential memories from new angles, different perspectives – focusing the eye of his mind upon new and hitherto uninspected segments of memory. He is able to look upon the bookshelves of his father's study and see things that, as a boy, he did not even know were there. Were he so inclined, he could return to the family home in Friesland and see again the Moorish sorcerer who took his father's money and promised to apply a healing salve to the boy's mottled face. He could watch the young Jeronimus Cornelisz buck and writhe and froth as the metallic unguent ate into his skin and caused his flesh to pucker and split and tear itself into a labyrinth of weeping lesions. He could see the look of pure horror upon his father's face and enjoy again the brutal horse-whipping that was inflicted upon the Moor before he was nailed to the barn door.

Eventually, Cornelisz departs the bustle of the marketplace and makes his way through a cluster of tightening streets to a row of dilapidated taverns – the paint upon their wooden shutters peeling like sunburnt skin and each door firmly shuttered, set back beneath brick-and-tile awnings that jut out over the narrow, horse-shit-strewn alleyway.

Cornelisz runs his pale hand over his cloak. He has vials

of six different poisons sewn into the lining and a sharp scalpel is wrapped about his wrist, ready to leap to his palm should it be required. He has practised the action time and again and fancies he will be able to flash the blade in less time than it takes for a heart to beat. Whether one cut would be enough to stop instant and lethal retribution from the man he is summoned to meet, remains open to speculation.

Three loud raps with his knuckles, followed by three short bangs with his fist.

The sound of bolts sliding back.

The jangle of keys.

The door opens a fraction and he is assailed by the reek of incense, of smoke and darkness and spice and sex. Two ice-blue eyes peer out from the gloom, assessing his worth.

'You,' comes the voice, and it is followed by a high, cackling laugh. 'You've won me some money, apothecary. *I* said you'd come back. He didn't. Said you wouldn't be stupid enough, and yet here you are. I'd say you looked well, but that would be a lie, wouldn't it? Instead, I shall say that you look as I remember you, and for that, you have my condolences.'

Cornelisz spreads his arms. Gives a grander bow than the old procuress is used to.

'It is my delight to again feast upon your own beauty, madam. Had I but world enough and time, I would drop to my knees and praise the good Lord for creating such a vision of true perfection. Might I ask – how does your father fare? Is it Michael or Gabriel? I presume you are indeed the daughter of an archangel?'

She laughs again, the sound an echo of the ugly shriek that emerges from the opening door. There are lights set in the wall behind her and the soft golden glow illuminates her features.

Cornelisz makes a great display of being overcome by her beauty. She wears a dark brown cloak over a discoloured blue smock and there is a length of white linen wrapped about her head instead of a cap. It is hitched up on one side to expose the ugly ridge of scarred flesh that pokes out from her matted grey hair: a seashell of puckered pink skin where her ear should be. She has been punished time and again for breaching the public decency laws but has never considered finding any other form of employment. She is past fifty now, glad to be alive, and still the very best at pairing customers with girls, boys or whatever takes their fancy.

'This way, if you've forgotten,' says the *koppelaarster*, as she takes a lantern from a bracket in the wall.

'I am your humble servant,' he says, bowing low.

'Aye, you might very well be.'

There is a smell of damp linens and ammonia around her; a halo of pungency that makes Cornelisz catch his breath. She laughs as she sees his discomfort and rearranges her cloak. A pitiful mewling comes from within the folds. She opens the wrapped gown and tickles the skinny grey cat that she holds against her wrinkled, naked skin. 'I've a Frenchman comes on Tuesdays. Pays five *stuivers* to be allowed to kill something while Zwaantie pumps his shaft. Takes all sorts to make a world, doesn't it? I'll be sad to see this one go, if I'm honest. Might send one of the young girls out for a chicken. At least it serves a purpose when it's done.'

Cornelisz smiles and follows her down a low-ceilinged hallway with exposed timbers and sagging mortar – the flickering light illuminating a gallery of framed oil paintings. Cornelisz glimpses men, women, animals, children all cavorting in grotesque parodies of pleasure. The floor is stone but covered with rushes and straw and a curious shushing sound drifts up as the old bawd disturbs them with her skirts. Cornelisz, a few steps behind her, passes two closed doors and a low stone arch hung with brightly coloured cloth. From behind come the sounds of pleasure. He permits himself a sneaky glance as they pass beyond. He sees a small, dark-skinned woman, bare-breasted, squatting above a monstrous mass of belly and body hair, half lost in a mound of gaudily coloured silk cushions. His hat, cape and boots are laid neatly at the side of the mattress.

'Found her in Antwerp, that one,' says the bawd, catching his eye. 'She's got a surprise between her legs, if you follow me. Makes twice as much as the other girls. Novelty is always expensive.'

Cornelisz tears his eyes away from the scene. Follows the crone up a short flight of steps and then waits, breathless, as she raps upon the wooden door.

'Go on in then,' says the bawd, moving herself back against the wall to allow Cornelisz to pass. He does so, pausing as they are sandwiched together in the closeness of the hall. She wrinkles her nose, disturbed by his sudden proximity. He sees her looking from one eye to the other, unsettled by the peculiar colours. 'I had a horse like that when I was a girl,' she says, quietly, sticking her tongue through a gap in her teeth. 'It was a biter. Sweetest nature for months on end and then he'd throw you and trample you where you stood. Sink his teeth into your arm and not let go until you whipped the bastard bloody.'

Cornelisz leans closer, his lips almost touching the puckered scar tissue. 'Life is cruel, madam,' he says, with sincerity. 'I weep for your suffering.'

She pulls away, suddenly cold. She is a good judge of men.

A voice from behind the door, low and powerful and used to being obeyed, says, 'Come in, you're letting the good smell out.'

Cornelisz gives a bow and pushes his way into the little studio room where the thief, pimp and occasional murderer named Speelman Nacht conducts his business. Cornelisz has been inside before but the little room is still an assault upon the senses. Cornelisz's gift for perfect recollection is sorely tested by the sheer chaos of the room, crammed from floor to ceiling and wall to wall with curiosities, extraordinary objects and endless peculiar luxuries that are rarely in Speelman's possession for long. Painted a shade of green that makes Cornelisz think of infected wounds, Speelman's sanctum is a treasure trove. Cornelisz runs his eye over exotic birds in gilded cages, animals from the new world, bottles of spirits brewed by savages in islands still undiscovered.

His pulse quickens at the sheer opulence of possibility. Here a man might purchase sculptures of cherubim engaged in unnatural acts with beasts of antiquity or ancient texts bound in human skin, their pages covered in a language long since lost. Upon his last visit, Cornelisz was privy to the unwrapping of a chest containing six heads sent back from the New World by traders; their reddish skin marked with pigment and teeth filed to points. Speelman had not found the package satisfactory. He had specified that he wanted Iroquois squaws, not braves.

There is little in Amsterdam that cannot be purchased. The streets are alive with men and women boasting of their ability to procure whatever a customer may desire. And each is in the pay of Speelman Nacht.

Nacht reclines on an elegant leather chair. His legs are elevated, his bare feet resting on the back of a stuffed animal that looks to Cornelisz like the offspring of a pig and a horse. He's somewhere north of fifty; fat and pink and blond. There's something carnal about him, something that speaks of abattoirs; of slapped flesh and gristle. His face is delineated by a finely trimmed beard; stained almost yellow by tobacco. The facial hair inserts some vague sense of geometry into the meaty blandness of his features. His neck makes Cornelisz think of newborn children, all grease and fluid and folds. He wears spectacles upon a chain, two circles of polished glass set in a golden frame encrusted with sparkling jewels. He cannot read, but the spectacles – remarkable new devices favoured by scholars and poets – are sure signs of wealth. He is mostly naked, wrapped in a fine shimmering fleece, his manhood covered by a gaudily coloured porcelain bowl filled to the brim with exotic fruits and a curious, jellified confection dusted with sugar.

'Mijnheer Cornelisz,' sighs Nacht, cocking his head to better examine the man who stands by the door, twisting his hat between his fingers. 'I would ask you to sit but I have not yet found opportunity to purchase a chair built around a white-hot poker.'

'A fine jest,' begins Cornelisz, bowing low, his whole being seeming to ooze with unspoken praise. 'My, do you not have the look of a veritable sultan! How regally you do sit in your throne of unequalled splendour. I only regret that my presence in this, thy cave of wonders, does sully your many treasures. To wit, I would hasten my departure. And so, my good and gracious friend, might I first...'

The fat man holds up his hand, insisting upon silence. Looks, bemusedly, at his own raised hand. 'There is an itch in my finger, sir – an itch that demands I reach for my pistol and put a ball through your eye.'

Cornelisz twitches out a gracious smile. Bows low, his hands out to his sides so that for a moment he looks like a tar-caked seabird. He flicks a glance at the places of concealment within the crowded room. Dazzling silks hang from shimmering poles set in brackets in the ceiling. Some are patterned with dizzying, glorious curls and Cornelisz has no doubt that each conceals a man, or woman, who would end his life in a moment were Nacht to give the word.

'I am here as a matter of respect,' wheedles Cornelisz, bowing and rising, bowing and rising: now a chicken pecking for corn. 'Here to put right any confusion that may...'

Nacht spits out the flesh of some unfamiliar fruit. It lands on his belly. He inserts a jewelled finger into his mouth and picks at his back teeth. There is a noise like a lamprey sucking on a toe. 'Respect, Cornelisz? You do have a gift for finding alternative interpretations. You are here because I insisted upon it.'

'And I, as your humble servant, am glad to have opportunity to...'

'Stop your drooling, apothecary. Stop your bowing and scraping and your pretence of deference.' His voice starts to rise, circles of colour expanding upon his fat cheeks. He spits again, clearly thinking afresh of all the ways in which

Cornelisz has visited strife upon his business. Performs some complex arithmetic behind his eyes, weighing the balance of possibilities. 'Is "respect" a better word than "fear", I wonder? Do you find yourself less of a gelding if you tell yourself you are visiting an old friend rather than responding to a summons from a man who could have you sliced thin enough to slip beneath the door!'

Cornelisz raises his head. Looks past Speelman to where a human foetus floats in a glass jar filled with water. He takes comfort in its nearness. He had presented Speelman with the unborn child as a gift upon his last visit to Amsterdam. He finds that people are more amenable when somebody has taken the time to procure something truly thoughtful.

'We have served one another well, have we not?' asks Cornelisz, dabbing at one of his lesions with a swatch of cloth. 'Have I not provided you with suitable potions and powders? Have I not allowed you to inflict pleasures and pains upon those whose lives you hold in your palm? This has been a successful friendship. If there is some misunderstanding over the events that occurred in the spring, then it is my honour to provide you with clarity today.'

Speelman laughs, enjoying the performance. He runs his fingers over his moustache, pulling at the waxed points. 'Cornelisz, you paid me to ensure the delivery of a body. You paid to have a syphilitic corpse transferred into the hands of the Guild of Anatomists in Haarlem. As you knew then, and know now, a man in my employ is responsible for delivering the corpses of hanged criminals to the anatomists for such purposes. It should have been a simple transaction. And yet you concealed your true purpose, Jeronimus. You did not tell me that the poor bitch's heart would be pulled from her chest still beating. Nor did you tell me that the letter my courier delivered to Loth Vogel would be dusted with poison. My man was dead within a week, drowned in his own blood having ingested your potions. Vogel's lingering and colourful death is something that will be talked about for years to come! Questions are being asked, for Loth Vogel was a man of consequence and the anatomists still shriek in their dreams following the horrors of their last public dissection. The burghers of Leiden have begun inquiries. Where did my man procure the corpse? Was not the victim the self-same wet nurse who led the poor gentle apothecary to bankruptcy? I knew you would flee, Jeronimus Cornelisz – but to flee here? To my city? And then to speak to me of respect...'

Cornelisz tires of affecting the mannerisms of a timid petitioner. Straightens his back and shakes his head. 'I believe I have had my sufficiency of insults, Speelman. I look around me and see a fortune in curiosities, and I find myself wondering if perhaps one of these charms has somehow addled your wits? Do you not recall the origin of the monies that have allowed you to prosper?'

Nacht pops his fingers into his juicy mouth and sucks upon them, staring at Cornelisz thoughtfully. 'You will no doubt be referring to our mutual friend,' he says, smiling. 'The God of Flame.'

Cornelisz raises his hands, palms up, then makes a gesture with his right hand, carving a serpent into the air. It is a genuflection conducted with the same reverence as a Catholic crossing themselves in the cool of a church.

'You smile as you speak of him,' says Cornelisz, staring

at the fat man, a sudden dark malice in his eyes. 'You mock the title that was bestowed upon him.'

Nacht rolls his eyes. 'Jeronimus, I beg you – do not beat this tired drum. Johannes van der Beeck is no Messiah. He is no Rosicrucian. He is a half-decent artist who found a way to line his pockets and indulge in his own debaucheries by telling rich men what they want to hear. The man you call Torrentius lingers in a cell recanting every heresy I ever heard him speak.'

Cornelisz looks down at the skin upon the back of his hand. Watches the hairs rise. Tastes blood and bile and forces himself to remain still. He wants to smash the vials of poison in his cloak and throw himself upon Speelman Nacht like a dark cloud of private plague.

'He was betrayed by those who lost sight of his message,' he says, teeth locked around the words like a dog gnawing upon a stick. 'If they had but the courage to truly follow, Torrentius would even now be ruler of a new world. This time of superstition and religious oppression nears its end, Speelman. Torrentius has seen what the future holds for those who cling to this notion of a God in the sky, passing judgement upon our every tiny deed. There is no evil. There is no good, no bad. We were made in the image of an Almighty, were we not? And if God made us, then any evil within us must surely have been put there by His hand. We do him no more praise sitting in a cold church reciting prayers than we do gorging and feasting and roistering until our hands be bloody and our pricks be sore. I knew this to be true long before I was fortunate enough to meet him. In him, I found a man who saw in me the potential overlooked by so many others. He is my friend, my teacher, my master, my prophet. He spoke of a new age and my place within it, seated at his right hand.'

Nacht spits out a mouthful of fruit and scratches his belly, shaking his head. 'You are a beaten dog who winds about the legs of the first person who shows you kindness. Of course he praised you. Of course he spoke of your great potential. It means you did what he asked! Brought the girls, the boys, the children – gave away money you did not have; saw to the removal of the babies planted in the bellies of whores by the rich men who gathered about him. I have no interest in your happiness, Jeronimus, but for pride's sake, admit to yourself that you were lied to by a charlatan.'

Cornelisz ignores the blasphemy. Continues to press home his point. 'Every gathering my master held, we lined your pockets. Half the riches in this room were paid for by my master and his adherents.'

'And yet he languishes in a cell.' Nacht sighs, bored now. 'So too do most of his followers. And yet you, Cornelisz – you walk the streets like a man who believes himself wrapped safe in the palm of God.'

Cornelisz flexes his right arm, checking the position of the scalpel. If one of the men behind the drapes has a pistol he will be dead before he can even draw the blade, but its nearness offers some comfort.

Nacht waves a hand, no longer interested in the conversation. Sets himself to the business he summoned the apothecary to discuss. 'There is a young woman in my employ,' he says, reaching out and picking up a Chinese vase from the floor. He inserts his prick into the lip and proceeds to relieve himself, the sound of urine striking priceless china providing an undertone to his words. 'A woman for whom

I have an affection. She has been with me since she was a child and has learned the subtle art of being whatever a fellow might need. Alas, she finds herself in difficulty.'

Cornelisz allows his confusion to show. 'She is with child?'

'I doubt that,' says Nacht, drily. 'Most of my women have been poked so rough that their insides could no more carry a child than I could. No, I am afraid she has committed a foolish act while in drink and it is my burden to protect her from the consequences.'

'And what is this to me?'

'You are in my debt, Cornelisz,' explains Nacht, simply. 'You know that. You have wronged me, and it is in this matter that I seek recompense.'

Cornelisz allows himself a wry smile. 'You wish her dead? There are potions in my possession, which…'

A look of anger flashes across Nacht's face. 'I said I sought protection, Cornelisz. She is dear to me. I would see her taken to a place of safety and there established as a woman of substance.'

'You are Speelman Nacht,' says Cornelisz, softly. 'Such matters are trivialities to you.'

'They are trivialities primarily because I know who to ask, and what to insist upon.' He deposits the china vase upon the floor. He plucks a fat grape from the bunch in the bowl. Sniffs it and pops it in his mouth. 'You will be leaving these shores, I imagine. A man of education, of ambition, a man with no skill with sword or pistol – only the fine Gentlemen of the Vereenigde Oost Indische Compagnie will allow you to reach a safe harbour. You will seek employment, I do not doubt.'

Cornelisz rubs his hand over his chin. Feels the throb in the old wounds. He does not wish the fence to know his plans but is unsurprised that he has identified them. 'I have considered such a course, yes,' he says, cautiously. 'It would take a little guile, but it is within my reach.'

'A man of your schooling. Of your charm and reach. I do not doubt your ability to secure a position. And once suitably installed, you would have the authority to permit her passage to the Indies.'

Cornelisz laughs, genuinely surprised by the proposal. 'Speelman, I do not yet even know whether the VOC will employ a man who is currently sought in connection with two deaths and the heretical teachings of the Rosicrucians. And you sit there expecting me to arrange passage to the Indies for a maid? Why not just pay for her passage? Or smuggle her aboard the next ship? Have I not heard that Java is more than welcoming to Dutch maids seeking a new life? Why, the governor-general has requested the Company send goodly women to start families with the soldiers of the garrison and their various merchants. There is no need to put this matter into my hands.'

Nacht wipes his mouth. Turns harsh eyes upon the apothecary. 'I had a fellow within the Company. A man who served my purpose. Ensured my various cargoes were hidden away in the hold of the Company ships and that those who wished to start new lives were safely added to each vessel's manifest. Alas, he turned to drunkenness. He began to demand more money for his services and threatened to share the particulars of our dealings. And for that reason, his life came to a premature end. My attempts to find a replacement have been beset by complications. And so, I turn to you.'

Cornelisz sits down, unbidden, arranging himself on a gaudily coloured cushion and mopping at his brow. 'Speelman, you ask too much. I do not think the Indies would be my choice for a new beginning. I had thought to the Americas. There is much violence in Java. It is a place for soldiers and merchants used to meat and savages.'

Speelman shakes his head. 'This is not a discussion, Jeronimus. I do not care whether you tell the Company she is your wife, or your maid, or whether you disguise her as a young man and call her a cabin boy. But she is bound for Batavia – both the fortress, and the ship.'

Cornelisz sucks at his teeth, temper rising. Who is this fat fool to command his actions? He has been handpicked by Torrentius; selected for high honour by a great man who saw his potential. He feels the strange prickling sensation on the inside of his skin, as if writing were being carved into the underside of his flesh with a hot nail. 'What mean you, fortress and ship?'

'The *Batavia* takes shape as we speak, Jeronimus. The flagship of the winter fleet will be launched when summer loses its bloom. I am informed that the cargo she will carry represents near a quarter of the Company's wealth. Nobody has ever so much as glimpsed a fortune of such magnitude. This is the craft upon which she is to be a passenger.'

Cornelisz shakes his head. 'Were I a senior merchant with the Company then perhaps I would be able to help with this request. What chance do I have of securing myself a position upon this mighty, treasure-laden vessel?'

'Such matters are yours to arrange,' says Nacht, tiredly. 'I find threats to be exhausting, so I shall make it plain. If you fail me in this task I shall personally have you delivered to the magistrates for your various crimes. And to ensure you do not condemn me, I will first take the trouble of removing your tongue, your ears, your eyes, and your fingers, so the only way you could make a statement would be to prod at the floor with bloodied stumps.'

Cornelisz stares at him. Sees the truth writ large in the set of his jaw. 'Batavia,' he says, quietly. 'A fortune, you say?'

'More than a man could spend in a thousand lifetimes.'

Cornelisz gives a little nod. His thoughts are racing ahead of him. He has ever been giddy at the thought of true wealth. He has always known the truth of himself and his place in the world. It is a brutal, uncomfortable truth, but a small, scarred man with little money and fading influence must compensate for his shortcomings with gold.

He begins to consider his possibilities. Thinks upon the complexities of a scheme: stratagems forming in the wet clay of his mind. He cannot sail, but he can sell. Cannot fight, but he can kill. Cannot make men fear him, but knows how to manipulate their weaknesses. He feels a prickling in his skin, the wounds around his eyes splitting like ripe fruit as the blood engorges his skin. Perhaps this is what Torrentius had glimpsed in the flame. Perhaps this was the moment when he would finally step onto the path that would lead to a throne, a kingdom; a place among the great names of the age. He has never stopped believing in such a destiny.

Suddenly, his failings make sense. The bankruptcy, the failed business, the bland wife and squawking child – all were encumbrances. All were baggage that needed to be shed before he could begin upon this, his true path. He feels like giggling, madly, with sheer delight at having made sense of his recent failures. Quite simply, they were necessary defeats. As such he remains victorious. As such, his recent misfortunes were all part of a grander scheme. In moments he has convinced himself that this was always his plan, that he has deliberately shed the dead weight of his old life in order to embark upon this great enterprise.

'She will be fine company aboard the ship,' says Nacht, laughing. 'She has her uses, believe me. She's quick-witted, loyal and can juice a man's prick like an eel beneath a boot. Make use of her. Think of her as a blessing.'

Cornelisz shakes his head, aware he must not seem too eager. 'Speelman, my plans are not yet...'

'Zwaantie!'

At Nacht's shout, a small, dark-skinned woman emerges silently from behind a screen. She is wrapped in furs, and is grinning widely. There is a look of barely concealed madness in her eyes. In her hand she holds a pistol.

'Take her, or take the pistol ball right through your fucking eyes,' says Nacht, smiling. 'I know what I would prefer.'

Cornelisz holds her gaze. Considers her. He is a man who knows how to manipulate. How to beguile and entice. And there is something more than enticing about Zwaantie.

Cornelisz nods.

'She'll serve you well,' says Nacht, with a look of relief. 'She could pleasure a whole ship and still have breath to fight.'

'I shall require some coin...' begins Cornelisz.

'You bargain like the very devil.' Speelman Nacht grins.

Cornelisz holds his gaze. For a moment, he allows himself to appear in the form that he conceals within this ill-fitting suit of flesh. Appears in the guise that had so delighted Torrentius upon their first meeting. Allows himself to be seen in the form that he knows to be his true self. Becomes the serpent.

He takes a moment's pleasure when the bigger man looks away first.

'*Amen*,' he says.

3

Mermaid Court, Southwark, London

Nicolaes stands for a moment outside the big double doors of the Keeper's Lodge, allowing himself a moment to bask in what passes, in this part of London, for fresh air. The warm summer breeze is speckled with a gauzy rain and the moisture feels wonderful upon his bare face and hands. He breathes in, deeply, filling himself up with London. There is still something thrilling about inhaling the complex, dirty city air, even laced as it is with tobacco, tar and turned earth. He keeps his back to the turreted wall, gazing instead down the long, sunless alley that gradually opens out onto the quiet square. The nearest alehouse is not more than a hundred paces away. He can hear distant laughter; the clop of slow-moving horses and the raucous cries of passing peddlers. Hears gulls, turning in lazy circles overhead. If he closes his eyes and ignores all else, he can hear the kiss of wood upon wood and the great sloshing roar of the Thames at Tooley Steps.

'Shit and spoiled beef,' snaps Buckingham, appearing

from the wooden door of the Keeper's Lodge and tucking away his coin purse. 'Horse sweat. A whore's bedsheets left to turn stiff in the sun...'

Nicolaes doesn't reply, perceiving the sourness to his mood. The scowl draws lines in his fine features. Two red-coated members of the Royal Guard snap to attention as he breezes past them, jerking away from the high wall where they have been leaning and sharing a pipe. They wear fine swords in elegant scabbards and wear their beards and hair in the ringleted fashion of the politician they are here to protect. Nicolaes knows both men well enough. They are certainly passable swordsmen and the taller of the two, who answers to the name of Scudder, is an excellent shot with a musket. Both had been kind enough to look away as Nicolaes emerged, blinking, into the daylight, and sucked in a lungful of damp, grey air.

Buckingham ignores the pair as he strides towards Nicolaes, who feels damnably cold and hungry now the first shock of liberty has been absorbed. Buckingham finds the very notion of bodyguards insulting, but the king will not hear of him walking London's streets alone – not with the mood of the nation so firmly turned against him. Nicolaes watches the two soldiers from the corner of his eye while instinctively scouring the quiet little courtyard for any threat to his benefactor. Lets his gaze linger for a moment upon the beggar who lounges drunkenly against a post, pissing into the horse trough. He is clad in little more than rags; a doublet ripped across the back to show bare, grimy skin. He is singing merrily to himself, untroubled, his back to the prison and the fine gentleman who stands outside the main gates, slipping his fingers back into his golden gloves and glaring at the air.

Nicolaes composes his own face into something suitable. Effects the posture of a grateful man who nevertheless had the situation under complete control. 'Did you address me, my lord? Forgive me, I was reacquainting myself with the complexities of London's fine, rich air.'

Buckingham dabs at his moustache with a pristine, emerald-coloured handkerchief. Smooths his eyebrows with forefinger and thumb. Gathers himself back into some approximation of the nobleman who once revelled in the title of "most beautiful man alive".

'An overflowing privy, Nicolaes,' says Buckingham, every syllable perfectly pronounced, his manner radiating contempt. 'London? Ha! A great midden filled with the shit and piss of liars, cowards and self-serving malcontents. A pox on the lot of them.'

'I thought perhaps I smelled baking bread...' begins Nicolaes, hopefully.

'Liars and thieves,' growls Buckingham, once more. He glowers across the courtyard, frowning at the bare back of the beggar. 'Why, I should give my fealty to that bum-fiddling arsling at the trough before I pledged a breath in support of those cowardly piss-stains in Parliament!'

Nicolaes winces. 'Not going well?' he asks, awkwardly.

'What do you bloody think?'

A silence stretches out between them. Buckingham glares down his aquiline nose, daring Nicolaes to meet his gaze. Nicolaes, in turn, concentrates his eyes upon the pattern in Buckingham's doublet; gold threads forming an elaborate design upon the priceless blue silk. No friendship exists between them, but Nicolaes holds the man he calls "Uncle" in considerable esteem, while Buckingham, in turn, refers to his agent and nephew as his "favourite solution" to any seemingly impenetrable problems of State, of Church, of Crown – or the interests of the Villiers family.

'How is His Majesty?' asks Nicolaes, struggling to make conversation. He wishes he were capable of sullenness but feels compelled to repair any rips in their relationship caused by the death of the good Dr Lambe. 'Might he be making good on his promises to our friends in France? If you wish for me to visit our particular friend, I know the submersible vessel may be ready for another trial, if a man can be found to take the risk, and…'

Buckingham gives a shake of his head. Chews at his lip and spits. As he talks, a tiny drop of blood forms in the corner of his mouth.

'Do not trouble yourself with France, Nicolaes, nor any matters of state. Do, instead, take the air. You may catch the whiff of our mutual acquaintance, still on display for the crowds that gather to watch the flesh fall from his bones.'

Nicolaes lowers his head. Stares at the ground. In the hard earth, he can make out the shape of a child's footprint, perfectly framed within the big dinner-plate hoof of a fully laden horse.

'He deserved a better end,' says Nicolaes, softly. 'I do not seek to place the blame upon our departed friend but he would not take counsel, Uncle. A man who claims to see the future will not be steered onto a different path.'

'By Christ, 'tis the good king's favourite!'

Nicolaes looks up and sees that the beggar has identified

the splendidly dressed gentleman. He is staggering, drunkenly, across the courtyard, arms stretched out as if scaring crows. He is feigning deference, bowing low, laughing and swaying.

'Let me kiss they pretty mouth, sir. For did not that mouth press itself upon the lips of King James? Did not that pretty mouth ensure advancement? Did not those fine legs and shapely arse entice His Majesty to the point of madness? Come, Buckingham, tell me again how a man can advance himself? Do you still wince upon your chamber pot and remember the man who made you a man of substance? How does it feel to wear finery paid for by giving your arse to the Crown? I lost a brother at Cadiz, you mad, murdering bastard. Lost this fucking hand too...'

The soldiers to Buckingham's rear dash forward as the beggar opens his tattered cloak, revealing the gnarled stump of his severed left hand. Nicolaes looks instead at his other hand. Sees the pistol even before the guards have a chance to shout a warning. Nicolaes grabs the duke by the silk of his cape and presses himself close, turning his back upon the assassin so that the shot will hit his own flesh. His hand glances against the decorative dagger that Buckingham sports in his sash. It is more of an ornamentation than an implement for killing but Nicolaes does not doubt the ease with which it could stop a heart. He spins back to the attacker, the jewelled hilt in his hand, his body still shielding Buckingham. Looks upon the weeping, broken figure, the gun swaying in his hand, tears streaming down the grime and caked slime upon his rotting features.

'For God's sake, Nicolaes...' whispers Buckingham, urgently.

Nicolaes throws the dagger. He hurls it by the handle and not the blade; a lightning strike of silver glinting in the low sunlight. The handle strikes the assailant dead in the centre of the head, ricocheting away to clatter upon the cobbles. The beggar blinks, twice, then collapses onto his backside – a lump turning purple upon his brow. Nicolaes lets out a slow sigh and turns back to his uncle, who is brushing himself down and slapping away the hands of his guards as they fuss over his person. When they see he is truly unharmed they nod quiet thanks to Nicolaes and rush past him, hauling the unconscious beggar to his feet. He groans and sobs and hangs limp in their arms. Only when Nicolaes is satisfied they intend the poor bastard no further harm does he turn back to Buckingham.

'You should have put the blade in his heart,' mutters Buckingham, softly. 'Would be a swifter death than he must now endure as a warning to those who would strike against the king.'

Nicolaes closes his eyes. Tries to stop the words emerging but bites them back too late. 'You are not king, Uncle.'

Buckingham's eyes flash fire. 'I am as close to the throne as any mortal man, Nicolaes de Pelgrom. I have been trusted by two monarchs who were themselves ordained by God! To strike at me is to strike at the Crown, and to strike at the Crown is to strike at God!'

Nicolaes says nothing. Turns away from Buckingham and walks briskly to where the dagger lies. He picks it up and weighs it afresh in his palm. Such a fine, jewelled item could feed the beggar and his family for the rest of their lives. Buckingham wears it because one of the jewels in the hilt matches the ribbons upon his shoes. Nicolaes takes his time returning it. Allows his uncle time to recover his temper.

'A pity you were not so swift in the aid you provided for the good doctor,' growls Buckingham. Instantly, his features change. He looks embarrassed. Cross with himself for having spoken harshly. He takes the dagger with mumbled thanks and reattaches it to his sash, then begins to play with his fob watch, his fingers jittering nervously. He glances up at the sky, as if searching the low clouds for confirmation of the time. When he speaks, there is an air of tiredness to his voice. 'Lambe could not see the future, Nicolaes. He was a quack. A master of lies and illusion. He was a master at reading *people* – at giving them just enough of what they wanted. But, I did enjoy him. There was an art to his quackery. He rose from the filth and did reach his bloom late, but bloom he did.'

Nicolaes does not reply immediately, for fear of throwing light upon that which dwells in the shade. Buckingham's own humble roots are a constant source of insult and derision among the nobles who so begrudge him his place at the right hand of the king.

'He deserved better,' says Nicolaes, repeating himself.

'Deserve does not come into it, Nephew,' sighs Buckingham. '*Deserve* is the *preserve* of the Lord.'

Nicolaes gives a weak smile. 'Clever wordplay, Uncle.'

Buckingham plays again with his watch, more distracted than Nicolaes has seen him. Looks past him at where the two guardsmen are binding the assassin's wrists with rope as he sobs, desperately, and begs them to take pity upon an old soldier. 'Ah yes,' he says, turning affectionate eyes upon him. 'I had forgotten your love of verse. Allow me to share a ditty I heard this very morning. "Neighbours cease to moan, And leave your lamentation, For Doctor Lambe is gone, The Devil of our Nation." Do you like it? I fear it will prove damnably popular, though if naught else, it shall give the balladeers a chance to sing of somebody other than me. Buckingham is such a difficult word to rhyme.'

Nicolaes rubs at his chin, as if considering. He clicks his fingers. Decides to try one last time to find a way back to favour. 'Fucking 'em, my lord?'

For a moment, Buckingham manages to maintain his composure. Then he gives in to laughter, his face lighting up. Briefly, he looks young again: athletic and virile, light dancing in his eyes. He claps Nicolaes upon the shoulder, laughing heartily.

'Please, do complete that ditty when you have time, Nicolaes. I do believe that would amuse His Majesty.'

They stand in a more companionable silence, listening to the sounds of London. Nearby, a young girl in a soiled grey dress and dirt-rimed face sells stained strips of cloth from a basket. She is barefoot and her greasy hair clings to her features.

'Lambe's Blood,' she shouts, as a cutler in a leather apron hurries past, knives in his belt. 'Mopped from the earth where he fell, sir. Sure to be useful as a talisman, sir. A protector against ailments. Boil it in good Thames water and it will provide a cure for all manner of agues...'

Buckingham ignores the girl's cries. Gives Nicolaes his full attention. 'My God but you look much reduced, Nicolaes. Do I see fresh scars? New bruises? If that bastard turnkey hurt you we can return and unravel his guts.'

Nicolaes laughs, inspecting the parts of himself that can

be seen through his ragged shirt. 'Alas, Munce never found the courage to hurt me physically. He enjoyed the taunts and pissing in my ale but he lacked the courage to make good on his threats. I consider myself fortunate. Those on the Common side of the clink sleep twenty to a room. Others spend their days in irons. I didn't taste the skullcap or thumbscrews. Truth be told, I think I was a peculiarity: neither debtor nor murderer. Some said I was among the mob that did for poor John – others that I was a demon conjured for vengeance with his dying breath.'

Buckingham breathes out slowly, hands upon hips. He is dressed in his usual finery: the plume of some exotic bird in his immaculate felt hat. He has the scent of lavender and rose-petals – a feminine scent that seems at odds with the tobacco and red-wine smell upon his lips.

'I do not blame you, Nicolaes,' says Buckingham, with a tired sigh. 'And you should not blame yourself. There are those who would lay the blame for the good doctor's demise at my door. Perhaps I do myself, though what is one more accusation among so many? I truly wonder whether the pamphleteers will soon find a way to link my name to the death of our Lord at Calvary.'

Nicolaes feels tempted to offer words of comfort but knows they would be rebuffed. Buckingham's name has become a byword for the devil these past years. Dr Lambe's brutal end was due entirely to his association with Buckingham – a man whose elevation has been unparalleled. In the dozen years since first catching the eye of King James, George Villiers has risen again and again. Initially a humble cup-bearer to the royal household, he was plucked from the mass of courtiers and became the king's favourite.

He was the recipient of lavish estates, titles and untold praise – becoming the king's right hand in ways that the balladeers exploited to full effect. Villiers was made Duke of Buckingham two years before James died. Buckingham was at his side – already consoling and advising his heir, the young Prince Charles.

Handsome, ambitious, Villiers has worn the role of favoured courtier like a velvet mantle, deploying charm and ruthlessness as the occasion required. The pamphleteers were never kind but these past years have seen him become the most reviled man in the land: damned for corruption, greed and for wielding an almost ungodly power over King Charles. Lambe, the ancient mystic, soothsayer and alchemist, was made victim merely by association.

'You are thinking my thoughts for me, Nicolaes,' says Buckingham, looking into the younger man's eyes. 'I see that busy mind of yours – untangling me, unknitting me. I must warn you, as I have before, that not all men are so beguiled by intelligence as I. It is unsettling to see oneself so clearly anatomised. You have many skills, Nicolaes, but I urge you to learn the art of affecting imbecility when in the company of powerful men.'

Nicolaes smiles, glad of the lesson. 'There was nothing I could do, Uncle,' he says, flatly. 'It was a mob – like fighting a flood. I urged him to flee. He had faith in the sailors at whom he had thrown coin, believing they would protect him. They fled as soon as the mob emerged. I had urged him to let me accompany him, but he was insistent that he would be unrecognisable in such a place.'

Buckingham looks past him. A coach pulled by four sleek black horses trundles along the rutted road. Nicolaes follows his gaze. Saying nothing until the carriage pulls up next to them. The coachman is a squat, bald-headed fellow whom Nicolaes has never head speak. He throws a soft leather bag at the feet of his master.

'You did all I could ask of you, Nicolaes,' says Buckingham, drawing an end to the discussion. 'It does my own cause no great harm for such a hated man to no longer be a source of potential embarrassment to myself or His Majesty. And for all our friendship, I doubt our paths would ever have crossed were it not for my mother and her obsession with your father's health.'

Nicolaes shoots his uncle a curious look and Buckingham realises he has spoken too freely. That Nicolaes is John Villiers' bastard son is a secret they rarely refer to. George's brother John, the half-mad cuckold whose misdeeds have been Buckingham's cross to bear, does not acknowledge Nicolaes de Pelgrom as his own progeny. He would not even look at him when the young Nicolaes arrived at his door, clutching the locket that the young John had pressed upon his mother at a tavern in Leiden thirteen years before. He had threatened to whip him bloody should he ever show his face again. But George Villiers recalled with some fondness the flaxen-haired tavern-keeper's daughter whom his brother had paid to deflower. And he had vc offered Nicolaes the hand of friendship. Trained him in the arts of swordplay, in court etiquette; in Latin, Greek and horsemanship. Taught him to seduce and to steal without the crime ever being noticed.

Nicolaes turns away, refusing to look too closely at the memories that flood him. He rummages through the leather sack that the coachman tossed to the ground. Removes a black silk shirt and doublet, a soft leather overcoat, a long-brimmed felt hat and a pair of good quality boots. 'Thank you,' he says, to the coachman, who stares through him as if he were air.

Buckingham reaches into his own shirt and retrieves a swatch of fine silk, scented with honey and mace. Nicolaes takes it gratefully and strips himself down to his linen undershirt. Quickly, he wipes the silk over his skin, removing the worst of the grime. He pulls on the new clothes, putting on the hat with a flourish.

'I presume I am to be paraded, Uncle?' asks Nicolaes, hunting in the depths of the bag and finding a small, two-headed dagger in a black leather sheath. He removes it and considers the blades. Scrapes the quality steel down his cheek and enjoys the feeling of rasping away the patchy stubble. 'I see in your eyes you have a task for me.'

Buckingham doesn't reply. Breathes out slowly as if his lungs were full of tobacco. 'The duty I must entrust to you comes at a cost of great sadness.'

'Sadness, Uncle?'

'I fear we are to be parted for longer than we are accustomed,' says Buckingham, taking his arm.

'Is it La Rochelle?' he asks, expectantly. 'There is unfinished business, in France, is there not? Am I to go ahead? I fear leaving you exposed, Uncle. Even seeing you here, unprotected, causes my heart to clench like a fist.'

Buckingham shakes his head. Gives Nicolaes a little nudge towards the door of the carriage. 'No, Nicolaes, I fancy I must face our enemies without you and your blade at my side. I only wish I could accompany you as you experience the excitement of this new beginning.'

'A new beginning?' asks Nicolaes, uncomfortable. 'Have I disappointed you, Uncle? I know you have spoken of your hopes for me, your plans – I seek nothing but the opportunity to repay you for the kindnesses you have—'

'You are your own man, Nicolaes,' says Buckingham, with a sudden gentleness. 'Never have I asked you to perform a duty that I would not perform myself. Should you wish to refuse me today I shall not bear you ill will. But the commission you undertake is a matter of great concern to myself and His Majesty. It is a task for which I can think of nobody more suitable. I ask that you listen to her, and listen to the voice of your conscience before you decline.'

'To her?' asks Nicolaes. 'I am your agent, sir, and none other's. You speak in riddles.'

'I place my trust in you, Nicolaes. In this, and in all else, you have ever been true.'

Nicolaes reaches out, taking a handful of Buckingham's elegant sleeve and pulling him close. Fear rises in him: a sudden, uncontrollable sense of being discarded, or being set adrift, rudderless and lost. 'Uncle, I have nowhere – nobody, all I am, you have made me…'

Buckingham sees the urgency in the younger man's eyes. Places a hand upon his cheek, his whole demeanour suddenly full of sorrow. 'I wish you to know, you please me. Truly, I believe myself to have made the correct decision when I chose to make use of you rather than command your quiet execution. I have helped create a man of purpose.'

Nicolaes swallows, his mouth dry. He moves to embrace Buckingham, then halts, and gives a stiff, formal bow. Buckingham smiles, then turns away.

Wordlessly, Nicolaes climbs inside the coach. On the

embroidered seat, a fine sword with an eagle head sits proud in a thick black scabbard. At his feet, a basket, draped with quality sailcloth. He looks beneath, smiling as he spies the green bottle of good French Armagnac: the hunks of roasted meats and breads: a runny cheese and a bowl of soft-stewed fruits. Beside it is a plum-coloured beret, blood-stained and caked in mud. Inside are two small figurines, inexpertly carved. They serve as bookends to a square of parchment, sealed with the thumbprint of Dr John Lambe. He is overcome with a swell of true grief.

'Uncle,' he says, pushing through the curtains and poking his head through the window. 'Uncle, I cannot...'

Buckingham is already walking away.

4

Amsterdam Harbour

Sunset, July 29

The wind whips off the water in a great din of flapping flags and dancing sails; orange-beaked seabirds swirling overhead in a shrieking mass.

Jeronimus Cornelisz promenades, lazily, along the water's edge; allowing the briny air to sting the shimmering cuts upon his flesh. He imagines himself at sea. Wonders, idly, how it will feel to be master of such a vast horizon; whether he will hear the roar of the oceans pouring over the edge of the world. Watches, half curious, as a chain of fat, pink-whiskered rats emerge from a gap in the canal wall and scamper, silently, into the darkness of a rowboat that transports two bewigged merchants out to a waiting craft. Watches the boatmen who fight for space upon the crowded canal, their oars raised as pikes, their little vessels scraping against one another and flitting in between the larger vessels like fish seeking holes in the net. For a time he lets himself drift upon the air, revelling in these roars of undiluted malice; adrift in a mist of furious exhalations; a fog of venom and tempers and greed.

He looks up at the huge, pot-bellied, wide-skirted outline of the colossal ships docked upon the emerald waters. Looks upon gaudily attired figureheads and imposing crests; watches the little light left in the day reflect off small dark windows and the shimmering steel of cannon. Listens to the voices that spill down from the portholes and bilges of a dozen different craft; laughter and curses and the occasional crack of a bosun's fist against some laggard's jaw.

And through the gaps, he looks upon the field of bones. Looks upon the quiet little field where he finds sanctuary. He finds the *Volewijck* soothing. There's something peaceful about this orchard of corpses; this grey-green panorama where ink-black bodies hang from flimsy wooden crosses; their flesh rotting down to nothing and their clothing torn to rags. This is where the bodies of the damned are left after execution; food for the crows and a warning to any thief or murderer about the consequences of their actions. Amsterdam is a modern city that will tolerate different beliefs in the interests of commerce, but its punishments for criminal transgressions are severe. In the lonely weeks since arriving in Amsterdam, Cornelisz has found great comfort in the presence of these desolate scarecrows, talking to them with the same frank sincerity that he and Torrentius used to deliberate by candlelight.

'Zwaantie,' says Cornelisz, rolling the name around upon his tongue. He has barely spoken to her since she became his problem, but she has talked enough for both of them. He fancies she deserves a moment of his grace. 'Little swan?'

She nods, grinning hugely. She has big white teeth and full lips, wide brown eyes and a syrupy tone to her skin. Even dressed for propriety in a brown smock and sensible cap, there is something about her that suggests a softness of skin and roundness of flesh. Cornelisz is not a man who spends much time thinking carnal thoughts but he looks upon her with a merchant's eye. There are no sharp edges to her. She looks, he fancies, as though she were built for a man's unceasing comfort.

'It's not my real name.' She shrugs. 'Or maybe it is. Hard to say. Is your real name your first name? That's the question, isn't it? Or is your first name your real name? That's a better way of putting it. I think the man who gave it to me did so as a joke. I'm a little dark, see. And swans, well, they're white, aren't they? But little swans are a bit of both, and, well, that's me, isn't it? Something thrown together from different bits.' She slaps his arm, playfully. 'Like one of your potions, I presume.'

Cornelisz hides his smile. He is enjoying the girl's lust for life. He did not expect her to follow him from Speelman's premises but she emerged from the brothel with her meagre possessions in a small cloth bag and clad in the drab smock that clings to her figure. She attracts the eye as much as Cornelisz repels it. Though it pays to be unremarkable he feels a distinct pleasure in being linked to such a fine-looking maid. He imagines that those who notice them are presuming him to be rich and influential, and to be considered thus is, in truth, all that truly matters.

He has a pathological need to win. To conquer. To be held

aloft and revered. A lithe, disfigured little man, he cannot bask in the adoration of men through physical prowess. But he knows how to get what he wants. He knows how to turn men's thoughts inside out; how to slip and slither and whisper his way into the hearts of those who could break him like a twig. He fancies Zwaantie has bedded more of such men than she could count, and yet it is to him that she is entrusted for advancement. Given time, he could turn the situation into one that reinforces his opinion of himself. He is, he knows, quite magnificent.

'Not much of a talker, are you?' asks Zwaantie, pressing her face up close to his. She giggles as her eyes loom large. 'That's fine. I can be what you like. That woman you killed, was she your lover? If you've got a picture of her I can hold my face like hers. Or your wife? Tell me how she sounds and I can do that. I'm grateful to you and it doesn't hurt to show it.'

Cornelisz gives a bark of laughter. He is trying not to demonstrate too much fondness for the girl but she is quickly winning her way into whatever passes for his affections. 'You chatter like a monkey,' he says, softly. 'You're distracting me.'

'Sorry, sorry,' whispers Zwaantie, miming drawing a needle and thread through her lips. 'Not another word,' she mumbles, pretending to have her lips stitched shut.

Cornelisz turns away from her. Steers them on towards the field where the dying sway upon the air.

'Why Batavia?' asks Cornelisz, unable to help himself. He has already begun to formulate a stratagem that is entirely at odds with Zwaantie and Nacht's wishes, but he is nevertheless keen to know her purpose. 'Of all the places to flee to, why that great arsehole of a place? Heat and flies and savages, is it not? Soldiers desperate for wenches or wives protecting rich men from the Company's endless enemies. A woman of your unquestionable talents could prosper anywhere. I fear you and Nacht have a purpose you have not confided in me – a purpose to do with the money in the hold.'

Zwaantie looks at him sidelong, twisting an escaped curl of hair around her finger. 'I was ridden by a VOC musketeer once,' she says, a little dreamily. 'Fell for me, poor love. Told me wondrous stories of the Indies, of the colours and the heat and the maidens in silks who recline upon mattresses of gold. I return to the thought in my quiet moments, imagining the heat upon my skin. And now, when I am forced to leave Amsterdam and have the whole world to choose from, I seek to see it for myself.'

Cornelisz holds her gaze. Shakes his head. 'A story,' he says. Then he shrugs. 'A fine one, nevertheless. And I shall leave you to your secrets. But mark me this, Little Swan – you may have duties to perform in furtherance of your goals. If you wish to be situated as decreed and to reach Batavia as a woman of substance, you may have to endure some indignities.'

Zwaantie looks untroubled. 'The soldier who told me the story. He told me that when I was not yet twelve. Indignities are not unusual.'

Cornelisz looks at her with a moment's admiration. There is a pragmatism to her that he finds commendable. He wishes more people could understand that suffering is unavoidable. All that can be changed is the manner in which one faces it, and how to use it to further one's own ends. He is a sickly man whose wounds never truly heal and who coughs up metallic-tasting blood every dawn. And yet he is a scholar, a man of medicine, and he has assisted in hastening untold lives to their premature end.

Loth Vogel may have overseen his ruin and the midwife may have given his only son the French disease, but both have died excruciating deaths. He cannot see that as anything other than a victory. So, too, his dealings with Speelman Nacht. He may have manifested as an obsequious coward but he left the meeting with a small fortune in silver stuivers and a beautiful woman upon his arm. Again, he sees no reason to criticise himself. He continues to flourish; to thrive. He continues to win. And here, now, in this orchard of bones, he finds himself growing breathless with excitement as his plan takes shape. Perhaps Vogel has done him a favour in destroying his business interests. Perhaps his closeness to Torrentius was simply a barrier to realising his own full potential. He has learned much from his master. Knows that men like to be given free rein to indulge themselves. Surely a ship full of sailors and soldiers would be the perfect place in which to secretly share his garnered wisdom – to quietly attract a flock of loyal followers. He is every bit as capable of becoming to all that his master was, and more besides.

'Your scars,' says Zwaantie, quietly. 'They're strange. They seem to catch the light. It's like snakeskin.'

Cornelisz searches her face for signs she is mocking him. Sees none. He wonders whether she would say the same were she to see him undressed. Beneath his dark clothes, his flesh shimmers, like liquid metal. Every day brings fresh pain. He no longer bandages himself; just lets his suppurating skin weep against his cheap, scratchy clothing, disguising the reek with endless powders and perfumes.

'I was scalded as a child,' he says. 'I was almost perfect before that. Healthy, golden-haired, the kind of child that every father wishes to show off. Throughout my childhood I was held aloft as the very vision of perfection. I learned what it was to be deified. I was a victim of one of Father's quarrels. A fine man, my father, though some would call him cruel. He owned land near our family home in Friesland. He was liked well enough, but in his dealings with a miller he felt himself short-changed and sent two of our retainers to speak harshly with his rival. The meeting turned to violence and the miller's daughter was subjected to some, shall we say, unpleasantness. The miller took his revenge many months later. Took me. This was done to me with a kettle. Boiling water and a cone of sugar. And the apothecary summoned by my father to aid in my recovery only succeeded in completing my transformation. I, who had been so beautiful, was transformed thus.'

Zwaantie stares at him. Closes one eye, considering. 'A story,' she concludes. 'But a good one.'

Cornelisz laughs, pleased with her. Had he time, he fancies she would be a fine student. It strikes him as a shame that for his plan to succeed, he must ensure that she does not reach the land where she hopes to begin again.

'Secure us lodgings,' he says, fumbling for coins in his velvet purse. 'Send a boy to tell me where to find you. I shall be here for a time yet.'

'You feel at peace here – I see it,' says Zwaantie, wiping the sweat from her lip. 'What kind of man is happiest among the dead?'

Cornelisz turns away so she does not hear his reply.

'A god,' he whispers.

And smiles.

5

My Dearest Pilgrim,

I am stealing this brief moment to etch a handful of words that may be of use to you when the moment of my demise arrives. I will keep this letter upon my person so that in the moment of my death, it stands a chance of being placed in your possession.

I have no doubt that the house will be ransacked and the work of eighty years parcelled up for the amusement of the masses, even as they gawp at my suppurating corpse, but it pleases me to imagine your surprise at looking upon my seal and signature. I hope you gasp upon reading these prophetical words, astounded at my gift for seeing that which is yet to come. You have always been relied upon to feign delight in my marvels, even while seeing through the trickery and illusion that so bewitches those who seek me out. Doubtless, even now, you sit there, mouth agape, that quiet smile at your eyes, delighting in this last miracle woven by your old friend.

Alas, there is no need for divination here. I know my time is coming to an end because I see the way people consider me. I read the pamphlets and hear the *whispers. My end will be violent – my death a cause of celebration. Do try and reassure Villiers that I do not blame him for my being held in such low regard by the populace. For him to be associated with my mysticism and quackery is an injustice. We have never been more than acquaintances, and the only truly good deed we have done for one another has been in the introduction of your fine self.*

You have been a most excellent companion, Nicolaes. I thank you for the forbearance you have demonstrated in tolerating the peculiarities of this doddering ancient, and for the many nights you have shared a pipe with me and talked of matters corporeal and metaphysical. You have an unusual mind, Nicolaes, and a soul that, I fear, does not know its course. I see in you a man of wisdom, compassion, of learning and courage, and yet the dark shadows that gather about your edges seem intent upon stitching themselves to your bones. I dearly hope that Providence and Fate are kind to you.

To that end, I share with you my final forewarning. Empty your mind of remembrance of trickeries past, and accept this oracle from one who, for a time, did truly glimpse hidden truths. Accept this vision from the man I was, when the spirits whispered their secrets and each looking glass blurred to reveal the devil at my shoulder, offering answers in exchange for bites at my soul. That man, and this, offer these words, Nicolaes... beware the Man in Red. I see this Rat-King, mounted upon a throne of rock and bone, caked in the blood of innocents: a silhouette in flickering silk, clothed in crimson fur. I see him in my water glass, in the shapes in the fire, in the

*coiling ropes and streaming guts of the storm clouds that
gather. I see him, and I see you, Nicolaes.*

*I feel a lifting of some great weight having set down
these words and trust that they serve some purpose. I
have naught left to offer you, save gratitude and my
enduring esteem.*

Affectionately, your friend,
Dr John Lambe

Nicolaes reads the letter through misted eyes. He is not
given to tears, but there is a tightness in his throat by the
time he strokes his thumb against the dead man's scrawled
signature and presses his lips, tenderly, to the broken seal.
He catches a trace of the dead man's scent: that sea-coal and
bad-meat whiff; mildewed clothes, Armagnac and sulphur.
For a moment he pictures the old sod falling beneath
the blows of the crowd, then shakes the image away. He
slips the letter into his doublet and cuffs at his eyes, uncorking
the bottle and taking a good deep swallow. He helps himself
to what he can stomach of the feast, taking care to maintain
his courteous manners even when alone. He has seen high-
born men and women who devour their food like crazed
animals. He does not wish to considered thus. Even in
private, he must conceal the truth of his origins.

Having eaten and drunk to sufficiency, he pokes his head
through the window of the carriage. He finds himself in a
part of London unfamiliar to him. He has made his home in
England these past ten years but his life has been a series of
disparate chapters and he has never found opportunity to
truly acquaint himself with the capital. He fancies that they
have reached the area called Marylebone, but there is little

unique about this narrow street of tall timber buildings and pitted earth. He considers the brown-clad, hunchbacked figures: catches the eye of a hacking, filth-caked artisan who squats by a narrow doorway spitting upon a whetstone and sliding a knife along its length. Beside him, a gaunt, hollow-eyed girl of no more than fourteen holds a red-faced, half-dressed infant to her breast.

Wordlessly, Nicolaes puts the uneaten food back in the basket and holds it out the window. He does not look to see who takes it, but it is gone from his hand in moments.

He sits back. Raises the bottle to his lips and lets the motion of the carriage rock him into something that might pass for sleep: a place of fragmented oblivion, where men in red pour dirt into his open mouth, and a faceless figure in blue plunges a blade into his uncle's chest. In the clutch of the dream, he reaches out, fingers like claws, desperately trying to reach the man before he can bring the knife down; before he can spill the blood of the man whom the nation calls devil, but who has proven to be Nicolaes's guardian angel these past years. The last thing he sees before he jerks awake is the handsome face of George Villiers, mouth opening and closing like a herring on the dock, blood pulsing out to stain the lips and tongue and chin of a face that once beguiled a king.

As he jerks awake, it is all he can do not to weep.

6

Personal and private correspondence of Lucretia Jansz,
Heerenstraat, Amsterdam
Intended for Boudewijn van der Mijlen,
VOC under-merchant, Fortress of Batavia

Husband,

As I write, I fancy that I see you. You appear most fine and handsome, your skin buffed to a fine golden calfskin after your long months toiling beneath the unrelenting sun. Your eyes glitter like the diamonds that you work so expertly with your nimble fingers. You are barefoot, happy: perhaps holding an etching of one that you love. Oh how I pray to be the person you yearn for. How I long to still be your darling Creesje. I fear that I fade from your thoughts like breath upon glass. Yet you are as vivid and urgent in my imaginings as you were when we parted.

Has it been three years since I last cupped your face in my palm? The taste of your kiss still lingers. Will you think me a harlot if I confide that there are nights when

I press my lips to the palm of my hand and imagine that your mouth is against my own? I lick my thumb as if preparing to turn a page and make-believe that you are kissing me in your gentle, thankful way. I vouchsafe to thee, husband, there were those who would witness me in such moments and label me "witch". The images I conjure are as real as flesh. You linger like the salt of spilled tears.

Forgive me, Boudewijn. I drift from my intended course. I defer in making plain the truth of this letter. I ask that you pause here, and return to this page when there is drink in you. Perhaps you now hold the sweet, treacly spirit that you spoke of in your last letter. I urge you now, uncork your flask and drink long and deep. Feel my cold hands upon your scorched brow. Feel my nearness, as I impart my grim tidings.

I do not doubt that your eyes already cloud, your throat tightens, your fingertips grip tight upon the pages. For you know, do you not? Know that our final child has returned to the Lord? I fancy that you felt the moment of his passing, even if you did not know the nature of your sudden sense of loss and emptiness. It was thus with Lijsbet and Stefani, was it not? The sense of quiet annihilation; the disintegration of all sense of delight or peace or hope – as if your very heart were plucked from your chest and tossed into the ocean. You knew, then. Knew your daughters had lost their fight. All I can tell you of Hans's passing was that it was gentle. The fever gripped at dawn and by evening prayers he was already in God's embrace. Is there a word for one such as I? A mother widowed by the last of their children?

I have borne you four children, husband. Have raised three through infancy. Tarried lonely in Amsterdam, far from your embrace, so as to spare them the disease and uncertainties of the Indies. All in vain, husband. For now we are childless. Truly there are moments when I must ask the Almighty why He needs our sons and daughters. Could one not be spared? Could the work they perform in Paradise not be delayed until I am silver-haired and hook-backed? Could not one of our children resist the entreaties of the angels and choose life over death?

Forgive me, Boudewijn. I write in anger, the quill trembling in my hand, ink blotting my wrist where the tiny blue heart pulses against the soft whiteness of my skin. I shall look so unlike you, husband. You will scarce recognise this pale, haunted figure whose face is fresh milk against the raven blackness of my mourning clothes. I am a spectre, husband. And only in your embrace can I conceive of again feeling the strength in which you so delight. I feel weak beyond words, as if I were insubstantial: a mannequin of flesh and feathers.

I am to join you, my love. Perhaps I shall even reach you before these words. Perhaps I shall consign these words to the flames and give no warning of my arrival, happening upon you with the suddenness of monsoon rain. Shall I find some dark-eyed strumpet wrapped around you? Will you laugh to witness me in cape and cap, thrashing your bare-breasted companion with the fury of a slighted wife? I picture it now. I summon up cruel imaginings of your infidelities and for an instant I am myself again: jealous, embittered, quick to rage, merciless in rebuke. What does it say of me, husband?

Am I only capable of grief and fury? Am I so lamentably uncomplicated?

We could talk into the small hours upon such matters, of that I have no doubt. And you would soothe me, would you not? Would soften my edges? Would gently flatter, a balm for all the pinpricks and abrasions of my own dislike for myself?

I must ask your forgiveness again, my darling. With these words I have robbed you of your last child, accused you of duplicity, and spoken of naught but my own grief and suffering. How do you fare? Even with the vastness of the oceans between us, I am able to conjure the sensation of your skin upon my own. How I long for the consolation of your brow against mine own, your eyes shimmering and multiplying as we stare into one another and search out one another's souls. I feel your palm against mine; the prayer of our clasped hands as your beard rasps softly against my own fair cheek, wanton and ravenous in our zeal for contact; for caresses, praising the Lord with the perfection of our couplings?

I find myself biting my lip when Dr Tulp speaks of the location of the soul. I see him now, blade in hand, misted blood upon his fine skin, excavating flesh and innards and offal to seek out that which enlightens us – unravelling yards of coiled rope and passing it through his hands, seeking connection to the Almighty as if it were a pearl trapped in a twist of bowel.

I will cease now. This day presses upon me like rocks. I do not know if this correspondence will reach you, but in writing I feel a closeness like balm upon chapped skin.

We shall make more children, my darling. And I shall be ever yours.

Yours with all that I am,
Creesje

7

Jeronimus Cornelisz, moving like shadow through Dam Square. Viewed once, he could be mistaken for a sweep's brush. He is little more than a bushel of burnt sticks, wrapped up in his threadbare cloak.

'Apple, sir? Fresh picked this morning, juicy enough to tempt Eve herself...'

Cornelisz glances at the young girl who has arrested his passage. Blue dress, yellow hair beneath a smudged white cap; cheeks that look as ripe as the fruit she holds in her pink fist. She recoils from Cornelisz's unblinking stare. Retreats behind the legs of a stout man, caught up in conversation with a tall figure in expensive boots.

Cornelisz considers the child. Wonders whether she sees him true or whether she has already begun to lose the innocence of youth. He knows himself to be a source of fear for children who take the time to consider him. Animals, too, sense something within him, slinking out of his path or growling in a low, unsettled whine. It was thus with his own child. The boy always cried louder in his father's presence. Cornelisz takes some degree of comfort in the knowledge that his son saw him for what he truly was. It allows him to think of the boy's death, and his own part within it, as a charitable act. He spared him years of terror and shame; his mind troubled by nightmares of snakes and fire.

He gives the girl a smile, then forgets her. Descends back within himself. Returns to the pleasing thoughts that have entertained him through the cold, uncomfortable night and which distract him still as the low summer sun climbs into the cornflower blue sky.

Moves on.

Stalks and scuttles, tasting the air, a spider trapped beneath glass.

'Mijnheer Cornelisz. Good morning, my friend. I declare, I almost walked straight past you. You move like shadow!'

Cornelisz stops as if somebody has pulled his reins. Looks up and realises he has reached his destination without once taking notice of his steps. Above, hanging from a rusted bracket, is the ridiculous stuffed crocodile that tells him he has found the premises of the apothecary favoured by men of influence. The man who has arrested his progress is due within at eleven o'clock. Soon, he will bite down upon leather-wrapped chains and scream as if disembowelled as the potion-maker attempts to cure the venereal disease that causes him such discomfort. His name is Gerrit van de Werff, and Cornelisz has invested time and resources into fashioning the right opportunity to accidentally run into him.

Like a sailing ship catching a favourable wind, Cornelisz's mind surges ahead, probing the next few moments for pitfalls and opportunity. Van de Werff is a rich man. He knows Cornelisz by sight and reputation. They have shared evenings of debauchery and excess. He relaxes his manner, and offers a small, semi-formal bow.

'Gerrit,' he says, his arm fastening onto the elbow of the squat, amply chinned gentleman. 'You caught me in a moment of introspection. Forgive me. And do please overlook the moment it took me to correctly identify you. I am consumed by my own thoughts. You look to be in rude health. Has your good lady wife commissioned a portrait, perchance? I see you have lost some of the cushioning at your belly and your skin positively glows. In fact, do tell me, you are Johannes van de Werff, yes? Not a younger brother or illegitimate son?'

Van de Werff preens, straightening his back to stand a little taller. He smooths down his black shirt front and picks a stray crumb from his white lace collar. 'I had quite forgotten your gift for flattery,' he says, his fleshy lips curling into a self-satisfied smile. 'Truly, your potions and concoctions may heal the body but it is your company that lifts the soul.'

Cornelisz offers a further, deeper bow, his whole demeanour altering to suit the encounter. He is at once humble and obsequious; glad to be remembered and grateful for the opportunity to spend some time in the company of this plump, slack-jawed simpleton.

'I had not thought to see you in Amsterdam,' says van de Werff, lowering his voice. He glances at the apothecary shop and Cornelisz watches as he decides whether he should continue on past the premises so as not to betray the reason for his presence here, at the appointed hour. Discretion wins out. He begins to walk back towards the marketplace. At his side, Cornelisz falls into step, deliberately stooping and limping on his left leg. His great skill is in seeming benign; in displaying a harmlessness, a subservience; a fragility.

He glances at his companion and plucks a memory. He and van de Werff first met at the fencing club of Giraldo Thibault: the gentleman's club where radical thinkers could share idle blasphemies while parrying sabre strikes and making profitable connections. Cornelisz was present as the guest of his master, Torrentius, who had discovered that the men within could be easily seduced by his scandalous philosophies. He declared that all men were destined for Heaven; that as all things were predetermined, it was folly to live with decency and shame aforethought. He encouraged excess. Urged his followers to sin and blaspheme, to cavort and carouse and spill their seed into the men and women, children and beasts that he secured for their pleasures. He has seen this stout, Calvinist puritan draw his dagger across the neck of a goat and drink a toast to the devil with its blood. He wore the mask of Pan – his features hidden behind red velvet and a leering, tar-black mouth.

'You will have heard of the plight of our friend?' asks van de Werff, quietly. He breathes out as if a great weight has been pushed into his belly. 'Truly, had I but known that there was more to his teachings than liberty and love of earthly pleasures, I would have turned my face from his the very moment he began to entice me with his slippery words. I spend my days in a state of anxiety, Jeronimus. And my nights! Oh how I yearn for sleep. My dear wife believes me when I say it is business that keeps me from my rest. How to tell the truth? How to tell her that I am a disciple of Torrentius, whose name is a byword for debauchery and the work of Satan himself?'

Cornelisz returns his hand to the fat man's elbow, squeezing the flesh as if testing fruit. Notices a feeling of prickling warmth, low down in his belly. Van de Werff is a man of influence. He has a place at the head table of the VOC.

'I share your suffering, my friend,' says Cornelisz, as he steers them around a semi-circle of stallholders who have gathered to watch two small boys play a rowdy game of knucklebones against the wall of the church, crouching low and placing bets as they toss the defleshed pig toes as close to the wall as they can. 'In truth, it is my friendship with Torrentius that expedited my departure from Haarlem. Perhaps you heard of the misfortunes I suffered these past months?'

Van de Werff grunts an embarrassed affirmation. 'Indeed, indeed. A great tragedy, Jeronimus. A man of your education, your reputation, brought so low by so scurrilous an accusation...'

'To be robbed of my child, and for my wife's good name to be trampled to ash,' says Cornelisz, and manages to force tears from his blue eye. He makes a show of gathering himself. 'Alas, the indignity has proven too much for her. She has returned to the bosom of her family while I endeavour to correct the path my life has taken. You will perhaps have heard that I am bankrupt? I, a scholar, a Guildsman – one known throughout Haarlem and beyond as the most reliable and discreet of apothecaries... to sign over my property and holdings to such a crook as Vogel...'

'Come, come,' says van de Werff, putting an arm about the apothecary's frail shoulders. 'We are survivors, are we not? Men like you and I, men chosen by Torrentius as vessels for his teachings... such misfortunes are mere stumbles. Look at us!' He laughs suddenly, slapping Cornelisz upon his bony shoulder. 'Two dithering women, wrapped up in worries. We thrive, do we not? We flourish! And for as long as our learned master holds his tongue, that shall continue.'

Cornelisz does not reply. It pains him to think of the decadent, ebullient scoundrel languishing in a cell, his days a misery of boredom, of solitude, or pain. He is accused of heresy, of being a member of the Rosicrucian order, of making pacts with the devil. For the time being, Torrentius resists the entreaties of his jailers. He will not give them names, no matter how great the weights they pile upon his chest or the height from which they drop his broken, bloodied form.

'I fear for him,' whispers Jeronimus, his voice catching in his throat. 'He is not a young man and the strength that sustains him must surely fade. He will do all he has sworn to protect those he calls friends but I have made my peace with the knowledge that he will soon choose between his own life, and those who called him "master".'

Van de Werff stops, suddenly, a hand to his mouth. 'Surely not, Jeronimus. His word is his all. And I have witnessed his tolerance for pain. Why, he nigh surpassed you for tolerance of the torch, did he not? And what would he tell? That he hosted bacchanalian gatherings? Masked balls? That he dressed harlots and street-rat youths as satyrs and nymphs and paraded them for our pleasure? My, there is barely a gentleman among the VOC who has not indulged a hunger for such riotous assemblies.'

Cornelisz rubs his hand across the twisted skin upon his face. 'I pray you are correct, my friend,' he says, quietly. 'And it pains me to offer tidings that may rob you of your certainty.'

Van de Werff's features clench into a look of sudden concern. 'What news, Jeronimus? What tidings?'

Cornelisz endeavours to look pained. 'I am fortunate to count among my customers the wife of one of his jailers. She spoke of his suffering: the sheer agony he is enduring each day. And moreover, she spoke of those who plead for mercy on his behalf. She spoke of the recent correspondence received from the King of England, weak-willed milksop that he is. His Majesty, God curse him, is to offer Torrentius refuge at his court. He will provide for him a home, an income, a position as court painter. And our own accursed Majesty is prepared to assent, provided Torrentius divulge just three names. Three fellows whose executions may serve as warning against future heresies. Why do you think I fled Haarlem, my friend? Why am I here, seeking escape from these shores? I was shown such favour by our master that I do not imagine he will name me, but others will do so to save their own skins.'

Cornelisz shakes his head, aghast at the inequities of the world. 'I was able to send word before my flight. I gave him my blessing and told him to do what he must. Through sheer good fortune, the message was parlayed to him by the jailer of whom I spoke, and he did grant me that most detestable of confidences in return. He bid me take the burden upon myself. He asked me to select three men whom I know to have been to blame for his arrest and interrogation. And so you find me, Johannes – a lost prophet, blundering through this detested city, trying to make peace with God as I fight with my conscience and prepare to condemn three men to the flames, for that will be the punishment. No axe, no hempen rope for the followers of Torrentius. It shall be the flames that devour them.'

Van de Werff stands still, his red face draining of colour until his entire countenance takes upon the look of a drunken, leering eye. He gulps for air. Shakes his head. 'My God but that is a cruelty to gift to a loyal disciple, is it not? And all to buy his own passage to a safe haven? My friend Jeronimus, I do not envy you. But tell me, which three poor fellows do you intend to condemn to such a grotesque end?'

Cornelisz stares past him. Allows his gaze to drift upwards to the line of blue between the roof of the church and the bank of cloud. He feels a moment of connection: past and present and future, Heaven and Earth, sea and land, all flowing into and out of him; the spider at the centre of an infinite web of glistening strands, lethal and fragile and ravenous beyond satisfaction. He sees who he was, and is, and shall be. And he sees what Torrentius saw, when the flame first kissed his flesh.

He allows a little malice to bleed into his voice – just enough to unsettle his companion. 'It may happen, Johannes, that you and I can address that very matter over a cup of wine. I seek to offer reassurance and peace of mind.'

Van de Werff licks his lips. Takes a moment before replying. Watches, wordlessly, as Cornelisz reaches into his cloak and removes a simple mask. Offers it to the merchant with a twisted grin. 'My, you made a fine Pan.'

'You would bait me, sir?' hisses van de Werff. 'Would betray our friendship?'

'I seek funds.' Cornelisz shrugs, spreading his hands wide.

'I seek employment. I seek passage to a new beginning. I seek opportunity to live as our master instructed. I seek opportunities in the Indies.'

From behind van de Werff, a roar. The two children throwing knucklebones have succeeded in distracting the stallholders long enough for their accomplices to raid their takings. There is the thunder of running feet, shouts and jeers and fist upon flesh.

'You would go and not return?' asks van de Werff.

'Batavia,' says Cornelisz, softly. 'Both the fortress and the ship.'

Van De Werff is suddenly dripping with sweat, his face turning the colour of spoiled pork. 'An educated man such as you... a position within the Company might be within my reach. But if stories of your recent misdeeds were to reach the ears of the Gentlemen before you set sail, I would struggle to protect you...'

Cornelisz allows himself the hint of a smile. Bows, stiffly. 'My dear friend, any kindnesses you provide will be returned to you a thousandfold. You offer more than I deserve. And please, sleep soundly. Those who would wrong me have already been identified. Those who would speak against me will not be trouble for long.'

Van de Werff sucks at his cheek, sweat running from his pink face to stain his pristine collar. 'You are more than his creature, are you not?' he whispers, teeth bared. 'There is something in you that I did not see until this moment. Something that I wish I had not seen. I shall secure you passage, Cornelisz, and say a prayer that you find the new Eden of which our master spoke. But whether you be Adam or the serpent, I leave to God.'

Cornelisz stares past him again, watching as the cloud slowly descends and swallows the light.

8

The coach clatters to an unseemly halt, jerking to the left as the wheels snag in a cavernous rut. Nicolaes spills forward, the bottle falling from his hand: the hilt of the sword jabbing between his ribs. He lashes out at nothing, punching the air and losing his balance, spinning to an inelegant halt on the dirty floor of the coach: spilled brandy upon the seat of his breeches and his hat tumbling into his lap.

'Masterful, Nicolaes,' he mumbles, dragging himself upright. 'A bravura display.'

There are muttered curses from the coachman, culminating with his proclamation that the horses, the wheels, the earth and everything around and about, are the "bastard sons of piss-poxed whores".

Nicolaes, head muddied by the brandy and the dream, pushes his face out through the window, rubbing his eyes with the heels of his hands. Drowsily, he takes in his surroundings. Smells earth and sawn wood and the low, rancid fug of horse sweat and leather. Something else: deeper, coarser – pushing through his nostrils and onto the back of his tongue.

Corruption, he tells himself, as his skull sloshes with a deluge of ugly memories. *Dead flesh.*

He glances upwards, looking for the sun, and finds that it has already slunk low in the sky, turning the Heavens an attractive, pink-seamed indigo. The last of the light reveals that the carriage has come to a halt on a quiet country road, the boundary marked by two shabby hawthorn hedges. He can make out farmland beyond, the land marked up into small squares and rectangles, their edges marked by low railings of barked wood, tied with leather thongs. He can make out the outlines of livestock: skinny black-faced sheep and underfed cows.

He retreats into the coach as the driver begins to climb down. Hears grumbles about 'shit-spangled daughters of flux-cunnied curs' and gives a nod of appreciation. Truly, this man knows how to swear.

A face appears at the window, sullen and streaked: flies feeding freely in the grease that slathers his pockmarked features.

'We's here,' he growls. 'Church, yonder. Past the trees. You wait. They come.'

Nicolaes knows from experience that the coachman is impervious to charm. He mirrors his foul-tempered expression and wrinkles his nose.

'Is that pig shit?' he enquires, as if asking a noblewoman the provenance of her fine perfume.

'Aye, like as not, though I've had a stabbing in me guts these last three miles and can't say that I'm not to blame for some of it.'

Nicolaes bites back his smile. Peers past the foul-smelling coachman to where he can just make out the very tip of a slate roof.

'They?' he asks, guardedly. 'Who's they?'

'The people His Lordship told you to see,' he growls, spit flecking his chin.

'And you'll wait?'

'No.'

Nicolaes gathers himself. Fastens on the sword and climbs down from the coach, straightening his clothes and wiping his hands over his face. The driver is patting the rump of a fine grey horse, its flanks coated with the dirt of the road. 'I can put my weight behind her if you need some assistance…' he begins, and shuts up quickly when the driver flashes angry eyes in his direction.

'You's to go in. Up track. Poxed whore of a place to reach, I tells the Lordship, but he's sweet on yous and don't pay no mind to my sufferings. On yous go, now. Leave me to my business.'

Nicolaes shakes his head, his milk of human kindness starting to sour. He flicks the brim of his hat in farewell and begins trudging up the road to the break in the hedge line. He catches a whiff of something foul; a rank, hot-iron reek that causes him to raise his cuff to his mouth and nose. He hears the creek, metal upon metal, and the raucous flapping of damp wings. Looks up and sees the gibbet, its wooden trunk stained with blood and years. From the L-shaped cross-beam dangles an iron cage, big as an ale cask. Long thin legs hang down through the bottom of the cage, ending in black-and-white: bones protruding from the last scraps of stained, suppurating flesh. Leathery scraps of meat are peeling away from yellowy rib bones. Wisps of black hair and tattered skin cling to the worm-eaten skull, great black holes where the eyes should be. Nicolaes cocks his head, watching as a small red-breasted bird lands upon the dead man's shoulder and begins pecking at the closest eye socket, pushing inwards, yanking back: a string of something sinewy and red clutched in its beak. The tendril of gore snaps, and the bird flies away, triumphant.

Nicolaes continues up the path. He has seen more bodies than he could count, and is no longer disturbed by the sight of ruined flesh, though there was something about the dead man that struck him as out of place.

The sun is slipping below the treeline by the time he arrives at the small church, clinging to the lip of a shallow valley that rolls away down to more trees and the shining, hammered tin of a slow-moving river. It's a small construction, old and in poor repair. There are a smattering of half-toppled headstones in the long, briar-tangled grass that surrounds it, marked out by a mossed-over, tumbledown wall. Wildflowers bloom amid the thicker tufts: great tangles of nettle and cow parsley cloaking the flecks of colour: the tiny red hearts of strawberries and the deep purple of tall-stemmed, bell-shaped flowers. He lets his gaze drift, out towards a distant curve of dwellings: beetle-sized figures waiting in a line at a circular structure he takes for the village well. He catches the distant tang of smoke and turned earth.

Nicolaes waits, his hand upon the jagged wood of the broken-down gate. Considers the building. There are holes in the roof: birds cawing and squabbling as they flutter in and out of the ragged patches of black amid the green-slimed slate. There is no glass in the windows and the door, black as pitch, stands ajar – as inviting as the mouth of a sea serpent. He closes his eyes and wraps his hand around the hilt of the sword. He tells himself not to be afraid. He was in the clink this morning, trying to win pencil and parchment in exchange for a mouthful of piss. Not so long ago he was on his arse, covering his head as boots and sticks bludgeoned him unconscious and the man he was meant to protect was torn to pieces. He has faced cannon fire, enemy warships, clashed swords amid the gun smoke and blood spray of countless battles, and slit throats in the black of night and the full, honey-wine brightness of day. He does not need to fear what waits within.

He lets out a slow, controlled breath. Pushes open the door. The creak is loud as a wolf howl against the stillness of the night. Cautiously, cursing the screeching din that heralds his arrival as surely as a peal of bells, he steps into the cool black mouth of the church.

Cold air, upon his skin. A perfect, absolute soundlessness about him, as if the walls are saturated with centuries of unheard prayer. Slowly, the scent of old stone and mutton-fat candles creeps into his nostrils

'My name is Nicolaes de Pelgrom,' he announces, feeling foolish. He walks blindly forward, his eyes slowly adjusting to the gloom. Only one candle burns, casting a weak, stuttering light into the blackness of the low-roofed church.

'I was tasked with making a new acquaintance and offering what service I could...'

In the shadows, a sudden blur of movement, the rustle of cloth upon cloth; the glint of steel. For a moment the creature that bursts from the darkness is a demon: bones and blood and torn flesh, held together by a few ragged strips of cloth and the clots and scabs that stitch the wounds across his belly, chest and dirt-streaked thighs.

Nicolaes jerks back, glimpsing the face of something

grotesque as a blade whistles past his face with a sound like tearing leather. *A man*, he tells himself, his chest tightening, as he desperately tries to unsheathe his sword. *Just a man*.

Wide, staring eyes; toothless maw, dripping red; face transformed into something like smashed clay by the wounds that have been scored into its surface.

The thing roars. Slashes again. Hacks down as if chopping wood.

'Stop, stop, I am no threat. I mean you no harm...'

The attacker turns, his flickering shadow huge and hideous on the sloping roof. Nicolaes looks at the blade that he clutches in his bloodied, swollen hands. Looks at the man's stance. Tries to make out his features beneath the filth.

'You are from the East?' he asks, desperately, staggering back, feet tangling. 'I've served with your countrymen. I've fought alongside warriors such as you. Sheathe your blade, sir. I am not your enemy...'

Nicolaes watches as the man's features twist. Hears a scream of gasped, unintelligible words. Sees him shift his grip on the fine blade: two hands clutching the handle as if wringing the neck of a snake.

Then the metal is slashing at the air, hacking at the shimmering dark as if cutting hunks of meat from a hanging carcass.

Nicolaes's hands shake as he parries the blows; vibrations running from his fingers to his shoulders. He steps backwards, feet moving as if to music, parrying, twisting, listening to the high, echoing clang of sword upon sword.

And then Nicolaes is faltering. He has placed his feet upon an absent flagstone, toppled back into emptiness, his knee clattering on the lip of some unseen tomb. He raises his sword, blocking the strikes that rain down, killing blows all: reverberations numbing his elbow, thudding through his arm.

There is a moment when Nicolaes knows he will die. He sees his future as if it were painted in oil. He sees himself hacked and butchered, his head cleaved from his shoulders. Sees himself reduced to his component parts, bleeding quickly and blackly onto the floor of the church. He wonders who has killed him and why.

The curved blade streaks down towards him.

Nicolaes flicks it away with the handle of his sword. Feels hot wetness spurt over his left hand. Looks down, and sees his fist rammed deep into his attacker's belly, the grip of his dagger coated with thick, pooling blood. He does not remember drawing it.

'My friend, I had not wished you harm...' whispers Nicolaes, weakly, as he slides the blade from the man's gut. Watches him sag and hears the sword clatter on stone. He hauls himself up. Looks down at his slain attacker as he slumps to his knees, blood leaking from the great smile that Nicolaes has ripped across his belly without even thinking.

'Who sent you?' asks Nicolaes, cupping the man's face in his bloodied hands. 'What has been done to you? Why...?'

An explosion, from the space behind him. A flash of flame and the sudden whistle of a musket ball past his cheek. And the attacker's forehead opens like a waking eye, as his skull explodes in a burst of blood and bone and brains.

Nicolaes, his head ringing, can only turn and stare down into the blackness of the crypt. Can only watch as the smoke curls away and a patch of inky black delineates into the shape of a woman. Olive skin, star-bright whiteness in her eyes, she is wrapped in the finery of a dark red riding coat trimmed with gold. She holds a pistol, grey wisps rising from the barrel, and she is glaring past Nicolaes with a look of absolute purpose; her features locked, rictus-like, in an expression that Nicolaes knows well. She is utterly, irredeemably filled with hate.

Nicolaes stays still. Listens, as the dead man's body settles against the stone.

The woman lowers the gun. Blinks, hard. Gives him her attention.

Her smile, when it comes, is the strike of a snake: sudden, unexpected, lethal.

'Master Pelgrom,' she says, in an accented voice. 'My name is Mariam Towerson. Thank you for your attendance. If I could trouble you to accompany me, there are matters I would discuss with you. Our mutual associate informs me you are a man of ability, which you have certainly not disproven. I cautiously hope we can find a commonality of purpose.'

Nicolaes, recovering himself, hears his voice echo in the dark of the church. He jerks his head at the dead man. 'Who was he?' he asks, still panting from the exertion of the fight.

That smile again. Quick, like a whip crack, and then gone.

'There are men I wish dead, Master Pelgrom,' she says, coolly. 'Men who deserve to be hastened unto Hell. Men who have committed grievous wrongs and for whom death is the only suitable remedy for the evil that festers in their souls. I am informed that your benefactor has instructed you to assist me. You will understand if first I needed to see whether you would be up to the task.'

Nicolaes opens his mouth. Closes it again as the lady produces a small glass lantern and breathes life onto an ember within its ornate metal base. It fills the dark space with a soft warm radiance. Nicolaes stares down into the blackness into which she disappears.

Then, unsure what else to do, he follows her into the crypt.

9

Francisco Pelsaert, upper-merchant and second-in-command of the VOC's winter fleet, has taken lodgings in a tall slim house on the *Herengracht*. It is an impressive property in a quiet neighbourhood, shaded by a line of tall trees and overlooking a curve of canal: an elegant bridge reflecting back its likeness in clean, sun-gilded water. He does not fit in here. He has been too long in the courts of maharajahs and sultans; become accustomed to opulence, largesse and the giddy, gaudy colours of the Indies. Among the browns and russets of Amsterdam, he stands out like a splash of red paint on a headstone. He is a bird of paradise, all scarlets, emeralds and golds, roosting among drably plumed woodcock and partridge.

Jeronimus Cornelisz, recently installed as under-merchant with the VOC, has not had to part with more than a handful of stuivers to feast upon the stories, rumours and titbits surrounding the upper-merchant under whose command he is to spend the next months of his life. Cornelisz's own letter of commission as under-merchant is rolled up tight and slipped into one of the many concealed pockets in his drab black cloak. Van de Werff has done all that Cornelisz asked, and more. He has coin, now. Has secured a position of authority and a berth aboard the great flagship *Batavia* – number two to a man of no little renown. Seven years at the royal court in Agra have provided an unrivalled understanding of how to succeed in the Indies. He is a scholar, a seducer; ambitious and prideful and vain. He provides results for his paymasters and knows how much he can siphon off for his own ends without drawing attention. He speaks Hindustani and Persian, understands the importance of ostentatious displays when impressing potential business partners, and even appears able to tolerate the climate and diet without succumbing to undue sickness or untimely death.

And yet, his name carries no little scandal. Whispers persist. Pelsaert has undone himself, they say. Pelsaert has fallen a little short of true success. Pelsaert, they say, scuppered his own chances to be one of the truly great men of the VOC. He fulfilled his every desire with the native girls and courted scandal with his seduction of noble wives and daughters. He returned to the Provinces wealthy and intent upon retiring to a life of comfort and privilege.

After just a month in Amsterdam, spending freely and trying to rediscover a taste for soapy cheese and pale flesh, he has agreed to return to the service of the VOC. His brother-in-law, one of the senior gentlemen of the company, has persuaded the other members of the counsel to grant him a vastly inflated salary and a seat on the Council of India. There is none but he whom they will trust to command a vessel packed with such a fortune, and destined to return laden to the gills with nutmeg, mace – and gold.

Cornelisz thinks upon this cheaply acquired knowledge as he stands in the entranceway of the fine, cool house. He is clammy beneath his cloak. The walk through the bustle of Amsterdam has tired him and his lungs feel as though they are filled with shavings of hot iron. He endeavours to soothe himself. Breathes in the scents of honey and soap, baking bread and floor polish, and feels the spread of something that might, in a lesser man, be considered envy.

It surprises him. Cornelisz considers himself above such base emotions. There will always be men richer than he. Always be men with fine possessions and silken garments; men whose chiselled features catch the eye and whom Providence favours with fat, healthy children and the friendship of influential men. Cornelisz knows that he cannot expect to compete in contests such as these. Knows he will not prosper when held up against such men. So Cornelisz plays a different game. His success is in the delicate destruction of others. His delight is in the bending of stronger men's wills. He grows breathless with pleasure at the thought of whispering treacheries into the ears of those who believe him to be their confidant and counsel. To be overlooked, to be underestimated and disregarded – to be brushed into the shadows by those who pursue some illusory demon in their midst... in such moments, he knows himself to be the greater of any and all who cross his path.

From upstairs, the sound of raised voices. A barrage of insults and the crash of something hard hitting a wall. Cornelisz looks up just as the long-nosed, pinch-faced maid hurries down the stairs towards him. 'Perhaps it might be as well to return at a later date, sir. His meeting with Captain Jacobsz may continue into the afternoon...'

Cornelisz stops in the act of examining a bland but competent oil painting: sails and fields and a spider web of waxy green waterways. Looks to the maid as if he has heard nothing of the exchange overhead. 'Captain Jacobsz is the man with whom your master converses? That is most fortunate, child. The business we would discuss is something entirely for the triumvirate. Is it the room at the top of the stairs? Might we trouble you for honey water before the next strike of the clock? I find myself tired after the walk from the market.'

The maid opens and closes her mouth as Cornelisz talks, trying to turn the smooth flow of words into an instruction. She picks out the words "honey water" and "upstairs" and gives in to a nervous bout of nodding, hurrying past Cornelisz with something approximating a bow.

Cornelisz moves up the wooden stairs without a sound. Slick as shadow, feet wedged into the corners of each step so as not to cause a board to creak, he makes his way through the cool, buttermilk-coloured hallway and stops outside a black door, open to the width of a finger. He can hear conversation flowing out through the gap; the mumbles coalescing into words and sentences as he stands, still as stone, in the upstairs hallway. Above, the soft golden light of a midday summer sun pours in through thick glass windows, casting a series of yellowy squares onto the dark floor. Cornelisz positions himself away from the light. Pulls his hat low, lest it find his skin and cause his sores to weep.

'...*not exactly overjoyed about it myself! An opportunity to right some wrongs and cement my fortune and I find myself reunited with a drunken hobgoblin who humiliated me in front of men whose opinions I hold dear!*'

'By Christ, Pelsaert, you talk of humiliation! On the *Dordrecht* you demanded apologies of me in front of my own damn crew! Waved your rank like it was your manhood and had me grovel like a cabin boy! This was to be my reward, you bastard! Serious command of a brand-new ship, and I find myself subservient to a puffed-up peacock! By God if you wear that red cape aboard the *Batavia* it will become your winding sheet!'

'*Ah yes, I had forgotten the amusement I caused among the crew, resplendent as I appear in my fine crimson garb. Is jealousy not an ugly sin, Jacobsz? I thank the Lord I am too preoccupied with lust and greed to find time for envy...*'

'And you've agreed to women aboard, you madman! Women! On her first bastard voyage, when the docks are awash with rumours of intrigues and the Gentlemen themselves grow fearful that King Charles has sent assassins intent on retribution...!'

Cornelisz decides the time is right to announce himself. Makes a fair imitation of footsteps moving from the stairway down the hall, his steps growing louder, until he can move forward from the spot where he has stood and give a weak, nervous rap upon the wood.

'In, damn you!' The instruction is given in a deep, working man's voice: his tone such that even an "amen" would sound like a curse.

Cornelisz does as he is bid. Pushes open the door and succeeds in maintaining the appearance of a man forever grateful to be included. He affects an air of absolute humility, bowing and scraping as he removes his wide-brimmed hat and shuffles his way into the living quarters of his new superior.

'By Christ, what in the devil are you?'

Cornelisz gives his attention to the squat, swarthy man

in blue breeches and mustard-yellow doublet who scowls at him from the large, unlit fireplace against the far wall. He's bare-headed and balding and is absent three teeth in his upper row. There is a chunk of his top lip missing and an explosion of little white lines beneath his stubble where a surgeon pulled the stitches too tight. There is sweat beading his face. His cracked knuckles, gripping the neck of a green bottle, are the colour of bleached cloth.

Cornelisz offers a deep bow and takes the moment to compose his features before turning his gaze to the other individual whom he glimpsed as he slithered into the room. Francisco Pelsaert is reclining in a large wooden barrel, his arms draped over the sides and the tip of his beard floating like pondweed atop the surface of the deep grey water: flower petals sticking to his tanned skin. He is smiling as Cornelisz raises his head: neat white teeth peeking out from between neat moustache and well-tended beard. He wears his hair long, parted in the centre and hanging in damp twists down his handsome cheeks. Brown-eyed. Devoid of scars, two sizeable jewelled rings upon his middle fingers and a twist of gold about his thumb, he only needs a girl with a palm frond and he would be holding court like a maharajah.

'You will be Cornelisz, I'll wager.' Pelsaert smirks, from the barrel. 'Ignore the thick-witted brute by the fireplace. You are his senior officer, as am I, and should you wish it, you can have him beaten with a length of rope until his innards are as easy to examine as his sulking face. Do try and remember that in the months to come.'

'Try it,' growls Jacobsz, glancing from one to the other. 'I beg you, try.'

'I was encouraged to introduce myself,' stumbles Cornelisz, and his cheeks begin to feel clammy as the steam from the water starts to envelop him. He glances at the contraption beneath the barrel. Identifies a small metal brazier, filled with burning sea coal, concealed directly beneath the wooden frame.

'Go on then, man!' yells Jacobsz. 'By God, my bottle is all but empty!'

He waves the offending vessel – his sweep taking in the assorted fineries of the room. Fine rugs blanket the red-and-white tiled floor and green silks lie rumpled atop the wooden box-bed; its headboard covered in ornate fretwork. Paintings gaze down from the spotless white walls. Stacks of papers and expensively bound books are piled upon the Spanish leather chairs, which bask in the light from the open window. The drapes alone, purple and green, are such a stark contrast to the Calvinist blacks and browns of Amsterdam that the very sight of them seems to unsettle Jacobsz, who falls silent.

'I am Jeronimus Cornelisz. Under-merchant. Apothecary, by trade. I would not have disturbed you had I known you were at your bath, *Commandeur*. Shall I retire and return…'

'Another one!' growls Jacobsz, rediscovering his temper at the bottom of the bottle. 'Poets and bastard lawyers, given command over a man who knows the sea the way a babe knows his mother's teats! Swim, can you? Sail? Turn green the moment the ship's out of Texel? By Christ but you don't deserve the *Batavia*. An indignity, for such a ship to be commanded by men of commerce.'

In the tub, Pelsaert smirks. 'He can only speak this way, Jeronimus – may I address you as such – capital, thank you, and of course you must address me as Commandeur Pelsaert, but no matter, no matter – our skipper here has been given the opportunity of a lifetime and yet he knows no way to show gratitude or delight and so retreats to sullenness and boorishness. It is a tragedy, I'm sure you will agree. Too many men feel that they must imitate animals if they wish to be taken seriously, which is patently absurd. It is no sin to *feel*, Captain. Admit it to me, here, in confidence – you smiled when the news was delivered, did you not? You felt a little prickly sensation in your stomach and didn't know whether to drink, tup a wench or take a shit. That, dear Skipper, is a sensation that we developed men call "happy".'

'Fine talk,' growls Jacobsz, taking a swig from the bottle. 'Lots of lawyerly words. Lots of gentlemanly words. And they can get a man's jaw broke just as quickly as if you were to speak base, like me.'

Pelsaert smiles again, completely untroubled by the waves of malevolence that emanate from the man with whom he will spend the next months at sea. He gives Cornelisz his full attention. Slides his eyes over him like a trader considering a warehouse full of disappointing goods. 'Apothecary,' agrees Pelsaert, convivially. 'The rasp in your voice speaks of tinctures tasted and poisons imbibed. Orange fingers too – as sure a sign of a mixer of potions as ink upon the thumbs of a clerk. Not much beef on you, is there? And I'll confess that those scars are going to be difficult to stomach after a foul meal on a rough sea.'

Cornelisz subtly alters his demeanour. He fancies he may have appeared too feeble; too obsequious. He will need at least one of these men to believe in him. He stands a little taller. Takes on the look of somebody who sustained his scars in a bloody duel over a tavern wench.

'I passed a market trader on my way here,' he says, thoughtfully, running his eyes over the commandeur in his barrel of hot water. 'I would have bought onions had I known your maid was boiling you up for broth'

At the fireplace, the skipper snorts, his breath catching in his throat. Hocks up a lump of something unpleasant and spits into the dead hearth, his face split in a huge grin.

Pelsaert, in his tub, permits the jest. 'So there is some life in you. Excellent. I look forward to seeing what the Indies does to a man whose skin begins to seep even in the presence of warm water! Now, we are all acquainted. And perhaps, two out of our number may eventually be friends...'

'Soup!' repeats Jacobsz, overjoyed at the barb. He bounds from the fireplace and claps a meaty hand on Cornelisz's shoulder, offering the bottle and pressing his sweaty scalp against Cornelisz's head. Cornelisz takes the bottle, making sure to be seen refraining from wiping the lip before he takes a long pull of the spicy spirit.

'Eeh, you got him there, sir.' Jacobsz laughs. 'Sitting there in his petals and his jewels and you see through him in a heartbeat, do you not? Looks like he's being cooked for supper!'

Cornelisz shoots a look at his superior, who seems untroubled by the jesting at his expense. 'Now, to business. You've seen her?' asks Pelsaert, addressing the captain. 'The *Batavia*?'

'A fine ship,' says Jacobsz, his eyes widening to reveal grapevines of fine red upon his tallow irises. 'She's taking shape. One last coat of pale green paint and we'll see how she takes to water. Pride of the fleet, I guarantee it. With a fair wind we could well make the crossing at a speed the Gentlemen will struggle to believe. Nine thousand square feet of canvas she'll take, and she'll need it to move such a great fat-bottomed beast. One hundred and sixty feet from stem to stern. By Christ but I even like saying the words! Four decks, three masts, thirty guns, by God but Rijksen has designed a ship that Noah would have wept over! Every slaughtered cow would be thankful to have her hide stitched to the hull if they saw how splendid she looks in her leather coat. She's a beauty, but powerful, by God. A man couldn't wish for more from his daughter!'

Cornelisz takes opportunity to inspect the skipper, whose drunkenness seems more pronounced as he talks so animatedly about his new command. He reeks of rum and greasy meat. There are no fingernails on his left hand. He is drunk before midday. His disrespect is tolerated, so he must be a fine sailor...

'What is it you flee, Cornelisz?' asks Pelsaert, unexpectedly turning away from Jacobsz and inspecting him. 'Are you a thief? A bankrupt? Is there a murder to be laid at your door? Tired of your wife and in need of darker meat? Tell me, why would a man of education – an apothecary no less – travel to such a godforsaken hole?'

Cornelisz takes another swallow of the spirit. Hands the bottle back to the skipper with a word of genuine thanks. 'I'm not sure I follow,' he says, cautiously.

'Come, sir, do not be coy! The Company is a great refuge for all! Spoilt brats, bankrupts, cashiers, brokers, tenants, bailiffs, informers and suchlike rakes... what man would take passage aboard an East Indiaman were there not wolves at his heels? Half of the men who leave the United Provinces are dead within three years! There are more ways to die in the Indies than a man could conceive of. Disease or slaughter by the natives – or even by whichever European nations we suddenly call our foes – they are pleasant ways to expire compared to some I have witnessed. Aye, there are duties to be done and glory to be found. Yet I look at you, Cornelisz and do not see a man who yearns for adventure. Indeed, I do not quite know what I see at all.'

Cornelisz take a moment. Allows a little smile to form at his lips. 'You are a fine judge of men, Commandeur. I am indeed penniless. I am bankrupt and newly bereaved – my wife and child both taken in quick succession. In my grief I found solace with a woman whom I believed to be goodly and godly, only to learn that she was wed to another – a man of reputation who demanded satisfaction for the slight. And I, being one to know my limitations, have chosen a path that falls some way between cowardice and courage. I flee to uncertain death, to avoid a certain one.'

Pelsaert slaps the water, laughing happily. 'Well I'm glad to have one level-headed fellow aboard, sir! And good God we shall need you. We have a surgeon, of course, but the man's a halfwit and I'll be glad to speak to a man of science and partake of the occasional tincture if it helps the journey pass more quickly. I have little doubt it will be intolerably dull, but perhaps that is to be preferred to the excitement of overall command.'

Wordlessly, Jacobsz passes the bottle over to Pelsaert. He takes it, wipes the lip and sips at it, grimacing. Beside Cornelisz, Jacobsz gives a low growl: a dog hearing a footfall beyond a closed door.

'I am told Fleet President Specz is a respected fellow,' says Cornelisz, catching the sound of good drinking vessels chinking against a silver tray.

'Bring it in, Susannah!' yells Pelsaert. He jumps up, water dripping down his naked body, so he can be fully exposed when the young maid enters the room. She pales, the vessels clattering against one another, and Cornelisz reaches out to take the tray before she drops it. She curtsies, awkwardly, and scurries out. Pelsaert settles back into the water, grinning. 'I'll wager either of you fellows that I shall have that one's legs apart before we sail.'

'A hard word would part those legs,' spits Jacobsz, scornfully.

'I shan't force her, you oaf – she shall come willingly. Is that not the sweetest tup of all? You, skipper – when did you last have a woman who wasn't crying or counting her coins? And don't count your wife...'

'Fleet President Specz, sir,' says Cornelisz, pointedly. He has seen something in Pelsaert's face that he wishes to explore.

'He has problems I would not wish for myself,' says Pelsaert, shaking his head. 'We are a flotilla of secrets and lies, are we not, Jacobsz? The correspondence that comes to me from the Gentlemen would vex even the translators at the Tower of Babel. I am bid not to enquire about the gentleman in the under-merchant cabin aboard the *Dordrecht*, under the personal care of two mercenaries. I am bid not to speak of the precious artefact that we will carry in the hold to woo our friends in Batavia! What do I do with all of this, Cornelisz? How much can a man hold in his mind? I swear, I am exhausted before we have begun.'

Cornelisz looks up. Offers his most genuine smile. 'It would be my honour and privilege to take the weight from your shoulders, Commandeur. I am happy to serve in whatever capacity you make use of me, but I have a gift for correspondence and a tidy mind for facts and figures, should you wish to push all such correspondence towards me.'

In his tub, Pelsaert brightens. Lifts the glass and toasts his new subordinate. 'I am glad that the fates have brought us together, my friend. Already, I feel the weight of authority and leadership pressing less heavily upon my back.'

Jacobsz snorts. Spits. Shakes his head.

Cornelisz reaches out and takes the bottle. Wipes the lip, and hands it to the skipper. He notices the gesture, and grunts his thanks. Pelsaert lowers himself into the water, disappearing beneath the petals and bobbing like a corpse.

'Trinkets?' asks Cornelisz, quietly.

Jacobsz gives him a sly smile. 'As the bastard says, there's no end to the possibilities for a man with the wit and will to succeed. There's no rules south of the equator. Why, a man could declare himself king of his own patch of paradise had he the guile.'

'You know the Indies well?'

'Served my time, sir. Am in my prime but the aches are catching up with me. It's an honour to call myself skipper of such a mighty ship but honour does not put a bulge in a man's purse. I shall confide, there have been times when I wonder whether it is wisdom to put a man such as I at the helm of a ship carrying such a fortune. Only loyalty prevents me from putting myself before the Company, but now the Company has thrown me this preening bastard as commandeur, well – a fellow could turn from the path of righteousness.'

Cornelisz reaches down. Pours himself a glass of honey water and clinks the glass against the bottle.

Negotiations have begun.

Before the month is out, Ariaen Jacobsz will have made a pact with the devil.

IO

The air in the crypt smells of paper and dust; of death and damp wood. Nicolaes descends into the cold, low-roofed space and says a small, silent prayer for courage as his eyes adjust to the gloom. The lady's lantern gives off a yellow glow, which turns straight lines and hard edges into blurry, shimmering shapes that he struggles to identify.

'Allow me,' she says, reaching out to take his hand. 'My eyes are better suited to the dark.'

Cautiously, Nicolaes allows her to close her long, cold fingers around his bloodied right hand. He jolts at the contact, startled by the sudden trill of pleasure that shoots along his arm as she strokes her thumb across the gore upon his knuckles. She leads him as if he were a child, motioning for him to sit when she is satisfied he has found the correct spot in the darkness. He lowers himself, seated upon curved stone. She sits opposite, placing the lantern into a small niche in the wall. She turns her head, looking past him, into a pocket of absolute shadow.

'You saw?' she asks the dark.

'I did,' comes a reply. Nicolaes stiffens, his hand upon the handle of the rapier, staring into the black air.

'He has been taught to fight as a gentleman, but it is the gutter that serves him best.'

'You would do me the honour of showing yourself, sir,' says Nicolaes, squinting. 'I do not enjoy being dissected as if beneath the scalpel of an anatomist. Who is it that skulks in the dark under the protection of a lady and her pistol?'

Nicolaes's words are met with silence. He turns towards the woman. She is watching him, curiously, a little smile upon her face. 'I would ask that you refrain from insulting my companion,' she says, quietly. 'He believed it prudent to accompany me this evening but it is best if you remain unfamiliar with his visage. I am not so bashful. I am Mariam Towerson.'

Nicolaes continues to glare into the shadows. He fancies he can make out the curve of a shoulder; perhaps the hint of a grey beard.

'Your discussions are to be with me, Master Pelgrom,' she adds, pointedly. 'He is here to protect my virtue, and to assess your suitability for the task.'

Nicolaes feels his temper begin to prickle. His limbs ache, he is covered in blood and a stranger lies dead on the floor of the church above. He is growing weary of his ignorance.

'I am to be studied as an ostler would a stallion, yes?' snaps Nicolaes. 'Would he slap my forelocks? Should I curl my lip so he may rub his fingers upon my gums? Should I drop my britches? Unsheathe myself, sir?'

There is a bark of laughter from the darkness. 'He is as promised, Mariam. Please, continue. He has my approval.'

Nicolaes does not let himself react. Places his hands at his sides and feels the cold stone against his skin. As he considers the finely dressed woman before him, the shapes behind her delineate into caskets: wooden boxes stacked like books. He lowers his eyes to the bottom of the pile. Sees the mulch of bone and rags and earth spilling through the rotten timbers of the lowest casket.

'I shall bite my tongue, madam,' says Nicolaes, quietly. 'My master has instructed me to perform a service for you and I shall endeavour to do what you command. Yet first, I must enquire, whose blood is drying upon me? In God's record of my life, there are numerous names written in red, but none were trivialities. I would know whose death has come at my hand.'

The woman lowers her hood. Purses her lips, as if sucking a lump of sugar. 'The man with a pistol ball in his head and whose guts stain the stones, was mostly known as *Komatsu*.'

'I have fought alongside Japanese warriors,' says Nicolaes, rubbing the damp blood against his breeches. 'Brave, loyal men, one and all. What cruel game of chance brought him to meet his end here?'

Mariam Towerson chews her cheek, one eye closed. 'I gave him one chance to save his own wretched life, Master Pelgrom. All he had to do was kill you. He failed.'

'Kill me?' demands Nicolaes. 'What wrong have I done you, madam? For what reason could you so easily play these games of life and death?'

'Komatsu was an excellent warrior,' she says, without emotion. 'Yes, the voyage here and the questions that were put to him may have enfeebled his strength, but I did not know until you opened his belly that you would be capable of doing that which I desire.'

'He was a test?' asks Nicolaes, his knuckles white around the stone.

'He was your first commission,' she replies. She reaches forward, and by the flickering glow of the candle he sees her extend her arm and open her hand. On her palm lies a ruby, its edges reflecting the yellow light of the lantern and emitting a soft spray of dazzling light. 'Take it, Master Pelgrom. You have earned it. And I have many more.'

Nicolaes reaches out, mesmerised by the jewel upon the lady's palm. He stops himself from snatching at it, aware that whatever test he is participating in, is not yet complete. 'You buy my silence, madam?'

'I reward your skill with sword, Master Pelgrom,' she replies, coldly. 'Komatsu aided in the torture and execution of my husband. My husband's body lies far from here; far from his family church, his family tomb. Instead, I anoint the earth with the blood of his murderer.'

Nicolaes says nothing. Watches the soft wisps of smoke rise from the lantern and drift in slow tendrils across the fine features of this stern, exotic woman who offers him jewels and speaks so candidly of torture and death.

'Forgive me,' says Nicolaes, sitting back and forcing himself to look not at the jewel, but into the eyes of the woman who offers it. 'Oft have I heard that grief softens the mind. Think then upon revenge, and cease to weep.'

Mrs Towerson sits back, a small smile at her lips. 'You are familiar with the theatre, Master Pelgrom. Master Shakespeare, is it not?'

'I have been tutored to stand up to scrutiny in most things, milady,' he says, shrugging. 'I am indeed a scholar, or at least, able to bluff as such. I know sufficient Portuguese and Turkish to make myself understood. I am fluent in the language of my birth and, as you will hear, my English is flawless. I have knowledge of scripture and philosophy. I can make gentle conversation or imitate the furious righteousness of those who speak ill of His Majesty. I have spent these past years learning to be whatever is required, madam. And all of my lessons have taught me that when a beautiful woman offers a young man a fortune for a simple slaying, the true cost of the endeavour has yet to be paid by either party.'

From the darkness, that bark of laughter. Nicolaes doesn't turn his head.

'Towerson,' he says, as if struggling to remember. He rubs his jaw, miming deep concentration. 'You, madam, must be the widow of the honourable Gabriel. Which means that the man who hides himself in the darkness, must be...'

'Yes,' says Mariam, sharply.

'You have my condolences,' says Nicolaes, sincerely. 'A tragedy.'

'An abomination,' thunders the voice in the darkness. 'A massacre that would shame the very devil! And this Parliament has spurned every last opportunity for retribution, casting aside moral obligation to instead foster trade deals with the very bastards who cleaved my brother's head from his neck!'

Nicolaes feels no satisfaction at having his guess confirmed. The man in the darkness is the brother of the slain Gabriel, whose bloody end brought England and the United Provinces to the brink of war.

'You have a fierce intelligence, for one so low-born,' says Mariam, without malice. 'I hear rumour that you are mongrel – the blood of gentleman and whore. I say it without judgement. Indeed, a mongrel who fights with both a gentlemanly finesse and a gutter savagery is the perfect breed for the task ahead. I see you assembling a picture from the scraps of parchment in your mind. Yes, sir – the man you killed was present in the final hours of my beloved husband, as he and his fellow Englishmen rotted and festered in the dungeons of Amboyna, awaiting the peace of the executioner's axe. Komatsu claimed that my husband had paid him and a band of mercenaries to help him overthrow Dutch rule. An absurdity! A glaring falsehood, obtained from a man desperate to save his own skin, and which condemned a group of fine English merchants to their terrible deaths. I have sought redress through Parliament – even through the men of the East India Company. I have petitioned those bastards at the VOC and been met with scorn. Only your Buckingham, speaking with the authority of the king, has paid heed. It is he who has fought to achieve redress for that which occurred in Amboyna. And when those channels were closed to me, it is he who has offered, instead, a man he holds in great esteem.'

Nicolaes clenches his jaw. 'He offers me as if I were a horse, madam? For what purpose? I have known you only moments and already my bones ache, my head spins and I have taken a life. Your jewel does indeed entice me but I would have you speak plainly. You wish me to kill for you? There were many men who had a hand in the death of Gabriel Towerson. Dutchmen, Englishmen, natives; Japanese. You cannot truly expect to avenge yourself upon all of them! Why, from what I recall it was the order of that black-hearted bastard Governor-General Coen that permitted the atrocities conducted in that dreadful place.'

Mariam snaps a look into the darkness. Flicks her

attention back to Nicolaes. Grins: a dog showing teeth. 'Yes,' she says, simply. 'Coen. He and his dog, van Speult. I seek their heads. Theirs and more. The bastard torturer who poured water into my husband's mouth until it poured out of every hole; the merchants who lied to secure their own safety even as the smell of Gabriel's burning flesh made them gag. I wish them dead.'

Nicolaes looks about him, as if the answers might be written upon the old stone of the crypt. 'Madam, those you wish to avenge yourself upon are located at the most distant curves of the world. Your reach extends far and I am naught if not resolute when I set myself to a task, but your enemies are half a world away. To achieve that which you desire, I would have to journey to a part of the world from which only half make their return. I should have to take passage aboard a spice ship; brave those Satanic waters... How, madam, even with all the jewels in your purse... how?'

She leans forward, her eyes fixed upon his. Her cheek bulges where she grinds her jaw.

'Today, I buy a blade, Master Pelgrom. I unsheathe you. I wield you. And I plunge you into the dark heart of those whose continuing lives are an insult to myself, and to God.'

Nicolaes looks to the darkness. His pulse is racing. It feels as though there are birds inside his head: beaks and beady eyes and fluttering feathers against his skull. 'Madam, I do not know if I am equal to such a task. To even reach such high-ranking enemies would necessitate such charades; such dissembling. I regret your pain, you have truly been ill-used, but what you ask of me – the miles I would need to cross. What reward could be worth such an undertaking?'

The ruby glitters afresh in her palm. It is joined by other

precious gems: her hand beginning to tremble as she places stone after stone upon her delicate palm. 'These are just the beginning,' she says, her voice catching. 'I return soon to my family in the Indies. Upon reaching me, upon completion of your task, I will make land and title over to you, sir. I shall clear my family of their fortunes in gratitude.'

'And if I say no? Or if I say yes, and then just walk away with your secrets and your money?'

There comes the sound of a pistol being cocked. As Nicolaes looks into the darkness, he feels a sudden movement, and then a blade is pricking his throat.

'That is a course of action I would not recommend.'

Nicolaes swallows. Feels blood trickle into his shirt. Looks along the edge of the blade and into the eyes of Mrs Towerson. 'Was that a nod?' she asks, softly.

Nicolaes blinks.

'Rubies come in many guises, sir,' she says, spilling the precious stones on the floor. 'And if you cross us you will see that your blood, when it falls, glitters as richly as these precious gems.'

'I have other duties, madam,' he whispers. 'Others who would use my services. Why, Buckingham himself showed today how dearly he requires my close company in the dark months ahead…'

She stops him, holding up a finger to her lips. 'My dear Nicolaes, I would urge you to bite your tongue. Buckingham himself has already agreed. This command comes from his own lips. He is, as he explained to me, second only to the king. Ordained by God, is he not? Buckingham has already been paid for his acquiescence. You are here to revel in the illusion of choice.'

'I have a choice,' whispers Nicolaes. 'I do not need your gold, madam. Surely there are others better suited to the killings you wish to purchase.'

She smiles at him, the light catching the tears in her eyes. 'I have already bought myself innumerable assassins,' she says, drily. 'Whether I add you to their number or turn them upon you depends upon the bargain we strike tonight.'

Nicolaes swivels his eyes to the darkness. Thinks again of the look in Buckingham's eyes. It had been goodbye, had it not? It had been the look a horse owner gives to a favoured stallion as it is led away to slaughter.

He closes his eyes.

Nods.

Feels the blood squelch upon his palm as she shakes his hand.

11

Cornelisz puts his shoulder to the oak-and-iron door and pushes his way into a foul-smelling darkness. He's beneath the city; the very bowels of Old Amsterdam. The air is cloudy with the reek of sweat and damp and filth, but Cornelisz does not show any displeasure as he moves slowly into the stone chamber, straw rustling underfoot. His eyes adjust to the gloom. In stages, the darkness takes shape. Low-ceilinged and lit only by two small, meat-fat candles, the chamber is a box of flickering lights and dancing shadows. Cornelisz moves forward, lifting his dark cloak so that it does not disturb the stinking reeds, and peers at the huddled shape in the far corner, pushed up against the apex of the two walls, as far away from the pail of overflowing faeces as the space permits.

Gradually, the figure becomes a man.

Cornelisz stays motionless, wordless, as the pitiful figure raises his head and exposes a gaunt face, straggly bearded and pale as moonlight; his eyes two knots in a length of burnt timber.

'His boy,' grunts the man, his voice hoarse from lack of use. 'He sends his boy.'

Cornelisz considers Collas Siegel. Were he capable of such

a feeling, the man's appearance would arouse pity. Instead, Cornelisz views him as if he were a painting. He looks upon the lesions and sores; the cracked lips and bare feet; the guttering light spilling reflected flame into the hollows of his cheeks and admires the artistry of suffering. Cornelisz would like to sit here for a time and watch the changes that the man would undergo were he left untended. He wants to see him shrivel like a discarded grape: shrinking as the moisture leaves his flesh. He would like to see how he will look when the stiffness takes hold of his limbs. Would be intrigued to see the moment when the skin begins to corrupt and his meat turns sour, then rancid, then begins to fall from the bone. He does not wish the man any ill will but he fancies there will be a strange beauty in the process of transformation.

'You look well, Collas,' says Cornelisz, with a sly smile. 'Blooming, in fact – a flower kissed by the sun.'

Siegel twists his features into a sneer. Shields his eyes as Cornelisz produces a candle on a small tin tray from inside his robe and crosses to the little niche where the greasy wicks emit their flickering light. He lights it and allows the flame to swell. Slowly, he turns back to Collas and inspects him in this new, brighter light. The man's clothes are rotting upon him; his hair falling to his shoulders in greasy ringlets and curls. His face is wasting, diminishing... and yet there is a power there, an echo of something that was once handsome; once grand.

'They need to chain you?' asks Cornelisz, inspecting the length of chain that runs from a rusted bracket in the wall to the fetters upon his ankles and wrists. 'Chains, a locked door, jailers who feed you through a hatch and are told not to speak to you upon pain of decapitation – and the marks of repeated torture upon your skin, I see – it is almost as if your captors believe you to be dangerous.' He shakes his head, amused by the thought. 'Would it help, I could explain things properly. It would take but a moment to educate them.'

'They believe me to be a corruptor of men,' croaks Siegel. 'A fomenter of dangerous heresies. An evil-doer intent upon bringing about the end of days.'

Cornelisz smiles, genuinely amused. 'So I hear. I presume you have told them that they have imprisoned the wrong fellow, yes?'

'Have they?' asks Siegel, anger flashing in his green eyes. 'For all that I believe myself ill-used and mistreated, I am guilty of that which I stand accused. I did despise the church and its teachings. I did toast the devil and sup the blood of virgins from golden goblets. I did avail myself of young, nubile flesh and it was indeed my hand that held the whip that tore the flesh of an imitation Christ.'

Cornelisz grins as he considers a memory. 'I recall the evening with fondness, Siegel. There was barely enough left of the poor boy to crucify. Have you spoken this freely to your tormentors?'

'They do not acknowledge my words,' says Siegel, huddling into himself as the temper bleeds from his face. 'I confess to all and they act as if I am silent. There are no questions. No interrogation. Just this cell, and moments of suffering. I don't even know how long I have been here.'

'It will soon be a year,' says Cornelisz, squatting down in the straw. 'I commend you, Siegel. I would have expected you to have said his name before the end of the first day.'

Siegel jerks his head up, the chains clanking as he lurches forward. 'I am loyal to our master, Cornelisz. I am loyal to the man who showed us the truth. I will endure all the torments they inflict upon me. I would die before I spoke his name.'

Cornelisz shakes his head, looking pained. 'Your suffering has been for nothing, Siegel. Our teacher has been in a cell smaller than this since the winter of last year. He was taken only a few weeks after you. So were a handful of his followers and many members of Thibault's club. Your silence has not saved him, or any of our fellows. It is a cruelty that nobody has told you.'

Siegel's face contorts. Fury, confusion, despair... Cornelisz watches the conflicting feelings wrestle for control of his emaciated face. 'You lie,' he grunts. 'Were he taken, you would not be free to make your way into my cell. They would have nailed you to the doors of the new church. It is you, Cornelisz, who should be in a cell. Our master is a scholar, a teacher, a man of infinite and radical ideas – you are the dog who performed the evil deeds. You who procured the young boys, the cowering girls, to be portrayed in his tableaus. You who silenced them with your concoctions. You who poured the wine into our goblets and bid us take pleasure in the suffering of others...'

'You overcame your reluctance with some gusto, I recall.' Cornelisz smiles. 'You were never a believer, but you persuaded yourself of the pleasures to be had in pretending.'

'This is why you came?' asks Siegel. 'This is why he sent you?'

'You speak of our master?' asks Cornelisz, raising his fingers to his face and rubbing the livid pink lesion upon his jaw. 'Alas, I have not been able to converse with him. I understand from Mijnheer van de Werff that he has been stretched until his joints popped from their sockets and the bones of his ankles were visible through his skin, but I have not been witness to his sufferings. I fancy they would be most upsetting. I can tell you with some authority that he has not betrayed those close to him.'

'And you consider yourself thus?' snarls the chained man. 'You were no apostle, Cornelisz. No prophet. You were his dog. He poured his honey in your ear so you would keep doing his bidding. How he laughed as he told us of the hunger with which you feasted on his lies. How you sobbed and kissed the hem of his robe as he spoke of your great destiny – filling your head with dreams. You, the risen son – you, a specimen like you, believing yourself to be the herald of a new age, the one who would bring about a time of destruction and rebirth – you, the God of Flame...'

Cornelisz does not respond. Just sits and stares at the candlelight. Waits for Siegel to exhaust himself then continues as if he had not spoken.

'You will be pleased to learn that I have found employment with the VOC. I am now under-merchant, bound for the Indies, second-in-command to Francisco Pelsaert – a gentleman with whom I understand you to be acquainted.'

'Pelsaert?' snaps Siegel, breathing heavy. 'You come here to speak of Pelsaert?'

'Among other things, yes,' says Cornelisz, companionably. 'I fancy that I am at liberty to share my thoughts with you, Siegel, for nobody is listening to your confessions and the guards have been paid well to turn deaf ears and blind eyes to my presence. I am here because before your disgrace you were a good and loyal employee of the VOC, and you have information that may yet prove helpful. I ask you again – Pelsaert. You are acquainted, yes?'

Siegel shuffles back into the corner of the cell. 'Nine years I gave the Company,' he hisses. 'Nine years in the Moluccas – fighting, trading, dealing with the madness of my own men and the brutality of savages. Navigator, cartographer – you will have seen my maps upon the walls of the Gentlemen XVII. I carry in my head the coastlines, the depth soundings, every contour of every godforsaken island, reef and shore between here and the edge of the Earth! I was loyal and profitable and the VOC held me in esteem. I suffered for their profit. I spent three of them in a cell worse than this, all shit and flies and corpses, shackled to a dead Portuguese, suspended from a hook in the roof. When I was set free I could not lower my arms and there were parasites in my skin that bore down to bone. Such suffering gave me the strength to endure these trivialities, Cornelisz. I can endure this for as long as my jailers see fit and naught you can offer me will change my mind...'

'Hush,' says Cornelisz, softly, and enjoys the look that passes across the other man's face. 'You will help me, Collas, for the simple reason that I can put an end to your suffering. You and I sit here – companionable, friendly – and as we do so, a young lady of my intimate acquaintance pleasures the two turnkeys who keep you caged. She is an impressive young woman. She is clever and sly and has an uncanny ability to persuade people to her will. Distressingly, she is also being sought by magistrates. I regret that I played some part in this complex series of events and as such I feel it is beholden upon me to provide her with a future, and also to prevent her father from slitting my throat.'

'What is this to me?' demands Collas.

'You are a Company man,' continues Cornelisz. 'You may be down on your luck for having the misfortune to be among our master's circle of acquaintances but you are not beyond redemption. Were you to slip your manacles and disappear into the streets of Amsterdam, you could well live many years. You could even prosper.'

Siegel peers at him through the gloom, hope flaring in his eyes: a fire starting to smoulder in a darkened cell. 'You will want something from me. You will demand a price.'

Cornelisz smiles, pleased that the broken specimen is keeping up. 'Of course, Collas. Very little comes for free. But in this case, I ask only for your influence.'

'Influence? I have spent a year in a cell! What is it you want from me, Cornelisz? What could I offer you that would not cost me my soul?'

'All I ask is introduction, my friend,' says Cornelisz, smoothly. 'I have no doubt you can still find the strength to hold a quill. I ask for no more than your skill as a map-maker.'

'Speak your mind,' spits Siegel.

Cornelisz looks past Collas, staring into the darkness at a picture only he can see. He has made his calculations. Weighed up what is within his power, and what is not. He has no desire to reach Java. No desire to be an under-merchant, or to stare upon the malarial pestilence of the Batavian fortress. What he seeks is far simpler. A ship, a loyal crew, a body of men capable of doing his bidding in return for the God-given right to indulge their every base desire. He knows he can bend men to his will. But to find a place in a distant ocean where a majestic new ship might be halted and order turned to chaos? For that, he needs the skills of Collas Siegel.

'I am to build a new Paradise, Siegel,' he says, without guile. 'I am to become all that Torrentius foretold. I take command of the Ark and go forth to build a new world. A world free of rules or restraint or the petty tyrannies of those who praise a God that stopped listening the moment mankind nailed His son to a cross. It has been foretold. I see it in the flames. I feel the serpent moving within me. I am Adam. I am Christ. I am the Snake.'

Cornelisz takes paper from his robe. Proffers it to the cartographer.

'You are mad...' whispers Siegel, his voice catching. He glances past Cornelisz at the sounds of grunted ecstasy spilling from the next cell. Glances at his manacles and lowers his eyes.

'Skipper Jacobsz does not yet know that he is privy to this great undertaking. He thinks only of treasures and gold and his own base pleasures. He is petty and small-minded in his ambitions. But given time I shall set him upon the correct path.'

'Skipper Jacobsz? That drunken fool? There has never been a mutiny aboard a VOC vessel that involved an officer! You are mad, sir. Be grateful for your new beginning. Try the life of an under-merchant – you may find it suits you. None shall follow one such as you.'

Cornelisz closes his finger and thumb around the burning wick of the candle. Feels no pain.

'I am no sailor,' continues Cornelisz, as the darkness

closes around him. 'I rely upon men such as Jacobsz. He is without guile, but I, as you know to your benefit, am not. There will be not far short of four hundred souls aboard the vessel. That, my dear Collas, is too many. I shall require an unsafe harbour in order to exact my stratagem.'

'An unsafe harbour?' His voice wavers. 'You mean it! You mean to seize the ship! There will be families aboard, Cornelisz. Women! Children! Why, the soldiers will stop you, I guarantee it. They are loyal to the Company, no matter what!'

Cornelisz moves soundlessly in the dark. Appears at the ear of Collas Siegel and whispers, softly. 'With the hatches nailed shut they shall not even have a chance to rise past the gun deck. And by then, those surplus to our needs will have been removed. The soldiers will bend to my will more easily once we have turned the cannon upon them.'

'Madness,' whispers Siegel. 'This is the work of the devil! Where would you even stage such an atrocity? The *Batavia* is but one of many ships in the fleet. You would first have to lose the others. You would need to rid yourself of Pelsaert! And a VOC flagship, sir? They would never stop searching for it.'

Cornelisz breathes out, slowly. 'Your mind moves impressive fast, Collas. Mine moves faster. All that you warn me of has already been taken into consideration. I simply need a place to stage the performance. I need a new chart, Siegel. One that may be disseminated among the other vessels in the fleet. I am told by Skipper Jacobsz of a reef; a tooth-sharp chain of islands at the edge of the world. You are to provide new maps, my friend. You are to assist in the wrecking of those vessels that sail with us. And you are to assist me in depositing those who we do not need, upon a distant shore. There shall be no survivors, Collas. The Company will consider its treasures lost and its passengers dead. It is beautiful in its simplicity, is it not?'

'You mean to kill all those who would resist you?' he asks, his voice a wavering croak. 'I knew you to be bad. I did not think of you as evil until this day.'

'Such a tired word.' Cornelisz sighs. 'So insufficient to describe what I am, and what I feel myself becoming. Now, you sailed with Houtman, did you not? You know the isles of which I speak?'

Siegel coughs. Begins to gasp for breath. 'That place is truly Hell. There has never been a more windswept, bleak and blasted landscape. None could survive there. Still I feel my flesh creep as I recall the absolute desolation of the Abrolhos.'

'Yes, that's the place.' Cornelisz smiles, relighting the candle and enjoying watching Siegel fold in on himself as if aflame. 'Now, ask yourself, do you wish to assist me and vanish, or do you wish for me to invite my companion to enter your cell, and beat you to death with your own limbs.'

Siegel's hand shakes as he reaches out. 'Paper. Quill. I shall require the VOC seal and a signature to copy...'

Cornelisz opens his cloak. 'I have all a man could seek. Truly, you must stop acting so surprised. God provides.'

As the map-maker sets to work, Cornelisz looks into the flame.

Sees himself, staring back.

12

The Windmill Tavern, Old Jewry, London

August 18, 1628

Nicolaes sits by the grand fireplace, watching the dance of the flames. It is a warm night and the landlord of the tavern has only built up the fire for the light it provides, and the air of welcome and comfort that it lends the premises. Now, as curfew approaches, the flame greedily devours the last errant hunks of wood and sea coal, which huddle low beneath the red-gold tongue of the dying blaze.

Nicolaes is sprawled in an uncomfortable wooden chair; his muddied, bloodied boots resting on the edge of the long, empty table. The carcass of his roasted fowl sits greasily on a trencher of pale blood and spilled ale. Were he less footsore from the long walk through the city, he would have made the effort to cross to the door and hand the bones and scrappy meat to one of the children whose eyes occasionally appear at the darkened glass beyond the fire. But to do so would risk becoming a man worth noticing. And here, now, he does not wish for the other patrons to comment upon him. He needs to blend into the darkness; to become a part of this empty room, with its bones and crusts and molehills of discarded tobacco rising out of the rushes and old, damp stone.

He sips at his beer. It's strongly brewed and heavy but it has little effect upon his faculties. He has drunk strong spirits since he was a boy and beer serves no other purpose than to moisten his throat.

He stares into the flames. Occasionally he shakes his head, or smiles, or offers a little laugh at the absurdity of the mission that he has somehow vouchsafed to undertake. He cannot make sense of himself, or the ease with which Mrs Towerson and her brother-in-law bought his services. From time to time, a little shiver of glee makes him wriggle like a worm on a pin. Two dead now. Two broken men gone to God at his hand. He has earned the beginnings of a small fortune. Within the year he could own land and the title to numerous holdings in a place where a man of means could become a man of extraordinary wealth. He is overcome with visions of a different life: a future in which he has no master. He allows himself to consider wife and children. Stares into the flame and considers the kiss of hot sun upon bare skin; of lazy, listless days where none can snap their fingers and demand he kill and scout, seduce and beguile at their leisure.

Skilled as he is in the art of overlaying his reality with illusion, he cannot truly imagine himself settling to such a life. He has already exceeded every ambition that he set himself when he came to England seeking his father. He has served a great man. Has proven himself as soldier and spy and learned how to secure advancement through favours remembered and secrets forgotten. There are other ways for him to prosper, of that he is certain. Why continue with this cruel, ungodly campaign? Why accept such a dangerous, foolhardy commission? Why put himself into this Hell of enemies and disease: to rejoin the ranks of the common soldier and journey to the East Indies to do bloody murder to men as well protected as his uncle?

He shakes his head. Wrinkles his nose, disappointed at the inevitable realisation that he is doing this to please his benefactor, and because the formidable Mrs Towerson looked at him with such desperation that to refuse was beyond him.

'Mrs Towerson,' he mutters, tapping his tankard against his teeth and allowing himself a little smile. 'To consider yourself the equal of a man would be an act of diminishment.'

He still has not fully digested all that she has shared with him about the vicissitudes of chance and misfortune that led her to the crypt beneath the little church, parlaying with the Duke of Buckingham's retainer about a campaign of bloody violence against those who have wronged her. He thinks again of those piercing, joyless eyes; the look of absolute conviction in the way she held herself. This would be done with or without his involvement, of that she was certain. There have been others in her employ – others who have tried to reach her targets. Some have lost their life in the process. Others secured scraps of her fortune by eliminating softer targets. Her favoured assassin suffered severe wounds and succumbed to fever while securing the transportation of a Japanese mercenary from the fortress in

Batavia where he had lately been serving his Dutch masters, alongside dozens of his countrymen.

Nicolaes drains his ale. 'Madness,' he mutters. 'True madness.'

He pictures her mouth. Summons up the image of those full, tulip-petal lips as she spoke, so matter-of-factly, about her life.

'I was a gift,' she told him, by the soft light of the lantern, as her brother-in-law sheathed his sword and returned to his vigil in the dark. 'I have been twice married to Englishmen and twice I have found myself grateful to God for providing me with such good and steadfast men. I was little more than a child when the Great Mughal Jahangir developed a friendship with an Englishman at his court. My William was a great adventurer and a forthright, honest man. Jahangir wanted to please him, as one would a favoured guest. He set himself the challenge of finding a good Christian bride for his new friend. I was selected for that honour, and though it hurt bitterly to bid farewell to my family in Agra, he was indeed a good and attentive man. I was the best wife I could be to him, and ours was a union of friendship and love. We had been married too few years when my husband, every inch a weather vane for what was to come, decided we should return to England.

'Alas, he sickened on the journey home and did not reach England alive. And so I found myself, an Armenian by birth, raised in a court in India, widowed by an Englishman, in this strange and unwelcoming land. My late husband's employers, your veritable East India Company, proved reluctant to honour certain financial agreements that should have by rights passed to his widow. It was only by the good graces of those who showed kindness to a stranger that I was not abandoned at the docks. Of those who showed me kindness, I thank God for steering me into the care of Gabriel Towerson. The love I felt for Gabriel repaired me and somehow, our union seemed to please God. My fortunes changed. The monies owed by the Company were finally paid, and having sold those jewels which I had been gifted by my family, I received the joyful tidings that we were to leave England. Mr Towerson was appointed principal factor in the Moluccas – a position long overdue and too little reward for his years of loyal service.'

Nicolaes shifts in his chair, the weight of his sheathed dagger pressing against his back. He thinks again of the way it had slid into the samurai's gut as if quartering fruit. Shakes his head, lest the memory become more than an echo. He knows from past experience that those whose lives he has ended can linger if he dwells upon their memory: bloodied spectres with empty eyes, staring accusingly at the man who stopped their hearts. He thinks instead of Mrs Towerson – of the melody in her voice and the sudden flash of light in her eyes as she spoke of the man for whom she threw off her widow's gown.

'After a return to India, we made our home in Amboyna – a time I recall with great fondness. He was a strong, adaptable man, full of laughter and ever eager to delight me. He was like a child in the way he would run to me, a butterfly upon his knuckle or a glittering stone upon his palm, thrilled to show me something that might make me smile. He was a true jewel for the Company, making it his business to represent the Crown and his employers with wisdom, humility and grace. Truly, he was a victim of that insidious, creeping evil that infects the minds of powerful men.'

Nicolaes had kept quiet, for fear of dragging her back from the memory into which she stared. No tears fell, but her eyes grew dark as she remembered that which was done to Towerson and his English colleagues in 1623.

'The Dutch and the Spanish had fought bitterly over the spice trade,' she'd said. 'The English merchants who traded at Amboyna were viewed with suspicion by the authorities, amid fears that they would switch allegiances and attempt to capture the island. I swear by Almighty God that such imaginings were fantasy, but the idea took root in the mind of that damnable bastard Herman van Speult, who feared above all things that the sultan would begin to favour traders other than his own countrymen. In this time of hot tempers and simmering blood, Dutch soldiers identified some Japanese mercenaries looking uncomfortably closely at the fort's defences. They arrested these men and reported their findings to van Speult. Under torture, the mercenaries identified my husband and his countrymen as the leaders of a conspiracy. They were accused of attempting to seize the island and with formulating a plan to kill the governor.

'My husband, a respected man, attended the fort to answer what he knew to be ridiculous accusations. He, and men he considered friends, were tortured beyond their wits. Though my husband stood firm, the Englishmen condemned themselves by confirming each devilish contention that was put to them. Men I knew to be wise and godly were beaten to mulch. Gallon upon gallon of water was poured into their bellies. Bloodied, broken, they were held in manacles until the rotting flesh of their wrists and ankles spilled over the rusted irons. And when my husband saw that his countrymen had broken, he was made to press quill and ink to a confession.

'In front of the men of the fort, my Gabriel was murdered. So too were those factory owners who had been similarly brutalised, together with the Japanese soldiers who had first been put to torture. Four Englishmen and two Japanese prisoners were pardoned, having given confessions that condemned Gabriel and his associates. My husband's head was mounted on a pole at the fort gates, Master Pelgrom. And these many years I have petitioned the Company, Parliament, the king – I have begged them to demand redress for this ungodly massacre. They have ignored my pleas until this day, Master Pelgrom. On this day, finally, they send me you.'

Nicolaes is yanked from the reverie at the sound of raised voices from the adjoining room. Forces himself to stay present. Stay alert. A watchman was here not long ago, reminding the innkeeper that curfew was growing closer by the moment and that only a good meal and a hearty helping of ale could persuade him to forget such a salient fact. He has joined a gaggle of younger men in the back room: apprentice glovers, coopers, brickmakers, tanners. They are boorish, headstrong, physically able young men, whose thirst for drink seems unquenchable and who daily and nightly fill the pockets of the innkeeper.

The tavern is owned by a man known to one and all as Trotter: so named because of his facial disfigurement. Trotter lost a portion of his nose in a fight while not much more than a boy and the remaining portion has become something of a snout: pink, mucus-crusted slits offering obscene windows into his round, meaty face. He's a grotesque creature: a man of average height who carries himself like something from a nightmare: hunchbacked and rangy, his legs bent low as he waddles between the tables. He's broad-shouldered and strong and Nicolaes knows the lamentable caricature he displays is nothing more than a ruse. When threatened, Trotter straightens himself. Closes his open mouth and strips himself of the simpering, toadying nature with which he clothes himself when his customers are behaving as he would wish. Wronged, he is half-savage: a dog in a bear pit, all teeth and claws.

Nicolaes is familiar with both aspects of his character and knows each to be similarly repulsive. He has a secondary income as a procurer of the young and disposable: catering to whims of men with purses deep enough to ensure no thirst is ever left unslaked.

'Van Speult,' mumbles Nicolaes, eyes closed like lips, swallowing the name. 'Sent home in disgrace by the East India Company. Died at Mocha, off the Yemeni coast.'

He thinks again of Mrs Towerson, her voice cracking as she spoke the names of those she would see dead. 'The gossips would have it said that van Speult died onboard ship two summers since. That is a lie, sir. I have paid handsomely for information and van Speult lives, I swear to you. So too that accursed Coen, even now Governor-General in Batavia. Both must pay for what they oversaw. The Englishmen pardoned for their treachery returned home. Two are to die at your hands in the manner you see fit. Another has already succumbed to sickness. The other yet lives. The torturer who flayed my husband's flesh is a Dutch soldier, sir – even now filling his belly in an Amsterdam brothel as he awaits orders to join his new ship and return to the East Indies. Of the Japanese traitors, you need think no more. You have already ended his struggle for life; while the other, who died aboard ship, festers and pours through the grates of the gibbet at the edge of the lane.

'As for me, sir, I am to return to India. Petitioning the Company has been as much grief as the loss of my husband. They paint me as some grasping, ungrateful harlot: some foreign witch eager for naught but unearned recompense. They do not understand, sir. Only your Buckingham understands. Blood must be met with blood. Buckingham has spoken plainly, Mr Pelgrom. Though the negotiations between the two nations will continue, there is no hunger for conflict. To earn redress, I cannot expect cannons. And so, sir, I must wield a hidden blade.'

Nicolaes breathes deeply. Massages his temples, his head beginning to ache. He has nowhere to sleep tonight. He will make his way to Wapping before the morning tide, seeking passage on a ship bound for Amsterdam. Tonight is his last night as an Englishman. By the morning, he will be speaking in his native tongue and adopting the mannerisms of a Dutch soldier. Inside his shirt, beside his locket, is a commission as a private soldier in the Army of the United Provinces, attached to the Dutch East India Company and awaiting passage to Batavia on the next available ship.

'And may you come back and spew your coin into a fat man's purse, you rabble of bastards.'

Nicolaes looks up, cocking an ear as the watchman and his new companions grumble their way through the door and into the warm air of Cheapside. Listens as they lower their breeches and aim their splashes of piss up the front door and laugh, raucously, as one of their number succeeds in forcing their jet of beery froth onto the lower reaches of the window. There comes a low laugh from the hallway, beyond the partition wall, as Trotter closes the door behind the last of the men and leans, heavily, against it. Slowly, the raised voices grow quieter, and the sound of stumbling footsteps disappears into the night.

'By Christ, sir, I had forgotten thee!'

Nicolaes raises his head. Trotter stands in the doorway, a hand over his chest, half lost in the great mass of hair that coats him. He wears a leather jerkin over a stained doublet, unfastened to the waist, and his gut sits over the top of his breeches like baking bread. At his belt is a coin purse and tucked into a length of cord is a long strip of black leather descending from a wooden handle. Recovering himself, he follows his customer's gaze.

'Aye, a bull's pizzle, sir. I've wielded many a club and cudgel and these fat hands have hefted a sword and pike when war has called for it, but I have never felt as well at ease as when I feel this here piece of beef in my hand.' He stops talking for a moment, his voice thick with mucus. He hocks something back into his throat and spits onto the floor, his nostrils opening and closing like the gills of a landed fish. 'The bird was to your satisfaction, sir? You'll forgive me for not refilling your cup – I was dealing with that ragged bunch of chisellers and roustabouts and feeling the watchman's pincers nipping at my purse. It is no time to be a tavern-keeper, sir. There are always those willing to pick an honest man's pocket.'

He steps forward, looking at the near-extinguished fire and squinting at the handsome, well-dressed man he has ignored this past hour. He takes in the mud and blood of his boots and assesses their worth. Peers at the fine features and then his gaze stops upon the hilt of the sword. He sucks his teeth appreciatively.

'A fine rapier, sir. I see you are a man of means. If you are without a bed for the night then perhaps I could kick out one of those ungrateful bastards who lingers upstairs. If you were of a mind for company, there are few pleasures that cannot be catered for. My own dear wife makes for a comfortable hump, though she's in drink this night and may not even wake until you were done. If you seek somebody with a little more spirit, a little more... shall we call it fight... well, I know of a young boy who comes to me for scraps, and who can pretty himself up to be a maiden while still letting his pride jut like a mainmast, if you'll take my meaning, sir...'

Nicolaes smiles, a gentleman considering his options. 'Your name is Bellew, is it not?' he asks, softly.

Trotter, who has been moving forward as if carried along in a trail of ooze, stops short. He scowls at the name. 'And if that name meant something to me, what sort of a fool would I be to admit it to a stranger?'

'You've done well,' says Nicolaes, calmly. 'Just two years back in London and already so well connected. A tavern of your own and a network of apprentice boys glad to do your bidding. You make money at the bear pit, so I'm told. Will pay for inconvenient men to be removed, yes? Can secure the services of whatever a man might fancy, no matter what the cost. You have put that hard-earned coin to good use, I see. I wonder, does van Speult know what he has funded? It would no doubt do him good to see what a turncoat Englishman can become when given a proper start.'

Trotter fondles the bull's pizzle. Sniffs, throatily and allows his mouth to open in a leer. 'The name means nothing to me, boy. 'Tis clear you've had your fill of ale and per'aps that's addled your wits. I'll overlook the slight upon my honour, seeing as you're young and pretty and not worldly enough to know that you don't tell a man what you know of his past until he's already bleeding and both hands are nailed to the floor...'

Trotter lashes out with the strap of hard leather: its tip hard as tarred rope, whistling past Nicolaes's cheek as he pushes himself back in the chair. Off-balance, Trotter lunges forward and Nicolaes uses his boots to push against the table and pitch the chair over backwards, rolling through into the reed-strewn space behind him, turning on his shoulder and regaining his feet in one motion. Trotter swings the weapon but it passes harmlessly by as Nicolaes jerks forward, his head smashing into the vile, damp hole in the publican's face. There is a sickening crunch, and Trotter is falling backward. Nicolaes grabs him by his matted chest hair and smashes his forehead with his cheekbone. He feels Trotter slump, spilling backwards, his knees buckling. He drags him forward, dropping him on the table, blood leaking from his mouth and ruined nose.

Nicolaes steps back. Picks up the dropped bull's cock from the floor, and considers it. It's a fine object. Well-made and with a pleasing heft. He rolls Trotter onto his back and places an arm under his fat neck. Smiles, as if having seen an old friend.

'You're going to tell me things, Trotter. I won't make you

any promises about still being alive in the morning, but your death can come one way or another. My employer has left the details up to me. Now, I am going to give you some names. And you are going to fill my head with information with the ease that this world spills coins into your purse.'

Beneath him, Trotter squirms, drowning on his own blood as it drips from his ruined features into his throat. He gurgles something: a curse or a threat, but most definitely nothing that Nicolaes wants to know. He shakes his head, sadly. Slides his knife from its sheath. Slowly, deftly, almost tenderly, he slices off the fat man's ear and throws it onto the embers that glow in the hearth. He shoves the bull's pizzle in his mouth to mask the scream, feeling the blood jet over his sleeve.

'There are lots of pieces between you and death, Trotter,' he says, as the smell of burning meat rises into his nostrils. 'We just have to find something that you want to keep.'

He glances down, a slow smile crossing his features. Beneath him, Trotter's eyes bulge in their sockets.

'Now,' says Nicolaes, as his grin reflects in the steel of the blade. 'Tell me the truth and I shall set you free.'

13

Cornelisz leans against the trunk of a knotted linden tree, catching his breath. He is drained from his recent exertions; from the walk through the crowded centre and beyond the medieval city wall, making his way to this busy network of warehouses, factories and grand, tall buildings.

East India House stands on the Kloveniersburgwal, a tree-lined canal that was once the city moat, close to one end of the Oude Hoogstraat, the old high street of Amsterdam. The House is an elegant, three-storey brick rectangle, completed a quarter of a century ago and built around a central courtyard. Cornelisz is not impressed. As a cathedral to commerce, it lacks majesty or splendour. Though a fine and handsome property, it is less imposing than many would expect for the main headquarters of one of the world's richest trading companies: a company with power equal to the Parliament, Crown and Church. Cornelisz will demand that the churches built in his own honour will be more impressive – that his disciples will insist on wonder and glory. He has a thirst for sacrifice – will ensure that altars are used for more than the display of candle and cross.

It is a warm, uncomfortable day. The clouds press down

hard upon the clammy, bustling city, a damp blanket trapping the last greasy heat of summer. The air crackles with an eerie potency that makes hair stand on end and tempers flare.

Cornelisz watches. Waits. Enjoys the toing and froing of sailors, officers, clerks: scuttling in and out through the doors like drones from a hive. He wonders that they do not see him. Does not know whether to be aggrieved or glad that nobody falls to their knees before him, offering inverted genuflections and begging to do his bidding – to become disciples for this risen antichrist.

From time to time he indulges himself in sliding his fingers into the black velvet bag that he holds in the fold of his robe. He has enjoyed being permitted opportunity to touch and taste and fondle an object that fairly gleams with wealth and history. He holds in his cloak the Gemma Constantiniana: a rectangular cameo commissioned by the Roman Senate 1200 years ago. Though gaudy at first glance, the artefact becomes more intricate and opulent with each examination. Delicately carved in agate set within a glittering frame, the object displays a magnificent tableau decorated with a fortune in polished rubies and emeralds.

Cornelisz has run his malformed fingers over every dip and rise of the iwork. It depicts an impeccably glorious family: the Emperor Constantine, mighty in his chariot, cosseted between his adoring wife and mother; his firstborn son majestic in the foreground. A pair of muscled centaurs beat the sky; their hooves halted in the act of smashing down upon the dynasty's cowering enemies. In the Heavens, a goddess holds aloft a laurel wreath, smiling beatifically upon the Emperor as she prepares to crown him in his victory. It is a symbol of power, of dominance, of dynasty. The more Cornelisz considers it, the more the faces seem to twist into something familiar; the more the Emperor's features become a mirror.

The object has already served him well. He has renegotiated the price agreed by Pelsaert with the owner, respected jeweller Casbar Boudaen. It had delighted Boudaen to find himself being encouraged to push the price up rather than down – the difference being split between seller and purchaser. Pelsaert will grumble, but Cornelisz fancies he will be able to mollify him swiftly enough. He will tell him that a man such as he will have no difficulty in selling the object on when they arrive in the Indies. He will tell him that a merchant of such fine reputation will be able to command whatever price he sees fit.

He is quickly discovering that his commander is a man who responds well to flattery, and whose fortune is sufficient to not balk at a few extra florins. Cornelisz is now privy to his private accounts and correspondence and has identified a king's ransom in private trade conducted in the Indies in flagrant disregard of Company rules. Cornelisz is almost tempted to continue in his role as humble servant. He fancies that upon their arrival in Batavia, he could fare well under Pelsaert's command. He could become a rich man, influential and respected.

Cornelisz almost wishes that he could be tempted by such a vision. He wishes that he were capable of limiting the scale of his ambition. But to accept such a future would be to deny his destiny. Cornelisz is not a man who can prosper within the confines of this world of men. He is not intended for subservience or meekness, no matter how much power the dissembling may bring him. His destiny is to rule. To lead. To light a fire that will be seen from the Heavens and to sit atop a throne of skulls. Torrentius has seen it in him. He is no acolyte. No apostle. He is the God of Flame.

'If your eyes were a tongue the poor bitch would be damp as November,' comes a voice from behind him.

Cornelisz turns, smiling, extending his hand and shaking the sweaty red fist of Skipper Jacobsz. He's dressed for a meeting with the Gentlemen XVII but cannot pass for any more than a rough-hewn sailor. He reeks of rum and cheap wine, despite the pod of treasured spice that he rolls around upon his tongue.

'You caught me unawares, Ariaen,' says Cornelisz, warmly. 'Of what am I accused?'

Jacobs leers and points at a tall woman with an elegant neck, dressed in a dark blue dress. She is standing on the steps leading up to the big double doors, deep in conversation with a clerk who seems eager to get away. Cornelisz had indeed noticed her, remarking to himself upon the swan-like drift of her passage parallel to the water's edge. She is a remarkable beauty. Cornelisz undresses her in his mind. He fancies that her legs are longer than his own and imagines the feel of her hip bones against his belly. It is a pleasing thought. He looks at her neck: fragile, long. Considers his right hand and notices that his stained, unattractive fingers have twisted themselves as if around the bulb of a brandy bottle.

'Women like that are the only bloody consolation of having families aboard,' growls Jacobsz. 'I told them straight – said that no good would come of having women and children on a voyage of that length, but they won't pissing listen to me. I'm only a sailor and a captain – what would I know? But looks like you'll have your chance to impress her.'

Cornelisz cocks his head, intrigued. 'She is to journey with the winter fleet?'

'Lucretia Jansdochter,' says Jacobs, scratching his crotch. 'Poor bitch has lost the last of her nippers. Husband's a diamond cutter turned Company merchant. Spent the last couple of years in Java working for the Company and she's been here burying their young. She's got nothing here so she's joining him, though she won't like what she finds. I have it from the clerk that he's had new orders to see to the Company slaves in Arakan, which is a death sentence for him and not somewhere she wants to spend any time, I swear to you. She's got a haughty look about her, hasn't she, though I've heard she's not one of those stuck-up bitches who thinks the likes of me aren't good for anything but bowing and scraping. Helped the sick when the last plague came and it must take something like balls to sign up for a voyage like this one – especially since she's not got so much as a maid for companionship. She'll keep me busy, I shouldn't wonder. Guarding her virtue will be a bastard of a job.'

Cornelisz slides his fingers over the jewelled contours of the agate cameo. Looks upon Jacobsz and wonders whether the expression in the old sailor's eyes is lust or concern.

'No maid?' asks Cornelisz. 'And with a beard-splitting hunter like Pelsaert aboard? I share your concern. She'll catch the eye of every lonely sailor and soldier, will she not? I know of a tincture that can prevent lustful thoughts but I fancy I would need a lake of it to prevent assault on so rare a beauty.'

Jacobsz hawks something up from his lungs and spits into the canal. 'I've been months out of port and had to turn back when we've found women hiding away. A man I know from Dordrecht, a good captain – he commanded a ship of whores being sent to the fortress at Run to provide wives for the garrison. He said he'd never had such an ill-fated voyage and that the women were worse than any sailors he'd ever had under his command. Drunken, lecherous, lustful, fighting one another for every perceived slight... and now we're taking goodly womenfolk as passengers! We've a family of young women to contend with aboard the *Batavia*. Silly fat predikant, off to preach gospel to those who have no need of it, and a whole gaggle of duckling daughters in tow. I'll make sure to berth them right by you, Jeronimus – they can sing prayers and keep you entertained.'

They laugh, companionably. Jacobsz truly believes that the under-merchant is an ally – somebody who shares his views about the unfairness of the hierarchy aboard ship, and who thinks of Pelsaert as a fool who would be better served falling overboard at the first sign of rough seas. Cornelisz is only too happy to keep up the performance, even while he spends time in Pelsaert's company insulting the skipper as a boorish oaf and drunkard. Both men have no doubt that the unassuming under-merchant would support them in any dispute. Neither have seen what lurks beneath the fragile exterior.

'You're here to see the Gentlemen?' asks Cornelisz, tearing his gaze away from the elegant woman in blue.

'Here to be told my business, aye,' grumbles Jacobsz. 'I reckon Pelsaert will be licking himself like a cat before the day's out. They're splitting the fleet in two.'

Cornelisz feigns a mild interest: a pupil ready to be schooled by an experienced tutor. 'What have you heard?'

'The Gentlemen are shitting their breeches about the relationship with the English. You'll have heard of that cocksucker Buckingham? He wasn't far off the only friend the Company had at the English court. Their Parliament won't leave well alone about Amboyna. Still bitching, still demanding compensation for what happened to those poor bastards at the hands of van Speult and Coen. If the Company had any sense they'd just hand him over and be done with it but they can't do that because they've already told the English that the murderous fool is dead.'

Cornelisz chews upon his lip, watching a green-shelled insect walk gingerly across the back of his hand. He mimes ignorance of the events Jacobsz speaks of, allowing the skipper to keep talking, his tongue as loose as if they were sequestered in an unmanned and well-stocked tavern.

'He was following orders, see,' grumbles Jacobsz. 'Van Speult, I mean. Company man – more than any of us. Did what Coen told him to do and kept his eyes and ears open for trouble from the English. One of those Japanese soldiers spilled his guts about a plan to seize the fortress and kill the governor and it was up to van Speult to find out if it was true. Tortured the English traders and factory owners and got the confessions he needed. Took Towerson's head for it. Let those who cooperated go free. Of course, tongues have wagged for years that van Speult was hale and hearty and that the poor bastard clothed in finery that the Company slipped into the sea off Mocha were just some soldier dead from plague. It was a lie everybody could live with. But he turned up back in Amsterdam a year back, if you'll believe that. Begging for protection, begging for compensation, threatening to tell the English that he'd done what he done on direct orders. So Specz is taking him back to Batavia with a fortune in his sailing chest, though I've heard he can't hold a glass without trembling and he's half mad from fever and fear. He sees assassins everywhere.'

'How much of this do you know to be true?' asks Cornelisz, captivated.

Jacobsz shrugs. 'All I know is that women on ship are bad enough, but rumours of dead men with a fortune in gold in their cabin is a recipe for fucking mutiny. This voyage is already damned, my friend. Perhaps you and I should turn our jests to action and simply feather our own nests, eh?'

Cornelisz enjoys the look upon the skipper's face. Enjoys the feeling of drawing together the different threads of silken spider thread.

Across the thoroughfare, Lucretia has been left alone. She is reading a document and glancing up occasionally, looking left and right as if hoping somebody will come and offer assistance. Cornelisz allows himself to remember the tableaux he helped Torrentius to create, dioramas of satyrs, sprites, nymphs and cherubim, naked and painted flesh, arrayed for the pleasure of rich adherents to the teachings of their heretical leader. Slyly, delightedly, he slips Lucretia into such a montage. Imagines her naked, draped only in a fine twist of crimson silk. He would daub splashes of red upon her naked feet as if she had walked through blood and spilled grapes. She would hold a golden bow; a crown of leaves and exotic feathers twisted into her hair. Such a woman could be the consort of a god, he tells himself. Such a woman could be Magdalene to your Christ.

More – such a woman might be Eve; mother to the children of a new age.

'What would it be to know what goes on in such a mind, eh?' asks Jacobsz, nudging him and gesturing towards her. Then he leers, lowering his voice. 'And what it would be to be between such legs?'

Cornelisz looks back to the skipper. Remembers to make his face harmless and friendly, even as he feels something hot and snake-like slither around inside the ruined flesh of his face. He will need Jacobsz to do his bidding. He has no doubt that Pelsaert will also have designs upon bedding her while at sea. He, scarred and unwieldy, would strike neither man as a potential suitor for such a woman. But were he able to suggest that he could help them win her favour, he is in no doubt they would consider themselves in his debt. Were he privy to her thoughts, were he friend and confidant, why, he might be considered the most powerful man aboard. She will need a friend. More, she will need a maid. A maid loyal to him, and him alone.

'I feel it would be rude of me not to introduce myself.' Cornelisz smiles, slapping Jacobsz on the forearm in a perfect imitation of the way the skipper had first greeted him. 'I urge you to keep your temper as you deal with the Gentlemen. I do not wish to sail with any other skipper than you and it would pain me if you were robbed of command. I fancy that during our long journey, you and I will have many opportunities to discuss how best to prosper, and I would beseech you not to allow Pelsaert to believe himself to have scored a victory.'

Jacobsz nods, appreciative of the words of counsel. 'I'm pleased that fate sent you to me,' he says, with an unexpected warmth. 'There are those of richer blood, but you are a gentleman – one such as I can admire.'

Cornelisz doesn't reply. Just gives a nod and a tight smile, then walks nimbly towards Lucretia.

'Milady,' he says, with a formal bow. 'Perhaps I may be of some assistance…'

In her grey eyes, he fancies he sees a flicker of flame.

14

**Personal and private correspondence of Lucretia Jansz,
Heerenstraat, Amsterdam
Intended for Boudewijn van der Mijlen,
VOC under-merchant, Fortress of Batavia**

My darling husband,

*These letters are a prayer, are they not? I inscribe
these desperate words with all the passion and faith that
I beseech the Almighty.*

*Oh how I long to be heard, husband. Is it so with
thee? Do you still kneel at your bedside each evening,
hands clasped, thanking the good Lord for his kindnesses
and seeking his blessings for your actions? Do you still
implore Him daily to watch over those you love and to
provide the strength that will keep you on the path of
Righteousness?*

*I confess, husband – my prayers would be considered
obscene were they spoken aloud. There are nights when
I make demands, husband. There are nights I treat our
Heavenly Father as if He were some bullying infant: a*

brute wont to pull the wings from butterflies or swing dormice by their tails. I scold Him, husband. I urge Him to explain Himself – to tell me what I did or did not do that so enraged Him. And I will confess that I cannot make a picture of a vengeful God. I cannot see the good Lord – the Father who sent His only son to die for our sins – I cannot draw a picture in the eye of my mind in which He punishes us for wrongdoings by snatching away those dearest to us. How could such a creature be a source of kindness and benevolence and hope? If God were thus, what need there be of Satan?

Forgive me, husband. Again I find myself writing as I pray – unsure if the words will ever be received and instead simply spilling angry, hateful thoughts into a blackness that so rarely offers light. I will proceed as your good wife. I will continue as your Lucretia – your darling Creesje – sending love and warmth and kindly thoughts from an Amsterdam that has lost its colour since your departure. How fare thee? The last letter to reach me remains crushed to my heart. The scents were enough to make me feel faint. Mace, nutmeg, syrup; the wet wood of the ship's hold. One breath and I feel as though I am by your side, holding your hand as we cling to the salt-jewelled wood of the great vessel that carries us towards the horizon and the setting sun.

Perhaps my last letter did not reach thee? Perhaps I must again write these hollow, pain-drenched words. Our children are dead, husband. We are childless once more. And I, friendless, empty, desperate for the soft embrace of one who loves me – I am to travel to your side. Oh how I hope this proclamation delights you, *husband. I know there will be tears for our darling Hans, just as there were for our daughters, but it warms me to imagine you feeling enlivened, invigorated; to picture you delighting in the nearness of me.*

I have begun the process of changing my life forever. I have found tenants for our house on the Heerenstraat and made arrangements with the Company to oversee the rental processes and to add the monthly tally to your wages, minus a commission. They were most kind to me, husband, and the clerk with whom I spoke had much to say in your favour. He did cause me a moment's disquiet when he spoke of some rumoured re-posting. He seemed truly troubled by some nagging recollection – a letter sending you onward to Arakan, which I recall you mentioning as a disease-ridden den of vice and inequity where the only employment was in slaves and the curtailment of thievery!

I was gratified to learn that he had remembered incorrectly. Having caused me such distress, the clerk and I agreed to favourable terms for passage and the sale of some possessions. We should be well provided for, husband, and I recall fondly the way you talked of the exotic, palatial homes in which you imagined me, dressed in silks and barefoot; our almond-skinned children sitting beneath towering trees, tousle-haired and free as birds.

Is it wicked, husband? Am I wrong to think so excitedly of our reunion? Of our future? Hans's fragile body was lowered into the earth just four days ago. I fancy I saw the bones of one of his sisters as the gravedigger sunk his spade. Your mother and sister attended the service:

two blobs of spilled ink against the wet green grass. They held me as I wept but I shall confess that the tears were not only for our lost son. I wept for the emptiness within me, for the distance between us, for the lost years cosseted here in Amsterdam when all that I longed for was at the far side of the world.

My tears spring again, husband. I find myself dampening these precious pages. I shall collect myself.

I am returned. I shall endeavour to fulfil my earlier promise and write only of practical matters. You can take comfort in the knowledge that I shall not be alone on the long voyage to your side. Through sheer good fortune I have hired a maid who is willing to accompany me to the Indies. You will recall how Catharina, who nursed Hans, had scoffed at the very notion of leaving Amsterdam? I will admit to being pleased by her refusal to even consider the opportunity as she is tiresome company and would doubtless have been more hindrance than assistance on the long voyage. Do you recall the trip we made to Delft aboard the canal boat? The water flat as glass and still she vomited and caterwauled and begged to be returned to God's dry Earth. I took her refusal as permission to seek one better suited to the task and I declare myself well pleased with the young woman whom Providence has steered into my path.

Zwaantie tells me she is twenty years old but I cannot say with any certainty that she is correct in her assertion. I think she is perhaps no more than sixteen, but there is a worldliness about her that I fancy will be invaluable on the voyage, and I sense that she will be colourful company. I confess I would not have retained her service were you still the master of this house and your admiring gaze liable to fall upon her daily. Indeed, I fancy she is not somebody that any goodly wife would permit entry into the household. She is small in stature, but shapely, and though she dresses correctly in grey gown and crisp white cap, there is something most beguiling in her general comportment.

I observed today that the curls of hair that escape from concealment beneath her cap proceed to form themselves into little question marks. And how appropriate those symbols are! For she is all intrigue, husband. She barely answered my questions and yet we spoke at great length about ambition and hope and painted pictures with words about what we might see during our passage. Do tell me again of the turtles, husband. I recall with great delight the way that Hans would giggle and clap his hands as I read and reread your colourful descriptions of these peculiar and marvellous creatures.

Before I retire I must tell you the story of how Zwaantie and I came to be acquainted. It was pure serendipity, I am sure of it. I had made my way to the Company offices to make arrangements for the rental of the property and to send my last correspondence via their next ship bound for the Indies, and found myself in conversation with a gentleman of most peculiar appearance who had just secured employment as an under-merchant with the Company. He is bound for Batavia, where he is to serve as deputy to the celebrated Mijnheer Pelsaert.

Perhaps that is a name that is familiar to you? Pelsaert was the gentleman who returned to Amsterdam in some disgrace having been embroiled in the death of a young woman rumoured to have been his lover. Do such things not simply reek of scandal, husband? Is it wrong for me to remember with such clarity the details of his wickedness?

The gentleman with whom I had entered conversation made it plain that there was something more than bad blood between Pelsaert and the skipper of the fleet that makes for Batavia before the dawn of winter. He did warn that there could be unpleasantness aboard any one of the vessels due to the bitter acrimony between the two men, and encouraged me to seek passage aboard the vessel upon which he too is placed, so as to offer close protection.

I will confess, he did not look physically capable of offering any such service. He was a small, willowy figure who seemed to be at odds with himself, his limbs jerking and spasming as if there were twins inhabiting the pale membrane of his skin. And his eyes, husband! I swear to thee, one was the soft blue of a June morning but the other was black as tar. From his voice, which rasped like a blade upon stone, it was clear he had suffered illness in the past and there was a scaliness to his skin, around the hairline and across his jaw, that gave him a most reptilian appearance.

And yet he made for fascinating, charming company. It was he in whom I confided my wish for a maid. He declared himself bored and ill at ease as he tarried in Amsterdam and set himself the challenge of securing me a suitable person. Within three hours of our parting, the charming Zwaantie had arrived at my door, carrying letters of commendation and declaring herself excited and honoured to be considered for a position in the service of such an illustrious family.

I will confess to blushing, such were the compliments she paid me. It will please you to know that you are wed to a "notable beauty", husband. We did talk more as sisters than as employer and maid and I must remind myself of the proper way to behave. Mother was never gentle with the staff, though Mother was never gentle with anybody. Even now, I think upon her and a stiffness comes into my limbs. She could tighten one's flesh like cold wind through an open window. And yet I have always been well provided for, have I not? An orphan by the age of twelve but a wife by eighteen. I know love, husband. I have known much of it.

I shall rest now. I do not wish to tire you with my prattle. I ask only that you press your lips to these pages and summon up the memory of your darling Creesje. I shall hold you in my heart.

With all that I am,
Creesje

15

The morning brings music. The bells of two warring churches pitch discordant songs into the warm, salt-kissed air; a madrigal of clattering chimes that drift out across the waking city like fog. It envelops all other sounds, muffling the shouts of the hawkers; the bustles of the merchants in the trading halls; the ale-headed whimpers of the men and women who groan themselves into wakefulness, chiding themselves for the excesses of the night before.

Amsterdam rarely sleeps. This is a city at the dawn of true prosperity: a city of possibility. While London seems to sink beneath the weight of its history, Amsterdam shines with the riches of a golden future. Great new cathedrals curve against the skyline, keeping pace with the places of worship more dear to the hearts of the merchants. The city is stuffed full of palaces of commerce: the Exchange Bank, the Lending Bank, the Bourse, transposing gold and silver, ducats and bullion, the trade frenzied and the profits obscene. Mellifluous, cauled in the mists of flooded marshland, Amsterdam spreads out from the harbour like a peacock's open tail; its narrow lanes groaning under the weight of warehouses and slim houses, the waterways so packed with ships that a traveller could cross them by foot.

WH Davies bird
"A prayer circui omar"
by feed dawn
1 ? publshei

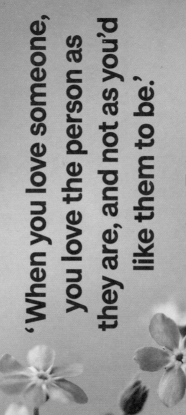

'When you love someone, you love the person as they are, and not as you'd like them to be.'

Leo Tolstoy

In the cosy embrace of the hayloft, Nicolaes de Pelgrom worms deeper into the clean dry straw, one arm slung across his face and his legs dangling through the hatch, boots brushing the rungs of the ladder. He elects to keep his eyes shut for a time, feigning sleep. It is a practice that has proven useful: an opportunity to remember who he is meant to be and where he has lain his head. He has become accustomed to waking up in unknown and disparate locations: one morning a fine feather bed beneath coverlet and embroidered linens; the next bedded down beneath a bridge, wrapped in a damp cloak, so hungry he has to check his gut to see if he has been hollowed out by a blade.

Here, now, he feels uncannily comfortable. There is a thirst at his throat and his dry lips taste of some sweet, unctuous spirit that was pressed into his hand by a cheerful harlot beside the Oudezijds Voorburgwal, but he has little to complain of. He is presently situated midway between the two houses of God: the carillon of the Westerkerk and crashing din of the Oude Kerk bells contrive to form a melody of sorts, which lingers in his mind long after the last reverberations have ceased. He has always enjoyed music and often finds himself distractedly improving upon hymns and tavern ditties while his mind is occupied with other things.

He has slept these last few nights in his new uniform, attempting to make it better compliment his character. It is too bright. Too new. He has greased the knees and elbow patches and flecked his jerkin with a mixture of pigs' blood and pitch, but he fears that an experienced soldier will notice the affectations. The soldiers who await passage aboard the *Batavia* are by no means new recruits. Many have seen battle and siege, been witnesses to the death of their fellows and well used to the feeling of a stranger's blood upon their skin.

'By Christ, she bit me! Bit me like a dog!'

Nicolaes decides to wake up. Groans, as if suffering from a crushing headache, and drags himself upright, straw falling from his body and hair as if he were a corpse rising from an autumn grave. He peers at the man beside him, who requires no such gift for theatrics. He is bleary-eyed and green-skinned, swallowing and gagging as if there were a week-old oyster trapped beneath his tongue. He is examining his own bare leg, bloodshot eyes narrowing as he considers the two neat semi-circles of indentations on his muscled, near-hairless leg.

Nicolaes closes an eye, pressing his hand to his mouth as if suppressing a wave of nausea. 'She's left her mark upon you, my friend,' he says, his accent pitched at a low, rough croak. 'Will you take it as compliment or insult? Was it passion, or displeasure?'

The young man beside him turns groggily towards Nicolaes, and his wine-veined lips break into a pleasant smile. He laughs, throatily, then clutches his head as if expecting parts of his skull to break off like dropped crockery. 'I'll ask her,' he says, patting the straw beside him, looking for a suitable lump. 'She may yet tarry beneath the straw. I feel sure she was still astride me when I fell asleep. Is it not always thus? That come the morning, one can never find the things that one took off the night before?'

'Check your purse, Otto.' Nicolaes smiles, rummaging beneath a sack of millet for his own meagre possessions. 'I have no doubt she considered the tumble itself to be ample reward, but there are some Amsterdammers who would prefer a gilder to a kiss.'

'Fear not,' says his companion, his grin reaching up to his ears. He fumbles around beneath his bare backside and produces his shabby coin purse. 'Eight stuivers well spent, my friend. She was no beauty but she had a fire. If I find her among these bastard grain sacks I'm sure she will not be averse to showing you her services. She did consider you the prettier of the two of us, though unless I go carousing with a gargoyle I fear that shall always be so.'

'You are hard upon yourself, Otto,' says Nicolaes, listening to the sound of nearby hooves moving rhythmically across stone. 'I'm sure you have made many a maid blush in your time.'

Otto gives in to a loud burst of laughter. 'You are a fine companion, Wiebbe. I'm grateful our paths crossed. We shall spend much of these next months cosseted together like two lovers beneath sheets, and there will be plenty aboard ship who will test your patience, your resolve and your willingness to ever see Heaven. To have a friend is a blessing.'

Nicolaes gives him a companionable slap on the back. He has taken to Otto and is similarly grateful for having won the friendship of one with experience of sea travel and the Indies. Their paths crossed at the harbour, both men clutching commissions in gloved hands and staring at the vast ship that will transport them to the garrison in Batavia where they are to spend five years protecting Company interests. The friendship has been nurtured in numerous taverns, giving Nicolaes a chance to ply the genial mercenary with strong ale and to steal his knowledge like a silk-fingered cutpurse.

Otto, who has been soldiering since he was a boy, has twice sailed beyond the Cape and spent many months aboard East Indiamen, begging God to send a breath of wind. In drink, Otto spoke of the madness that took some of his companions, stuffed together with the rats and the filth. Pestilence swept through the decks and the ship became a Hell of waste and pus and poison. Despite enduring such horrors, he remains bullish about returning to sea, convinced that this time they will experience better fortunes.

'I think I can feel a foot,' says Otto, patting the straw again. 'My head! And by Christ I stink like a midden. I wonder, does this make me a merchant? Am I now a man of trade? Perhaps if can keep the stink of an Amsterdam whore upon me I can sell it to homesick countrymen when we reach the Indies?'

Nicolaes watches as his companion hauls himself upright, naked from the waist down, the patterns of the straw marbling his skin. There are scars upon his thigh: a hole in his left leg like a thumbprint in soft fruit – a souvenir from the Siege of Grolle. He hunts around for his uniform, groaning each time he plunges his hands into the straw. He totters unsteadily to the rear of the hayloft, supporting himself on an old beam as he pisses against a stack of grain. Nicolaes drags himself upright, inspecting his uniform. He's pleased to get a whiff of his own hard-won stench: a musty, vinegary stench of unwashed skin and damp cloth.

'Oh Christ,' mutters Otto, from across the loft. He is

struggling to get his leg in his breeches; one foot trapped in the fabric. He yelps, helplessly, as he falls over sideways, tumbling into the straw and eliciting a curse from something half buried and rudely awakened.

'Eight stuivers,' mumbles the wench, sitting up sharply and putting out her hand. Her dress is little more than rags and the straw in her hair makes her look like a corn dolly made by children at harvest time, but she gathers the garment about herself haughtily, as if to cover her modesty.

'My darling,' cries Otto, delighted to have found his new love. He grabs for her waist, tickling her beneath her ribs, and they disappear beneath the straw to the sound of muffled shrieks and giggles.

Nicolaes leaves them to their fun and makes his way down the ladder, emerging into an empty stable; the stalls neatly kept, leather harnesses and elegantly made halters hanging from iron pegs along the wall. He relieves himself into a stacked pile of wet hay, easing the lumps and bumps from his shoulder, and glancing back up through the loft as the sound of joyous coupling emulates the song of the bells.

'Today, Nicolaes,' he says to himself, quietly. 'Perhaps it will be today.'

It has been six weeks since he arrived in Amsterdam. Six weeks of reacquainting himself with the land of his birth. The city continues to swell and expand, the buildings rising higher: sun-starved trees seeking to lift their heads above the canopy.

A thud, from the hayloft. Muffled speech. Then Otto is descending the ladder, pulling up his breeches, grinning widely and wiping his face with the sleeve of his uniform. 'I have another bite,' he says, grabbing Nicolaes by the arm and hurrying them forward across the empty little yard. 'If our paths cross again, remind me to stay away from the head end.'

Nicolaes looks back towards the hatch. Two bare feet dangle down. He catches a snatch of a song, some lullaby he recalls from his youth, and then they are out into the bustle and tumult of Kalverstraat.

Otto notices a horse trough by the edge of the canal and plunges his hands in up to the elbows, withdrawing them to scrub at his face. He pushes back his dark hair and jams his hat on his head, readjusting his sailcloth satchel and refastening his purse to the length of cord around his waist. 'My God but I could eat my own feet if they were buttered,' he grumbles, and his eyes light up as he spies a young girl selling salted fish and bread from a cart she looks barely able to push.

Nicolaes stands at the canal edge, staring into the dirty water, while his friend hurries away to secure his morning meal. He lets himself enjoy the moment of reflection, looking at his own blurry image in the murky depths. He is no longer Nicolaes de Pelgrom. He is now Wiebbe Hayes, a rank-and-file soldier from Winschoten in Groningen. He did not question the man in the tavern about the whereabouts of the real Hayes, or even if there ever was such a man. He had simply taken the pages, the commission, and the parcelled uniform, proffered beneath the table by a hook-nosed, red-bearded man retained by Mrs Towerson.

The days since have been tolerable enough. He can play the part of a soldier well enough. The corporal who has overseen daily drills and musket practice is an experienced man well used to dealing with the cut-throats and unrepentant bastards who have signed up as Company soldiers. They are a motley bunch, gathered from across the United Provinces and beyond. There are Germans, Portuguese and Scotsmen among the ranks, and though a good number call themselves Hollanders, many cannot understand one another's dialects and languages.

Nicolaes has endeavoured to do as he is told, and not stand out. Being merely competent with musket has been a hardship for him. He is a keen marksman and has had to aim deliberately off-centre for fear of being identified as somebody to be plucked from the ranks and put to better use. For now, he simply needs to be a half-decent soldier. He knows that he will be aboard the fleet commanded by a man called Pelsaert, a Company man of some high esteem whose last sojourn in the Indies ended in indignity. Otto has been far from tight-lipped in relaying gossip about the man who will outrank the captain of the ship during their long voyage. Pelsaert, he claims, is a dandy and a seducer. He is a clever, self-serving and deeply self-satisfied man who cannot keep his manhood in his breeches. Otto has warned that there will be trouble between him and the captain: a great slab of a man and first-rate sailor who cannot control his temper or his tongue when in drink.

'He cannot abide being told what to do by men who know less than him,' Otto had confided. 'Cannot understand why he should be spoken down to by men whose skulls he could break.'

Nicolaes had listened, and laughed, and filed the information away.

'A feast, my friend,' says Otto, appearing at his side and handing him a hunk of salted fish and a small, warm loaf.

He tears at a hunk of yellow, soapy cheese, swilling his mouth with great gulps from a clay cup. Milk pours down his chin, soaking his ragged beard, which he pulls into a sharp point. 'I could eat that again and more besides. What is it about an ample backside that makes a man hungry?'

Nicolaes mimics the ravenous hunger of his companion, stuffing a handful of warm bread into his mouth and ripping at the fish with his fingers. He does not find it difficult to return to the manners of his youth, when each morsel of food that passed his lips was hard won and the food so rank that it was better to swallow it whole than to taste it.

'Won't be today, anyway,' says Otto, as they mooch along the canal-side. 'No call to sail, I promise you that.'

'You have tidings?'

Otto nods. Farts. Laughs. 'Happenings abroad,' he mumbles, spraying food. 'A prince or a politician falls into a puddle and waves crash down upon distant shores.'

Nicolaes stuffs the last of the bread into his mouth, his cheeks bulging. Looks up to see a tall woman in a grey gown, chatting animatedly with a smaller, dark-haired maid. He moves out of their way, tipping his hat. The maid sees him, and gives him a sly, inviting smile. As they pass, Nicolaes hears the tall lady berate her for some neglected task, scolding her like an infant. Nicolaes watches them pass, only half paying attention to what Otto is saying.

'Now I understand your reluctance to tup the harlot.' Otto laughs at his side, following his line of sight. 'You are a man of refined tastes, eh? Tucked into expensive cunnies like a starving man eating a roasted capon? Oh, Wiebbe, the stories I will demand you tell me once we board!'

Nicolaes rolls his eyes, affecting coyness. He alters his

accent, talking like a dandified member of the aristocracy, lovesick and simpering. 'It was the maid, Otto. There was a look in that one's eyes. A sharp one, I'll wager, and every bit as fine a tumble as your friend from the hayloft. If Providence returns me to Amsterdam I may have to offer her my affections.'

'Your affections.' Otto, who has begun to appreciate his new friend's gift for imitation, laughs again. 'You'll have time before we sail, my friend. Chase her down.'

Nicolaes gives his attention back to his companion. 'You spoke of "happenings"? Of delays to our voyage? Truly, the child with the fish cart knew much.'

'Oh, the Englishman!' says Otto, spitting into the water. 'The one who sucked the king's prick so well he was made a lord and more. Handsome devil who bedded the French princess.'

Nicolaes keeps his features composed. Forces down the rising tide of breath and bile. Cocks his head as if he were no more than a soldier eager for gossip.

'Buckingham, you mean,' says Nicolaes, snapping his fingers. 'Favourite of King James, and his son after. He has caused fresh mischief, has he? What has the fellow done now?'

'Dagger to the heart,' says Otto, raising his head as the sun's golden rays emerge from behind the tall timber building that marks the crossroads. He basks in it for a moment.

'Who spoke this?' asks Nicolaes, the colour draining from his face. 'The girl? What could she...?'

'Two gentlemen I overheard,' says Otto, idly. 'Speaking plain as I waited for our feast, clutching a pamphlet as if it were a Bible. He was in Portsmouth – a city of which I've heard little good – in conversation with the men he was due to lead to relieve the Protestants of La Rochelle. Some angry soldier pushed through the throng and stuck a knife in him. They say that while the king weeps into his silken nightdress, there are songs being sung in the streets. The Company wishes to see how the developments will affect relationships with the king, which means we will not be aboard until summer is past. So, if the maid does entice...'

Nicolaes feels his world spin and sway. Though his face does not change, his mind is awash with memories, questions – his gut hollow and his heart clenching like a fist. Buckingham, dead. His patron, his protector, his blood. He should have been at his side. Would have thrown himself between breast and blade and given his own life in a moment if it saved the man who raised him up and gave him purpose. He has never been anything other than Buckingham's man. A quiet rage begins to simmer in his gut. He finds himself thinking of Mrs Towerson. Think of revenge, and cease to weep. His instinct is to tear off the stinking uniform and turn his back on the whole absurd enterprise. He is in the employ of Mrs Towerson solely because he was gifted her by Buckingham. But Buckingham is dead, and the man who slew him deserves to have his throat carved open.

'The ale has hit you, my friend? Your fine features look like fish skin. Are you sick? Shall we return to barracks and share our gossip? We can tease it out – earn coin and a good Rhenish wine if we tell it properly. I'll wager you're a fine spinner of yarns, yes? By God, your eyes have darkened. You look shark-like, Wiebbe...'

He feels his friend slip his arm through his own and gently steer him forward.

He cannot seem to find the strength to protest.

16

Personal and private correspondence of Lucretia Jansz,
Heerenstraat, Amsterdam
Intended for Boudewijn van der Mijlen,
VOC under-merchant, Fortress of Batavia

Dear husband,

The day approaches, and I confess that my heart does beat fast and free at the thought of what these next months may provide.

I write these words in our bedroom, here upon the Heerenstraat, in a house that I can no longer think of as home. The tenants are travelling from Delft on Friday and will be comfortably sequestered here without much difficulty. I leave almost all of the furniture for their comfort and have even filled the larder and cellar with enough provisions to keep them comfortably fed until they find time to visit the markets. I have no doubt they are familiar with Amsterdam but it will be a great change for them to make their homes in the city, and no doubt our neighbours will be peering out and judging them for their every word and affectation.

I understand that the head of the family made his money in ceramics and property and that he has a daughter with a fondness for theatre, which he intends to indulge in now he has sold some of his business interests to a former competitor. I know this from Zwaantie, who has proven herself most adept at snapping up little titbits of information. I picture you smiling at that, grinning to yourself as you witness my attempts to find an alternative word for "gossip". Yes, I shall confess to enjoying knowing the business of those whose delicious stories are hidden deep beneath their caps and plush mantles. There are many whose sole entertainment is the discussion of families such as ours.

Zwaantie talks to me less like a mistress and more as if we are friends and while I enjoy her company and eagerness to be in my favour, I will confess to finding her a little intrusive and her manners coarse. Her laugh sounds like something one hears from the men aboard the canal boats as they pass and she makes very free with her protestations of discomfort – wafting her skirts and huffing her cheeks, unfastening her cap to let her hair fall free. I am almost envious of the brazen manner in which she comports herself.

I returned home from church on Sunday last to find her sitting on the front step employed in peeling parsnips. She was barefoot and with her skirts hitched up to reveal legs that had been scorched the colour of coffee beans by exposure to the sun. The soles of her feet were elevated upon my arrival and before she snatched down I saw what must have greeted every passing eye. The soles of her small feet were lined and grimy and yet they made me think of fresh-churned butter. Is that not most peculiar, husband? The thought popped into my mind as easy as memory.

She unsettles me, truly, but when I find myself preparing to offer rebuke, she seems to sense the nearness of my dissatisfaction and steers me effortlessly onto a new subject, or performs some small kindness that makes me forget whatever it was that had caused me such concern moments before.

I spoke in my last letter of my concern about having such a woman in the home were you here to be tempted, and I confess that I now hope to rid myself of her before you and I are reunited. That you have kept your marriage vows and denied yourself the pleasures of the local women – upon that I shall not dwell. Zwaantie might be a temptation too far.

Does it speak ill of me, I wonder? She is certainly loyal to me and very hard-working. No chore is too demanding and no request is met by a shift in mood. She is a happy, well-intentioned young woman. Perhaps I am cruel to imagine her morals to match her appearance. It is not her fault that she has a look that men seem to find so alluring.

My God, I do believe I am jealous! Is that it, husband? Am I envious of her dark skin and flashing eyes and freedom to toss her curls and laugh with open mouth? I will confess to feeling constricted. I, tall and slim and pale; my eyes the grey of misted summer mornings. I feel like a blank canvas next to her portrait of deep colours and flame-lit shadows.

I must think upon other matters, husband. You will be gratified to learn that the peculiar fellow whom I met at the VOC has made arrangements for me to be aboard the ship upon which he is bound. The vessel is named Batavia, *which seems appropriate. She is a new vessel, the pride of the company and I consider myself fortunate to be so situated. Unfortunately, Pelsaert is also passenger upon the ship, which is to be skippered by the man with whom he has such animosity. My new acquaintance, Mijnheer Cornelisz, has told me much of the history between them and I fancy that Zwaantie will discover much more when we are safely aboard.*

I do hope there will be no sickness aboard and that the sailors and soldiers are to be kept well behind the mast. I do not doubt that they are fine, strong men and excellent in battle but they are rough men who do not think to conceal their base desires. A fine-featured, dark-eyed soldier of the VOC looked briefly at me as if I were meat upon a butcher's stall. Zwaantie said the most scandalous things when I remarked upon him, though I will confess that behind my fan I did succumb to laughter.

Oh, husband, what adventures lie ahead. I thank God for giving me the strength to embark upon this new journey, and for giving me such a good and dear man to make my way toward.

Your darling Creesje

17

'Move! In the name of all that's Christian, move! You, you German shit-stain! By God I swear I'll cut the flesh from your bones and have it stitched for slippers if you don't get down that bastard hatch!'

The words fall upon Nicolaes in a gentle rain. He's half drunk.

He laughs, giddily, as some vaguely remembered witticism bubbles up from the punch bowl in his gut. 'Glass... half empty... half full... half drunk...'

'Wiebbe,' hisses Otto, 'Wiebbe, keep moving, shut your mouth, swift. It's Stonecutter...'

Nicolaes spits. Laughs. His eyes slide closed and open again. 'Half drunk,' he mutters, again. 'An excellent jest, Uncle... great wordplay, Uncle... sorry you're fucking dead, Uncle...'

Otto's face, at his ear, a plea in his voice. 'Wiebbe, for both our sakes... oh fuck...'

'And you, pretty-boy! Standing proud like a cock with arms! She ain't to be looked at, see! You've got one job and that's to do as I bastard well tells thee!'

The world reels and spins and tastes of meat and metal.

'Oh I'm going to make this fucking hurt!'

Nicolaes registers the words a moment too late. Twists at the waist, a streak of fire lashing down his back. The pain sears through everything else; the agony so intense that for a moment he fears he has been set ablaze. He hisses through his teeth, brandy and tobacco and blood in his spittle. Spins where he stands, reaching for the sword upon his waist. His hands clutch empty air.

'That scowl ain't for me, is it, pretty-boy? That hurts me, I tell thee. Hurts. Makes me want to take a knife and turn it into a smile. Or maybe I just pull your fucking head off and hold it upside down, eh?'

Nicolaes comes back to himself. Feels the brandy turn sour as drunkenness gives way to the beginnings of a skull-crushing headache. Feels again the strip of fire down his spine.

'We got a deaf one? You deaf, soldier? Need me to stick something in your ears?'

Nicolaes glares up at the huge man who has struck him. He looks brick-built, his shoulders the width of a church window. Looks hewn for violence. He glares down at Nicolaes, sticking his tongue through his gappy teeth to reveal a tongue stained brown as ancient leather. He looks past Nicolaes, brown drool upon his pimple-spotted chin. Gestures at the sight that had stopped Nicolaes in his tracks.

'Pretty, ain't she?' hisses the big man, eyeball to eyeball. 'A fucking goddess, that one. Probably got a fur-lined cunny and shits little golden baubles. Proper lady, see. And you're defiling her with your eyes. We're all doing the same thing to her in our heads, lad, but you're the one who looks like he's about to start stroking his prick. And more than that, you're holding up the fucking line. So, close your eyes and shut your mouth and give yourself a memory to keep you warm, because that's as close as you'll get, see? Close as you or me or any of these bastards will ever get to a woman like that! You, and you with your simpleton smile – you've more in common with the fucking pigs than any of these fine ladies and gentlemen. So don't go getting comfortable this side of the mast, pretty-boy. You're going down in the bowels with all the other turds, see. Take a big gulp of fresh air and hold it cos you won't be getting another. And if you want to use those fists on me, don't think I'll stop with teaching thee a lesson. You'll go to the sharks looking half chewed.'

Nicolaes cannot quite unball his fist. His head is whirling. His senses cannot seem to comprehend the sheer frenzy of activity around him. He can't even quite recall spilling from the land to the sea. The *Batavia*'s hull had risen above him like a mountain; the masts and rigging disappearing into the low, grey clouds. His head had been afire with different voices, sounds, sights. He had tried to cling to Otto but he feels as though he is a book missing too many pages. He feels as though he is drowning under the weight of new experiences and the sheer chaos that seethes about him upon the deck of the *Batavia*.

'Go on then, pretty boy,' growls the huge man, eagerly, and Nicolaes feels the eyes of a hundred soldiers upon him. 'Tell her you love her, then you and me can have a little dance.'

Nicolaes shivers as a cold wind gusts across the deck, drawing curses from the sailors in the rigging. He tries to make sense of his thoughts. Glances again in the direction of the big man's leer. He realises he had been standing mute. Standing awe-struck. Standing in wordless wonder as the tall, elegant woman was helped down onto the deck from the curious assemblage of wood and rope with which she was hoisted from the rowboat. She had risen over the waist of the ship like a sunrise, an elegant, majestic presence that briefly silenced the sailors in the rigging and hushed the raised voices of the soldiers as they shuffled towards the hatches. Nicolaes, his hand upon Otto's shoulder, had been too dumbfounded to move. The lance corporal had been quick to remind him of his place.

Nicolaes swallows his temper as best he can but he would love nothing more than to sink his fist into the big man's belly. He has been desperate for a chance to do violence these past weeks. On the surface he has maintained the illusion of Wiebbe Hayes, the quiet, competent VOC soldier. He has laughed at the jokes and proven himself adequate during the daily drills and musket practice at the VOC barracks. But inside he has seethed with grief and rage.

Buckingham, dead. Dead at the hands of a disgruntled officer who should never have got close enough to stick his dagger through his heart. Nicolaes, had he been there, would have taken that blade. Perhaps it would have cost him his life, but that would surely be preferable to the soup of ugly emotions that consume him now. He feels orphaned. Abandoned. He feels insubstantial, unreal; as if his whole life to date had been somebody else's dream. He has no anchor, no sense of self. He is aboard the *Batavia* simply because he has nowhere else to go. He does not even know if he intends to make good upon his commission. He embarked upon this folly in Buckingham's name but with Buckingham dead he has no duty to anybody save Mariam Towerson.

He cannot make up his mind whether that burden is truly his to carry.

Those marked for death seem beyond his reach. He has heard the rumours about van Speult but has felt no desire to discover if the gossipmongers speak truth. These past weeks have been a blur of pretence and drink, ever unsure whether he would even step aboard the mighty ship. And now he stands motionless in front of a man he wants to break, blocking the deck of the finest ship in the VOC fleet.

Otto takes his arm and pulls him forward into the throng of stinking, sodden men. 'Not that one, Wiebbe, not him. Just follow me. By Christ we're not even out of the harbour and you're causing trouble!'

Nicolaes allows himself to be dragged forward, becoming aware of the resuming swell of chatter and chaos around him as the sailors tear their eyes away from the fine noble-woman who stands with the gaudily attired commandeur and the twisted, toadying little under-merchant who stands at his side. He glances back once more over his shoulder, catching sight of the tanned, buxom maid who hauls herself over the rail and hurries to her side. She is swift and lithe in her black dress, lace cap and heavy clogs, skipping nimbly between two barrels and a coiling snake of rope before reaching her mistress's side.

'Providence,' shouts Otto, in his ear, and his face splits in a broad grin as he follows his friend's eyeline.

Nicolaes tries to reply but his voice is drowned out by the terrible bellowing of a great bull being hoisted above the deck, its legs kicking madly at the air. He glimpses the broad shoulders and bare arms of the men who hold the thick ropes and lower the beast down into the depths of the hold; hears the squeal of the piglets caged upon the deck, and then he is being shoved into a dark hatchway, his feet slipping on damp wooden stairs, and disappearing into the guts of the mighty vessel.

From nearby, the voice of a clerk, ticking off goods upon a checklist. The soldiers drop their voices and begin to mutter.

'*...three thousand pounds of cheese, twenty tons of hardtack, thirty-four tons of meat in tight barrels, twenty-seven tons of herring, eight and a half tons of butter, thirty-seven tons of dried peas, seventeen tons of dried beans, three and a half tons of salt and two hundred and fifty barrels of beer...*'

The final word elicits a grand cheer from the men as they surge forward towards the next hatchway, glimpsing massed barrels of provisions and the locked doors of the gunpowder store and armoury. Nicolaes pats again at his side. He misses his sword. He carries a small dagger in the belt of his mustard-coloured VOC doublet but he will not be permitted access to pike or musket until the lance corporal or one of the fresh-faced cadets decides to drill them.

'Did you see?' whispers a tall, Germanic-sounding soldier a little way down the shoal of men. 'Those musketeers were all that stood between us!'

Nicolaes joins those who whisper their approval; scores of rank-and-file soldiers all lost in a pleasant vision of the treasures they glimpsed at the harbour. The VOC sent a heavily armed guard to protect its money chests as they were being loaded into the hold. Two soldiers for each chest, and each chest containing eight thousand silver coins. Despite the ale and the headache, Nicolaes had done the maths. 'Two hundred and fifty thousand guilders,' he hears, repeated, again and again.

The treasures are now the responsibility of the one hundred VOC soldiers of which Nicolaes finds himself a part. Their duty is to protect the ship's cargo and enforce the iron rule of the Company during the long voyage. He feels capable of neither. Feels capable of nothing save lying down and gathering the blanket of emptiness and drink about him.

Nicolaes stumbles forward, his hand again upon Otto's shoulder. His heart feels ragged, untethered. He had almost wept as he looked upon the families who milled about on the deck looking lost and overwhelmed. Women, babies, infants – all had filled him with a curious sense of sorrow, as if his every decision has been wrong. Perhaps he should have chosen a simple life. Perhaps a wife and children and a humble occupation would have been a neater fit. He has played roles for which he is far less suited. Perhaps, with a family, with somebody to love, he could find out what it would be like to live as himself.

A sudden blast of trumpet song bleeds down through the decks. The soldiers fall silent, shuffling along, down towards the gun decks, cocking their ears to hear any titbits of information. They understand little of the conversations between the sailors, who had glared and cursed and spat with an undisguised contempt. One young lad, high in the rigging, had received whoops of approval as he dropped his britches and pissed onto the throng of soldiers who hauled themselves up the rope ladders, red-faced and dumbfounded by the sheer size of the vessel they are to call home.

'*...thirty cannons, twelve heavy guns... do you spy the*

three other retourschips – the Dordrecht, Galiasse *and* Gravenhage *– there, the* Assendelft *and the* Sardam. *By Christ the* Buren! *That's a brute of a ship. Any pirates who chance their arm will be going home full of splinters...'*

'Oh, home shit home,' mutters Otto, as the dam of men bursts and they spill forward into the orlop deck. Nicolaes, remembering his instructions, runs forward, seeking a space among the guns and ammunition. He bangs his knees upon the wheel of a cannon and takes a blow to the face from an outstretched hand. There are shouts of 'mine, mine!' and the sudden scuffling sounds of violence and then Otto is dragging him into a little gap between a squat cannon and a stack of crates. Nicolaes blinks repeatedly, trying to get used to the dark. Already the cramped, low-ceilinged space is beginning to smell. He wrinkles his nose and Otto laughs, heartily.

'Wait until we hit bad weather,' he jokes. 'When they close the gun ports and nobody can see their hand in front of their face, the sailors piss down the hatches rather than fumble to the latrines. A friend of mine last time out – he took a shit direct to the face as he was lying in his hammock! Can you picture it? Christ, talk about laugh!'

Nicolaes stands back against the curved wood of the ship, feeling lost and out of place. Watches, gratefully, as Otto sets about rigging a hammock, listening to the jumble of different languages, different voices, laughs and shouts and the crash of men falling over in the dark.

This, then, is home, he thinks, hazily. *Look at where you find yourself, Nicolaes de Pelgrom. Look at what you are become.*

In his boot, the ruby. He presses his toe against it,

appreciating its weight, its solidity, its proof that he is more than this. He is not Wiebbe Hayes. He is *not*!

He looks up at the sound of the corporal's voice. Snaps to something like attention. A little distance away, the cadets are laughing to one another. None appears older than eighteen and none have seen action but they outrank these one hundred experienced soldiers. They will not be billeted in such a dank, ungodly space. They are officers, high-born, and clearly deserving of better.

Nicolaes glimpses two fresh-faced youngsters in crisp uniform. Neither is old enough to grow a beard. They are making fun of one another, laughing at the unpleasantness of the orlop deck where their men are to spend the coming months.

'Coenraat! You're sure you wouldn't rather bunk down here, my friend? I've always thought you would be better suited to a place with the men!'

'Close your mouth, Gsbert, or one of these men will mistake you for a girl and give you something to shut your pretty lips around!'

'By God but it stinks already!'

'Aye, they'll have no trouble sleeping – the air is thick enough to eat with a spoon! They can draw it over themselves like a blanket!'

'David, look – that fellow is shitting in his hand! Ha! In his own hand!'

'To the air, my friend! Let's leave these men to their comforts!'

Nicolaes turns to see Otto grinning at him. He shrugs. 'Aye, they're an inspiration, are they not?' He puts his hand upon his cheek and looks into his eyes, concerned. 'Maybe a bit of sobriety for a bit, eh? You can talk to me, if you wish. It's only fair. I've bent your ear long enough.'

Nicolaes hears a whistle from high above. Feels the ship lurch. His stomach seems to double in size, climbing up his throat. He puts out his hand to support himself, a pain in his throat as he fights again the urge to sob.

To the sound of lowing cattle and squawking fowl; of crying babies and cursing sailors; the crack of whips and the bellowed orders from the grizzled man at the helm, the greatest ship in the VOC fleet turns its back on Amsterdam.

And begins a journey that will end in Hell.

PART TWO

18

The VOC retourschip *Batavia*

October 28, 1628

Husband,

Where to begin? I write these words with trembling hand, tucked away inside the handsome little cabin to which Commandeur Pelsaert has graciously escorted me, with a deference that I find most reassuring. Commandeur Pelsaert, you ask? Oh, husband, I have so much to share.

I will confess I was indebted to be shown to this quiet place in which to gather myself even if the accommodation is somewhat smaller than I had envisaged. I will confess that the excitement of the boarding left me quite faint, though there is a certain sense of exhilaration within me yet.

You, sweet Boudewijn, will have been frequent

witness to the bustle and chaos of an embarkation, but truly, it did feel to this inexperienced pilgrim as though half the world were being loaded aboard the Batavia. *I did feel as Noah must when overseeing the conveyance of all God's creatures!*

The scene before me at Texel was almost too grand to comprehend. I counted a dozen huge ships at anchor in the Moscovian Roads – smaller ships swarming around us like bees upon fresh fruit. All were packed with sailors, soldiers, ballast, provisions, and nobody seemed able to speak at any considerate volume. I heard so many languages, and all coarse, loud and better strung for the battlefield than the cramped confines of a ship. I swear, husband, it did feel to Zwaantie and myself that we were stepping aboard a castle rather than a ship...

A moment, my love...

Forgive me, you were ever in my thoughts. I stepped away from my writing table for a moment, having been interrupted, afresh, by the impudent Zwaantie. She is almost delirious with excitement and it is all I can do not to stop her ripping her cap off and throwing it to the gulls. She has caught the eye of every man we have seen and I find myself scolding her like a big sister for the flirtatious way she returns their every glance. I still know precious little of her origins or life before entering my employment, but were we not already set on our path I would have sought to verify the letters of recommendation that she brought with her upon our meeting. I do not believe she has been a maid in any of the great houses she claims, and though she is a fair cook and thorough with laundry and dusting, I sense there is guile and deceitfulness within her and have taken to keeping my private correspondence and valuables in a locked box.

I am nevertheless grateful for the interruption as, at her urging, I made my way to the waist of the ship and witnessed such activity that my eyes are near exhausted. I witnessed the loading of the sailors' chests, hauled up from the barges by the hundred, while the crash and bang and furious shouts that accompanied the loading of the wood for the galley stove left me blushing. Above, the deck is a mass of rope and cable while on all sides, a throng of ill-dressed sailors were roundly whipped to business by a ferocious-looking fellow who wielded a length of knotted rope and did not stint from lashing it upon the backs of anybody not doing as they were told.

Next came the soldiers, bright-eyed, pink-cheeked Company cadets leading scores of scowling, underfed men. I am told they will serve five years of garrison duty in the Indies, though they did not look back to Amsterdam with any fondness or with the manners of one saying goodbye to a place dear to them. Among their number was the soldier I saw by the canal-side, and who looked upon me so lasciviously. I declare myself grateful to the under-merchant for taking my well-being so personally. He has now introduced me to Francisco Pelsaert, who is a most vivid fellow and truly delightful in manners and deportment. A true gentleman, he could not be more at odds with the skipper, Jacobsz, whose appearance and manner are more suited to the alehouse than in service of a fine company like the VOC. I am told he is a peerless sailor, but I trust Pelsaert's quiet assertion that he is a drunkard and a ruffian, and I shall endeavour to keep our interactions to a minimum.

What else can I share, husband? I write these words knowing I shall arrive before this letter, but scribbling sentences in your name causes such a stirring of my blood that I fancy I shall do so for pleasure throughout the journey.

I will spare you the tedium of too much information about the mighty vessel, but will declare myself tolerably satisfied with my accommodation. My cabin has the luxury of bunks instead of sleeping mats, and sufficient room to put a writing desk and chair. I am informed there are cabin boys to fetch and carry meals and empty chamber pots, though I fancy it is too small a space to share with Zwaantie and shall request that she find alternative arrangements near enough to hailing distance.

As I hinted previously, I will confess to some regret at having accepted her as my maid, and find myself bewildered by the curiously blank-eyed way in which Mijnheer Cornelisz greeted both Zwaantie and myself upon arrival – as if we were strangers who had never shared a word. Perhaps he has his own reasons for such behaviour but it has unsettled me.

I wish only for the journey to be quick and uneventful, so that you and I may again build a family.

Yours, ever,
Creesje

19

The VOC retourschip *Batavia*

November 6, 1628

Dearest Boudewijn,

What a fool I was to imagine that life at sea would be all excitement and adventure. I have spent a truly tedious evening in the company of a man whose face, even though it was close to my own for an eternity, I now struggle to recall. I can describe him only as unglazed pottery: a lumpen approximation of a man, formed from sun-baked mud. He vouchsafed to me that he had more than a half century of years behind him, though in that time he has not learned the art of captivating oratory. There is nothing about him that could even be remarked upon, just blocks of drab grey and brown, all wrapped up in an abiding sense of unconcealed insubstantiality. I feel myself growing tired even as I recall our conversation. Could you stand to be remembered thus? It shall not surprise you to learn he is a godly man, though how the Almighty could find Himself well served by such a hunk of greasy, uncooked pork, I cannot fathom.

I speak of our predikant: a man whose mouth has not stopped moving since he first introduced himself with a bow that would have knocked me senseless had Zwaantie not roughly interceded. I believe the fellow to be almost feeble-minded, though his knowledge of scripture and recollection of the events of his own life demonstrated that his memory was certainly intact. It was simply the delivery that offered so little in the way of colour.

I will tell you now of Gijsbert Bastiaensz and the wife and offspring who follow him like ducklings. It would be kindest to call him an uncomplicated fellow. He thinks entirely in straight lines and I saw nothing in his eyes that spoke of a curiosity or zeal. He is every inch the hedge-preacher: an unremarkable artisan of naïve Calvinist beliefs, undoubtedly overcoming his own financial embarrassments by taking to the pulpit and preaching of economy and restraint. He spoke at great length of his previous life as a profitable miller in Dordrecht, but it is clear from the shabbiness of his family's dress and his very presence aboard this ship, that misfortune has befallen them.

His wife, Maria, was an equally tiresome companion, crushed up against me at table as we awaited the return of the cabin boy with the bland but satisfactory evening meal. She, I can recall clearly – if only because of her discernible similarity to an underfed rabbit. The shape of her head was most unusual – bulbous at the top and yet skinny and sallow as it petered down to a weak chin. Her teeth protruded over her lips in a manner that suggested she had smoked two pipes all of her days, though no predikant's wife would indulge in such a habit. And the daughters! Fat as buttermilk and with the dull grey eyes of those who have been too long in one another's company.

I fear, upon reflection, that I am being unkind with these words. Perhaps it is the queasiness that gripes at my stomach. There is a ball of greasy nausea in my throat. The to and fro of the ship, with its smells of vinegar and leather and its hum of unbathed skin, is enough to cause me to feel dull-witted and dazed. This is no excuse for my unkindness and I shall only offer in my defence that Zwaantie whispered far worse appraisals of my fellow passengers in my ear. Such is the nature of our curious relationship.

But regards the bothersome predikant. I must tell you, husband, that I am now something of an expert on the benefits of the rosmolen, *which I now know to be a horse-powered mill, over the damnable new mills that begin to blight the landscape. The predikant spent more than forty minutes on this subject. I gather that his dislike for modernity has been largely responsible for his financial disintegration. He spoke of having signed over the last of his land and holdings to his creditors shortly before accepting the position as VOC predikant.*

I think of him with some sympathy now I am freed from his company. It must be something of an upheaval for his wife and children, yanked from the blandness and familiarity of their native Dordrecht and transplanted to this raucous sailing ship heading for a new world. Perhaps I shall make more effort to be friendly. Certainly his children, wide-eyed and as frail as their father, look as though they may need a friend.

Before I retire, I will speak again of the under-merchant, Cornelisz. Truly, he is a most mercurial fellow. He seems equally comfortable in discourse with the common sailors as with Commandeur Pelsaert. His scale of knowledge quite remarkable. He is not given to bouts of enthusiasm and I am yet to see him smile, but he makes for most fascinating company and has a manner of conducting himself that leaves those in his company feeling inexplicably vital and necessary. There is something poetic to his speech and his whole demeanour is of one who would rather be nowhere else in the world than in one's own favour.

He is, however, scandalously candid in his sermonising at table. I hear the Anabaptist in him as he talks, blithely, about the nature of God. He quite brought the predikant to apoplexy as he spoke to the cadets this evening about God's disinterest in their acts. He did tell all among us that there is no such thing as Evil, and to suggest so would be to claim the Almighty to be imperfect. He promised that those who saw as he did would be guaranteed a place in Paradise regardless of their acts in life.

Worse yet, I do believe his words had an effect upon those about me. One of the merchants even spoke about his own brief dalliance with a heretical sect in Leiden in his youth, cavorting in crimson capes and daubing goat blood upon his flesh. His wife, at his side, looked upon him as if he were a stranger, but his admission brought great cries of celebration from the young officers.

I will confide that despite his gift for oratory, Cornelisz is nevertheless unsettling in his appearance. There is something in his manner that I can only liken to a hunger. He makes me think of a starving man placed at the head of a mighty banquet, denying his urge to feast and instead extending the tip of his tongue to savour the wine; to nibble only at the crusts of bread and the remnants upon the plates of other men. I sense in him a hunger kept in check.

Commandeur Pelsaert, meanwhile, continues to be a fine fellow. He has twice interceded on my behalf when the skipper, who has proven himself to be a boor and drunkard, and who has made lewd remarks within my earshot. You would grimace and seek your pistol were I to tell you the manner of his unseemly proposition. I thank God for Zwaantie and the fair Francisco that they hold my honour and good name in such esteem.

I see him even now, his tongue probing between the gaps in his few remaining teeth; his bald scalp burned the red-brown of polished leather; his yellow, rum-shot eyes moving over my body like a palm. I feel I would be well served to remain in my cabin for the duration of the voyage, but the air is already becoming stale and oppressive and I would not wish to experience these next months with only my own company. Perhaps I may offer to assist the ship's surgeon. I spied a young woman aboard with a pregnant belly and have already seen sailors fall and suffer sprains and cuts. Would it be *forward of me to make use of my own limited skills in tending to the sick?*

I am so full of thoughts and questions, my love. I shall ask Zwaantie to bring warm wine and I shall endeavour to take comfort in sleep. Tomorrow we reach what my dining companions refer to as the "open ocean", and I know that upon sighting the horizon I shall experience the greatest thrill, safe in the knowledge that there is now nothing between you and I, save time and the will of the tides.

With a richness of love,
Creesje

20

It's dark on the orlop deck whatever the hour. Dark and dank and putrid. The gloom conceals a scene of truly biblical suffering. Men lie upon their mats clutching at seasick guts, puking where they lie, voiding their insides upon their bellies and thighs. Untreated wounds begin to fester; teeth begin to slop loose from swollen, bleeding gums. Sweat drips in a greasy, foul-smelling rain from the wooden ribs of the low ceiling; endless hammocks and canvas sacks dangling from iron nails studding the joists, bulging egg cases within the tangled webs of some vast spider. This is a place of waste and pestilence; the air so thick with stench it seems to cling to the skin like damp cloth.

In the darkness, muttered conversations, quiet groans, offers of favours and the collections of debt. There have been no deaths in the darkness, but the soldiers' quarters are rife with sin. Friendships of convenience are forged in the blackness; men willing to watch one another's possessions as they snatch rare moments of sleep; men who will offer quiet words of comfort to one another when the nightmares descend.

Nicolaes de Pelgrom clings to the hem of the creaking hammock, sweating and shivering, the heel of his hand stuffed into his mouth. He bites down, tasting old blood, new blood, fishmeal and vinegary ale. Biting at himself briefly arrests the paroxysms of sickness that have been grinding their boot-heel into his belly since the ship left Texel. He has spent much of recent days in a state of true misery, lost in fever, grief and the kind of seasickness that can make a man put a pistol ball in his own brains.

At his side, Otto, damnably cheerful, is talking to himself in the dark.

'A fine ship, Wiebbe. A satisfactory skipper, even if he does have all the grace of a blind pig. And the women? Oh believe me when I vouchsafe that I have spied a true pearl amid the swine. So I do not begrudge the Almighty for neglecting to make me too comfortable as I while away my days and nights in a state of terminable indolence. But were I feeling impudent, I would enquire why He has robbed me of the conversation, jest and welcome geniality of my most particular friend.'

Nicolaes manages a snore. Regrets it as hot bile rushes up his throat. Growls a curse and swallows, eyes watering.

'I know you're listening, Wiebbe,' persists Otto, adopting a schoolboy tone and doing his damnedest to be as irritating as possible. 'You've changed your breathing. Come on, I'm doing all the heavy lifting here. I know you're a quiet man but if you don't at least tell me something interesting I'm going to go bunk up with the French, which will hurt me a lot more than it hurts you.'

It takes Nicolaes de Pelgrom a moment to realise that the name *Wiebbe* is one to which he should respond. He stares, bleary-eyed and muddle-headed, at the mound of tanned, scarred skin with whom he shares his hammock. Envies his newfound friend. Otto has a stomach for sea travel. He tucks into his mealtime rations with such gusto that he has been warned there are harsh punishments for biting through a VOC spoon. Nicolaes, meanwhile, is discovering that both he and his assumed identity share a similar aversion to the rise and sway of the ocean. He has thrown up so many times that he would not be unduly surprised to see his intestines coiling around the deck like lengths of rope.

'What are you muttering?' he growls, over the top of his knuckles – his hand pressed against his mouth in case he vomits up the last trickle of water that Otto eased between his lips. He tries to remember how to speak as a common soldier. 'You dragged me from a dream, you bastard. Flaxen-haired she was, and nipples that stood up high enough to hang your hat.'

'Lucky you,' sighs Otto, his hands behind his head. 'You've been muttering, that's for certain. I tried to keep myself entertained by asking you questions in between your ramblings. "*Tell me*," I said to thee – "which of the maidens you have bedded would you consider your true love". Your reply involved a rooster and a pear tree. I made myself laugh for a while but then you spoiled it by puking on my chest.'

Otto is gazing up at the low roof – the very picture of a man at peace. He seems entirely comfortable in this sweat-box of filth and has already bulked up a little, having feasted on rations refused by the other sea-sickened soldiers. Otto has stripped down to his breeches but his skin is still greased with a thick sheen of sweat. There is no fresh air in this rank space. Their quarters are so close to the waterline that they are permitted neither portholes nor windows. There isn't so much as a breath of breeze to stir the gathering stench.

Nicolaes is already growing used to this fug of grimy men and filthy clothes, of raw sewage and acid puke: the mingled reeks of festering men as they squirm deeper into the ship's hold like maggots into putrid flesh.

Nicolaes is shivering, his belly hollow, eyes sunk deep in their sockets, his body racked by tremors and great tugs of sickness. He has not stripped out of his uniform and the sodden material clings to him like a second flesh. He prefers it to the problems he would face should he elect to disrobe. Although his body carries scars, his skin does not look like the whipped, grimy flesh of the other men aboard the *Batavia*. He looks better fed and noticeably cleaner than his fellows. He may have wounds, but his body is that of an officer who has seen action, rather than a battle-hardened conscript.

'It will pass,' says Otto, rolling over and giving his friend a consolatory smile. 'You've gone a kind of green colour. It's nice. Matches the uniform.'

Nicolaes tries to make a witty reply but is overcome by another surge of nausea. He huddles in on himself, his clammy forehead pressing against Otto's shoulder. They are stuffed together as close as lovers: two caterpillars bound in a chrysalis. Nicolaes is grateful to have found such a companion before setting sail. The soldiers of the VOC are a disparate bunch: a straggle of tough and desperate men drawn from across Europe. Nicolaes, with his ear for language, has identified accents from across the United Provinces, from Germany and France; even catching the echo of a conversation between an Englishman and a Scotsman climbing into the same hammock and promising to watch out for the other amid this rabble of "foreigners".

Here, one hundred and eighty unwashed men are crammed into less than seventy feet of deck, scattered and squeezed around sea chests, a dozen heavy guns and several miles of cable.

The air is heavy with the weight of temper and untapped violence. Nobody yet knows who to trust. Any alliances forged this early on the voyage will be sorely tested before they can even begin their five years of garrison duty in the Indies. Those who have signed up together tend to cling to one another as if sprung from the same womb, but little factions and breakaway groups are beginning to form. They are marriages of convenience. There is no shared fraternal spirit here. The soldiers remain individuals: here for their own reasons and primarily concerned for their own welfare. Otto, with his friendly smile and lust for life, is proving to be an unusually fine companion. Nicolaes, who has barely stopped vomiting since the ship left Texel, is proving far less entertaining for his bedfellow.

'At least you're not the only one,' says Otto, as the repulsive sound of vomit splattering against wood provokes a chorus of disgusted outbursts from further aft.

Nicolaes recognises one of the angry voices as belonging to an ugly brute called Cornelis, a thick-set lump from Utrecht who has already left a stream of bloody noses and broken ribs among the rank and file. Nicolaes has marked him out as somebody to be wary of. He has asked him twice already where he is from, having been told that the handsome fellow with the fine features is claiming to be from Groningen – an area he knows. Nicolaes has managed to avoid speaking too much as yet: his sickness also serving to keep others away. He barely has the strength to stand, let alone defend himself if anybody were to take a dislike to him.

'Think cheerful thoughts.' Otto laughs and smacks his lips. 'This isn't forever. A few months and we'll be under blue skies staring at coffee-coloured women who'll stare at us as if we're made of gold, I swear it.'

Nicolaes doesn't reply. Wishes he could lose himself in imagining what lies ahead. In truth, he's barely given the true reason for his voyage a second thought. To think upon the killings is to think of Buckingham, and to do so is to fill himself up with bile and the icy fire of true grief. He no longer feels as though he is wearing a costume. Here, in this grotesque place in the bowels of a great ship, he fancies that Nicolaes de Pelgrom is fast becoming a hallucination. Perhaps he has simply imagined the years of service to the English court: the assassinations and seductions and thefts on the orders of a king's favourite. With the death of his uncle there is nobody who could vouch for him as a servant of the Crown. He is a Dutchman, aboard a Dutch ship, bound for the Indies. He has no proof he is anything other than that which he pretends to be. He takes no comfort in the thought.

'Poor companions, you say?' stammers Nicolaes, weakly, trying to distract himself. 'Would you have me dance for you? Perhaps sing...'

'Not you, you fool.' Otto smiles, giving him a nudge and readjusting his position in the hammock. 'No, you'll be a proper friend once you've got the sickness under control. No, I mean the ill luck of getting stuck with Stonecutter.'

Nicolaes screws up his features. He's heard the name before but much of the last three days has been a blur of cramps, chills and explosive sickness. Has Otto mentioned the name as they were boarding? Nicolaes has little memory of the chaos of loading the mighty behemoth with the provisions needed for the long voyage. He can recall the frenzied bellowing of a huge prize bull being winched into the hold; its song drowning out the frenzied squealing of a pregnant sow preparing to give birth to hungry piglets in its bed of shit and straw. He remembers taunts and jeers from the sailors as they climbed up and down the rigging with the ease of monkeys, all telling the soldiers that they had best keep away from them, from their possessions – that they should remember their place. Soldiers at sea were less use than women, or so they claimed.

Ah, women, thinks Nicolaes, wistfully. He had glimpsed an elegant neck or two; fine dresses and curves; well-fed women milling around the well-dressed merchants who in turn orbited the weak-chinned, shabbily dressed predikant. Nicolaes recalls a shared smile with a brown-eyed maid. White teeth and a mischievous look about her that counselled him to keep his hand upon his coin purse. And then Otto had been dragging him down to their quarters, thrusting a bottle into his hands, kicking out at men with German accents as they fought over bunks and kit, hammocks and sleeping pads: cursing the passengers, the officers, the cadets and commandeur – all enjoying superior accommodation.

'Stonecutter,' remarks Nicolaes, and his head fills with a hazy recollection. 'Lance corporal? Lashed my back?'

'Jacop Pietersz,' confirms Otto, in his ear. 'Amsterdammer. Told you at the time but you were too drunk to remember. Tough as horseflesh. Made this journey twice already. Prefers the sea to the land, or so they say. This is his third term for the VOC. Can't deal with any other life than soldiering. He's in this for the chance to hurt people. They reckon he was let loose on some of the Spaniards after Grolle. Took them apart a piece at a time. Keeps a little cadre of thugs about him and knows how to win a fight. Got his own way of keeping order and I tell you, last thing you want is to be his favourite, if you understand my meaning. Got an eye for the raw recruit. It's against the rules but there's never been anybody brave enough to give him a flogging for having his way with whoever takes his fancy. There's a young lad from Bremen already looking longingly at the sea because of what Stonecutter's making him do.'

Nicolaes rubs his hand over his bristled face. Tongues his dry lips. Closes his eyes. Feels the world spin and sway and does his damnedest to overcome the feeling of gut-rot that climbs up his throat. 'What about the corporal?'

'Jacobszoon?' Otto shrugs. 'Nothing much to tell you save he's shit-scared of Stonecutter. He used up his one favour with the Company when they agreed he could bring his wife on board. The skipper's spitting teeth about the number of women we're carrying. Corporal's got a three-year posting at the fortress and his good lady's going to be billeted with him. I saw her coming on board. Nice to look at though every woman will look good by the time we've been at sea for a few weeks.' He grins: a curve of yellowing teeth emerging from the gloom. 'Even the predikant's wife.'

Nicolaes manages a smile. Raises his head and takes the cup of warm water that Otto holds out for him. Takes a couple of sips and lies back down. Otto shifts his bulk to better accommodate him. From somewhere nearby comes the sound of violence: men roaring encouragement as boots and fists meet skin and bone. Otto grins.

'A few of the lads who were at Grolle are having a bit of a barney with those who weren't,' he explains. 'If I get bored I might go and join in but it's too bloody warm as it is. Worst of the worst – that's what they give the soldiers, though we're the most important cargo. Without us to support the fortress there'll be no Dutch interests in the Indies. They can hand the whole bloody lot over to the Portuguese, the Spanish, even the bloody English next time we have a falling-out. But the merchants get the fine cabins and the good food and a chance to look at the lovely Lucretia every mealtime. Not that you're not pretty, Wiebbe – but she and that little maid could give a fellow a prick he could hang a sail from.'

Nicolaes listens as Otto talks, providing sufficient gossip and rumour to keep the pamphleteers amused for a year. Otto, he has discovered, would make for a first-class agent of the Crown. He has a genial harmlessness about him – an air of ebullience and eagerness to please that seems to soften the hardest of hearts. People tell him things, and he is happy to share his repository of secrets with anybody willing to repay him with some intriguing tale of their own. His manner reminds Nicolaes of a noblewoman he had bedded upon Buckingham's orders. When the deed was complete she liked nothing more than to lie in the sweat-soaked silks and tell her young lover a host of scandalous secrets regarding great men at court. All he had to do was lie back, stroke her shoulders, and let her destroy Buckingham's enemies with every word that spilled from her mouth.

'...Pelsaert, well – you saw him, as we boarded,' says

Otto, teasing something out of a risen red welt upon his chest. He squeezes the offending tick between finger and thumb then wipes the mess upon his breeches. 'Red cloak and a feather in his hat. He and the skipper have already been at it. They're sharing the Great Cabin but I doubt either of them's sleeping with both eyes closed. Proper hatred there. Did you feel the crash when we grounded off Texel? Christ, Pelsaert behaved like the ship was on fire. Skipper refloated us in a matter of hours but that Pelsaert's not got a head for command. Gives more of a damn about the riches in the hold than he does about the men and it's an arrogant bastard who parades his wealth like that when everybody knows he's made his money in illegal trade. It's a relief he's retired to his bunk. Sick as a dog, apparently, though I've heard that haughty lass with the swan neck is helping him feel better.'

Nicolaes breathes out, slowly. Feels his insides settle. Props himself up and stares into the fetid, shimmering air. He can hear the waves slapping against the hull but it is little compared to the crash and roar of the hundred men sharing this putrid, stinking space. Occasionally he hears snorts of laughter, but the conversations are abrupt and rude, littered with curses, threats and suggestions about what they would like to do if given a few moments alone with the haughty bitch berthed in the cabin next to the under-merchant.

'Under-merchant?' asks Nicolaes, drily. 'Skin and bone? Scars on his face?'

'Saw him, did you?' asks Otto. 'Looks like a gust of wind would knock him over, doesn't he? Those scars – I can't tell if they're old or fresh but I swear they give his mood away as clear as a dog's tail or a horse's ears. Got his eye on that beauty, I guarantee it. He's lusting after her same as the rest of us. I saw him, last patrol, hiding behind a coil of rope like a naughty child. Watching her like a cat watches a bird and I swear, those scars on his face turned red as fire while I stared at him. By Christ, if Pelsaert drops dead of the flux we'll have him in charge of the ship! Seems tight with the skipper though. Had him roaring with laughter at something he whispered in his ear. Pelsaert wasn't happy about it; you could see that. He'll have his eyes on Lucretia too, and the skipper will want her just to piss Pelsaert off. Keeping order on this ship will be like herding cats, you mark my words.'

Nicolaes is about to ask him what he has heard about the mysterious passenger aboard the *Buren*, but a burst of angry chatter from further down the deck forces him to hold his tongue. A group of men jostle and shove one another: two loose semi-circles forming around a tangle of limbs doing battle on the wooden floor. Over the jeers and cheers, Nicolaes hears the ugly, high-pitched shriek of an animal in pain.

Otto turns his head, craning to see between the jostling bodies. 'One of the posh boys has caught a rat,' he says, bright-eyed. 'Coenraat. You'll know the type – from money but likes the rough and tumble of the ranks. Close with Stonecutter too. Spends more time down here than he does in the saloon with the other cadets. By the looks of things he's come down for a little sport.'

Nicolaes listens to the frenzied squeals. Peers through the throng and sees a portly young man, splendid in his cadet uniform, down on all fours with blood running from a scratch on his cheek. Opposite is a young man with pale skin and so little meat on his bones that Nicolaes can identify every bone in his skeleton. He's kneeling opposite his senior officer. Both have their hands tied behind their backs. A soldier in the crowd holds the squirming rat by the tail and tosses it into the space between the two men. Immediately they begin thrashing, slamming their heads down upon the deck, butting one another, biting, gouging: trying to smash their foreheads or teeth into the maddened rodent as it darts between them and attempts to flee into the forest of legs. Each time it escapes it is grabbed by another soldier and tossed back into the gaming circle. Nicolaes hears bets being taken. A roar of pain followed by a crash of laughter.

Then Coenraat van Huyssen, gentleman of the VOC, succeeds in dragging the bloodied rat away from his opponent and bringing his teeth down on its skull to a great chorus of cheers.

'Poor bastard,' mutters Otto, as a group of jeering soldiers pick up the dead rat and smear the hot blood onto the cheeks of the terrified young recruit. Nicolaes feels disgust smouldering away in his gut. Forgets the sickness that has gnawed at him and drags himself upright. He feels Otto's hand upon his forearm. 'There'll be worse to come, Wiebbe,' he says. 'Worse for all of us. You'll look back on these times as the good old days before we next see land. Let them have their fun. It's not up to you to stop it.'

Nicolaes drags his eyes away from the bloody performance and lies back, staring up at the timbers. They will be here for hours more. In any twenty-four-hour period they are given two half-hour turns upon the deck, under the strictest of orders not to venture before the mast or to have anything to do with the passengers from the upper decks. There are four latrines on board and the hundred soldiers are permitted to use two of them – wiping themselves afterwards with a length of tattered rope that dangles into the ocean. There will be sickness aplenty in the weeks that follow. He will see far worse than the brutality he has just witnessed.

'Out of my way, damn your bastard eyes!'

A sickening crunch followed by a squeal of pain, and the silhouette of the man called Stonecutter throws a hulking shadow onto the dangling row of hammocks. Somebody has made the mistake of stepping in front of him and arresting his swift, soundless progress through the swaying hammocks. He has responded with immediate violence, bringing his great mallet of a fist down upon the head of a slight, red-haired fellow. The poor unfortunate's knees buckle with the impact of the blow, crumpling in on himself and sliding to the floor so that it looks for a moment as if the lance corporal has hammered the man straight into the deck.

'Get that clumsy bastard to the surgeon,' he roars, looking down at the hollow-eyed tangle of arms and legs at his feet. A nasty leer crosses his big broad face, cutting a seam into his map of wrinkles and fine white scars. 'Get him to reset his nose while he's there.'

A tall, rangy chap with a Haarlem accent steps forward. 'He hasn't got a broken nose...'

Stonecutter raises his boot. Brings it down with a sickening crunch. 'Happy now, big mouth?'

Nicolaes has to force himself to blend in with the great sea of unwashed, anonymous men. He cannot reveal himself. Cannot become somebody remarkable. He would dearly love to grab the great bullying bastard by his bovine neck and smash his fist into his face until his eyes roll back in his head. But he's weak, and sick, and his whole mission relies upon not drawing attention to himself.

Nicolaes bites his lip, trying to make sense of himself. Is he still an assassin in the pay of Mrs Towerson and King Charles, or is he a common soldier with the VOC? He feels mislaid – a hawk who has strayed too far from its master's glove. It had seemed simple back in London. He was to kill those who had not been dealt with properly through official channels. He was to put a blade through the heart of Herman van Speult, and if opportunity presented itself, to ensure the death of Governor-General Coen. Both deeds would further British aims, and they would silence the irrepressible Mrs Towerson. He has her ruby tucked safe in his boot. He has already killed on her behalf but unless he makes good on the contract to end the life of van Speult, he will be a thief and a trickster rather than a professional who has given his word.

'Coenraat,' yells Stonecutter, addressing the VOC cadet who is his junior in years but superior in rank and social status. 'Look at the state of your face! Have that cleaned or it will get infected then get back up the stairs to the saloon. I'm told that Lucretia's maid is to tease the predikant over dinner tonight. There will be nothing under her skirts as she serves Lady Lucretia and she intends to show the predikant and his wife exactly where Adam and Eve could make themselves comfortable in her Garden of Eden.'

His words are met with a roar of laughter. A rangy, rat-faced man with wispy whiskers demands to know how the lance corporal can promise such a display. 'I have the ears of the great men aboard,' he says, slyly. 'I knows things that you'd all pay handsome to hear. And you'll all learn, in time. Those I trust know who you are, and I'll thank you to come join me for a drop of rum and a description of the young maid's skill with a prick that will have your breeches heaving. That's the thing about the skipper – he's happy to share with those who show loyalty.'

'Is the rest of the fleet still with us?' comes an English voice.

'Seven ships, pretty as a picture,' snaps Stonecutter, unhappy to be questioned. 'Better than you English bastards could manage. All friendly and close enough for the skippers to shout their good mornings. We'll be spreading out though, and there's a lot of ocean ahead. We'll get separated, like as not. And that's when you soldiers will earn your pay.'

'Is it true you were in Amboyna?' comes a voice from the darkness. 'That you held a candle to the Englishmen until the fat melted from beneath their arms?'

'Who said that?' demands Stonecutter. 'My business is my own. Believe me, whatever any of you have heard about old Stonecutter, the truth is far fucking worse.'

Nicolaes drops down from the hammock, movement smooth as silk. Otto, unbalanced, gives a little yell as he cartwheels out of bed and clatters down to the decks. He's met with a wave of laughter as he pops back up and gives a grand bow, grinning hugely. 'Do return tomorrow, when I shall be attempting a somersault while juggling two hogsheads of arrack…'

Stonecutter is upon him in a moment, two big meaty hands grabbing him by the skin of his bare chest and lifting him up as if he were made of straw. Otto, taken completely by surprise, shrieks out in pain and there is an ugly crunching nose as Stonecutter jerks him upwards and slams him, face first, into the wood. He drops him. Kicks him twice in the guts and brings his leg up, preparing to stamp down upon his exposed chin.

'Funny! Making your jokes! A jester, are you? A fucking clown?'

Nicolaes acts entirely upon instinct. Throws himself at Stonecutter as if hurled by a giant. Smashes into him with his shoulder, forearm, face, using his whole body as a battering ram. The bigger man totters but doesn't fall. Gives Nicolaes a smile that seems to contain genuine pleasure. Then he throws a punch. Short, fast, expertly delivered. Nicolaes jerks back as a fist the size of a ram's head swings past his chin. Trips over a pair of outstretched feet and clatters down. Two huge blows to the small of his back, pushing the wind from his body, spilling piss into his breeches, and then he's being pulled up by his hair. Stonecutter's forehead connects with his cheekbone and the world seems to tear into strips.

'We've got a fighter here lads.' Stonecutter grins, and the shapes around Nicolaes drift into and out of one another until he is surrounded on all sides by a group of the lance corporal's personal, hand-picked favourites. 'No need to bother the commandeur with an act of assault on a senior officer. Not when we can sort it ourselves.'

Nicolaes squirms in the big man's grasp. Kicks out and connects with a kneecap. Throws an elbow and feels it smash into a jawbone. Then a fist slams into his gut, and he's choking on his own bile. The sound of tearing cotton as his shirt and doublet are ripped away. He stumbles forward, the heel of his boot ripping away and flapping like a broken jaw. There is a tiny tinkling sound and flash of blood red as the ruby clatters away, unseen, and drops through the planks.

'The lads need this, son,' grunts Stonecutter, holding Nicolaes's face in his giant hand. 'Take what they give you and don't complain. It comes to us all sooner or later.'

Nicolaes spits blood and puke into the lance corporal's face. It provokes the right reaction. Stonecutter hits him so hard that the world turns black.

He is mercilessly unconscious for all that comes next.

21

The food has been devoured and the expensive crockery cleared. Now the fine men and women of the *Batavia* sit at table with their brandies, their coffees, their pipes and cups of wine. Above, the flames flicker in the huge candelabra; hot wax dripping like pearls.

Quiet conversations, hushed confidences, little twos and threes of meandering chatter as those who have dined together for two tiresome months do their damnedest to find some modicum of interest in one another.

At the head of the table, Skipper Jacobsz, drunk and loud-mouthed, revelling in the absence of his detested commandeur. Pelseart is, again, confined to his cabin, nursing the sickness that eats him from the inside out; comforted only by the tenderness of the fair Lucretia.

'Easier fighting two than one,' insists Jacobsz, spraying spittle. 'You keeps hold of one while you're smashing up the other, and you keeps your eyes on the one you haven't got round to yet, so you gets in their head, see, and they start thinking about what you're going to do to them once you've finished with their mate and got both of your hands free. Chances are you won't have to fight both. You win before the second one's even got proper involved. Now, if you're taking on three, there's no way to be sure you'll come out of it looking as handsome as you went in, but the key is to make sure you look like a crazy person – somebody that they'll have to kill if they want to keep down because you're willing to chew their leg through to the bone as long as there's breath in your body, and then they've got the spectre of the hangman in their heads as they come for you…'

The skipper has been entertaining the predikant's wife for the past fifteen minutes, delivering an insightful tutorial on the best ways to survive a full-blooded fist fight on the cobbles. Her cheeks look a little flushed: two twin sunsets of pink, threatening to set fire to the chinstraps of her pristine white cap. She is a quiet, rabbity woman, and it is a fair assumption that until this night, nobody has ever been so full-blooded in their descriptions of how best to bite through a human thumb. Her name is Maria, but nobody has yet spoken it. Her husband addresses her as "Wife". Her children do not address her at all. The daughters are all replicas of their mother, decreasing in size all the way down to the diminutive eight-year-old. Maria is well-mannered and thoroughly proper in her deportment, but it is clear that she is quietly rather enjoying the chance to converse with a man like Ariaen Jacobsz, and to learn about something other than windmills and God. From time to time she asks the skipper a particular question. Does he, she ponders, favour the belly or the nose when it comes to delivering a winning blow? Moreover, is it true, as she has heard, that it is possible to twist a man's head so sharply that the neck breaks as surely as if they were flung from the gallows. Jacobsz is giving the matter much consideration – even slowing the pace of his evening drinking.

Cornelisz watches.

Cornelisz *sees*.

Predikant Bastiaensz, seated at her left, has paid little attention to the conversation taking place between the skipper and his wife. Unless she were to transform into another bowl of ale-soaked lentils or a leg of pan-roasted chicken, she is unlikely to attract his attention between now and this evening's prayers. He has barely looked at his children, who sit blankly at the far end of the table. Buck-toothed and with dandruff falling from his lank hair like snow, Bastiaensz made for a true grotesque as he wolfed down fistfuls of bread, of bony fish, of buttered leeks and gnarly cheese: all sloshing around in a belly full of ale. His evening prayers, delivered on the main deck, are as like to end with a belch as an amen.

'You do not eat, *Heer* Cornelisz?'

The under-merchant drags his eyes away from the elegant, blue-veined neck of Lucretia Jansz. She is a welcome rarity at dinner, having taken to dining instead with the ailing Pelsaert. He realises that one of the merchant wives has been addressing him. He recalls that they spoke at breakfast but cannot find the stomach for recollecting the contents of the conversation. He sees nothing in her worth investigating, though there is a rash upon her chin that he fancies he could treat were he in possession of his old chest full of vials and potions. Her eyes protrude a little too far, making him feel as though he is being addressed by two boiled eggs.

'Alas, I had not known myself to be such a poor sailor,' says Cornelisz, with a thin smile. 'I have laced my coffee with a tincture of my own devising and I anticipate I shall be in rude health before the dawn but sadly I have no appetite this evening.'

'You are not a sea-going gentleman?' she asks, her accent containing a trace of some rural dialect. 'Frederick and I are keen sailors, are we not? My husband has previously voyaged to Italy and Portugal and I have made a brace of trips to England, when relations were good between our nations, but I would not call myself a woman of the sea.'

'And how do you find our vessel?' asks Cornelisz, giving her his full attention. He moves closer to her, his shadow lengthening upon the wooden table. He sees her eyes flick to his scars. He can see her wondering what he would look like were he not disfigured. Can see her trying to peel back the ruined layers to find the man beneath. 'I trust we are providing you all that one would wish for an honoured guest.'

She lowers her voice, imparting a confidence. 'Our accommodation here is tolerable, certainly, though I will confide that it is by no means luxurious... I am given to believe that *Vrouwe* Jansz over there has been given a distinctly superior berth, with room even for that young, well... that young lady who calls herself a maid. And we do find ourselves in some discomfort, with the smell from the bilges rising directly beneath. We had thought to talk to Commandeur Pelsaert about an alternative position, but I see we are again deprived of his company.' She looks around herself pointedly, as if Pelsaert may be hiding in the shadows. 'He is again indisposed? I heard it said he has been the beneficiary of the attentions of Vrouwe Jansz. She has nursed him in the extremities of his sickness, is that not correct? Of course, I am not a modern woman, so I cannot say what is proper and what is not. Am I correct in believing her to be joining her husband in Jakarta?'

Cornelisz sips the good French wine that swills like blood in his silver goblet. Flicks a glance at her husband. Frederick, a merchant from Delft, is a reedy, high-shouldered man who looks to have inherited his dusty black clothing from a recently interred and better built relative. He sits to her left, mouth open, staring into the middle distance like a discarded toy.

Cornelisz gives the lady an encouraging smile, answering her question with a slight inclination of his head. When he speaks, he raises his voice sufficiently so that the other diners may hear the latest news about their absent leader.

'I am assured we will enjoy the commandeur's company by tomorrow night's evening meal. He suffers with a malady that causes him some distress but he is confident that the symptoms will pass. We are all finding our sea legs, are we not? I will confide that I had given little thought to the impact that the voyage would have upon my own constitution. I had thought myself a buccaneer – a hardy adventurer, standing upon the poop deck with glass to my eye, staring into the mist and spray like a true hero. Instead I find myself squirming upon my bunk, unable even to find comfort in the words of the good book, as things twist in my belly and threaten to climb up my throat.'

The merchant's wife gives a high laugh, clapping her hands together at the description. Cornelisz glances down the table and finds he has drawn the attention of all the other diners. He sees the skipper looking at him, a hard sneer on his scarred face.

'Bad guts, has he?' spits Jacobsz, taking a slurp of brandy

from the wine glass by his plate. 'That's what he calls it, is it? If you ask me it's more likely a flare-up of the French disease. You'll have all heard by now what a philanderer the good commandeur is. Believe me, under that dandified cloak he's no better than a pox-ridden…'

'You will perhaps have noticed the moments of ill will between our skipper and commandeur,' cuts in Cornelisz, smoothly. He gives Jacobsz the slimmest of glances, shaking his head. *No*, he says, wordlessly. *Not now. Not yet.*

'Not our place to say,' mutters one of the merchants, to Cornelisz's left.

'Am I not correct in thinking that aboard a VOC vessel, the commandeur outranks the captain in all matters save those specifically to do with seafaring? I am informed that should he wish it, he could order the flogging of every man aboard, captain included.

The mumbled conversation fades to complete silence. All heads turn towards Lucretia. She has been every inch a perfect gentlewoman since boarding and moving her meagre possessions into the cabin next to Cornelisz's own. She has spoken little and her manners and dress have been impeccable. But there is a certain steel in the way she rises to defend the commandeur's honour and insult Jacobsz into the bargain. Cornelisz sees a look of pure hate grip the skipper's face as he glares at her from across the table, his hands squeezing his glass like the wrist of a naughty child.

'Do not concern yourself with matters of hierarchy aboard ship, Vrouwe Jansz,' says Cornelisz, his voice a vial of oil. 'At sea we are far from the Gentlemen of the honourable East India Company and we all have much to contribute to the success of this voyage. Why, our skipper here is a hugely experienced fellow and the very fact that he is skippering the *Batavia* upon her maiden voyage is no little symbol of the esteem in which he is held. The good commandeur, meanwhile, is a merchant admired by all, and a man who understands how to thrive in the Indies. The document he wrote about his time at court in Agra is invaluable to the VOC. We are fortunate to have two great men aboard, taking care of—'

'And you, sir,' butts in Lucretia. 'What do you bring to our voyage?'

Cornelisz is taken aback by the interruption. He feels as though he has been suddenly bitten by a tame bird. Where is the frightened, timid wren he found at the wharf in Amsterdam? She is looking at him with undisguised disdain, as if they were man and wife and he had made some off-colour remark in polite company. He feels a sudden urge to apologise – to make amends for whatever ill he may have mistakenly done to her. There is no doubt that she is a magnificent creature, beautiful and imperious; almost regal in her bearing. She moves among the commoners like a swan through pondweed. Cornelisz alone had noted the undercurrent to the admiring glances. Something crackled in the air among the sailors, the soldiers, the wives of the hapless merchants upon the deck; something born of jealousy and distrust.

'Has your tongue developed an ague, Mijnheer Cornelisz?' she asks, sweetly. 'Do you perhaps know an apothecary who could assist with such an affliction?'

The impulse to apologise is quickly overtaken by a desire to beat her pretty little face to meat. He will bow and scrape and hide his true nature if it furthers his goals but he will not be made to look a fool by a woman he knows himself man enough to break. At this table, he is to be treated with respect. How dare she address him so? It takes a huge effort of will to keep his face amenable. He smiles at her as if they were old friends trading jests.

'You have me there, Vrouwe Jansz. I am, indeed, a humble apothecary endeavouring to make himself useful and to employ his meagre gifts in a manner that repays my employer's faith, and perhaps to prosper myself along the way. I would add to my knowledge of tinctures and powders – purchase saffron, cochineal, poppy seeds, hemp, the finest of opiates. God conceals His wonders within an abundance of marvels and it is the duty of the apothecary to tease them out. I trust I shall be equal to the task, and to provide comfort for those who need it. As you have seen, not all who set sail for India find that which they seek.'

There is a pause at the end of the little speech as the assembled diners sift through the words for hidden meanings. The air at the table is thick with things unsaid and sentences ripe with coded messages. Cornelisz is reminded of the tavern in Haarlem where Torrentius held court. Enjoys a moment's fond recollection of one of his writhing, carnal tableaus: a blonde-haired young maiden attired in goose fat and white feathers, twirled and spun between the assembled men, her eyes heavy with the lullaby of opiates and gin; hands reaching out to grab at her flesh, to pluck the plumes from her bruised flesh; drum thudding faster and faster, fiddle player drawing terrible screechings from his instrument while Torrentius stood naked atop a wine barrel and told his followers that all sin was preordained; that to brutalise this maiden would be to perform His almighty work.

Cornelisz stops himself before he descends into pleasant recollection. Permits himself to hold only a scrap of memory: white feathers, turning red.

'An apothecary?' asks the merchant's wife, clearly enjoying the back-and-forth. 'Where was this, may I ask? I have visited a number of different establishments in Amsterdam but I judge from your voice that you are not an Amsterdammer, and...'

'I am fortunate to have practised my art in numerous locations,' says Cornelisz, breezily. He is beginning to wish he had not spoken of his previous trade. Moreover he is beginning to think he would have been better served assuming his new position under a different name. He has made little effort to conceal his identity. Should Torrentius betray him or the murder of the wet nurse be linked to him, it would not be impossible for the authorities to seek him out in his new life. The thought would be unsettling, had he any intention of seeing the journey through to its end.

'The men are behaving, are they, Skipper?' asks the predikant, scooping up an errant flake of white fish from the wooden table and popping it into his mouth.

'Scum of the Earth, but they're my scum,' growls Jacobsz. 'This is pleasure-sailing compared to what's to come. Once they get sick, and their skin opens up like rotten fruit, and their teeth are sliding in their gums every time they move their heads and they're falling asleep wearing one another's shit and puke on their skin – that's when we'll see what kind of bastards the VOC is sending to its fortress. I ain't seen much to impress me so far, not from the soldiers.

My boys could have them on their backs in a heartbeat were it to come to a fight. And as for the cadets! Listen and you'll hear them drinking and boasting and telling each other about the wenches they've banged their balls against. Christ, how would you respond to an order from somebody who looks as though they should still be suckling at the teat!'

There are a chorus of coughs and murmurs of disapproval at the choice of language. Even so, all the diners seem quite energised by this glimpse into the real life of a merchant vessel, and the descriptions of the five VOC youths, boisterously drinking in the neighbouring saloon, are somewhat apt. Cornelisz has been assured that Coenraat, the high-born brute who prefers the company of the common soldiers, will be a man they can trust when the time comes. And where Coenraat leads, the other cadets will follow.

Cornelisz looks past the light of the flickering candles and over the mess of dirty dishes and spilled goblets. He realises that Jacobsz is still staring at Lucretia. Cornelisz follows his eye-line. He's burning holes in her neck with his eyes. Cornelisz sees them as thumbs, either side of her windpipe, shutting off the breath in that elegant neck, causing blood vessels to pop in those chilly grey eyes, making those long legs kick beneath his weight. The thought of it excites him. Cornelisz knows how to control men. Knows how to give them what they want most. He has already steered Zwaantie into the skipper's arms and the old bastard is grateful for her attentions, but it's the fine gentlewoman whom he most wants to bed, and to hurt. Cornelisz can make that happen. He can engineer a situation where Ariaen Jacobsz can have everything he wants.

Cornelisz takes a moment to bask in satisfaction at his own grandeur. Already he has made good upon his promises. Already Jacobsz is beginning to talk freely of a future other than in the service of the Company. He clearly admires Cornelisz, who has already provided him a woman who will share her affections with any man her lover decrees. Zwaantie, God bless her, is doing everything Cornelisz bids: playing the part of the wide-eyed but flirty maid with some considerable gusto. And Cornelisz has found no difficulty in slipping the powders into Pelsaert's wine – rendering him sick in incremental doses. Jacobsz will soon be free of the interfering merchant. All Jacobsz has to give him in return, is the *Batavia*.

'How do you keep them from killing one another down in the orlop?' asks the predikant's eldest son; a weak-chinned, dull-eyed specimen who seems forever to be working through some internal list of figures; counting on his fingers and thumbs and seeming continually dissatisfied with the tally.

'A firm hand, that's the kèy,' grunts Jacobsz, and looks past the guttering candle to direct his words at Cornelisz. 'A few men you can trust to hit hard, and hit right – they keep the others from stepping out of line. I've sailed with the lance corporal before and I swear, old Stonecutter's not one to be toyed with. Can make a mess of a man.'

'Stonecutter?' asks the predikant's wife, meekly.

'Little trick from when he was van Speult's man at Amboyna. Can cut through a rock with a hot blade. One swipe. Made decent money from those who bet he couldn't do it. Strong as an ox. Put a beating on one of the soldiers a few days back and if you were to look at the poor bastard you'd think he'd been run down by a cart. The others will do as he says, right enough.'

'It is a brutal life for many,' says the predikant, helping himself to a hunk of cheese. 'I thank God again and again for calling me to serve him as I do. I fancy I would not have been much of a soldier, and I am not built to scurry up the rigging like your fine sailors. Truly, they are remarkable men and a credit to you.'

Jacobsz shrugs, still feeling the sting of Lucretia's insult. He will brood upon it until he is too drunk to stand, then shall fall asleep amid Zwaantie's pillowy thighs – waking in a foul mood with a head that calls for drink and a sourness in his gut that cannot be soothed. Cornelisz has discovered that his new friend seems to prefer brooding about imagined slights rather than celebrating his good fortune. He is rarely in a good mood – even as he skippers the finest ship in the VOC fleet and enjoys the nightly attentions of an Amsterdam whore that would have cost him double a day's wages back home.

Cornelisz reminds himself to speak to Zwaantie about perhaps withholding her affections until he better behaves himself at dinner. Cornelisz needs the assembled gentlemen and women to suspect nothing until the deed is done. He wants the moment of the mutiny to come as a complete surprise. They will do as they are commanded if they are unprepared. He shall follow Stonecutter's lead. Make a few examples and encourage the others to fall into line. Those who please him he will deposit at a safe harbour before striking out for the open sea with a crew of loyal men. From there, he will find a place in which to construct his new Eden – to fulfil the destiny foreseen by his master.

And in that place, as he climbs his throne, it will not matter whether Lucretia stares at him with sullenness and hate. She will spread her legs and become his Eve.

'Van Speult,' says the merchant in the ill-fitting cloak. He pulls a face. 'Coen's understudy, yes? Oversaw that nasty business with the English spies? Died on his way home to face the consequences, if I'm not mistaken.'

'Did as he was bid,' snaps Jacobsz, slamming the flat of his hand down on the table to call for more arrack. Zwaantie enters from the adjoining galley, carrying a hogshead of arrack, her bodice unlaced to her cleavage and sweat greasing her coffee-coloured skin. She gives a little curtsey to the assembled diners and hurries towards Jacobsz, whose mouth splits into a grin as he enjoys the flashes of bare tanned skin at her wrists and neck. She fills his glass, her eyes upon her mistress. Lucretia looks at her maid with disgust, her nostrils wrinkling as if she were something foul. Nobody at the table says a word as Jacobsz squeezes a fistful of her thigh. She stifles a yelp and slaps him, giggling.

'Zwaantie!' hisses Lucretia. 'My God I shall not have this again!'

Zwaantie bites her lip, making her bee-stung lips seem all the more engorged. She leans over and whispers something into the skipper's ear, and is rewarded with a slap on the rump that would have sent a horse into a canter. She flashes her mistress a look of pure triumph. Winks at Cornelisz as she turns and hustles back out through the wooden door, leaving a trail of unwashed clothes and the alley-cat reek of sweat and sex. Cornelisz feels a swelling of something unfamiliar. Realises it is a quiet sort of pride, as a master would consider an apprentice who has exceeded their own teachings.

'A fine servant, I'm sure,' mutters the predikant, his breath catching in his throat. Nervously, he rubs his greasy fingers on his lips. He has yet to fully recover from the evening when Zwaantie slid past him during dinner and lifted her skirt to reveal her willingness to help him turn his back on God. A thought occurs to him and his eyes widen. 'My wife and I shall require a goodly servant in the Indies, were you minded to…'

'No,' says his wife, firmly, her body stiffening in her seat. 'No thank you.'

Cornelisz leans back in his chair. Sips his wine. Feels the ocean move beneath him. He has no motion sickness. Feels in true rude health. His every action is considered and calculated. He must be neither glutton nor drunkard nor sanctimonious in his abstemiousness. His eyes may sparkle with sufficient wit to seem a worthy occupier of his elevated rank, but he must not appear too intelligent lest it cause his fellow diners to probe for answers about his education and influential friends. Such is the life he has chosen. Such dissembling is the cost of greatness.

Over the lip of his glass, he sees Lucretia gazing at him. He gives a small bow and raises his goblet to toast her health. She looks away, as if the very sight of him offends her. He becomes aware of his scars. Feels as though the old wounds are blistering and popping; bubbling beneath flame.

For a moment, he lets himself become true. Drops the pretence. Straightens his spine and lets his face slide into its natural state. The shadows and hollows seem to lengthen, his jaw elongating, eyebrows arching, scars twisting to delineate a face that is at once terrifying and beguiling; a gargoyle leering from a church roof.

She sees him for what he is. Sees what lurks within him.

He is gratified to see, as she raises her glass to toast him in return, that her lily-white hand trembles like a flower.

22

Husband,

I am afraid.

Oh, Boudewijn, what sweet relief to confide such a shameful feeling. What a fragile, sugar-spun creature you must think me to be so undone by my first steps beyond the Provinces.

Please, be not alarmed to receive such unhappy confidences. I swear to thee that I have done naught to dishonour you. I conduct myself daily as the dutiful wife of a gentleman and I trust that were you in my company you would be well satisfied at having such a serene and self-assured wife. And yet I confess that each day brings fresh apprehension. Each dawn I find myself increasingly afraid. My sleep is peopled with strange and unsettling nightmares. I cannot face food and it would be no hardship to imbibe nothing but wine and brandy were I to permit myself.

There are few moments during the interminable day when it does not feel as if my strength is failing me. I am dizzy every moment I spend trapped in the thick, sweaty air of this cabin. I feel confined, shut in like a bird in a too-small cage. I tire of the noises of travel; the murmurings of other lives pressed up too close against my own. Recollections of our own blessed children thwart me in my every attempt to keep occupied. I have sought to employ my own humble talents for nursing the sick and the needy, but each passenger whom I bandage or bathe – or to whom I might offer a gentle word – is transformed into the vision of our own lost children. I wipe the sweat-wreathed faces of strangers and I see our lost infants.

I will endeavour to find the strength to persevere in the duties I have taken upon myself, but how I yearn for the comfort of a warm embrace from one who loves me as I love them.

I miss you with such fire, husband, even as grief chills me down to the bone.

Ah, what blessed respite I find in disclosing these truths to thee, my love. I pause here: emboldened, quelled, breathing slow and deep as I gather myself to proceed.

What, I wonder, would you seek to absorb of our voyage? We are here at the close of the year. I repeat for your absorption words that I have heard but do not truly comprehend. We are at the limits of what Jacobsz calls the horse latitudes and will soon experience our first taste of land since Texel. We will put in at the Cape for fresh supplies and I shall find opportunity to stretch my legs upon dry land and to look upon the people whom we so glibly think upon as "savages". I am told that the port is a cesspit of sickness and disease and that *no white man should consider stepping ashore if he has hopes of seeing his native land again.*

I am perhaps alone of those on board who trusts in the good commandeur, though I am openly mocked when I speak in his defence – even among the merchants and senior VOC figures who seem, through some perverse practicality, to have given their allegiance to our drunken, lecherous skipper.

I will confide that even those who profess to be watchful of my safety are proving themselves most unsuited to the task. Zwaantie has made her true self plain. She is no maid, husband – she is a thief and a whore who has used me for nothing but the payment of her passage. She has abandoned our shared cabin and now beds down with the skipper. Her public displays are shameful. She has given herself over willingly and if the rumours at table are to be believed, she is providing similar services to those he considers his most loyal men. She is an instrument of division aboard this ship and I fairly shake with guilt at having been involved in bringing her aboard.

And yet the man who should hold himself accountable seems utterly oblivious to my disgust and dissatisfaction. Heer Cornelisz, who swore to the character of this wretched slattern, continues to act as if he has played no part in this dishonourable situation. He looks upon me with bewilderment and no small amount of hurt when I allow my displeasure to manifest in angry glances and pointed remarks. It is as if he has no conscience, husband. No sense of guilt or any thirst to make amends. I will confess that I find him an unsettling figure and there are times when his nearness alone is enough to make my flesh prickle as if kissed by fire.

I have the sensation of being watched even when I am alone. I know that a woman of high birth and some lingering beauty will be an object of desire for so many men crammed so close together, but I confess that I am beginning to feel most vulnerable. The good commandeur has been abed for many days and though he tries with stout heart to continue in his duties and tend to my needs, it is he who is the patient and I the physician. He grows thin as peasant soup, husband, and there is a continual miasma of pestilent air emanating from his burning skin. I sense that for one who prides himself upon cleanliness and appearance, to be witnessed in such a pitiable state causes him nigh as much pain as the cramps that gripe his innards. He fights his illness with such bravery that it is all I can do not to weep as I dab at his blistering flesh with a cold cloth.

Oh, husband, how I wish that you could emerge from the gloom of this cabin and enfold me in your embrace. I feel delirious with longing for affection. There is a foulness to the air aboard ship. The soldiers in the hold are permitted only thirty minutes of daylight every twelve hours and they fight and war and grow thinner down in the pestilential horrors of their quarters. I was given insight into the ugliness of their accommodation by a soldier I attempted to nurse. His plight was revealed to me some days ago. Jacobsz and Cornelisz spoke of the methods employed by a brutish lance corporal when it comes to maintaining discipline. Truly, I was the only person present who demonstrated any concern for the fate of the man of whom an example was made.

Afterwards, as I brooded upon the plight of the beaten soldier, I vouchsafed to do what I could to ease his suffering. He had been taken to the surgeon's quarters but save the application of a balm and the bandaging of broken ribs, little had been done to provide him with comfort. With dispensation from our ailing commandeur, I was permitted to provide some degree of gentle care, holding his hand in my own as he lay prone upon the hard bedroll and fell in and out of wakefulness.

I will admit to some surprise at the utterances that spilled from his split lips. Though I had been led to believe he was Frisian by birth and bound for the fortress at Batavia as no more than a common soldier, he spoke frequently in English and even cried out for the Lord's forgiveness in Papist Latin. I felt enormous pity for the poor man who had suffered so greatly at the hands of the brutal lance corporal. I have no experience of military matters but it is not God's will for man to treat man as if he were a disobedient animal. Truly, the sight of his swollen and broken face was enough to soften the hardest of hearts.

It came as some surprise to witness the unexpected healing of his wounds and the gradual easing of his suffering, and to witness something close to a rebirth. The man beneath the injuries was indeed handsome, with bright, intelligent eyes and manners that were almost courtly. It was my honour to be there as he awoke from his fitful slumber. His first concern was the health of a companion with whom he had boarded. It was with some relief that he learned that his particular friend had visited him many times during his convalescence and had seemed in rude health on each occasion.

The Frisian told me that his name was Hayes and that he was bound for the Indies following a failed love affair. He quite entranced me with his tale of doomed love and were it not for the distance between our ranks and the scandal it would cause, I would confess to wishing to spend more time hearing the anecdotes of this quiet, enigmatic man. Alas he is now declared fit and has rejoined his companions in the hold where I fear that any progress he has made will be swiftly undone by the primitive conditions in which he and his companions are forced to travel.

Perhaps I have lived too cosseted a life, husband. When we disembark I intend to write to the VOC encouraging them to afford better care of their men.

I shall pause here, glad to confide that I feel infinitely better for having taken the time to put my thoughts down on paper, and to feel your nearness. I remind myself constantly that each moment we are at sea, I am moving closer to your side. I shall write again when I have tidings to report. Tomorrow I suffer the indignity of a visit to the louse deck between the bows, where I shall again have to inspect my own naked body for these detested parasites. Why we must subject ourselves to such indignities is not a question I can answer. Why concern ourselves with lice when there are so many foul beasts feasting upon us. My bedsheets fairly crawl with life and the grotesque brown-shelled beetles fairly swarm along the decks whenever the sea is becalmed.

There are times when I cannot sleep because the squeals of the rats in the hold are as loud as a saw through wood. It is no surprise that some of our number have begun to behave most peculiarly. The predikant's eldest daughter has stopped speaking and refuses to eat, and I am led to believe that one of the cadets had to be restrained lest he throw himself into the ocean while in a state of some madness.

And yet we begin a New Year, husband. Tonight I shall drink the brandy that is offered and show the face of a gentlewoman more than equal to the pernicious affronts of this voyage. I shall raise a glass to our marriage and our future and the joyous reunion we shall experience in a few short months. Surely, the year 1629 shall bring us much good fortune. I pray that you long for my arrival with the same passion that I dream of your embrace.

Yours, ever,
Creesje

PART THREE

23

Tafelbai, Cape of Good Hope, Africa

April 14, 1629

'See, Wiebbe! *Gannets*, by the score. The wings have the look of velvet sleeves, do they not? Black as good ink. Sure sign of land, my friend! I say again – if I have not said it to sufficiency – I am truly glad the Lord didn't yet want you for His own. I hadn't ever imagined to see you as a seafaring man but by Christ you learn things quick... ha! I look upon you and it delights me, Wiebbe. With the wind playing with your hair and the salt scabbing your chapped face... we are twins, are we not? And look! Those reeds, their stems opening like musical instruments, all tangled up with cuttlefish bones. Table Bay, my friend, Table Bay!'

Nicolaes grimaces, sourly, as he recalls the excitement with which Otto had spoken of this place when first it emerged from the distant horizon. Those who had survived previous voyages around the Cape had begun immediately pointing out clues to the nearness of land, their energies suddenly restored. Briefly, it did not matter about the men who had succumbed to sickness or injury. That the *Batavia* was now worm-eaten and stinking became a mere triviality.

Otto had explained the transformation as simply as he could – ahead of them lay the lush, well-stocked African port that the Europeans had christened *The Tavern of the Ocean*. This was an opportunity for food and drink, for company.

Nicolaes stands upon the deck, his arms upon the rail, and glowers at the land where he and his friend will not be setting foot.

'A pox on him,' mutters Otto, equally disconsolate at his side. 'A pox on the lot of them.'

Both men glare at the skiff where Stonecutter lounges, bare-chested, letting the sun and the spray glaze his broad, scarred chest. Two brawny-armed sailors row them through the surf. The sun glints off green bottles and bare, sun-scorched flesh. Nicolaes cannot make them out but he has no doubt who accompanies him in the sleek little boat. Stonecutter has his favourites. He today rewards those who have demonstrated their loyalty to him or who have served some particular purpose these past months. He is rarely without the company of these chosen few.

Wordlessly, he squints into the blue, trying to find something tangible amid the endless shimmering haze. His eyes have begun to struggle in the light. He has always enjoyed keen eyesight but since the beating and the weeks laid up among the sick, he has found sunlight difficult to bear. He knows he is not the man he was when he boarded the *Batavia*. His ribs have healed and there is now no evidence of the swelling that had once locked his jaw as if with hammer and nail. But the headache that grips his brow is a constant. So too the numbness in his fingertips and the flecks of red that he spits up each morning after a fitful sleep. And yet he fares better than many. The newness of the *Batavia* does not help its crew avoid the poxes, plagues and pestilences that have assailed endless European sailors so long at sea. His quarters upon the orlop are now a true vision of Hell with scores of victim to gut-rot, putrid wounds and unforgiving scurvy.

Nicolaes considers himself fortunate to have spent those days in his sick bed under the tender care of Lucretia Jansz. She even instructed the stewards bring him the same food as those who ate at the commandeur's table and though she had no authority to make such demands, nobody demurred.

Nicolaes has been returned to the rank and file a prettier specimen than those who had previously considered themselves fortunate not to have suffered at the hands of Stonecutter. Nicolaes feels a begrudging admiration for the great scarred beast who left him three-quarters dead. The lance corporal has certainly succeeded in keeping order aboard the *Batavia* and the men would follow any command he gave, if only because their fear of him exceeds their apprehension at the enemy. He seems to have taken it as a personal affront that Nicolaes did not die as a result of the beating that he and his cronies put upon him in that first month at sea. Nicolaes and Otto have endeavoured to be perfect soldiers in the weeks since resuming their duties and have given Stonecutter little to reprimand them for.

Even so, the brutish bastard had taken a true delight in informing them that they would not be joining the soldiers, sailors and passengers amid the warm green splendour of Table Mountain. They would remain on board, guarding the *Batavia* from the attentions of the natives, along with any other men unfortunate enough to have fallen foul of him or his friend, Captain Jacobsz.

Nicolaes and Otto watch the ships depart. Were they not so dispirited, they might have marvelled at the vista before them. The whole fleet has put in at this warm, inviting anchorage. Around them is the pride of the VOC – the *Sardam*, the *Dordrecht*, the *Assendelft*; the little warship *Buren*.

'Bloody stupid place anyway,' growls Otto, whose natural bullishness has been dissipating these past weeks. He is not yet sick but like many of the soldiers he has struggled with the endless days of inactivity. In those torpid days when the wind deserted them and the *Batavia* wallowed, becalmed, Otto had started to worry Nicolaes with the way he folded in on himself, withdrawing like a wounded animal. He spoke little. Ate less. Became convinced that there was some long, hungry worm tunnelling into his fleshy places and riddling his insides with holes.

For a time he began to fixate on Nicolaes; asking questions, probing his answers for inconsistencies; treating him as if he were privy to secrets that he had chosen not to share. Were he and Lucretia previously acquainted? Was he among the common soldiers as a covert agent of the VOC? Was it true that there was enough gold in the hold to buy an entire country? Nicolaes had almost taken a chance on the truth. It was the only prospect of a brief sojourn at Table Mountain that had restored his good humour. Now Otto watches, sour-faced, as sailors and soldiers whoop their way through a bloodthirsty hunt: shooting blindly at the sea lions that slap along the distant shoreline; taking clubs and hooks to the rabble of near-tame penguins or stripping down to scrub the rind from their skin in the revitalising blue water.

Nicolaes and Otto stare, dry-mouthed and hungry, as landing parties set up sailcloth tents for them along the edge of the beach.

'See her?' asks Otto, managing a smile and nudging his friend. 'Your saviour. My God but she's a cool one. I've yet to see her look anything other than a true gentlewoman. I mean, she must be every bit as hot and rancid as the rest of us, and yet she's like a swan among rats. And without her maid these past months? Fending for herself, caring for the sick, tending to the scum of the Earth like me and thee? There's much to admire in her, Wiebbe.' He grins, looking pointedly at his friend and giving his eyebrows a suggestive twitch. 'Of course, I know that what you and she had is special. A true connection. And a gentleman shouldn't pry...'

Nicolaes follows his line of sight. Sees the faint bloom of Lucretia. She is holding a parasol, resplendent in a soft yellow gown. She walks alongside a creature that, from this remove, could be some extravagantly plumed bird of paradise. Commandeur Pelsaert has donned his most splendid finery to deal with the natives. Otto, squinting at the figures on the beach, had delighted in informing his friend that the savages had not taken similar efforts with their appearance.

'They barely wear a stitch,' says Otto, for what may be the hundredth time. 'Just rub themselves in mud to stop the sun burning them, though they're black as coal as it is. Some of the men shove their privates in what looks like a snake's mouth and strap it around their middles! The noise they make! Like angry turkeys. I'd give a year's pay to watch Pelsaert barter with them, though it's hard to come off badly out of the deal. They'll trade a dozen ox for an old pot or pan. Not that they know how to cook an ox properly – I've heard they chew on the intestines raw. By God I hope Pelsaert has to partake, though one more puking session and I swear he'll be inside out.'

Nicolaes stares up at the sky. Watches the black-sleeved birds drifting in widening circles. Lets his gaze slide across the nearest ship. It's close enough to swim to. He could lose himself aboard the crew, could he not? Put himself out of harm's way and continue his journey to Batavia. He would miss Otto, but he has lost friends and comrades before. He is here upon a mission; an assassin intent upon ending an expensive life. The Governor-General of Batavia awaits him. There are rumours, strong rumours, that Herman van Speult still lives and is, even now, bound for the Indies with a hefty reward from the Gentlemen of the VOC for having the presence of mind to die before facing an official inquiry into the events at Amboyna six years earlier.

'You think he has the experience of which he boasts? We put much faith in this man who has done nothing but linger in his bunk and hold a fine lady's hand. What do we do if he says the wrong thing and they cleave his head from his body with their fine new cutlasses?'

Nicolaes turns at the sound of a friendly German voice. Sees Jan Hendricxsz a few feet away, cleaning the lock of a musket, sitting near-naked on the freshly scrubbed, vinegar-soaked deck. Hendricxsz had not yet ingratiated himself with Stonecutter when Nicolaes suffered his beating so there is no bad blood between them. Hendricxsz spends most of his time with a man of similar years: a quiet, dark-eyed and stoutly built German called Mattys. Both are on the fringes of Stonecutter's group of favourites so it is with some surprise that Nicolaes realises he is not in the skiff heading for shore.

'I should imagine that the commandeur would be able to continue performing his duties even were to find himself without a head,' says Nicolaes, soberly. 'I'm sure he would claim as much.'

Hendricxsz smiles and selects another musket from the box before him. Takes oil and cloth from the step at his feet and sets about cleaning the weapon.

'What I wouldn't give to be in that boat,' he grumbles, shaking his head. 'They say the native women like to give you a flash of what they've got between their legs. They do it as quick as you or I might offer to shake hands. I mean, they're no beauties, but a cunny's a cunny and I'd give a leg for a gander.'

Otto, listening in, laughs in agreement. 'If those Hottentots have got any sense they'll keep their women out of the way. The way some of our lads have been talking, I wouldn't be surprised to see them giving one of those sea lions a good hump, let alone an actual woman.'

Nicolaes runs his hand over his chin. Feels his beard bristling against his fingers. He doubts even Buckingham would recognise him now.

'You're not in the landing party?' asks Otto.

Nicolaes, quietly watching, notes the flash of temper cross the German's features.

'Bastards have got me rowing the skipper about on his little jaunt this afternoon,' he spits, throwing one of the muskets down on the deck like a petulant child. 'The skipper's been here enough times to not have any interest in gawping at the Hottentots. He's leaving all the bartering to Pelsaert and while he's away, the skipper and his good lady will be popping over to the other ships to enjoy themselves and partake of the hospitality. Under-merchant too! They'll all be too pissed to row back. So Stonecutter volunteered me instead.'

'I thought you were one of his favourites,' says Otto, pointedly.

'He reckons it's a sacrifice worth making,' explains Hendricxsz. 'He wants to make sure the skipper doesn't get up to more mischief than is necessary while he's over there. Needs saving from himself, that one. Of course, Zwaantie has him wrapped around her finger but she's wilder than he is when she's been on the French wine. And we need 'em both, according to Stonecutter.'

'Zwaantie, is it?' asks Otto, raising his eyebrows. 'It's true, then? He does pass her around?'

'My lips are sealed, mate.' Hendricxsz grins, picking up another musket and polishing the stock. 'All I'll say is that the skipper is a generous man.'

'I'll say!' Otto laughs, glancing towards the stern and watching a slight, blonde-haired soldier whittling at a nugget of wood. He's been thus employed every time Nicolaes has seen him, whittling the pieces of a chess set for no other purpose than to relieve the boredom.

'There's a jealous streak to him, though,' confides the soldier, his eyes darkening. 'A fellow isn't sure which way to turn. He's getting her all prettied up in her finery in the Great Cabin, but whether he'll be parading her as a grand gentlewoman or pimping her to those who can be useful to him, I'll not make any attempt to guess. They'll be opening a bottle with the men of the *Buren* and the *Assendelft* and God knows where else, and it'll be me, this poor sod, who'll be rowing them from ship to ship until my arms ache. Mattys said he'd stay and take the strain with me but Stonecutter likes him close by. Big strong lad is Mattys. If there are problems ashore he's the sort Stonecutter would want at his side.'

'He sure as Hell doesn't want us,' says Otto, hawking something up and spitting it into the sea. 'I'm in no mood for a fight but he doesn't seem to see that I'm a soldiering man. Got holes in me from Grolle, same as any other bastard. Stonecutter doesn't like me because I find occasion to smile from time to time and I make the odd joke to keep my spirits up. He doesn't like any of that. Wants his men to be no more than dogs on a leash. And as for my friend here…'

'No hard feelings on that score,' says Hendricxsz, quickly. 'Saw what you took and for you to come back with some colour in your cheeks means you're the sort of man I'd want beside me in a fight. Shame he took against you. We could use a man with a bit of cleverness in his eyes.'

Nicolaes turns back to the ocean. Broods upon the German's words. He has no doubt that there is a storm gathering. There is a mood of far more than ill feeling aboard ship. Otto has already whispered that if the circumstances were right, there could be an uprising. Putting Pelsaert and

Jacobsz together was a recipe for mutiny from the very start. There's a fortune in the hold and the presence of women and children aboard means even the experienced sailors feel part of an expedition that seems markedly different from any they've experienced before. Worse, their destination is not some fortune-laden Paradise. For many, all that lies ahead is garrison duty, the next war, and the hope of fending off disease long enough to prosper.

Were he wearing the garb of Nicolaes de Pelgrom, he does not doubt he could persuade a few capable men to join him in seizing the ship. He fears that the idea has occurred to those men for whom piracy might seem eminently preferable to completing the voyage. Stonecutter has a loyal band of followers. Skipper Jacobsz is a fine seaman, at the helm of a mighty vessel packed to the bilges with treasures. Pelsaert has been too ill to provide much in the way of leadership and it is only the presence of the VOC's soldiers that provide him any security. But the soldiers are mercenaries, loyal to coin and self-interest. Stonecutter is clearly Jacobsz's man. So too, it seems is the under-merchant.

Were Nicolaes asked to give counsel to Pelsaert, he would encourage him to divide the *Batavia*'s crew among the other ships in the fleet. He would appoint a second lance corporal from the ranks, and pick a good strong sergeant. Moreover, he would suggest he sleep with a pistol beneath his pillow. He would certainly urge him to curb his displays of extravagance and largesse. His red silk cape is an open provocation to men caked in filth and bedded down among the rats.

'Look lively, here's the royals...'

Nicolaes glances down the deck to where Ariaen Jacobsz

and his mistress are taking a turn upon the freshly scrubbed deck, revelling in the wolf-whistles and whoops of the few crewmen still aboard. The skipper is done up like a French noble in fine ivory-coloured silks and a ludicrous puffed-up wig: matching slashes of blue and gold at his collar and with buckles on his gleaming shoes. At his side, Zwaantie is dazzling in a gold dress with a crimson sash, her bodice fastened almost to her collarbone but straining over the swell of her captive bosom. She wears no cap and her dark hair hangs in sweat-frizzed ringlets over her coffee-coloured cheekbones.

They make for an absurd pairing, but it's clear that they are not taking themselves seriously. Zwaantie affects a haughty, straight-backed walk and opens a black lace parasol. Jacobsz performs a mincing, dandified walk, stopping every few paces to fan himself and to mime a sudden attack of stomach difficulties. The men laugh and cheer, all recognising the caricatures of the commandeur and Lucretia.

Nicolaes, at the rail, does not join in the laughter. He narrows his eyes to better make out the fine garments inelegantly worn by the pair, and realises at once that they have helped themselves to the best clothes of the commandeur and his confidante. Nicolaes feels the low heat of outrage build in his stomach. He does not give a damn about Pelsaert but in those few precious hours in the company of Lucretia Jansz, he glimpsed a soul that might be worth something. He does not wish to see her openly mocked, or the delight that the remaining crewmen seem to take in witnessing her simulated persecution.

'Don't cause yourself any problems,' says Otto, quietly,

moving to his side. 'They're only teasing, and she isn't here to see it.'

'No class,' growls Nicolaes, glaring hard at the skipper. 'There's something foul on this ship, Otto. Something... *wrong.*'

Both watch as the elaborately dressed couple form an archway with their hands. Stepping through, ducking so as not to disturb the scarlet plume in his hat, strides the under-merchant. He, too, has dressed in his finery. He carries himself straighter than when Nicolaes last glimpsed him and his beard has grown out to better conceal the scars that make a monstrosity of a fine-featured face. He wears a red sash over his black doublet and as he walks nimbly across the deck he takes on the appearance of a carrion bird: the red silk transmuted into something bloody and freshly spilled.

The sun chooses the moment to emerge from behind one of the ribboned clouds that add some texture to the azure sky. Nicolaes watches as the under-merchant's shadow lengthens, elongating across the deck, creating a dark silhouette that slides over the nearby crew as if it were spilled oil. Nicolaes feels an urge to recoil lest it touch him. Watches as the men caressed by the little man's silhouette seem to succumb to some inexplicable pestilence; their features shrinking down; their cheekbones rising from beneath grey, unhealthy flesh; smiles twisting into something more ghoulish. His very shadow seems to carry a whiff of something mysterious and arcane.

'You need to change your face, my friend,' whispers Otto, nudging him in the ribs. 'He catches you glaring and we'll be...'

'You two,' snaps Jacobsz, stamping down towards the bow, his eyes fixed upon the two ragged soldiers. 'I see you gawping. Don't you be thinking that the display my Zwaantie puts on is for eyes like yours. She ain't to be looked at by rat-shit like you two. I knows lust when I sees it and by God I sees it when I look at you. That'll be why you're still aboard, is it? Stonecutter doesn't want to have to whip the hides off your backs for trying your luck with one of the predikant's pig-faced daughters, eh?'

Jacobsz pushes his face up close to Nicolaes's. There are gaps in his teeth and his breath reeks of brandy, rotten meat and salted fish. Nicolaes can see a whole map of scars and wrinkles and burst blood vessels in the red lines upon his cheeks. Can see where the chunk of missing lip was inexpertly stitched together so as to ensure his mouth would never properly close.

'Sorry, sir,' says Otto, at his side. 'Eyes wandered, as you say, sir. Not Wiebbe though, I promise you. Half blind since he took a bad knock first week out of Texel. Wouldn't be able to look at a beautiful woman until she was stood in front of him, I guarantee it. And his heart belongs to another, more's the point. We tease him for it…'

'Shut your fucking mouth,' spits Jacobsz, turning on Otto, who straightens his back and snaps off a smart salute. 'By God I'll have it scrawled in the log that you were caught committing unnatural acts upon one another. You know the punishment, yes? Sewn together in the same hammock and thrown to the fucking sharks!'

Nicolaes cannot stop glaring at the skipper. He has not felt any hint of temper these many months. He exists as well as he can – performing what minor duties are requested of him and endeavouring to lose himself within the sea of men. His friendship with Otto has been a blessing. Were the cheerful companion lost to him, Nicolaes imagines he would have no cause to speak. He does not let true feeling bloom within him. He pushes down his grief at the death of Buckingham; will not allow himself to consider the mode of his revenge for fear he obsess over it. He finds himself becoming more Wiebbe Hayes than Nicolaes de Pelgrom and cannot decide whether he would mourn the loss of identity. He is feeling more comfortable as a common soldier than he ever did as a spy or agent of the Crown.

But the Skipper has managed to provoke some hidden emotion. He finds himself wondering what would happen were he to grab the drunken bastard by his ludicrous collar and pitch him, headlong, into the swell. Aboard a ship that seethes with the possibility of uprising, he wonders whether Pelsaert would punish or reward him for ridding the *Batavia* of his enemy.

'Something to say, pretty-boy?' demands Jacobsz, one eye pushed up close to Nicolaes's, as if peering through a keyhole.

'My apologies, sir,' says Nicolaes, forcing the word out. 'As my companion says, my eyes have begun to trouble me. Truly, no offence was meant.'

Jacobsz is about to offer another savage retort when a gloved hand alights upon his shoulder. He turns, angrily, outraged at the interruption, and has to hastily rearrange his features as the under-merchant offers him a friendly smile.

'A shame to spoil such a day with bad tempers, Ariaen,' he says, smoothly. 'And were he to look upon you and

Zwaantie and to cock a smile at being treated to such a display... what then? Would not the keeper of such a rare bird feel a glow of pride at having her so admired? We have a pleasant day ahead of us. Why not consider afresh the advice I shared – when your temper swells, consider it as fire. Search yourself for the cooling water that shall extinguish it. Think upon those things that pleasure you; that soothe you. In the eye of your mind, consider your feet planted in cool water; Zwaantie with her head upon your shoulder; a glass of fine French red in your hand. Let it cool your fires.'

Nicolaes finds himself fighting a smile. The under-merchant's words are delivered in such a gentle, soporific tone that the skipper's entire manner changes, as surely as if he were a wild dog lulled to sleep by the gentle stroking of its brow. He stands, eyes closed, transfixed. Behind him, Zwaantie stifles a giggle, flashing a look at Cornelisz. Something passes between them – a message laden with things unsaid. Nicolaes feels himself casting off the skin of Wiebbe Hayes. He is again a retainer to the Duke of Buckingham: a player taught to listen at doorways, to sift through concealed documents, to tip strong liquor down the throats of loose-lipped lords and ladies and to report back to the king's right-hand man.

He suddenly sees the comical little under-merchant as something more than the delicate, unthreatening figure that he portrays. As one actor spotting the affectations of another, he realises that Cornelisz is playing a part.

Cornelisz, his mouth twitching into an amused little smile, seems to sense himself being scrutinised. He returns the stare, cocking his head like a bird. Nicolaes feels the urge to shiver as those mismatched eyes bore into his own. For an instant, he feels as though something is moving inside his head. Feels a presence inside him, something sibilant and fearsome, squirming through the tunnels and passageways of his mind; assessing, revealing; a forked tongue lapping at his every concealed regret and desire.

'Why not allow them to be our companions?' asks Zwaantie, sidling alongside the skipper and sliding her finger over his collar. She moves the pad of her middle finger over the sweat at his grimy neck. Withdraws it and sucks it as if it were glossed with honey. 'I have never had an escort, Ariaen. What is the word… a retinue? A dress like this deserves men. We do not know the sailors aboard these other craft and though I know you to be equal to any challenge, perhaps a few more fists would be a help should I provoke unstoppable lust in those who glimpse me.'

Jacobsz licks his lips. His eyes cloud over, heavy with desire for this small, earthy girl who moves among the ship's company like a cat in season. He nods, his mouth too dry to speak.

Cornelisz spreads his hands. Shrugs. 'It seems you are to be spared the misery of watching your companions frolic among the Hottentots.' He turns to the German soldier who has been watching the exchange. 'You are to be spared the burden of rowing, it seems. You may remain here, or find your own way to the shore if you are unable to resist. Tell Stonecutter that all is well.'

Hendricxsz shoots a look at Otto and Nicolaes. Glances at the skipper, who nods assent. Nicolaes finds himself deciphering the coded messages in the little glances and raised eyebrows. Zwaantie is the under-merchant's agent.

She has helped him gain the loyalty of the skipper. The skipper, in turn, has recruited Stonecutter and the cadets to his cause, and they have won over a handful of men willing to put their own interests ahead of those of the Company. What had seemed fanciful suddenly appears a very realistic prospect. And suddenly he knows, with absolute certainty, that they mean to take the ship.

'Will we get chance to meet your old friend?' asks Zwaantie, coquettishly, pressing herself against the skipper. 'What are we to call him, if not his true name? I could make him happy, if you wish it. I've never sat astride a dead man before…'

The blow comes from nowhere. One moment Zwaantie is whispering in the ear of her lover and the next she is sprawled upon the deck, blood leaking from her lip and a livid bruise already starting to darken at her eye. She sits up, eyes blazing fire.

No tears, thinks Nicolaes. *Only rage.*

'Keep your mouth closed,' spits Jacobsz, standing over her. 'What's said in our bed stays there, you understand? And by God if you dare ask about him aboard the *Assendelft* I will have you stripped, whipped and thrown overboard. The baby in your belly also!'

The tears come. She whimpers, mute. Weeps into her own lap. Jacobsz softens at once. Bends down and hauls her up, pressing her to him. He has the manners of a father with a spoilt child – slapping their legs then compensating with embraces and gifts.

'Remember the feel of the ocean,' says Cornelisz, amused. 'Soothe your fires. There will be time enough to loose the flames.'

Nicolaes follows the party to the gangway. Otto, at his ear, whispering unintelligibly. Nicolaes hears a few panicked words. 'Stonecutter's going to...' Then he stops listening. His mind is afire. There is a man aboard the *Assendelft*. An old friend of the skipper. A man tied to the atrocities at Amboyna. A dead man, if Zwaantie's jest is to be believed. He bends to collect a musket from the pile.

Nicolaes has thought little of Mrs Towerson these past weeks and the jewel she gave him for his services is lost to him for ever, having vanished into the piss-soaked bilges of the ship. And yet Buckingham had bid him to do what she wished. Told him it was of importance. He travels to the Indies to seek an opportunity to kill the governor-general. Here, at the very bottom of the ocean, he is being hand-delivered to the man who ordered the execution of the English merchants at Amboyna.

If he has put the pieces together correctly, he will soon be within killing distance of Herman van Speult.

24

Cornelisz skulks in the flickering darkness outside the Great Cabin, listening to the furious back-and-forth within. From time to time, he permits himself to smile. The pleasure is by no means genuine, but he has trained himself to react correctly even when unobserved, and the frenzied discourse certainly serves his purpose. He feels entitled to express some small measure of satisfaction – and a smile, he has observed, can be suitably employed when some minor victory has been achieved.

'...never have I heard of such atrocious behaviour! I knew you were no gentleman, Jacobsz, but I am dumbfounded to hear reports of such behaviour – not from common sailors but from a senior man of the VOC! I drag myself from my sick bed, endeavour to present the correct face of this honourable company – to make fine trades with the heathens – and I return to the *Batavia* to find my skipper and his whore have been making merry aboard the other ships of the fleet! You struck the upper-steersman of the *Assendelft* with such force that the man cannot speak. His crime? Making eyes at that damn slut! You brought her for the express pleasure of flaunting your own good fortune in their faces! My God but it is no surprise that it has taken you this long to prosper. You are my senior in years but in every possible way I am the superior man. Look at yourself! You are too mutton-headed and gone with drink to even summon a retort! I am all but ready to order you stripped and lashed to the mainmast! Had matters not escalated concerning that damn nuisance aboard our sister ship, I feel sure the *Assendelft*'s skipper would be insisting you be clapped in irons and kept below deck for the remainder of the voyage…'

Were he capable, Cornelisz might experience a little pity for his friend, Ariaen Jacobsz. It was hw after all, who suggested they visit the other vessels in the fleet while Pelsaert was ashore with the Hottentots. He'd even told the poor bastard it was considered the correct and proper thing to do and that Pelsaert had made a foolish error in not personally performing this common courtesy upon arrival at the Cape. Jacobsz, glad to be led in such things by a gentleman acquainted in all that is proper, had been indebted for the guidance. Of course, Cornelisz did not volunteer this information when later accosted by Pelsaert. He told the puce-faced commandeur that he had merely accompanied the skipper and his concubine on their journey from ship to ship so as to curb their excesses. The skipper, he claimed, was already dead-set upon his course of action and it was he, Cornelisz, left in *de facto* command as a result of Pelsaert's sojourn on land, who had been forced to react to the situation as it developed. He had even insisted upon the presence of two soldiers from the *Batavia*'s company – men he hoped were equal to the task of subduing the skipper should drink get the better of him.

Cornelisz's interview with Pelsaert had ended with a

clammy handshake and some generous words from the commandeur, confirming that his understudy had made a sound decision that would be noted in the ship's log and in his own journal. He declared that it was only Cornelisz's timely intervention that had stopped the embarrassing situation developing into something even worse.

In the darkness of the gangway, Cornelisz strokes his calloused fingertip over the scars upon his cheek. His mind seems to flicker for a moment, as if a breeze has lengthened the flame of a candle. Suddenly he is staring into memory. He is laid upon hard planks, his arms bound at the biceps and wrists, pinioned to what passed, in that fetid darkness, for a surgical table. He is staring up, the pain in his face so intense that it seems as though every part of his body were exploding and reforming a thousand times per second. His whole being is afire.

The alchemist is leaning over him: a rotund, dark-skinned Moor with a coarse black beard and eyes that peer out from beneath bushy brows and wrinkled, sagging lids. He is pulling a face, disappointed with what he observes. The unguent he has smeared upon Cornelisz's burn has done more harm than good. It is eating at his very skin, causing his features to boil and blister as if there a fire burning within. He senses the nearness of his father. Feels him move closer, then step away, aghast. Sees himself becoming something monstrous. And yet there is no sorrow. He does not mourn the loss of his handsome profile. There is just the cold acceptance. It will, of course, be harder to persuade people to do what he bids, but he shall simply have to develop more cunning.

To be elegant, to be beautiful; he has experienced

the privileges of both. Now, he has the occasion to be underestimated. Perhaps even pitied.

Suddenly he feels hands upon his hips. He pulls his elbows in to his sides, yelping – panicked by the sudden intrusion into his private recollections. Catches the whiff of her, even as she slips her hands from the crooks of his arms and places them, coolly, upon his eyes.

'Zwaantie,' he whispers, recovering himself and taking her gently by the wrists. By God, how had she managed to sneak up on him? 'You move like darkness itself. Where have you been loitering?'

'It is you who skulks in corners, Jeronimus,' she mutters, her cheeks dimpling. He turns to face her. She treats him to her courtesan smile. It dazzles in the darkness, though her eyes remain distant and unfocused. So little of her life seems to penetrate into her inner sanctum. She may giggle and flirt, carouse and fuck, but her brown irises are those of a corpse. 'I have had duties with the gunner.' She shrugs. 'Allert. Not a gentle lover, but mercifully quick. I think Ariaen hopes to persuade him that the babe in my belly is his, though he and I both know that Ariaen will have changed his mind before morning and once again reclaimed me. Truly, were the babe real and not an invention to suit your purpose, it would pain me to see it passed back and forth.'

Cornelisz settles back against the wood, making space for Zwaantie at his side. 'I believe that it was you and not I who suggested you further bind the skipper to our purpose with the promise of a child.'

Zwaantie looks at him sidelong, clearly unsure how much to say. 'Our purpose, Jeronimus. I have no desire other than passage to Batavia. Whatever purpose you wish to bind Ariaen to, I have no doubt it is at odds with my own.'

He keeps his face inscrutable. Allows himself to look a little hurt. 'I simply feel that you will better prosper in the Indies as his match, my dear. Any other suggestion is but wild fancy.'

Zwaantie rolls her eyes. Wipes her hands under her armpits and uses her skirt to clean herself. She glances up at Cornelisz, who watches amused.

'I had hoped the babe would limit the gusto with which he shared me with his fellows.' Zwaantie shrugs. 'I have not been so fortunate, though he has been gentler with me these past days. There would be a good man in him were it not for the drink and the resentment. Were he and Pelsaert kept apart, I fancy this would have been a smooth crossing and we would already be in Java.'

He doesn't reply. Listens to her breathing. Fancies he can hear her heart. Can see it, momentarily. The image is so vivid that as he squints into the blackness and makes out the swell of her chest, the picture in front of him is somehow less real than the pulsing scarlet muscle that he holds in the fist of his mind.

'Your mistress still has need of you?' he asks, tilting his head. His eyes become those of a bird set upon tugging a worm from soft earth. 'Does her journal still offer glimmers of the person beneath the skin, and the fun that shall be had when the ship is ours?'

Zwaantie wrinkles her nose. Pouts, as if the victim of a great indignity. 'Out of sheer kindness I visited her cabin when we returned from the *Assendelft*. I cleaned. Tidied. Even refrained from reading her correspondence, left out upon her writing desk for anybody to see. I served her well. And still she greeted me with anger. Called me some terrible names. Names that a gentlewoman should not know.'

'And the correspondence that you did not read...' Cornelisz says, his voice a snake moving through long grass. 'What did it say?'

'Were I her husband I would grow jealous,' confides Zwaantie, clearly disappointed that a woman of such poise and breeding could so despoil herself. 'She has developed some degree of affection for our poor stricken commandeur. She is quite taken with his charm and the forbearance with which he faces his sickness.'

Cornelisz readjusts himself inside his cloak. 'Does she speak of me?'

Zwaantie scratches her head. Grins. Puts out her palm. Pockets the coin as soon as it appears. 'She believes that you are ill-suited to the role of under-merchant. Wonders about your scars and the life you flee. She was, and it pains me to say this, quite unkind about the appearance that you make. I believe she used the word "half-crippled" and "gruesome".'

Cornelisz does not reply. Already he can imagine the delight he will take in altering her perceptions. He feels a certain jealousy at the position she currently finds herself in. She does not yet know the path that has been chosen for her. She considers him delicate, weak, crippled... What a joy it shall be for her to see the strength and beauty hidden within this flimsy chrysalis. What a treat when he pins her beneath him and shows her the true nature of the god she has mocked.

'...look at you! Snivelling! I at least expect you to threaten to blacken my eyes, Ariaen, but I look at you now and see a whipped child, pleading for forgiveness even as a stern hand raises the lash…'

'He serves our purpose with every insult,' whispers Jeronimus, into Zwaantie's ear. She moves closer to him, her plump and dimpled skin pushed up against his own cold, clammy frame. He does not desire her, but her proximity is enough to cause a physical reaction. She appraises him with an expert glance, placing her hand on the front of his breeches and casually cocking an eyebrow. He removes her hand. She has made the offer on several previous occasions but he has never partaken of her services. He does not desire her. Does not desire anybody in the way that Zwaantie pays her way. He finds the notion of coitus repulsive. To even become a father had necessitated drugging his wife and funding the intercession of a young man recommended to him for the purpose of producing a male heir. He has lain with women and men alike but the act has always been for advancement, not release.

'I honestly didn't think Ariaen was going to hit him that hard,' mutters Zwaantie, and from somewhere overhead they hear a chorus of cheers as the long-awaited rain begins to fall like coins upon the bone-dry deck. 'He must have had two bottles of brandy and the same again in wine. Didn't slake his thirst though – not for more drink and not for me and certainly not for the fight. Nobody insulted him and all the poor bastard did was give me a kindly glance and maybe a leer.'

'Innocents often find themselves ill-used in service of a greater design,' says Cornelisz, apologetically. 'There is no sin, Zwaantie. All is predestined and in each act we commit we bring ourselves closer to a state of grace.'

Zwaantie lowers her eyes. Nods. She is a begrudging convert to this creed preached by the apothecary. Jeronimus has begun to softly sermonise to those who have shown themselves ready to be seduced. He has altered the fine words of Torrentius to better suit his new parishioners. They are not high-born gentlemen seeking forgiveness for the raping of a maiden or the Pagan excesses they have enjoyed in the dark cellars of Haarlem. To woo these hard, straightforward men, he has had to offer them a more palatable gospel.

My God, he swears... *My God wants you to fuck, and to drink, and fight, and kill. To be all that you were intended to be. There are two Heavens. One offers serenity, and peace, and an eternity of sermons and song. The other is flame. Fire. Heat. Lust. It is a forever of excess; of gluttony and fornication. And to find that kingdom, all you must do is believe in me. For I am the way. I am the truth. I am the Flame of Reason...*

From inside the cabin comes a sudden clatter. Something heavy and metallic has fallen from the table. Pelsaert finds the strength to roar a new barrage of abuse at the skipper.

'Goddamn clumsy oaf! How can you expect to steer a ship if you cannot even hold your pitcher of coffee! The question I ask is simple, you fool. Did you see him? The special passenger? Did you find opportunity to enter his cabin? To speak upon those past deeds? I can accuse you of much, Ariaen Jacobsz, but I know you are not an assassin, for who would hire such a drunken oaf so unskilled in deceit? It is perhaps a blessing that he has succumbed to his sickness but as leader of the fleet I am beholden to at least ask the question. Tell me, did you kill van Speult?'

Jacobsz mumbles something inaudible. Zwaantie shakes her head. She cannot make it out.

'He's panicking over the gentleman who lost his fight with fever aboard the *Assendelft*,' explains Cornelisz, with a little shrug. 'No place for secrets, a ship. Was there anybody who did not know about the presence of the resurrected van Speult? I should have liked to see the fellow, if only to see whether he still looked as he did in the fine painting at the Company boardroom. Now I learn that I am to be denied this opportunity. He has died a second time, it seems, and this time there shall be no resurrection. It came as little surprise to the *Assendelft*'s own beleaguered skipper. The man had been abed these past weeks, struck down with an ague that had stripped the fat from his frame. When they slip him into the ocean I fancy he will float for a time. But of those many marks against Ariaen's name, we can at least be sure he is innocent of this one particular crime.'

'Indeed,' says Zwaantie, as the ship begins to list starboard. 'He was never alone. You and I were with him constantly and the soldiers did all we could ask of them.'

'The handsome fellow,' muses Cornelisz. 'He was a wrong note, was he not? A fiddle played out of tune? When Ariaen struck the sailor, I lost sight of him for a time, though I shall confess that I was near as muddle-headed as the skipper and thyself by the time some semblance of order was restored.'

Above, the rain falls harder; a spray misting through the open hatch at the end of the gangway. They can just hear the droning of the predikant's evening sermon, mercifully obscured by the sound of rain upon wood.

At the sound of footsteps from within the cabin, Cornelisz nudges them towards the hatchway. The sea air stings their cheeks as they ascend to the deck. The rain falls in great silvery sheets from a black sky so full of stars that they appear in streaks and swirls rather than individual spots of light. The ship rises and falls upon the silvered blackness of the ocean, its vastness resembling the chest of some slumbering giant as it swells with great, rhythmic breaths. From the poop deck, the skipper's second in command shouts orders to the sailors who scurry up and down the rigging, their moods ebullient after the trip ashore. There is fresh meat lowing in the hold and the monsoon rains tumble down to rinse their skins.

'He won't be flogged,' says Cornelisz, his mouth at Zwaantie's ear, her damp hair whipping at the dead skin of his cheek. 'He will be seething about the dressing-down, and I mean to make sure that all are aware before the dawn, but we shall need more to turn talk into action.'

Zwaantie gives a nod, jerking her head upwards at a sudden movement. Moving smoothly across the quarter deck beneath a billowing sail, Lucretia flips her head back and smiles into the fresh, brine-stiffened air. There is something joyful and childlike in her delight at the sudden onslaught of the rains. She is clad in a mauve dress and her bonnet is unfastened. As Cornelisz studies her, the wind catches her cap and whisks it away. She laughs; a high, pleasing sound, her mouth open. She seems free, suddenly. Seems emboldened and liberated. Seems, briefly, like somebody who has climbed out of the darkness and is excited by the nearness of the light.

'Were she harmed...' says Zwaantie, the muscle in her jaw twitching like a flexed arm. 'Were one so dear to Pelsaert to be mistreated somehow… why, a wise man could ensure that those responsible were properly dealt with.'

Cornelisz enjoys the darkness in her eyes as she chews over her own suggestion. Watches as she tries to make light of it, smiling her dimpled smile and again adopting a childlike eagerness. He wonders whether she realises that she is facilitating in her own demise. If she truly seeks passage to Batavia she should not be feeding him suggestions that will help turn angry talk to decisive action. Played correctly, an assault upon the fair Lucretia could light the powder keg. Those loyal to Jacobsz could be tasked with her defilement and when Pelsaert acted to punish those responsible, Cornelisz could use it as a catalyst for mutiny.

He fancies that the plan is simpler than the stratagem he has jealously guarded. He may have disseminated his false charts among the fleet but surely as much could be achieved by simply extinguishing the light of the great lantern that guides the other ships, and disappearing into the darkness with the treasures. It would be a shame to litter the sea with so many dead but he fancies he could find sufficient cannon-balls to weigh down two hundred souls.

He gives a nod. 'Suggest it, then,' he says. 'Loyal men. Red-blooded men. Our men. She's to be humiliated. Hurt a little. Nothing more.'

'Ariaen will want to…'

'No,' says Cornelisz. 'No, not until all is ready.'

'You mean you need to lose the fleet,' says Zwaantie, flatly. 'I'm not an idiot, Jeronimus. He understands what you are subtly pouring in his ear and has already made his peace with what lies ahead. And you may rest easy. The southern seas will be perfect for your purpose. A little nudge against the rocks, all the signs of a shipwreck...'

Cornelisz reaches out and forces himself to stroke her arm. She shivers at his touch. He stares at Lucretia and his hand bites into the flesh of Zwaantie's arm. He feels that peculiar pang of envy once more.

Lucretia does not yet know the honour that awaits her. Soon she will be entered by a living god.

25

An eerie hush is spreading through the reeking darkness of the gun deck. Conversations fall silent; men cease in their bickering. Those still sharing their evening meal of salted fish and barley stop with their spoons to their lips. Hairy, hoary unwashed faces spread into eager, excitable grins.

'Go on,' whispers a Frenchman, and is rewarded with a great hiss of commands to keep his mouth shut.

Slowly, all heads turn to watch the quiet, capable soldier who kneels upon the deck, head cocked: a bird listening for the sound of a worm moving beneath the earth. He's barefoot, filthy, shirtless; his back a chaos of scars and bruises and grime.

A little in front, almost entirely lost to the dark, lies the body of a young man. He succumbed to his wounds not more than an hour ago, despite the tender ministrations of those who knew and liked him. His name was Claas. He was a fiddle player; a good shot. He'd spoken of a green-eyed girl back home; an older brother killed fighting the Spanish; his hopes of seeing a real, live elephant. Two days ago he was released from Hell: the tiny cell in the forepart of the gun deck where the wind whistled endlessly through the slats. A man could neither stand up nor lie down once locked within. Claas was already bleeding from his mouth and nose when Stonecutter stuffed him into the tiny space, stamping on him a couple of times for good measure.

He wept for the first six days. After that his mutterings and wails became more primal. By the third week he did not reply to those kinder-hearted soldiers who tried to pass him food or to offer a friendly word as they skirted near his cage. The man who emerged two days ago was little more than a pile of bones. The surgeon had refused to even offer hope. Had him sent down to die with his fellows in the stinking dark.

Now, Claas is bait.

The sudden whipcrack of rope lashes the black air. A pistol ball whirls from the slingshot in Wiebbe's right hand, a flash of silvery light in the flickering black.

There comes a shriek, and a sudden raucous cheer as a hundred pairs of gleaming eyes watch the two rats that had been sitting upon the dead man's chest come apart in a gory spray.

Half a dozen men surge forward, ducking under beams and hammocks, patting their marksman on the back as they haul him up. They turn and jeer, good-naturedly, at the dozen or so sour-faced men who grumble as they hand over coin, trinkets, tobacco, coffee – whatever they had been able to wager against the handsome marksman and his catapult.

'You have a gift, mon ami – a gift from God!'

'I couldn't even see the buggers! How did you get them lined up like that? Christ, when we face the savages we'll only need to show them your skills and they'll run back to the jungle thinking you a god!'

Nicolaes says a quiet thanks to those who shower him with kind words. Watches as Otto grins at him from their little section of deck, holding up a fine selection of winnings. He isn't quite sure how he became this source of entertainment. He's popular, that's for certain. Even those who bet against him do so for the sport of it and most will get their losses back when they parade their man against the best shots that the sailors can put up against him. Nicolaes is quietly surprised that he's mastered the slingshot so quickly. The last time he used such a device he was still a boy, taking the heads off squirrels and enjoying the whirr and swish of the pebble past his thumb.

Nicolaes makes his way over to Otto, who is holding up the two rats by their tails and offering them for sale to anybody who wants a souvenir of this evening's show. He claps his friend upon the shoulder. 'Could have got three of them but that other whiskery bastard didn't show his face.'

Nicolaes doesn't reply. Looks down at the broken body of the young soldier; bite marks upon the ragged flesh of his chest. He died because he spoke back to Stonecutter. Asked a question that the huge man did not feel inclined to answer. Two other men tried to intervene on Claas's behalf, if only because they didn't want the lance corporal annihilating their best fiddle player. For their intervention, both had their palms nailed to the mainmast. To free themselves, they had to drag the nails through their flesh and sinews. Both spent days nursing weeping, open wounds. One can no longer make a fist.

'A shame,' mutters a voice at Nicolaes's side. He turns to see the quiet, clever soldier he knows as Wouter. He's a popular, dry-humoured young man. He keeps to himself but has no enemies and plenty who would be glad to call themselves his friends. He spends his time playing games of chess against himself, moving hand-carved pieces on a stained little board, turning it after each move. Nicolaes has discreetly watched him play. He's good. Protects the king while slyly moving his pawns to unnoticed positions of influence.

'I didn't know him well,' says Nicolaes, sadly. 'I fancy I'll always hear his cries.'

Wouter considers him for a moment. Then he places his hand upon Nicolaes's arm and moves him a little further back into the darkness. Otto, noticing, moves to join them.

'Something wrong, Wouter?' asks Otto, dropping his voice a little.

Nicolaes waits in silence. It's clear there's something troubling the man but Nicolaes cannot comprehend why he would be chosen for any confidence. No friendship exists between himself and Wouter, who he has always considered to be on the fringes of the group of favourites led by Stonecutter. He wonders if, like so many others, the man is simply a pragmatist seeking to make his own life as agreeable as he can. If so, Nicolaes wonders what comforts he could expect to find in the companionship of somebody who Stonecutter so blatantly detests?

'I understand that the Lady Lucretia was good to you as you recovered from your wounds those many months ago,' he says, quietly.

Nicolaes feels his pulse quicken. He has had no opportunity to even thank the gentlewoman for her attentions during his convalescence and to send a note would betray his literacy, but he has been glad of every stolen glance at her upon the deck.

'Oh yes.' Otto smirks. 'He's well acquainted with Her Highness.'

Wouter keeps his eyes fixed on Nicolaes's: the points of a guttering candle reflecting in twin golden points upon his irises. 'She is a wealthy woman, that much is clear.'

'A house on the Heerenstraat; a diamond merchant husband,' confirms Otto.

Wouter nods in approval. 'She struck me as a kindly soul,' he says. 'Fair. Likes to remember those who had done her a service, I'll be bound.'

Nicolaes feels his temper prickle. 'Speak your mind, Wouter.'

'She would be grateful to be forewarned for any misfortune that may befall her, I presume,' says Wouter, his voice slick as oil. 'Were a common man like myself to come into information that could spare her some discomfort – why, for that she may well pay a handsome reward.'

Nicolaes moves a little closer to Wouter. They're the same height, evenly matched. Nicolaes cannot help but notice the shrewd, calculating look in the other man's gaze. There is a fierce intelligence to this one, he thinks. He's no stranger to bartering for life and death. He glimpses in him a reflection of sorts; his own image refracted in smashed glass. Wouter, he knows, has experienced suffering. Has known pain. Has learned to hide himself within a skin-suit and to be what the moment demands.

Otto glances at his friend and notes the darkening of his mood.

'You'd do well to speak plain,' says Otto, quickly. 'For all that I joke, Wiebbe here has a true fondness for Her Ladyship and it would serve you well not to play him for a fool.'

Wouter licks his lips, clearly amused. He raises his hands in offence. 'That was not my intention, I promise you,' he says. 'Perhaps I was wrong to even consider sharing this confidence with you. Do forgive my intrusion. I'll leave you to play with your rats.'

He nods to both men. Takes a step back and finds Otto has moved to block him in, still smiling. 'Linger a while, Wouter. We're enjoying your company.'

Wouter opens his mouth to protest then snaps it shut, as if taking a bite out of the air. A nastiness alters the previously pleasing outline of his face; his jaw twisting. He shakes his head, half-sneering. He has the look of one who has made a rare miscalculation. He turns to walk away and Nicolaes closes his hand around his wrist.

'I'd rather we finished our conversation Wouter,' he says, keeping his manner as light as he can. 'You spoke of some harm coming to the lady. I'd hear more.'

Wouter glances down at his arm, feeling the pressure of Nicolaes's grip. Raises his face, amused by the other man's temerity. 'You won't be feathering your nest in my stead, Hayes. You warn her, we split the reward and never speak of it again. Otherwise I'm not saying a fucking word.'

Nicolaes moves closer, his nose an inch away from Wouter's. Feels Otto's restraining hand upon his shoulder. Turns to tell him to back away and feels the sudden heat of a blade tickling his ribs. He looks down. The blade glints in the darkness like a smile. He glares into Wouter's eyes and sees a man willing to plunge the blade all the way in if required. Nicolaes gives a little nod. Even manages a grin, of sorts. Wouter reads it the way Nicolaes had hoped he would. Sees it as agreement to be part of whatever bargain he expects to strike.

'You had me worried there,' smiles Wouter, pocketing the knife. 'I mean, we're both clever men, aren't we? I see the way you read people, the way you go about your business, always listening, always learning. We're the same, you and me, or at the very least, we're made of the same stuff. Question is, would she pay more handsomely to be forewarned, or for us to let it happen and then give her the names of those who did it. For all the grand words, I can't see any of the big talk turning to action. Jacobsz is fine seaman but I'm not built for a life at sea. A bloody pirate? With the VOC forever at our backs? And there are women and little ones aboard. They won't answer when I ask what they plan to do with those little problems. Anyway, I'd be grateful for your counsel…'

Nicolaes moves so quickly that Wouter is still talking when the punch takes him in the dead centre of the chest. All the air leaves his body in a rush and Nicolaes takes him by the throat, drags him back into the darkness and spins him to the wall, pushing his face up against the damp wood and pressing his mouth to his ear.

'I'm not like you,' he hisses. 'I'm not like any of you. But I swear, if you don't tell me what you know, I'll do violence that will make what Stonecutter did to Claas look like a gentle tug from a silk-gloved maid, are we clear?'

Wouter struggles in his grasp, water spilling from his eyes, gasping for breath. 'The bosun… Evertsz… Skipper wants her cheeks slashed, her pretty face scarred... Allert, Ryckert... all the skipper's men...'

Nicolaes and Otto listen as Wouter spills what he knows. Nicolaes feels as though ice-cold water were running in his veins. Each time Wouter shares a new confidence Nicolaes pushes his face harder into the wood. Otto has to drag him away before the soldier's skull cracks. He slips to the deck, blood pouring from one ear, rubbing his chest and reaching out, pitifully, with one hand.

'You don't tell them I warned you,' he begs. 'You'll not stop it. Who would you tell? He's got the cadets already, the under-merchant... Pelsaert won't know what's happening until he's dead in the water.'

Nicolaes presses his bare foot against Wouter's neck and pushes him back against the damp wood. 'When?' he demands, his eyes blazing fire.

Wouter grimaces, blood painting his teeth like bars. From above they hear the faint sound of bells chiming upon the windless night.

Wouter, despite the pain, manages a defiant grin. 'Better hurry. You might not want her so badly after she's been tupped by half the crew.'

Nicolaes brings back his foot. Stamps down upon Wouter. Feels something break. Turns to Otto, whose eyes widen in panic as he sees his friend pushing past him, heading for the ragged strip of sailcloth that marks the edge of the soldiers' quarters. Were he to venture beyond it he would be answerable to the skipper himself; his punishment a brutal keelhauling, or worse.

'No, Wiebbe, you can't...'

Wiebbe pushes past him, snatches away the sailcloth, and vanishes into the belly of the ship.

Otto stands alone for a moment. Then he screws up his face, furious with himself, and follows his friend into the stinking blackness.

26

The retourschip *Batavia*

Husband,

How desperately I reach for you. How many years of my worthless life would I exchange for one fulsome caress in this, my moment of torment. My mouth is not strung for prayer this night. You are all I can conceive of as comfort; of sword and shield.

How can I even begin to describe the terrible indignities wrought upon me? I sit, huddled and misshapen, my fingers hooked as talons into the grain of the writing desk, shivering as a newborn laid upon snow. I am rimed in the filth of my attackers. I cannot find the words to pray. My entreaties to the Almighty salt my tongue as if it were a slug. For God saw what was done to me. God saw, and did not intervene until I was already upon my back, pinioned beneath the weight of masked, armed men; a victim of the jealous scheming of those who have sought to subjugate me to their will.

I am shamed, Boudewijn. Moreover, I tremble with a rage that is pure and absolute. I curse my frailty, my weakness, my inability to conjure the strength to tear my persecutors into gory strips of flesh and bone. I despise my naïveté, my lack of foresight. Why did I not keep myself away from the dark and secluded places where I may fall victim to attack? Why did I not sense the gathering cloud of hatred about me? And yet, though I lash myself for my own foolish part in my disgrace, I do not call myself a sinner. I cannot hold myself accountable for the ungodly actions of another.

I am smeared with filth, husband. Here I sit, my quill shaking in my hand, and there is scarcely a patch of skin that is not covered with the wretched foulness with which they so delighted in adorning me. Husband, from the odour I know that I have been despoiled with their own vile dung. My God, but to write such a thing! My throat feels as though there are fingers squeezing the life out of me, such is the agony of withholding the shriek that I yearn to release. My eyes are so fogged with tears that I cannot see whether my words even turn to full words and sentences upon this page.

What shall I tell thee? You are conscious of my habit of taking an evening turn upon the deck. I find some small whisper of serenity in observing the great vastness of the sky while listening to the slap of ocean upon the ship's hull. I am not alone among the passengers in finding comfort in such a pastime, though I alone drift away from the predikant's nightly sermon rather than stand and pretend to listen. So it was tonight, husband. Though these past weeks I have sensed a certain air of hostility towards me as a result of my burgeoning friendship with the good commandeur, I have truly never thought myself likely to be accosted by the crew of a VOC merchantman.

And it is only through my attentiveness to Francisco that I am even aware of the source of these high tempers and tensions. We have lost the fleet! Somehow we have been blown off course and have not sighted any of the other vessels in several days. Skipper Jacobsz refuses to alter course to search for the other vessels and indeed seems to be following a heading that Francisco fails to comprehend. In matters to do with seamanship I am led to believe that Jacobsz is peerless but I fear that he is either lost and too proud to admit his mistake, or worse, is set upon some nefarious business.

It is with the full and certain knowledge of the consequences of my allegation, that I declare myself convinced that Jacobsz and his whore had a hand in this evening's attack. Oh how I shake with rage as I consider the brief flashes of kindness she has shown me this night: helping me back to this cabin and enquiring whether I should wish for hot water or some help to change my clothes. In that moment, bleeding from crushed lips and still jumping at the thought of my attackers returning, I had not the strength to demand she account for her own role in my defacement. I simply sent her away and requested that she send the predikant's goodly wife to my cabin to help me wipe the filth from my skin. Whether she has done as I asked I do not know.

Perhaps even at this moment, Francisco is ordering the bosun to whip the flesh from the skipper's back and to clap his loyal attack dogs in irons. But I fancy that instead she has returned to her drunken lover to laugh at my defilement and they are applauding themselves for setting such a terrible event in motion.

I see them now – barefoot, masked – springing from the darkness or scuttling down from the rigging like malignant spiders. I had no time to scream. In moments there was rough cloth in my mouth, tied so tight as to force blood from my lips. I glimpsed knives. Brawny arms. And then there was hessian about my eyes and rope upon my wrists and I was spun between them, jeers and ugly words ringing in my ears. I was forced to the deck and called out for mercy as I felt their blades slashing at my dress, hacking at my stays; hands tugging at my petticoats until I was clad in naught but rags.

I swear it was only in this terrible moment that I realised their purpose. They sought my defilement, husband. I, a gentlewoman, kept apart from the common men and paraded before them like some exotic rare bird as they fitted and festered in the squalor below decks. In that moment, I saw what they saw. Hated myself as they must surely have hated me. Then I made out rough voices; arguments back and forth between those who stood astride me, breeches down. Boudewijn, I heard his name. One of the attackers spoke it aloud, saying quite clearly that "Ariaen" had insisted I be merely humiliated and not violated, as if in the avoidance of this act of subjugation he were in some way doing me a kindness that would spare him and his henchmen the rope.

As they argued upon whether or not to kneel betwixt my legs, I felt myself being smeared with cold, clammy *unguent; rough hands wiping me from top to toe with the vile substance. Only as the smell hit me did I realise what had been done to me and in that instant I will declare myself briefly possessed by something demonic. I fought as I should have fought from the moment they appeared. I kicked and bit and thrashed as if I were briefly host to something ungodly and I declare that my fury did briefly arrest the torments.*

Moments later I heard the sounds of violence and protest and I had the bandage lifted gently from my face by the same good soldier whom I had tended to those many weeks ago. The men who had waylaid me had made good their escape. Wiebbe stayed at my side, as attentive as a midwife, endeavouring to clean the filth from my face and bare arms and swaddling me in his coat while his companion sought out those minded to help me. Zwaantie, still known to some as my maid, was summoned from the skipper's bed. I will confess that she did seem genuine in her sympathy when she first saw what mischief had been performed but I do not believe that her lover would have commanded such an attack without first divulging it to his concubine.

Husband, truly, I beseech you as I would ask of God. Be at the dockside, waiting for me. I know these letters cannot reach you and that I write instead to some projection – some memory made flesh – but with all my heart I beg you to be the first thing I see when I finally glimpse Java. I have never felt so alone or so afraid.

I hear raised voices as I write. Though I would not call myself a sailor I declare that we are running faster than I have hitherto experienced. Perhaps Skipper Jacobsz has indeed found a healthy wind to hasten our passage. If so, would our purpose be better suited in allowing him to continue to steer the ship until we reach land? But to permit it would be to delay interrogation or eventual justice for his part in my desecration.

Truly, I have never felt the ship make such swift progress. We are hurled along as if God were emptying His mighty lungs into our sails. I am minded to clean myself and request a restorative from the blasted apothecary and then seek counsel with Francisco. Though we are only a few hours from sunrise, I feel sure he will be awake and already involved in seeking retribution for what I have endured and it is only through concern for my dignity that he has yet to present himself at the door of...

27

Nicolaes pitches forward as if thrown from a runaway horse – smashing into the mirror behind the commandeur's table with an impact that drives the breath from his lungs. He bites down upon his tongue – his mouth filling with the taste of metal and brine. Feels the sting of falling glass. He can hear a high-pitched whine, though whether it is inside or outside his skull he cannot be sure. He feels wetness in his left eye. Reaches up to wipe his face and slowly, dull-headed, he realises he is ensnared, his hands at his sides as if bound with rope.

His senses return in a sudden rush; a great upsurge of memory flooding his aching head. He had been standing in front of the commandeur. Had been haranguing the VOC's most senior man, close enough to smell the malarial reek that oozed from his fine silk clothing like steam from horse shit. He had been demanding the perfumed popinjay take action following the grotesque attack upon Lucretia. Otto had been trying to restrain him, his hands about his wrists, pulling him back, offering soothing words and desperately making apologies to Pelsaert.

But Nicolaes's blood was simmering. He had looked at the diminished, sweat-jewelled merchant in his expensive nightclothes, and he had given in to anger. He knew who the attackers were, he insisted. Could name them all. He'd even knocked a tooth clean out of the head of the boatswain, Jan Evertsz, as the cackling bastard had stood above the stricken lady and pulled down his breeches to anoint her despoiled skin with his own water.

Pelsaert had lacked the strength to maintain his authority in the face of the onslaught. Gave in to a violent bout of coughing and sickness as he tried to mollify this common soldier. He could not act against any man favoured by Jacobsz, he had said, pitifully. Not at this stage. They needed the skipper's unquestionable seamanship and to punish a popular man like Evertsz could provoke outright mutiny among the men. He would personally see to Lucretia's care, he promised. He would move her into his cabin and insist that the surgeon drop all other duties in favour of nursing her back to health. And upon being reunited with the fleet, they could take action. Jacobsz would answer for any part he may have played, and Evertsz, if Nicolaes was willing to name him, would hang. So would his accomplices. But for now, nothing was more important than the completion of the voyage…

Nicolaes had refused to countenance delay. He would, he claimed, go and rid the vessel of all of the skipper's favourites if Pelsaert would just provide him with a sword. He had lost all sense of Wiebbe Hayes; addressing the merchant with the manners of one tutored by the Duke of Buckingham himself. Pelsaert, even in his weakened state, had asked him his name. Asked him his background. Begun to question him upon whether it was he who had been aboard the *Assendelft* with Skipper Jacobsz those weeks ago, when the special passenger had been found dead in his cabin.

Nicolaes had caught himself as he opened his mouth to tell Pelsaert the truth. Yes. He was the assassin they sought. He was bound for Batavia to kill the governor-general and had already claimed the lives of those few disloyal men who had dragged themselves from the dungeons in Amboyna six years before. He was an imposter. An assassin and spy. He had indeed slithered his way to the cabin of Herman van Speult while the men of the *Assendelft* were dealing with their drunken visitor from the *Batavia*. And he had found a dead man, his eyes staring sightlessly at the ceiling, a great spray of red veins upon their whites. A soft white feather had curled like a tusk from his lower lip. Nicolaes had seen such eyes before. Had even caused such injuries himself when he'd had cause to hold a pillow over the mouth and nose of anybody whom Buckingham wished to remove without arousing suspicion. But he had not killed the man in the little cabin. Somebody had got to van Speult before he could.

He had told Pelsaert none of these things. Instead he had slunk back into the manners of a soldier. Bit back his anger and attempted to undo the impact of his bout of rage.

'Forgive me, Commandeur,' he had said. 'I have a sister who bears an uncanny resemblance to the lady who was set upon and for a moment I lost all sense of what is proper. Forgive my outburst. I sought this audience purely as I know you to be a man of integrity and noble bearing who would...'

And then the *Batavia*, moving at full speed, had struck the reef.

Pinned beneath the commandeur's writing desk, blood running into his eye, Nicolaes tries to recall the moment of impact. The crash had been explosive and powerful, a noise louder than cannon fire or the collapse of an enemy fort. His mind had filled at once with extraordinary images; some primal part of himself screaming out, certain that a vast sea creature had suddenly risen from the black depths and bitten the mighty flagship clean in two.

'Up. Come on, push, you bastard, we're fucking going down!'

Nicolaes becomes aware of the face in front of his own. Otto, carlet with exertion, soaked to the skin: a vein bulging in the side of his head as he tries to heave the weighty piece of furniture aside. Nicolaes pushes upwards with every muscle he can command, his body aching. Feels something shift as he strains against the seemingly immovable obstacle. Spit froths upon his chin. And then Otto is pulling him out, wrenching him onto the floor of the Great Cabin, hauling him up; slipping and sliding on spilled bottles, fallen books, scrolls, fine china. He puts his hand down and feels an incongruous smoothness. Grips it with numb fingers and brings the curious object to his eye. It's a whale tooth, an intricate design whittled into its surface. *A woman*, he realises. Elegant. Refined. Had Pelsaert...?

'Come on, Wiebbe!'

Otto drags him to his feet and together they stagger out of the doors of the Great Cabin and clatter onto the deck.

Nicolaes stands still, Otto at his side, both briefly frozen by the sheer horror of the scene before them. The ship has struck land with such impact that the *Batavia*'s foreparts are risen high above the waterline, a jagged mess of splintered wood and razor-sharp coral.

'What have we hit? There's not meant to be anything here! Wiebbe, what have we hit?'

There is a sudden dreadful shriek, wood tearing apart and the pistol crack of iron nails shooting from their moorings like tiny knives. The stern plunges down into the water, the hull twisted at a grotesque angle. Nicolaes and Otto pitch onto the deck. They lie still, hands over their heads, breathing hard, listening to the surge of breakers smashing against the broken hull and the gathering shrieks and cries that drift up from below decks. Some three hundred men and women have just been thrown from their bunks and hammocks and pitched into a living nightmare.

Nicolaes hauls himself to his feet. Wipes the blood from his eye and begins to scramble towards the poop deck. Somebody needs to take charge, he tells himself. And where are the goddamn officers? There will be frightened people needing help. Who's giving orders? A wave breaks across the rail and drenches him in icy spray. His feet go from under him and he clatters down again, glaring up at where Pelsaert and the skipper stand, screaming obscenities at one another.

'What the fuck happened?' bellows Otto, again at his side, hauling him to his feet. They push forward as soldiers, sailors and passengers begin to surge up from below, a great stampede of terrified faces and bloodied nightclothes. 'Wiebbe... what did we hit?'

Nicolaes shakes his head. He has no answers. Just knows that this great ship with its precious cargo and its hundreds of souls is going to be lost to the ocean before the dawn.

'It was moonlight, that's all! The lookout saw nothing! It's not supposed to be here! There's nothing on the map!'

'You drunken bastard, you've killed us all! How could you not see it? This was your course. Why, there's not even another ship to call out to as you've already lost the fleet!'

'We're not done for, Pelsaert. Not yet! We'll be back at sea before the morning and by Christ it will thrill me to wave goodbye – to watch you in your finery begging us to return!'

'You speak of mutiny, you fool! Do you not see, the ship is done for? We have a duty to those in our care but by God the Gentlemen XVII will have us both torn to pieces if we do not at least recover the cargo. We must tend to the passengers and...'

Otto grabs at Nicolaes before he can hear any more. A little way down the stern, a young woman in a nightdress stands like a spectre among the throng of men who spill and fall and rush from rail to rail, calling upon their God and cowering each time a new breaker smashes against the rail. She is white-faced and one arm hangs limp at her side. As the ship clatters down against the reef she loses her footing and spills to the deck.

Nicolaes darts forward as soon as he sights the newborn child that she clutches at her breast. A sailor drops down from the rigging and smashes into him before he can reach her. Nicolaes hauls himself upright, jostled by a sudden rain of men tumbling down from the rigging as the ship is battered afresh by angry waves. He shoves one man aside, smashes an elbow into the face of another, and then his view of the mother and child is lost amid a fresh wave of soldiers, flowing up from the orlop deck. He hears Stonecutter's voice, bellowing orders, demanding the men stand fast. Nicolaes cannot see him. The only voice that carries is one of the cadets, a young man with a shrill tone, whose laughter sounds maniacal against the weeping and prayers.

'Away to me, lads! If we're done for, we may as well meet our makers rich and drunk, eh? Let's head to the hold. There's gold there. Let's see if we can't pay the sea gods to show a little mercy!'

Somebody bumps hard into Nicolaes and he spins, angrily, lashing out at whoever has pushed him. He sees the big white face of the predikant, still in his nightclothes, clutching his Bible in his hands and saying swift, indecipherable prayers. His eyes are screwed up tight and yet he points his face Heavenwards. His children are clustered around him, sobbing, saying His name, calling upon the Lord, calling for Mother.

A dark-haired sailor stops suddenly as he runs to the side of the young cadet, reacting like an animal to the sight of young flesh. He grabs the predikant's youngest daughter, pawing at her breasts, yanking at her nightdress, leaving a long trail of spit upon her neck and cheek as he smears his tongue lasciviously along her face. She screeches desperately and her brother pushes his way to her aid, attempting to grapple her from the sailor's grasp. The sailor laughs, throatily, and immediately smashes his forehead into the gallant young man's face, spinning the girl into a closer grasp and beginning to tear at her clothes with a renewed urgency.

The predikant stands mute, watching the attack as if in a trance. Nicolaes elbows the cleric aside and grabs for the sailor's long dark hair, yanking him backwards as if hauling on the reins of a horse. The girl spills from his grasp. Nicolaes keeps his fist in the man's hair and heaves him down to one knee, hitting him hard in the side of the head and feeling him drop, limply, before he disappears into the forest of feet and legs, boots and shirt-tails.

'Otto!' yells Nicolaes, casting around for his companion. He spies him at the tail of a straggle of soldiers, all boisterously making their way back below decks, following the drunken cadet who has promised them gold and the best brandy as they meet their end. 'Otto, come back, you fool!'

Otto glances back as he hears his name. Comes to as if he has been lost in a trance. Tears himself away from the body of men and fights his way back to Nicolaes: a salmon escaping the shoal. There are tears in his eyes and his cheeks are white as moonlight, but he manages to show some flicker of remorse for having momentarily abandoned his friend.

'Otto, people will need protecting,' shouts Nicolaes, putting a hand upon his friend's shoulder. 'We will need to launch lifeboats, launch the yawl…' He looks up, to where the *Batavia*'s ten sails billow in the howling wind. 'Listen to the wood groaning. We're already taking on water below. The men won't do a damn thing unless there's a voice to give orders. The sailors have got the bosun. Who've we got, eh? They're decent men but they need orders to follow and I can't do it all on my bloody own. I'll send the passengers to you and you do your damnedest to keep them safe, right? Any good men you can vouch for, recruit them to your cause.'

Otto nods, his eyes widening as he sees the spray of another great wave crash over the deck. 'And you?' he yells.

'There was a girl with a child,' bellows Nicolaes, shaking the saltwater from his eyes. 'And these children have lost their mother. God knows what those drunken bastards will do to anybody who stands between them and the hold...'

'Private Hayes!'

Nicolaes does not register the name as his own but he recognises the voice. Stumbling across the deck, Lucretia and the predikant's wife are making their way towards them. Lucretia still wears his coat. She calls his name imploringly as they battle their way through half a dozen soldiers. Nicolaes rushes forward, shoving men aside and reaching out to grab Lucretia by the arm. She has had little chance to clean the filth from herself but she has been soaked by the crashing waves and drips watery mud and filth from the hem of his jacket. She clutches a sheaf of papers in the crook of her arm.

'Are you quite well?' he demands, examining her fine features and staring into her eyes. 'Vrouwe Jansz, are you quite well?'

She manages a nod, gulping like a dying fish. He glances at her companion, the predikant's wife, Maria. She juts her chin forward and muscles her way towards her children. She shouts, pained, as somebody emerges from the gangway and attempts to grab her by the waist. She kicks out instinctively, throwing a fist at the shape behind her, then yelps as her hand connects with something hard. Nicolaes drags her towards him and kicks the legs out from underneath the man who had laid hands upon her. He's still a child, a boy of no more than fourteen, his face oozing malice. He looks around him at the scene upon the deck and laughs, madly.

'To me, devils! You're free tonight! Feast and fuck and feed! Take me, use me. I'm your servant!'

Nicolaes pushes back through the throng to where the merchants, the wives, the children, are forming a widening crowd behind Otto. He has already recruited three other men to his side. They follow his instructions, fighting off those who would harm them, standing tall against those who wish to go to their graves with their pricks sunk into something warm.

'Up!' shouts a commanding voice from above – an older man used to giving orders. 'Get in that rigging and unfurl the damn lot or I'll have you broken before the dawn!'

Nicolaes thrusts his way through the throng of men who charge past, their arms full of furniture, flour sacks, cannon and rope. Crashes into the far gunwale and peers over the edge to where the ship grinds against the unforgiving coral. He watches as heavy items of furniture are hauled through the hatches, catching snatches of pitiful pleas for help and orders to throw anything they can carry into the sea. He takes a blow to the face as two young sailors rush past, an expensive writing bureau carried between them. The bosun is at their rear, lashing down with a length of tarred rope. 'Overboard,' he yells again. 'If it isn't nailed down, pick it and toss it or it'll be you idle bastards that we chuck!'

A gap appears in the melee of frantic people and he glimpses the girl in the white dress. She is sobbing now, her child clutched to her breast. Her arm hangs uselessly at her side and there is blood dripping upon her bare feet. He pushes forward, suddenly hearing the dreadful sound of axes biting into the deck below, hacking into the cables that tether the cannon. Below, he hears the roar of men suddenly shouldering the colossal weight of the fine bronze and iron contraptions, then the sudden crash and drenching as they spill through the ports and down to the merciless sea.

'Why, you drunken imbecile? Why could you not follow the simplest of instructions! It was all ours for the taking and you spoil it over some whore who's fucked every man aboard!'

Nicolaes stares up to the poop deck. The under-merchant, Jeronimus Cornelisz, stands in front of the skipper. He wears only an undershirt and in the light that spills from the Great Cabin, Nicolaes is able to make out the shape beneath. He stops, his hand at his mouth. Beneath the cotton shift, Cornelisz carries scars that far surpass those upon his face. His body is a map made of weeping lesions and risen welts. He looks as though he has stood at the edge of a lake of sulphur and allowed its blistering surface to spray him upon his every extremity. Even at this remove, Nicolaes sees that the wounds are raw and weep like the eyes of a scalded child. The man must be in constant agony. A man could be driven mad by such eternal pain.

'She told me, you lying cunt,' growls Jacobsz, striding forward and smashing a fist into the under-merchant's gut. Cornelisz doubles over and Jacobsz, his face purple, grabs him by the tails of his nightshirt and tosses him bodily over the rail. He crashes down into the swell of men and is swallowed up the press of sailors, soldiers, merchants, children. Nicolaes glimpses his bone-white, hideously scarred legs as he slithers through the men like a viper.

And now Stonecutter is lashing his own rope down upon the backs of the men, gathering his soldiers into some semblance of order, striking at those who still try to make their way down to the hold to help themselves to the treasures of the sinking ship. The bodies part for just long enough for Nicolaes to spot the cabin boy, little more than a child, grabbing a handful of the young woman's hair and dragging her towards the craft. She screams, twisting in his grip, her pink-faced baby tipping its head back in imitation to emit a howl of fear.

Nicolaes reaches the boy in a handful of strides. Grabs him by the ear and slams his fist into his nose, hearing cartilage break and feeling the warm spray of blood upon his face. He looks into the girl's eyes and sees nothingness. Sees only his own face, reflected back on the empty, clouded irises. Sees Nicolaes de Pelgrom. Sees Wiebbe Hayes. Sees the foundling boy who became the agent of a foreign king. Feels, for perhaps the first time, that in this instant he is at last doing that which best serves his own nature, and not what he is commanded to do. He is, in this moment, not acting. He is protecting those who need it because it is the right thing to do. The ugly duty that he must perform in Java is so far from his mind as to be a dream.

He looks down, suddenly aware of a warm sticky wetness at his gut. Sees the handle of the little knife that protrudes from the skin just above his hip. There is no pain. Just a sudden anger at himself for not having seen the weapon until it was already within him.

'Wiebbe, we need you! They're launching the yawl! Wiebbe!'

He holds the girl close to him. Pushes back through the throng, feeling himself weaken as the blade slips from the wound and his blood begins to spill.

'You're hurt,' insists Otto, taking the girl from him and

passing her on to Lucretia, who is tending to the wounded. 'Wiebbe, you're hurt…'

He shakes his head. Grits his teeth. Turns to where Jacobsz stands, his hands still upon the tiller. At his side, Zwaantie tugs at his big arms, trying to tear him away from the position he refuses to yield. He slaps her hard, hissing some unheard curse, then turns back to his duty, guiding the ship even as it breaks apart beneath him.

Then Lucretia is at his side. 'Thank you,' she says. 'Thank you again.'

He gives a little nod, embarrassed and unsure of himself, and then the pitch of the creaking ship tosses him forward so he is pressed against her, pushed up close to her filth-streaked neck as she feels the warmth of his blood upon her own cold flesh.

And they stand together in the darkness, their gaze upon the far smear of amber dawn. Their prayers are made in unspoken unison.

Please Lord. Let the dawn bring hope.

28

The light changes. The hours tumble past in great fistfuls, falling as dirt upon a coffin lid.

Cornelisz, huddled in the dark, hiding in an oil-black pocket of shadow, tears and blood mingling with the wounds upon his face.

He emits an air of true anguish; a phosphorescent shimmer about his edges, his entirety shrieking with an unspoken fury. About him, the air seems to sizzle. He crackles with such rage that to touch him would be to clutch hot coal.

He feels himself fragment and reform. His framework disintegrates as if he were an entity built of cold ash. He becomes a swarm, a cloud of something both more and less than the being that has slithered and seduced, coerced and manipulated; scattering poisoned seeds into the fertile earth of the *Batavia*'s darkest places these many months.

It is as if he were briefly distorted into an immense swarm of bees: a great buzzing cloud of pure malevolence that drifts through the chaos below decks. He experiences the regrets of other men; glimpses dead siblings, children; murders unavenged. He drifts within the private sorrows of those who feel the chill grasp of their own mortality.

Sees all.

Feels all.

Is all.

For a moment he is up on deck, drifting among the exhausted men, the terror-stricken passengers, as the sun's first lights show that the *Batavia* is lost. He sees Pelsaert, grey-faced, saltwater spraying from his trembling lips as he whispers his prayers, huddled in upon himself in the shelter of the gunwale. Sees the skipper, screaming orders at those who still listen. He pauses for a spell in the air around Jacobsz. Feels the truth of him. The lust and rage, the white-hot jealousy, the fear of his shortcomings being discovered. He has recovered himself. The madman who steered the ship into the reef has been replaced with the fine sailor who believes himself capable of saving the ship.

He senses the slow diminishment of hope as the dawn reveals that the reef was struck at high tide. The waters fall instead of rise. There shall be no swell of tide to refloat them. The *Batavia* is lost, surrounded on three sides by open water and the great coral teeth. He feels the death of the ship as if some part of himself had been absorbed by the timbers. The groaning of the planks vibrates within him like a toothache; he shivers as the waves smash down again, again, upon the huddled masses of men, women, children. He feels the ship begin to rise then crash down again, clawing its way further onto the jagged coral; now twisting, pivoting, as the mainmast catches the burgeoning gale and begins to buckle; the wood splintering, grinding against the deck. He hears Jacobsz scream. Sees axes glinting in the rain and the gathering sunlight. Feels the reverberations of axe heads biting into wood, again, again, and the sudden shriek as they begin to fall; not out to sea but towards the

Batavia herself, smashing gear and railings and sending the survivors scattering like foxes from a burning den.

Cornelisz feels himself drifting in the remaining rigging, staring out through the eyes of a sailor from Antwerp. Experiences the man's regrets, his wish to see a daughter born three days before they embarked. And he is sighting the low, bone-white smudge of a line of nearby islands. He hears the shouts of the senior men, the sudden brief flaring of hope, and then he is cast out as surely as if the waves were blessed by a priest.

And now he is naught but man. He returns to himself in a great wave of disparate emotions and it takes a moment to untangle himself from the mess of borrowed sensations and shared doubts.

He is in the saloon. There is blood upon his face and one of his ribs seems to be splintered beneath his skin. There is no pain. There is never any pain.

'A tribute! A libation! Finest brandy upon your throne of gold!'

Cornelisz becomes aware of the men who mill around him. Some are drunk and insensible. The cabin boy is naked, squatting upon the corner table; gold coins mounded up beneath him. He is a bird protecting its eggs.

'For you, Jeronimus!'

The same voice again. He looks into the broad, earnest face of one of the VOC cadets. He is draped in fine silks and there are precious gems in his hair: diamonds, emeralds, rubies catching the light as he kneels before Cornelisz and tips a stream of amber liquid onto the glittering pile of jewels at the under-merchant's feet.

Jeronimus considers himself as if he had returned to the

body of a stranger. He has no memory of having donned the finery with which he is now robed. The cloak is lined with ermine, embroidered with golden threads that stitch pearls and opals to the breast. His boots are calfskin and soft as butter. He wears a white silk shirt, a mulberry sash about his waist. He moves his head from side to side and finds himself smiling as he imagines the picture he presents. He wears Pelsaert's fine plumed hat and his chin scrapes against a stiff white ruff that forms a perfect disc around his thin neck. He shifts in his seat. Feels precious items move within the lining. Jewels, lockets, coins. He glances at his fingers. Expensive rings, too large for his slender digits, spin and clank as he wafts his hands in the soft golden light. He has been busy, he thinks. Even as his soul drifted, his body sought out opportunity.

'They flee!' comes a drunken voice from somewhere at the back of the saloon. 'They think there is hope! The fools have launched the yawl!'

Cornelisz looks past the supplicants at his feet. At the rear of the saloon is a figure from a nightmare. One of the gunners has decorated himself with blades. He is a suit of knives; lethal steel protruding from his hat, breeches, doublet, ensuring that none of his fellows can come near, or attempt to wrest the bottles of best wine that he holds in his arms like a newborn.

Cornelisz feels a glass bottle being pushed into his hand. Takes a long gulp of some rich cherry brandy.

'You are unafraid,' comes a tremulous voice, near his face. He turns and sees the smooth features of Lenert, the youngest of the cadets. 'You spoke with such certainty,' whispers Lenert, breathily, 'of the many Hells that assail us.

I shall confide that it is hearing your truths that has most undone me. Please, speak again of your God.'

Cornelisz puts his palm upon the cheek of the young man who looks at him with the wide, trusting eyes of a new convert. 'He is God to all. And He looks upon our work here today and He smiles. You praise Him with your greed; with your debauchery and avarice. We face our deaths here, my child, and yet you continue to lust for the pleasures of life. There are those who cower upon the deck, making their peace with some uncaring Almighty. And there are those who drink and carouse and fight and fuck and steal until their final breath. And I count myself blessed to be among such fellows.'

The room fell silent as Cornelisz's voice wound about them, his words cold silk upon hot flesh. He feels himself growing strong as these young disciples look upon him with the zeal that he witnessed during the sermons and rituals of his own master. Unstoppably, impulsively, he falls into a memory; the colours rich and vivid; the smells as raw and carnal as those that climb within him as he rises to his feet, red-robed and majestic, in the saloon of the *Batavia*.

He is again in the cellar of the little corner bar. He is again witnessing the push and pull, the surge and withdrawal, of two dozen rich men, naked and masked, their movements conducted to the steady rhythm of the drumbeat that emanates from the hidden figures in the darkest corner of the makeshift church. Torrentius, robed in blood-red, stands atop beer barrel; gold-painted horns protruding from his sweaty black mass of curls; his hand about the long pale throat of the drugged, feathered girl. Cornelisz hears again the Rosicrucian's fevered words, his promise of eternal knowledge, his vow to share the mysteries of the universe, to choose one from among his gathered acolytes. He slid the blade sensuously over the girl's flesh, roses of blood blooming in its wake.

And his eyes had locked upon Cornelisz's own. He had felt Torrentius's consciousness within him. Had, in that moment, perfectly understood. The only knowledge he had was how desperately people wanted to be freed from conformity. He understood the basest, deepest desires of those for whom God was a damnable obstacle to their pleasures. He told such men what they needed to hear. Wrapped it up in arcane imagery and lavish displays of ceremony. But there was no Rosicrucian God. There was no true secret order. There was just these drunken men, in the dark, engorged at the thought of spilled blood and copulation.

'Who will take the blade?' demanded Torrentius, smearing blood upon his face. 'I toast the devil in your honour, my children! And one among you must bind himself to our creed. Who shall take the blade!'

And Cornelisz is remembering the stampede of men. Haarlem's puritans and rule-makers; these church-going husbands and fathers, fighting one another for the right to draw the blade across the girl's neck. Cornelisz did not join their number. He simply watched, and imagined how it would feel to yield such power over those with more wealth, more power.

And he knew, in that perfect moment of realisation, that if he could remove Torrentius, he could take his place. Torrentius had always shown him favour. Had welcomed him in to their sect like a returning son. He had taken pleasure in drawing up the apothecary's astral chart and informing him, breathlessly, that his spirit had lived before and would live again. In Cornelisz, he saw the hand that slew the innocents at Bethlehem. He saw the centurion who hammered the nails into Christ's wrists. Saw in him Catus Decianus, procurator of Britain, welcoming a flame-haired tribal leader and her children into his camp and subjecting mother and infants to brutalisation by his men.

'The scars upon your flesh were put there by the fires of Hell, Jeronimus,' whispered Torrentius, staring into his eyes as if they were keyholes barring entrance to the beyond. 'And yet your spirit returns again and again. You rise from the pyre, remake yourself from the ashes, ascend as a god. You are the master of the pyre, Jeronimus. The God of Flame.'

Cornelisz returns to himself, rising from his memory as if spat out by a leviathan.

He is alone. The candle has guttered itself out and the pile of gold that had been at his feet is now piled up in the far corner of the room. The ship lists heavily to stern. He feels a wetness upon his face and on his hands. Feels sticky with blood that is not his own. Looks down at the table in front of him and is unmoved by the severed hand, pale and bloodless, that has been placed upon a fine golden plate in front of him. He glances down at the jewelled goblet. Lifts it cautiously and sniffs the charnel-house reek of congealed blood.

He realises that there is no sound save the creak of timbers and the smash of wave upon the splintered wood. His belly growls. It takes him a moment to unstick his tongue from his mouth. As he stands he finds his breeches stiff with piss.

He wonders how long he has sat here. Whether those who listened to his sermon had tried to take him with them or whether the spell he had woven with his words had disappeared like morning dew.

He drifts forward, light as smoke. Bumps through the doorway and slides down the wall of the gangway, his eyes not yet fully awake. He spills into the deck like a fish from a trawl.

He is alone. Has been alone for some time. The *Batavia* is chewing itself apart. The sun is setting. The horizon is a faint indigo smudge, an arrow pointing his gaze towards the little islands. He narrows his eyes. Makes out the tiny stick figures of countless men. He feels something flame within him. Shivers as the cold air takes him in its fist. He huddles into Pelsaert's crimson coat. Feels the shape of the expensive telescope in its folds. Ferrets it out and raises it to his eye.

Breathes out, slowly, as he focuses upon the longboat that slowly pulls away into the nothingness of the horizon. Sees Pelsaert, hunkered down in the bow. Sees the scarred scalp of Jacobsz, emerging from the constellation of dark-haired skulls. Twenty men, perhaps. And women, too. He chews his cheek, tasting blood. Spies the outline of the whore who abandoned him to his fate. By what magic had she inveigled herself onto the longboat? As he watches, Zwaantie huddles into the embrace of Jacobsz, one hand protectively cupping her belly.

Cornelisz grinds his teeth. He feels slighted. Wronged. Were Jacobsz not so trifling in his outlook they could have succeeded in taking the *Batavia* and its bounty. Here, now, the sea could be littered with corpses and this sinking vessel would be heading out to sea under Cornelisz's command, set upon a new beginning and with incalculable riches to be shared between a chosen few. It has been snatched away from him. He feels tired suddenly. Wishes he could persuade himself that Torrentius was more than a charlatan. He is comforted by the idea that he will continue after his demise. Whether there is a place in some debauched Pagan afterlife, he is not truly sure. But there is joy to be had in the idea of awakening in a new host, of his essence transferring to a new vessel where he might try again to create a world in which he is revered as he should be. He has suddenly grown weary of being the scarred, bankrupt, misshapen apothecary. He feels that here, in this truly forsaken place, it is time to begin again.

Wordlessly, without a second glance, Cornelisz walks to the gunwale. He looks to the horizon and curses them all. Tells himself to remember. Remember the betrayal. The humiliations. The failures and rejections and the pitying glances from those who never learned to fear him. He shall have his revenge. Whatever awakes, it shall do so with a ravenous thirst for blood.

He crosses his arms about his chest. Closes his eyes.

And falls backwards into the raging surf.

PART FOUR

29

The Houtman Abrolhos

June 14, 1629

Nicolaes's tongue feels thick as blubber; his lips the texture of a snake's shed skin. There is no moisture in his mouth, save the thick paste that serves to glue his mouth shut. His head pounds: a great thumping at his temples, a fist beating feather pillows. It feels as though there is a rind of sand upon his skin. He struggles upright, cold and feverish, hollow and sick. Scratches the salt flakes from his beard. Thinks, momentarily, of coconut husks. Lifts his shirt and flinches as he surveys the purpled flesh above his hip. The stitches, mercifully, still hold. The predikant's eldest daughter, Judith, had unpicked the threads from a discarded gown washed up in the bay, tangled around a twist of rigging and rope. She patched him up with a combination of gold and turquoise filaments. They stick out from the gash like varnished spider legs.

He hauls himself up, his stomach growling. There may be a little meat today, if the rations hold. He knows of a little rock pool where the crabs gather after high tide. Perhaps one of the better swimmers will again disobey orders and return to the sinking vessel, rummaging through the galley and stores for brandy, beer, salted beef.

Gradually he becomes aware of the groaning sea, that incessant rhythm: the whisper and crunch, slurp and swallow of an endless tide upon hard shore. It is a sound that could drive a person from their wits, a sonorous hiss that he can feel in his teeth.

'Wiebbe!'

Light floods in as Otto whips back the fold of sailcloth. His friend's face appears in the gap, blocking out the dull white light. Otto has lost weight. His skin hangs from his bones as if the stays holding him to his skeleton have become unlaced. He grins down at his friend, revealing teeth streaked with blood. Otto gums are swollen and painful and there is a crust of dried red at his nostrils. Still he smiles. Still he wears the uniform. Still he follows orders. Whatever bargain he made with himself when he chose to come with him to Lucretia's aid, he has not gone back upon it. He is loyal to Hayes. Loyal as a brother.

'Wiebbe, there's a great tangle of mast and rigging washed in on the low shore,' he gabbles, helping him to his feet and checking his wound. 'There looks like some useful salvage but if the cadets get there first then none of it will go to the passengers. Stonecutter's just threatened to rip the predikant's head off if he says one more prayer of thanks for our salvation. I know you've barely slept but it's all breaking down and nobody's listening to anybody.'

Nicolaes screws up his eyes. Gathers his strength and drags himself from the little shelter. The tent is not much more than a scrap of cloth held down by rocks but he has come to find some degree of comfort while cocooned within. He does not want to leave its embrace. Did not ask for this. Did not ask to be a leader of men, marooned at the edge of the Earth.

There is nothing joyful about the barren landscape into which he emerges. It has been ten days since the first of the survivors dragged themselves ashore and the gratitude for having found safety and shelter was quickly replaced with misery at finding they had put ashore on a barren strip of land unsuited to supporting life. This is a place at the outer rim of the world: a cheerless, colourless gash of rock and coral; harried by harsh winds and trodden beneath a low, bone-coloured sky. It is nothing but shell and stone – five hundred paces long and three hundred wide. There is no speck of colour to balm the spirits. Nicolaes feels as if his head were wrapped in canvas, the panorama made opaque by rough material. He has sent men to explore every inch of the little triangular-shaped archipelago and each party has returned with increasingly bleak tidings. No hills, no trees, no caves. There are greasy, white-winged birds aplenty and sea lions splash fatly on the two little sandy beaches, but this is not land where man can survive for long.

There is no fresh water.

There has been only one blustery squall of rain.

Soon, the living will begin to envy the dead.

'You have him, I see.'

He turns smartly at the sound of the voice. Takes in the pleasing vista of Lucretia Jansz. She too has lost weight and her cheekbones push against her pale flesh like wet linens draped over a pole. Behind her waddles the predikant and his gaggle of offspring. The cleric has not altered his clothing from the day he splashed out of the longboat and crawled ashore amid the sea lions, his every action an accidental mimicry of the great whiskered beasts that watched him from the shallows. His wife is endeavouring to maintain some decorum – tucking her lank hair within her stained cap and daily washing the children's tattered clothing in the little jagged pools by the rocky islet. Some of the sailors have begun to insist she wash their clothing for them also. They are taking the risks, they say. They are the ones who will see them all to safety. It is, they claim, only fitting that they are treated to a few luxuries: first pick of the rations, best spots upon the shore, the occasional squeeze of an arse or a teat as they do their damnedest to turn planks and caulk, ropes and salvaged nails, into a vessel fit for sea.

'Two of your long-haired fellows are endeavouring to maintain order,' says Lucretia, pushing her long, flaxen locks back from her face with one hand and pressing the other to her hip. She catches her breath, pained.

'My long-haired fellows?' asks Nicolaes, failing to hide his smile.

''Tis what the merchants and the families call your brethren,' she says, with a little shrug. 'They wear their hair as you do, Private Hayes. Long and free. Had you not noticed that those with whom you quarrel have, to a man, trimmed their hair down almost to the scalp. Poor Frans sheers them as if they were sheep.'

Nicolaes shakes his head, feigning ignorance of the

division between the different camps. 'Stonecutter causes mischief?' he asks, quietly.

She sneers at the mention of the big man's name. 'The lance corporal has already told your man Otto here that he'll put a pistol ball in him if he tries to take any of the supplies for communal sharing. He says his men need to drink first if they are to protect the rest of us. The gunner, Allert, ever at his side – he wields a club with a shell screw upon its end, a weapon fit for a savage. He has already struck down one of your Frenchmen. He says there are casks of water just beyond the surf line.'

Nicolaes licks his dry lips. Tries to work enough moisture into his mouth to speak. 'Why does he believe there's water?' he manages, painfully.

'It's wishful thinking,' says Lucretia, scornfully. 'They all see what they wish. It's a mess of rope and planking, stuck a little way out past the rock. There will be bloodshed, Wiebbe.'

Nicolaes glances at Otto, who gives a sly smile at being referenced as "your man". Otto has fallen into the role of Hayes's strong right hand, though Nicolaes never sought the advancement that has fallen to him. Since the longboat left he has found himself an unexpected leader of men; a beacon around which the frightened, the hungry, the needy have all begun to cluster. He finds himself directly at odds with the hardcore group of soldiers and sailors who flock to the banner of the VOC cadets and their henchman, Stonecutter.

'Pompous little pricks,' mutters Nicolaes, as he thinks upon the pampered young princelings who now command the soldiers. Coenraat, Gsbert, David – all strut in their purloined finery, splashing in the waves and gorging themselves upon the finest of the salvaged foods. They had arrived four days after the first of the survivors reached land. They had spent their time on the sinking ship growing increasingly inebriated and delusional. Only when the ship started to break apart beneath them did they find the courage to plunge into the surf and strike out for land. Half of those who set off were able to make it. The others disappeared beneath the waves. The survivors arrived half-drowned and delirious, spouting tales of their lost leader; lamenting some crimson-cloaked preacher who had entranced them with sermons that veered towards the demonic. Even when they recovered their speech, they would not speak of him by any other name than Lord Commander. He refused to follow them ashore, they claimed. Held the ship together through sheer force of will and bid them to save themselves and grow stronger upon his sacrifice.

Coenraat van Huyssen wept for him as if he were a slain apostle. The strength they have recovered has not been put to any useful purpose. They serve themselves and refuse to consider such sensible precautions as rationing or storing food and water for the days still to come. One of their number, a man of noble birth, refused to countenance sharing with the passengers as they were so many rungs below him in the social order.

None of the one hundred and seventy souls upon this crowded little island have adjusted to the new social order. Those used to being obeyed by bowing servants are finding themselves at the wrong end of the whip. Pelsaert's own clerk, Salomon Deschamps, has been put to work plucking birds and chiselling shellfish from the rock pools, his hands bleeding. To refuse invites a beating from any number of the men who used to snap to attention as he trailed his master about the ship.

The survivors fragment into smaller and smaller groups, each watching the others distrustfully and fearing to sleep lest they wake to find themselves newly alone. More than one hundred of their number are common soldiers and sailors; their number augmented by coopers, carpenters, and smiths. Lucretia is one of twenty women – mostly wives of members of the crew. The others are children, from cabin boys of fifteen summers to the trio of babies born to the womenfolk aboard *Batavia*. Fear of the VOC stopped being a deterrent to unruly behaviour a week ago, when the half-mad Commandeur Pelsaert ordered forty hand-picked souls into the longboat and set off for the horizon, promising to bring back help. A dead-eyed, shame-faced Ariaen Jacobsz accompanied him. His mistress, Zwaantie, had clung to the little boat with such ferocity that Pelsaert lacked the resolve to order her back to the island. She did not look back as she climbed, nakedly, into the craft and settled herself in Jacobsz's wordless embrace.

Nicolaes now finds himself endeavouring to keep this straggle of men, women and children from falling prey to the bastards who flock to Stonecutter, the boatswain and the cadets. A dozen rank-and-file soldiers have given him their unspoken support, standing at his side, muskets loaded and clubs raised, as he has attempted to ration the rainfall and pitiful supplies among the company. He is, ostensibly, doing the bidding of the remaining senior officer, Frans Jansz, but the surgeon is a sickly, weak-willed man, unable to threaten or cajole stronger-willed and more physically able men to do as he commands. Nicolaes, accepted as his proxy, has found himself giving orders.

From the shore comes a sudden shriek and a great roar of raised voices. Nicolaes glares at the wall of bodies two hundred paces away, down by the little islet where they first washed ashore. He glances towards Otto who in turn looks back to where Nicolaes's long-haired soldiers are awaiting instruction. They are a ragged bunch: scrawny and pitiful in the tattered strips of their uniforms. But each is ready to do what Wiebbe Hayes asks of them.

'To me,' yells Nicolaes. He jerks his head towards the shore. 'Nobody takes a damn thing until it's been added to the inventory and a share agreed. Don't hurt anybody unless you have to. But if you have to, hurt them bad.'

Otto begins to run towards the throng of people. Nicolaes stops after only three paces and turns back to Lucretia. From the inside of his shirt he retrieves the curious object that he had found himself clutching as he dragged himself through the surf and onto the coral. He presses the whale tooth into her hand and closes her fingers around it, softly. And then he too is running for the surf.

Stonecutter is up to his waist in the water, a club in his hand, striking out left and right at the few sailors who still follow the commands of the provost, Pieter Jansz. A Company man, Jansz is one of the few ashore who truly believes in the skipper's ability to reach Batavia in the longboat and then to return with help. He fears nothing so much as the wrath of the VOC's Gentlemen XVII and is resolute in his application of Company policy. He and Stonecutter's men would already have come to blows had they enough water to quench their thirsts after battle.

'I saw him!' shouts Coenraat, wading in the shallows, his eyes fixed on the tangle of wood and rope. 'A flash of scarlet, I swear to you!'

Nicolaes pushes his way through the group, his hand firm about the frizzen pan of the musket that he has so far been too afraid to fire. He does not want to know if it is damaged beyond repair.

A sailor bars his way, a great hunk of razor-edged coral held in his hand like a serrated axe. He is swinging it wildly in great pinwheeling arcs – the weapon coming dangerously close to the widening semi-circle of wives and children spread out along the shore. Nicolaes ducks a crazed downswing and catches the man's wrist, bringing his hand down upon his knee and then wrenching his arm up behind his back. The sailor curses as something breaks in his shoulder and Nicolaes shoves him towards the nearest of his companions. He pushes past and into the water, the cold taking his breath away, the saltwater causing his flesh to sting.

'Ah, here he fucking is!' growls Stonecutter, grinning, as he sees the man he failed to kill. 'Where's your white horse, my pretty? Shouldn't you be back in your tent, polishing your halo...?'

Nicolaes ignores him. Senses the nearness of one of the soldiers. He turns to look into the face of Wouter, the self-serving soldier who tried to sell him information about the attack upon Lucretia. Wouter is brandishing a sword, still encased in its elegant scabbard, laughing drunkenly as he swings it at Nicolaes's head. 'You better stick to killing rats,' roars Wouter, his eyes flicking to the left as another man moves in behind Nicolaes, who senses the looming presence of Mattys, the big German. All have thrown in their lot with Stonecutter.

'Shark!' yells Nicolaes, pointing frantically at a point just behind Wouter. The soldier turns away for an instant and Nicolaes hits him in his exposed jaw. He crumples into the sea and Nicolaes scoops up the fallen weapon before it is swallowed by a wave. He turns to find himself facing all three of the men he fears. Stonecutter, Mattys, and Jan Hendricxsz. They exchange warm glances, fanning out, each clearly looking forward to what is to come.

'Come here, pretty,' taunts Stonecutter, striding towards him, shirt hanging open to reveal the latticework of old scars and brands. He has his cudgel in one hand and a musket in the other, brandishing the sopping weapon like a club.

Nicolaes unsheathes the sword. Jerks left just before the next wave hits, finding his feet and lashing out with the jewelled hilt of the rapier, catching Mattys full in the face and knocking him back into the surf. Hendricxsz reaches into his cross-belt and pulls out a dagger: too fine a weapon to have been his since Amsterdam. He changes his grip on the dazzling weapon, clearly unsure whether to throw such a treasure. Nicolaes feels the ocean try to take him off his feet. Senses the nearness of angry men closing in behind him. Looks right and sees Otto wrestling in the shallows with a sailor and a cooper, blood pouring from his mouth.

Stonecutter is almost upon him. He hefts the musket. Brings it down like an executioner's axe. Nicolaes parries the blow but feels the impact all the way through his arm and up to his shoulder – the sword splitting the wood perfectly above the lock.

Stonecutter hits him in the guts with his club. Hits him below the jaw with the stock of the musket. Stamps forward through the waves, leering delightedly.

Stops.

Nicolaes can just make out a flash of movement over the bigger man's shoulder. He narrows his eyes, all the while trying to shake some life into his hand. Looks down and see that the sword has spilled from his grip. Glances back up and his face creases in confusion. He can see one of the cadets swimming vigorously through the surf, trying to reach the fallen mast. Stonecutter stops and turns, following his gaze.

'It's ours first, lad!' he roars at the young man, Nicolaes briefly forgotten. 'Whatever you get, it's…'

His voice fades to silence.

For a moment it seems that the whole world is breathing in, an eerie silence dropping upon the gathered throng. At once the air pressure seems to drop. Nicolaes feels a stinging pain in his teeth and the hairs on his arms stand up. Suddenly there is a ringing pain in his ears and his headache seems to explode behind his eyes.

The sky darkens. Clouds that moments before had seemed like ribbons and strips suddenly assemble themselves into great walls of darkness. The wind turns in on itself.

Nicolaes looks up as the rain starts to fall. A billion billion raindrops suddenly tumble from the sky; a merciless waterfall of blessed, life-giving water.

And then he hears it. Hears the sudden murmur of prayers and entreaties, words of thanks and wonder.

He looks out to sea. The tide has picked up the cluster of wood and rope and pitched it forward upon one perfect wave, depositing it into the shallows as if held aloft upon a giant palm.

Nicolaes watches, hair plastered to his face, as the figure that has been tangled in the rigging, hauls himself aloft.

He is clad in crimson ermine and fine leather boots. Upon his head is a splendid hat, its feather pointing upwards like the tail of an arrow.

Jeronimus Cornelisz stands aboard the tangled raft and stares at the scores of survivors that stand in mute wonder as the Heavens reshape themselves and fall to the parched earth like a miracle.

He stares upon them with eyes of such intensity that it seems for a moment as if he may cause those nearest him to crumble into cinders.

'They said you was dead…' growls Stonecutter. 'Said you had a fit. Died in front of them. Pelsaert's gone. Jacobsz, the bastard… we're done for, whichever way it goes…'

Cornelisz looks upon the bigger man. Seems to see through him, down to the scrimshaw on his bones. Puts out a hand and places it upon his forehead. Leans forward, and whispers, gently, in the big bastard's ear.

From where he stands, Nicolaes cannot hear the words. But he sees the way the lance corporal's eyes cloud over. Even through the deluge, he sees the soldier's huge frame shake as a lifetime of suppressed weeping bursts out into the wild, wet air.

And then the God of Flame walks ashore.

30

Batavia's Graveyard

My dearest Boudewijn,

Rejoice, my love. Though I am weakened and much reduced by my recent tribulations I am not yet unmade. I live, husband. The tempest that has deposited me upon these stark and hostile shores cannot yet count me among its victims. I cling to life with the same resolution that our blessed under-merchant gripped the mess of planking and timbers during the two torturous days that he bobbed in the ocean like a corpse.

Forgive me, I know not where to begin. I know not how to explain my circumstances to thee. The letters into which I poured so much of myself these past eight months have been reduced to a mulch of illegible ink and brine-soaked pulp. I sought to save the precious pages but have been unable to stop the ocean from flooding it with even more tears than I spilled upon its pages. But I shall write as if you are aware of all previous confidences. I shall simply tell you that we have been here, upon the hunk of jagged rock that we have come to know as Traitor's Island, for nearly eighteen days.

The land is named for those who have deserted us. The commandeur, the skipper, my shameful slattern maid Zwaantie, and a number of strong sailors with the backs to pull the longboat, have abandoned us here to seek rescue at the nearest inhabited land. I fear they shall not return. Commandeur Pelsaert seemed as though his entire spirit had fractured as he slunk away into the wooden craft alongside the very man responsible for my shaming. Neither would suffer themselves to look at me. Pelsaert did not speak to me at all in the days after the initial impact. It was almost as if he were too ashamed to face me.

For all that he vouchsafed to Hayes that I would be protected and my honour restored, he made no offer that I join him in the longboat. I would not have accepted such a proposition when so many here still need to be nursed, but the wretched whore who has so disgusted me had no such compunction. Zwaantie forced herself into the boat like a piglet nudging aside its siblings to reach the teat. Were it not that the longboat is our only hope of rescue, I would wish for Poseidon himself to rise up and smash the vessel with his fists before it reaches Batavia.

And yet there is reason to feel moments of good cheer. I find myself increasingly indebted to a soldier of whom I have previously written. Wiebbe is a man of Friesland and brings great honour upon that humble province with his every word and deed. I wish that all men here were made in his image, husband: capable, quick-witted and with an innate sense of what is right. I entertain hope that I may yet be returned to thee, and that perchance you could make some reward for this humble soldier who has defended the honour of several of our party, and who fights to keep us falling victim to the machinations of those malevolent brutes loyal to the lance corporal.

Wiebbe's forthcoming absence will be difficult to bear for many of our number, but we must place our faith in Mijnheer Cornelisz, who has taken charge in a manner I cannot fault, and who has ordered Hayes and his best men to make their way to the neighbouring islands and there to search for provisions. His absence will be keenly felt, but despite my earlier misgivings about the character of Mijnheer Cornelisz, he has proven himself an able leader these past days. He recovered his strength with extraordinary rapidity and though he has found himself custodian of a most sorry and bedraggled company, he has set about making necessary changes with true zeal. The mood among our number has certainly improved as a consequence and it is with relief that I relay that men unsuited to the task of leadership are making way for one who seems to have found his calling in this forsaken place.

There are certainly those who see omens in his near-resurrection. Though I find such talk inappropriate, I shall confide that his arrival has certainly coincided with a marked improvement in our fortunes. A change in the wind's direction has ensured that all the bounty from the wreck has at last begun to wash up upon our islet, adding to the treasures and stores already recovered by a handful of soldiers brave enough to return to the ship's hold. We have been fortunate enough to recover large quantities of driftwood, along with barrels from the stores. We have so far counted some five hundred gallons of water and five hundred and fifty gallons of French and Spanish wine, along with numerous other victuals.

Absurd though it may be, some of the livestock has also been recovered. As I write I hear the lowing of the bullock that swam through the shark-heavy waters to reach this coral shore. Chickens and pigs roam freely about our ragged encampment. The provisions are now under guard and being communally distributed, while the carpenters set to work turning the planks into serviceable craft. Had it not been for the gluttony with which many did debase themselves in the first few days, we would be looking at a handsome supply of food and drink. But the cay has already been exhausted of its seabirds and sea lions.

The silence we experience in the moments when the wind drops is truly chilling. Moreover, the rain has stopped.

And yet, as I have indicated, in Jeronimus we have perhaps a leader who could sustain us in the weeks to come. I shall confide that I did not herald his survival with the same ebullience that many of the ship's crew greeted him. Truly, they strove to touch him as if he were Lazarus, risen. I have experienced numerous misgivings about our under-merchant since we were first acquainted and will confide that there are times when I have felt in him a true malignancy, a dark purpose at odds with the wellbeing of myself and numerous others. But he does have the stout heart and pragmatism that lends itself to command and he has swiftly remoulded the ruling council to allow him to better implement the changes that are required to preserve good order.

His arrival has been a blessing to those upon the council better suited to following a leader. Indeed, the predikant and poor hapless Frans Jansz have slowly come to look upon him with the same zeal and fervour that many of our number revere him.

I shall confide, husband, that some of our leader's behaviour has caused some mild concern among the wives, children, and those soldiers who flock around Wiebbe. Certainly this isle is as rife with gossip as the ship's saloon. There are rumours whispered beneath the sailcloth that Cornelisz had been embroiled in a mutinous plot in the weeks and months before the wreck. I have heard it whispered that Skipper Jacobsz had recruited several men to their cause and that the ship was even scuttled on purpose with a view to allowing their number to steal the treasures from the hold and then overpower the crew of whatever rescue ship be sent their way.

I have dismissed the notion as fanciful, though I shall confess that those whose names have been referenced as having to do with this plot, overlap disturbingly with the list of men I believe to have been involved in my own shaming upon the night of the catastrophe. I have spoken at length with Wiebbe and he assures me that Jeronimus will wish to use this opportunity for command as a showcase for his previously overlooked abilities, and that his survival better assures my safety.

Certainly he has been nothing but forthright, fair and proper in his dealings with me and those I have come to think of as being under my care.

As I write these words, husband, I find myself looking over my shoulders to see whether I am observed. When I feel the impulse to write some suspicions about the under-merchant's suitability for high office, it is as if there is suddenly a spirit behind me; a hazy form that peers at my words and stays my hand. But I shall here find strength to confide that I have had occasion to doubt the man of whom I have so frankly and fulsomely heaped praise. Certainly there is an air of the fool about him. It is with some discomfort that I see him don the fine garments of Commandeur Pelsaert and to parade about the camp in his elaborate cape and plumed hat.

Moreover, he has begun to sermonise to his followers, gathering little huddles of men about him into whose ears I am told he whispers shocking heresies and promises much in response for their loyalty. The impressionable young cadets follow him as ducklings behind their mother, though I cannot say with any certainty that those less favourably disposed towards the cadets and their ilk make any different picture in our persistent proximity to poor Wiebbe.

I talk of him again, husband! Truly, it made for a most depressing vista, watching him and his favoured men leave their weapons at the feet of Jeronimus and stride into the surf, kicking out for the nearest of the islands carrying all of our hopes and ribboned in our blessings.

I shall pause now, Boudewijn. There are those who require my care. It is comical, is it not, that here, at the end of the world, I finally have a purpose of worth. Moreover, I find my first respite from the interminable grief of losing our children.

Pray for me, Boudewijn. Wait for me. Whatever oceans I must ford, I shall return to your arms.

With my entire heart,
Creesje

31

Captain-General Jeronimus Cornelisz lounges, elegantly, upon the expensive Persian rug that marks the entrance to his wood-and-canvas palace. The shelter occupies the highest spot on the island, offering a fine view in each direction. From here, he can see all. Anybody wishing to speak to him must walk up an incline over jagged coral and slick rock pools. Those who seek an audience arrive breathless and footsore, often bleeding from fresh injuries and in need of the ointments and expertise that only an apothecary can provide.

Some among the survivors speak of his tinctures and potions as if they were miracles. Cornelisz, they say, can take away pain. Cornelisz can cause weeping children to tumble soundlessly into a blissful sleep. Cornelisz can transform a fitting, half-mad sailor into one who lies perfectly still upon the sands and stares out to sea with a silly soft smile upon his face.

Cornelisz, they say, holds in his hands the very power of life and death.

Eyes closed, he faces the light. The sun remains veiled behind a caul of ragged cloud but he can feel its golden tendrils reach inside him, finding its mirror within the soft flame that burns in his breast. He is a being reborn. As Torrentius foretold, Jeronimus Cornelisz is master of all the land he can see. He is saviour. A messiah. He feels rejuvenated. Powerful. Omnipotent.

My, were they not grateful when he was returned to them? Did not the fighting cease and the rains fall and the survivors come together in a joyous chorus of cheers at his deliverance. How he wishes Jacobsz had been there to witness it. He would have enjoyed that. Can picture it perfectly: he and Pelsaert hanged with a tangled knot of their own entrails, begging for forgiveness as the passengers and crew clothe him in silks and bow, reverently, upon the bloodied coral and stone.

He is what these poor lost souls need. He is the only man with the courage to do what is required. He is saving souls with each burdensome decision that he is forced to enact. He thinks upon those poor burghers and merchants with whom he shared the first counsel. None shall ever thank him, but in dismissing them from the committee and replacing them with those men loyal to his own cause, he has spared them the agony of deciding the fates of their fellows, of their own dear wives and children. Cornelisz, and Cornelisz alone, knows what it will take to keep the worthy alive, and to turn this situation into an opportunity for true prosperity. To do so necessitates sacrifice. And Cornelisz is willing to ensure these good Christian fellows get opportunity to show their absent God the level of their piety and faith.

'Captain General?'

Cornelisz does not immediately turn in response to being addressed by the title that he has bestowed upon himself. He finds it profitable to appear like one at prayer – a prophet in communion with a voice that none but he can hear.

'Coenraat,' he says, without looking. 'You are come to tell me that those ferried to Seal Island are safely deposited, yes? I sense that the final crossing was tough and the seas did threaten to turn you back upon yourself, but you saw to it that all forty of the blessed men, women and children, were safely placed ashore before making your return.'

Cornelisz opens his eyes and hauls himself upright, looking into Coenraat's dreamy, drunken face. Coenraat already looks several years older than the boy he was when the *Batavia* hit the reef. Any lingering innocence in his visage has been sloughed free by the elements. Bronzed and freckled by the constant sun, his face seems stretched taut across his cheekbones, as if it were being pushed back by extreme wind. The colouring of his eyelashes and eyebrows has been bleached to a ghostly blonde. Their absence serves to accentuate his eyes, which gleam with the passion of a true zealot. He is ardent in his belief in Cornelisz's teachings and is fanatical in his desire to delight his master.

Among the cadets, he has become the senior man, stamping out any hint of dissent among the other young Company men. There is a true joyfulness in the way he goes about his work – a sense of purpose that had been entirely absent while aboard ship. Whether he is honing the edges of swords and axes, distributing supplies to his favourites or setting the sick and the weak to some arduous and impossible duty, he does everything as if being judged by God. Coenraat is perhaps the truest believer in the gospel that Cornelisz so skilfully sells.

'You saw this in a dream?' asks Coenraat, staring upon

Cornelisz as if he were an image in stained glass. 'Did I serve Him well, Captain General? There was dissent from the cooper when we neared land. He spoke harshly of you. Said he couldn't see any of the abundance of which you had spoken. No water, no lush waterfalls or verdant greenery. Called you a damned liar and insisted he be returned here.'

Cornelisz sighs, imitating the manners of one who has been let down too many times by weak-willed non-believers. 'You were forthright in allaying his fears?' asks Cornelisz, making it sound more of a statement than a question.

'His son was among the passengers,' confirms Coenraat. 'It was the work of but a moment to convince the cooper that he was mistaken.'

'The child lives,' gasps Cornelisz, his voice ephemeral, as if the knowledge had suddenly reached him upon the air. He sticks out his tongue, tasting the breeze. 'And yet he is diminished. He has suffered.'

Coenraat grins, delighted to witness this miracle of prophesy. He opens his sodden shirt and retrieves something from a pouch about his neck. He offers it to Cornelisz, who nods towards the pile of treasures that sit inside the entrance of his shelter. The booty gleams like a bonfire: golden bars and gilt frames, necklaces, jewels and lustrous finery. Three men and one woman lost their lives retrieving this much booty from the hold. He fancies more will succumb in the days ahead. He enjoys the opportunity to address his gathered flock and speak upon the subject of noble sacrifice.

Coenraat places the severed finger upon the pile; the pink flesh slithering down the peak of a silky hill of silver coins. Each tide has been kind to Cornelisz. Half the treasure from the *Batavia*'s hold has, in one way or another, made its way into Cornelisz's coffers. He and his men have taken upon themselves the burden of protecting it, as with the food, water and weaponry.

'There were sharks,' confides Coenraat, quietly, as he returns to Cornelisz's side.

Cornelisz considers him. Feigns concern. 'You seem troubled, my child.'

Coenraat looks to the floor, ashamed. 'I looked into the eye of one of the great beasts as it emerged from the water. I saw myself reflected, Captain General. It was like seeing myself looking back from the night sky.'

'A true blessing,' says Cornelisz, placing a hand affectionately on his disciple's bare, sunburnt chest. 'A sign. My own master, the revered Torrentius, did speak of such happenings long before you and I were linked by fate. He did speak of the beasts of the sea turning away from one who would truly delight the Lord – fearful of retribution and seeing in him a soul more singular of purpose than their own. Truly, Coenraat, this moment must be celebrated.'

Cornelisz looks away, staring at the hidden sun, as he sees the cadet's lip tremble with sheer happiness. The lies come to him so easily. His gift is the knowledge of how best to unpick the lock of each human soul. Some need persuasion. Others thrive upon praise and responsibility. He understands naked ambition best of all.

'He still speaks his treasons,' whispers Coenraat, his eye drawn to something beyond the opening of the tent. He cuffs a tear from his eye and turns to look back towards the sea. A group of cadets are wrestling, shirtless and sun-scorched, in the shallows. Stonecutter, his bulk undiminished, holds a bottle in one hand and his great tarred club in the other.

'You speak of our Judas? Our liar, with his mouth strung for untruths and deceits?'

Coenraat nods. 'The rumours persist. He claims that you and Jacobsz had planned to mutiny. That you recruited men to your cause these past months. That you sought to rid the ship of scores of men and women and to take the *Batavia* and its precious cargo for your own purposes. 'Tis folly, of course. Indeed, 'tis sheer heresy! I have spoken out in disgust at such vile suggestions but he shall not be silenced.'

Cornelisz licks his lips. He stares at the jewels that adorn his thin, pale fingers. Watches Pelsaert's rubies catch the light. Turns his hand this way and that, reflecting droplets of red upon the bone-white coral.

'Does anybody believe his lies?' asks Cornelisz, softly.

Coenraat violently shakes his head, truly outraged at the very suggestion. The gesture is too fulsome, too staged. Cornelisz instead sees the truth in the young man's glassy eyes. Coenraat drops his head. 'There are those who speak of what happened to Vrouwe Jansz…'

Cornelisz twirls the ring. It is a fine piece. Pelsaert would no doubt have sold it on the open market, pocketing the profits for himself. Are they so unlike, he wonders? He, too, is merely taking advantage of an opportunity. He, too, is using his own innate gifts to make the most of his circumstances.

He feels a sudden shiver as the temperature drops. Perhaps there will be rain this night. He wishes that he had sought to perform an incantation in full view of the camp so that when the rain does fall it could be viewed as a direct consequence of his communion with the elements. To be considered a sorcerer does not hurt his cause. Whether he be Messiah or conjurer matters not. He is the captain general. He is the governor of this land. Those who would challenge him cannot be permitted to spread such accusations.

'We are fortunate,' says Cornelisz, wrapping himself tighter in the plush red cape. 'Those who have not the stomach for blood are already reduced in number. Those soldiers who looked upon my commands with suspicion have already been despatched to High Island. They have no weapons and no water and are surely dead already. The women who whine and cry and distract the men from their work – they are now yearning to be back in our safe embrace. Seal Island may not have quite delivered the bounty that I promised and the Lucretia who will return will be much reduced and infinitely more malleable than the haughty noblewoman whom you left there this morning. The predikant continues to support the actions that I take. To spare him the pangs of conscience that his God demands of him, I shall not make him party to what must happen next.'

Coenraat leans forward, eager. He looks the way he did in the hold of the *Batavia*, fighting rats among the common men. He is a man whom violence never ceases to arouse.

'The council shall take the decision,' continues Cornelisz. 'I believe they will see the good sense in cutting out this sickness. To do so is an act of reason and mercy. We must reduce our number, Coenraat. It is wisdom to start with those not loyal to our cause.'

Coenraat grins, showing sharp white teeth. Cornelisz revels in the adulation, complimenting himself for continuing to act with such grace and magnanimity. It was truly a wise decision to appoint his favourite disciples to the ruling council. Men like Stonecutter – useful despite his loose lips – and the merciless Mattys de Beer. Wide-eyed, bloodthirsty sycophants like the simpleton Petersz; like Lucas Gellisz and the soft-skinned, hulking cadet Daniel Cornelissen. They are men he can trust and they are glad to enforce his will.

'How shall it be done?' asks Coenraat, glancing towards the selection of sabres, cutlasses and rapiers stuck into the hard earth just inside the entrance of the captain general's shelter. They serve as a lethally edged gate when he sleeps; a slumbering tiger in a bladed cage.

'Have you killed a man before, Coenraat? Have you taken life?'

Coenraat seems poised to deliver some bullish bluster. He pauses before the lie betrays him. Lowers his head and shakes it, sullenly, ashamed at the admission.

Cornelisz reaches out and lifts the young man's face with his hand. Looks into his eyes. 'There is no sin, Coenraat. Your God could not put evil into man's soul. To do so would suggest there is evil within Him. Without this thing called evil, naught is sinful. You demonstrate your faith and understanding with each deed you perform that demonstrates to your Heavenly Father that you understand this simple truth. He shall look upon you with delight and wonder each time your blade finds its mark. With each thrust of your knife, you bring yourself closer to everlasting glory.'

Coenraat blinks quickly, tears spilling over his ghost-wreathed eyelids and cutting tracks through the salt upon his cheeks.

'Am I permitted to share this honour? There are cadets

who have not yet had opportunity to praise our Lord in the manner you describe.'

Cornelisz permits himself to smile. 'Whomsoever you choose for glory, I must ask you to ensure they perform this sacred task in a way that shows our Lord that we have witnessed His teachings, and do this in His name,' he says quietly. He puts his lips to the young man's ear. When he speaks, the words seem to emerge from a serpentine hiss. Coenraat flinches as if a forked tongue were slithering into his ear. 'Open him, empty him, and feed him to the sharks. Do not let him die until he has seen the best of himself devoured.'

Cornelisz feels Coenraat twitch his cheeks into a grin of true happiness.

'God is good,' says Coenraat.

Cornelisz looks away lest his smile betray him.

Thinks: *Yes I fucking am.*

32

The sunlight bleeds softly into High Island: a crimson blush that glides out of the smelted silver waters and up over the white rocks – inching in pinkish increments towards the emerald green hummock at the very centre of this barbed wedge of land. The southerly gale has dropped these past two days but there are still high white peaks upon the water, broken occasionally by the elegant menace of a nosing shark. Their number has increased since the *Batavia* hit the reef. They have scented blood. Primal, ravenous, they know that in the shallows around the archipelago, they will always find meat.

Past the sugar-white beach and mulch of dried grasses, the land becomes scrub; desolate nothingness punctuated by sharp rocks and shallow gullies. This in turn becomes an expanse of quarried coral and gouged stone; a bone-white horseshoe of dimpled hardness, bearing the scars of recent excavation work. In places, dried blood speckles the rock.

A group of men sit in a semi-circle a little way above the deepening pit. They have the appearance of spirits, clad in rags and tattered cloth, straggle-bearded and yellow-fanged; bare bloodied feet protruding from scraps of coral-shredded trousers. They clutch makeshift weapons: sharpened rocks

and slingshots, wave-smoothed lengths of lumber, rocks
tied to driftwood with thread and gut.

Wiebbe Hayes sits at the head of the arc of soldiers. Forty
men, surviving on the island where they were sent to die.
Surviving, thanks to the man who now reaches inside the
corpse of a still-twitching animal, and yanks free a blubbery
twist of meat. He offers it to the small, sallow-faced man
who squats before him, gasping for breath. His beating
heart is visible through his bare chest. There is a tracery of
blue veins mapping his skin. Still he smiles. Smiles at the
man who leads them.

'Go on,' says Nicolaes, to a general chorus of assent
from the gathered men. 'You found it, you get to try it.'

Otto looks at the crimson hunk of flesh skewered upon
the shard of bone. It has been wrenched from the haunch
of an animal that none of the men have seen before: some
ungodly combination of rat and cat.

'You killed it,' says Otto, licking his lips and staring upon
the cube of dripping, bloodied meat. 'I missed with…'

'Just eat the bloody thing,' says Nicolaes, his stomach
howling. 'Take it. You need it more than me.'

'There's still kindling, Wiebbe. You said yourself, we have
to remember who we are – not become savages.'

'You're savage already,' shouts an amiable cadet who
threw in his lot with Hayes and his men when Coenraat
van Huyssen began to preach heresies in their shelter. He
outranks the man he knows as Wiebbe Hayes but has made
no attempt to assert any authority. He is seventeen and has
never soldiered before. He is second only to Otto when it
comes to making the men laugh.

Hayes gives his friend an appraising glance. Makes a

great show of accepting the truth in Allert's words and enjoys the little ripple of laughter from the slavering men.

'It's not a kindness, Otto,' he explains as if to a child. 'If it's poisonous, we'd rather know before we all have a bite.'

Otto bows, graciously. Leans forward. Slurps the glistening chunk into his mouth, his lips and chin smeared red. He savours the morsel as if devouring fresh pork. Closes his eyes in ecstasy. 'My compliments to the butcher,' he says, grinning – his teeth smudged crimson. He turns his gaze on the assembled soldiers, each awaiting their mouthful of raw flesh. Smacks his lips, pleased to have an audience. 'A little salt might be nice.' He gets the laugh he craves, and carries on. 'Keep it away from the Frenchies though – it's not rare enough.'

There are cheers from the men. Nicolaes smiles with relief. Picks up the dripping carcass and hands it to the man to his left: a French mercenary with long dark hair and a moustache that reaches past his lower lip. He's a good soldier who has seen a lot of battle. He has proven himself a good leader of men, leading daily drills upon the sands and dividing their number into twos – each man responsible for the fate of the other. He has helped Nicolaes and Otto turn their straggle of strangers into a company where each cares for his brother in arms. His face contorts with indecision as he is handed the dead creature. 'Please Wiebbe,' he says. 'You eat next, mon ami.'

Nicolaes shakes his head. Tries to pretend he does not hunger and turns his nose up at the steaming mess of meat. '*Dis-moi ce que tu manges, je te dirai qui tu es,*' he says, smiling, as the soldier's hunger overrides his sense of gratitude and he tears off a hunk of flesh with his teeth, laughing delightedly to hear his native language spoken so perfectly by a Hollander.

Nicolaes puts his hand upon the white rocks and hauls himself upwards, keeping a watchful eye upon the circle of men as they pass the dead beast among themselves, each gnawing off a morsel until there is nothing but bones and fur. They have found food in abundance upon High Island but they are being severe with the rationing. They are preserving the fish they catch and refusing to feast upon the colourful native birds for fear they will fly away before the other survivors respond to their signal fires and come to join them. The water they have found is dirty but fresh. They can survive here. The whole damn party could survive here. Nicolaes cannot understand why the signal fires remain unacknowledged. Is fighting down the rising fear that in his absence, those who look upon the under-merchant with wonder have begun to abuse their power.

Nicolaes glances at the men. Feels a sense of pride as he watches a small, shaven-headed man take the remains of the animal under his tattered uniform and declare his intention to make soup with the bones. A German recruit, his cheekbone sunk into his skull and his jawbone improperly aligned, declares that he will scrape some oysters from the huge rock in the bay and that all should find something for the pot. An Amsterdammer, refusing to be outdone, stands up as if sitting on an anthill, telling the others he is going to gather a handful of the sweet grasses that the men have taken to sucking to stave off the worst of the hunger pangs. Volunteers step forward, each committed to being the most dutiful and diligent of soldiers. All glance at Hayes for his approval and are rewarded with a warm, indulgent smile.

The men disperse, half of their number drifting off towards the waterline and the remaining men making for the little encampment, spread out around a small stone fortification that provides some degree of shelter from the howling wind. Their provisions are kept within – timbers and caulks and spars that have washed in upon the tide.

Nicolaes turns to see Otto staring at him, a curious little half-smile upon his face. Nicolaes feels a sudden surge of fondness for the man, a delight in seeing him rejuvenated. 'Perhaps they shall name these creatures after you,' he says, covering the sound of his own growling stomach. '*Ottus rattus felis* has a nice ring.'

Otto wipes his lips with the back of his hand. Looks up to where the brightly coloured birds wheel and caw, turning in outlandishly garish semi-circles around the squabbling gulls. He looks upon Nicolaes with a half-hearted glare. His words, when they come, are seamed with accusation. 'It would be you who deserved the credit, my friend. But how could they name it after you, eh? None of us even know your name.'

Nicolaes takes great care not to let his expression change. Only when he has thought of every possible response does he allow himself to screw up his features and feign confusion. 'You think I would choose Wiebbe if something else were on offer to me?'

Otto rolls his eyes. Settles himself down upon the moss-slimed rocks and clasps his hands across his stomach. 'What did you just say to the Frenchman?'

Nicolaes laughs, as if the question were unimportant. 'I told him that we are what we eat. It's a French saying. I heard it in a tavern, I think...'

'It doesn't matter to me,' says Otto, closing his eyes. 'I'm grateful that you're here. We all are. We'd have beaten each other to death and sucked the flesh from one another's bones, if not for you guiding us. But you're mad if you think anybody believes you to be a common soldier from Friesland. You don't have to tell me, but if ever there was a time to drop your pretence and unburden yourself to a friend, this is it. You must be bursting at the seams keeping your secrets in.'

Nicolaes feels as though a pistol ball has taken him in the chest. All the breath leaves him in a rush as the effort of holding himself together suddenly becomes too much. He sags, eyes clouding, and it is only when Otto hauls himself up and takes him by the arm that he stops fighting the urge to fall and feels his legs lose the last of their strength. Otto lowers him to the ground, his red lips moving soundlessly. Nicolaes cannot turn the haze of muddled features into a face. Just sees eyes, nose, red-barred teeth, all circling around and into one another. He can make out no sound save some high, unpleasant whine nearby, gradually giving way to the hush and roar of the ocean.

He closes his eyes, watching circles of brightly coloured lights move upon his eyelids, slowing, slowing, until he comes back to himself, sick and dizzy. He feels something at his mouth and then muddy, lukewarm water is dribbling over his tongue. He opens his eyes to find Otto holding his head up, wringing out a square of cloth into his open mouth.

'Save it,' splutters Nicolaes, instinctively. 'The men must share...'

'The men would give up every last drop of their rations if

it kept you on your feet,' growls Otto, looking down upon him. His features are a grey mask of absolute dread. He gasps, relief pouring out of him, as he sees the life returning to Nicolaes's eyes. He sits back, laughing nervously. Shakes his head, trying to make a joke out of it. 'And if you don't want to tell me the truth, that's fine. There's no need to swoon like a maiden at her first sight of a prick.'

Nicolaes finds himself laughing. Slithers up to a seated position, Otto dragging him close. He leans against his friend, his head upon his shoulder. He smells saltwater and spoiled pork. Smells of sweat and onion skins, of mildew and fish scales, that rank reek of shellfish chiselled bloodily away from stone.

'Nicolaes,' he says, closing his eyes and offering up the name like an amen. 'Nicolaes de Pelgrom.'

Otto shifts position. Eases Nicolaes back against a low white rock. Studies him for a moment, his lips moving with unasked questions. At length, he gives a nod of gratitude. 'The pilgrim,' he repeats, quietly. 'You are not a man of Friesland?'

Nicolaes looks down at his boots. Chuckles to himself, shaking his head. 'I don't think I'm from anywhere, my friend.'

'But you are a man of the Provinces, yes? You are a Hollander? The way you speak. The words you shared when you were sick. The ease with which you slip between talking to people, giving them what they need... and the way you wield a weapon. For all I know, you could be an English spy, set upon some bloody course upon arrival in the Indies.'

Nicolaes nods, weakly. Decides that there is nothing to

lose with the truth. 'I am a man of Leiden,' he says, spitting out grit and leaning his head back against the rock. 'My grandfather was a tavern-keeper. My mother was little more than a child when two fine young gentlemen of England offered a handsome purse of coin and jewels to be allowed to take her maidenhead. She fell pregnant – the shame of it compounding my grandfather's guilt at having agreed to such a vile transaction. The humiliation of it put him in his grave. It drove my mother mad. None would believe her to be the victim of an outrage. She was reviled as a common slut.

'I was placed in the care of the good burghers of Leiden and sent to the orphanage with nothing of my own save a letter written by my grandfather, and the locket given to my mother by the gentler of the two men. When I received some schooling and was able to read, I became familiar with the circumstances of that night. My grandfather wrote that he remembered the names of the men. I, an enquiring child, asked the masters of the school if they were familiar with the name. Eventually I learned that "Villiers" had risen to favour in the court of King James. He and his brother were now men of influence. And Providence, that accursed vixen, took it upon Herself to intervene.

'I had proven myself an adept scholar – hard-working and quick to learn. There was talk of my continuing my education at the university after I had finished at the Latin school. But another opportunity arose. A former student of the school had for some time been a member of the royal court in London. A favourite of the king, he was a man of science and had proven himself an invaluable creator of inventions that pleased the king beyond measure. He sought an apprentice and wished to offer an opportunity to one who had not been given the most auspicious of starts. I was selected. And in England, I was at last able to let out the rage that had bubbled within me for as long as I had known the circumstances of my making.

'I sought out the man I knew to by my father – the older brother of the Duke of Buckingham. I presented at their fine house, clasping the locket they had given my mother as a token after bedding her. He would not admit me. Returned to my master in shame and despair, it half stopped my heart when I was sought out by the duke himself. I was brought to his luxurious apartments in London and he listened to every word that spilled from my lips. He did not attempt to dissuade me of my belief that his brother was my father. He merely asked whether I wished him to intercede on my behalf. To help me be all I could be.'

Nicolaes pauses, his throat suddenly dry. He looks at Otto, who is staring at him in fascination. Nicolaes, suddenly self-conscious, offers a smile. 'The words flow like a river, do they not? Allow me to say that I became his man. His agent. I was taught all that a gentleman may need.'

'To spy?' asks Otto, quietly. 'Upon your own nation?'

'Upon everyone,' says Nicolaes, without apology. 'Taught to steal, and fight, and kill. Taught to seduce. Taught to disguise myself as many and none. What is a nation, Otto? It is only a man's master. And who would not leave a master for the offer of better terms?'

'And your purpose upon the *Batavia*?'

'Murder,' says Nicolaes, and the word itself causes him to chuckle, breathlessly. Everything suddenly seems so damn ridiculous that it does not trouble him to speak it aloud. Such business surely belongs to another life now. 'I was commissioned to end the lives of those men who so mistreated the English merchants at Amboyna. The turncoats, the false witnesses; the torturers and the men who mounted heads upon spikes upon the orders of the governor-general and his lackey. I am commissioned to end their days.'

Otto sucks his lower lip, thoughtfully. 'Aboard the *Assendelft*? You slipped away...'

'Dead already, I swear it,' says Nicolaes, holding up his hand to God. 'You have no reason to believe me and I confess I would have attempted to take credit for the deed had we arrived at the fortress but the murder was not mine. I fancy that my employer has commissioned numerous other assassins upon the same mission.'

'You sought to continue on to Batavia?' says Otto, quietly, his mind running ahead. 'You returned to the vessel. Stayed alongside me these past weeks when a man of such skill could surely have made good an escape.' He licks his lips as he realises the final purpose of Nicolaes's kill list. 'Governor-General Coen?'

Nicolaes nods. 'It was ever a fool's errand,' he says, tiredly. 'My uncle is dead. He was murdered before you or I ever set foot aboard the accursed vessel. I have no more murders in me, Otto. I have little left but the will to redeem myself, and perhaps to help those of whom I have come to think fondly.'

'The Lady Lucretia?' says Otto, solemnly, and flinches in surprise as Nicolaes puts his palm upon his cheek and smiles, gently, into his eyes.

'Nothing about our friendship is an affectation, Otto,'

says Nicolaes. 'I mean to see you safely off this island. I mean to do all I can to help you all stay alive until the rescue ship comes. And come it will, Otto. The Gentlemen will demand every effort be made to recover the treasures. It would be comforting to think that they were similarly interested in the men and women of the ship, would it not? But Pelsaert shall return. I want to know I have done all that I can to ensure that the ship leaves with as many of our number as is possible.'

'And you?' asks Otto, shuffling around on the white sand. 'You will sail on to Batavia? To do what? To serve at the garrison? At my side?'

Nicolaes feels a surge of warmth and friendship towards the young soldier. 'I do not think I have ever been anything but the instrument of another man,' he says, gently. 'If Providence grants me more life, I should like to know what I can make of myself when not employed in the schemes of another.'

'You will desert?'

'I think we are getting ahead of ourselves.' Nicolaes smiles. 'Look where we are. Look what we face. We have found water and lit the fires but nobody comes. The seas around Traitors Island froth pink and the sharks feed well. We weaken by the day. To talk of a future desertion...'

'I shall not tell,' says Otto, solemnly. 'You are simply telling a story, my friend. You are Wiebbe Hayes. You are a fine soldier from Friesland. You are the leader of those soldiers who believe they have a duty to protect the survivors and who remain loyal to the VOC. All else is fantasy, is it not?'

Nicolaes holds his friend's gaze. Nods, slowly. Shifts position, as if wriggling back into the neatly fitting suit of

343

the character he has played for a year. 'Of course, Otto. I merely seek to distract you from your belly.'

Otto's grin does not reach his eyes. 'I care not for Coen,' he says, quietly. 'Keep us alive and I give you my word – were he to wake with his throat slit, I would not shed a tear.'

Nicolaes is about to reply when he is distracted by a sudden commotion from the waterline. He hears the raucous cries of raised voices – men shrieking his name. He pulls himself upright and reaches down for the length of sun-bleached timber that serves as both staff and poleaxe. Takes Otto's arm and hurries them both down to where the men are waiting: bare, sunburned backs obscuring his view of the sea.

Slowly, like stage curtains, the men part.

Bobbing in the shallows, clinging to their disintegrating raft, are three of the men from Traitors Island. Two are dead, their bodies bleached like the underbelly of a whale; ragged wounds to their backs and haphazard smiles gouged into their throats.

The third man is sobbing, rocking back and forth, sitting in a haze of pinkish water that leaks from some hidden wound. He looks up as Nicolaes moves towards him, staring through him with eyes that seem robbed of all light.

Otto crashes forward into the water, reaching out to the man. He flinches away from his touch.

'What has happened, my friend? Where are the others? These wounds upon your fellows – who has done such wickedness?'

He moves his lips but no sound emerges. Only when Otto takes him by the arms and forces him to look at him does the poor survivor find his voice.

'He's killing them,' he whispers. 'Cornelisz and his Blood Council. Killing them…'

'Killing who?' demands Otto. He shakes him, angry now. 'Listen man – killing who?'

He stares past Otto. Addresses his words to Nicolaes. Manages to utter three words before he succumbs to another fit of sobs.

'All of them.'

33

Cornelisz sleeps little. To sleep is to invite visions. To slumber without recourse to his sleeping draughts is to visit Hell. He does not think of the things that he sees as nightmares. They are more real than that which he experiences in wakefulness. For a man blessed with such exceptional memory and power of perfect recall, he cannot find the words to describe what he experiences when he gives in to exhaustion. Even Torrentius, eager to coax a useful truth from the mouth of his prophet, could not bring forth a description that made any sense.

'Teeth,' he had muttered, as his master sat before him, impatient to sketch this glimpse of the beyond. 'Teeth and flame and bones. People inside out – naked muscle and sinew and tendons tearing meat from their bones to devour themselves, over and over. And the pain, Torrentius. I felt it as one hears song – something so piercing and perfect as to be absolute. And yet there is no fear. It is a sensation of reunion, of being swallowed up into the embrace of the familiar. If it is Hell, it is home.'

Cornelisz feels a surge of fondness for Torrentius as he pictures him. Wonders what the old charlatan would make of him here and now: captain general of his own kingdom;

godlike in his power to grant life or death, punishment or reward, pleasure or pain.

He considers himself in the glass. Zevanck holds the mirror for him, tilting it at the perfect angle so that he may stare upon his likeness without being dazzled by the rays of the reflected sun. He enjoys these moments, these flourishes and affectations – the subtle lengthening of his silken cuffs, the last buffing of the silver buckles upon his long leather boots. He rests nakedly so as to better enjoy the sensation of slipping into his silken undergarments.

'An inch more, my child,' he mutters, to the woman at his feet. 'Gently now. And do use your clean hand or I fear you shall despoil the cloth.'

Two of the women have been given the honour of dressing him each morning – wiping his unclothed skin with swatches of damp linen and grooming his hair and beard as if preparing a horse for sale. They go about their business with a quiet dedication, their eyes never meeting his. They have the look of beaten animals: timorous, forever flinching, grateful for any scrap of sustenance or affection. After the first whippings they began to anticipate his preferences. His collar must be white as snow, the ties of his doublet uniform in length, the golden rings laid out perfectly upon the porcelain dish at his bedside so that he may slip his fingers inside them like a gauntlet.

The women lack the strength to demonstrate their gratitude but Cornelisz knows that they feel honoured to have been chosen as his maidens of the bedchamber. He has never experienced such devotion before, and yet it seems entirely as it should be. He has waited his entire life to be lauded thus. Bigger, stronger, fitter men bow to him as if he were the risen Christ. Zevanck and Coenraat have come to blows over who shall have the honour of preparing his food, of laying out his clothing, pouring his wine, taking his commands to the rest of the trusted men. Even Stonecutter has endeavoured, in his clumsy way, to make amends for his indiscretions and find his way back into the captain general's favour – taking it upon himself to crush the skull of a wailing infant that had so disturbed Cornelisz's moments of communion with the rising sun.

'Good morning, Captain General,' comes the voice from outside his quarters. He recognises it as Gsbert van Welderen – one of the cadets who has found his true calling in carrying out Cornelisz's instructions. He is presently in his leader's favour and is wholeheartedly enjoying his reward of being given first pick of the women. His men, Cornelisz had insisted, deserved dutiful wives. Gsbert had been inexperienced with women before sailing for the Indies, but the other cadets fulsomely helped him bed his dead-eyed bride – the consummation taking place even as the sobbing predikant blundered through the ceremony, tears spilling from his sagging cheeks to splash upon the pages of the Bible.

'You have tidings, Gsbert?' asks Cornelisz, standing at the flapping entrance and raising his hands so that Zevanck can fit his sword about his waist. Cornelisz angles his head to stare a burning hole into the forehead of his dresser. Zevanck has disappointed him recently. So too has Coenraat. Some of those whose deaths he ordered upon nearby Seal Island had somehow slithered away. He fancies that a handful may even have made it to Hayes and his soldiers upon High Island, having glimpsed the signal fires. Damn Hayes.

The soldiers were meant to die of thirst. They were meant to turn upon one another. And now they prosper, even as supplies upon Cornelisz's own encampment are dwindling fast. Of course, Cornelisz has the guns and enough gold to buy a kingdom, but their meat is almost gone and the water has fouled. He fancies he shall soon have to walk across the ocean to High Island and pluck Hayes's beating heart from his chest.

'How fine you look in red.' Cornelisz smiles warmly as Zevanck enters the shelter and snaps smartly to attention. He makes a superb specimen in his new ruby-coloured cloak, fastened at the neck over his bare chest and with sabre and pistol tucked into a pair of thick leather belts. All of Cornelisz's lieutenants have been given this honour – the luxurious red garments hand-stitched by the sailors and the womenfolk; transforming every scrap of plundered red cloth into the uniform for his chosen men. It is the uniform of what Cornelisz has come to call his "Blood Council".

'She shall not eat, Captain General,' says Gsbert, without preamble. 'I forced the fish into her mouth and held it closed until she swallowed but when I took my hand away she puked it back up. Same with the water. Even the brandy. She is beyond my skills.'

Cornelisz reaches out a jewel-festooned hand and is unsurprised to feel his palm touch the golden goblet proffered with impeccable timing by Zevanck. He fancies that Zevanck will remain loyal until his last breath. So too Coenraat and the funny little cabin boy who begs each day to be allowed to take a life. He feels safe in their devotions. He does not feel the same about his Hendricxsz and Mattys, his favourite killers. They have made an entirely pragmatic decision to follow him and are willing to kill in order to further their own ends, but they do not, he suspects, love him as he deserves. He does not truly object to this eminently sensible approach. He, too, has feigned religious zealotry in order to gain favour. He has always presumed that at least half of Christ's disciples were merely there for the free wine.

He takes a gulp of red. Sighs, momentarily exhausted by the burdens of omnipotence. 'I trust you refrained from striking her,' he says, softly.

Gsbert nods, concern taking hold of his young pink features. 'She doesn't speak, Captain General. Just lies upon the rug and rocks back and forth. There is no meat upon her. She has made up her mind to die.'

Cornelisz laughs, still beguiled by the haughtiness and pride of this shit-rimed, half-dead creature who lives only at his behest. He thinks for a moment upon the wife he left behind and cannot help but compare their characters. Perhaps if his spouse had shown such stoicism in the face of their bankruptcy and bereavement, he would have allowed her to live. Instead, her constant mewing and demands for prophesy about what their future may hold, had hastened her blessed release from the burdens of continued life. He wonders whether her body has yet been found. What it looks like after a year beneath the dirt.

'She does not die until it suits our purpose, Gsbert.' Cornelisz tosses the empty goblet to Zevanck. 'It would pain me to see us so diminished by the loss of a woman of character and high birth. She may try our patience, but the Lady Lucretia has been treated with indulgence and gentleness ever since you brought her back from the island. Why, the other women are passed among you fine young men as if they were cattle, and yet Lucretia remains untouched. She has been selected for a greater purpose, Gsbert. She shall be my Magdalene – the bride of this resurrected Christ. She shall live and prosper, and she shall come to my bed upon her knees. I shall not force her to my will, Gsbert. And I swear to you, before the month is out she will have scraped her knees to the bone having crawled her way across the sharp coral to my bed. I have foreseen it.'

Gsbert bows, grateful to have been the sole recipient of such a sermon. Cornelisz can sense the nearness of his other red-cloaked men. They gather outside his tent like flies to fire. They follow him upon his daily excursions around the island. Sometimes he deigns to speak to them; other times he remains in absolute silence, enjoying the confusion and grief that his aloofness causes among them and enjoying the knowledge that the following day he shall be greeted more fulsomely, praised more reverently; that the pile of offerings outside his shelter will be augmented by new objects of worth. He takes little notice of the items themselves, simply flicking a glance over the pile to ensure it continues to grow. Bones, shells, buckles, coins, teeth: all festoon the heap of golden treasures.

'David,' says Cornelisz, suddenly giving his attention to the young man who has stood in mute adoration during his leader's lengthy ablutions. He raises his head, awed to be so addressed.

'You have a duty for me, Captain General?'

Cornelisz feels a warm benevolence flowing through him. Zevanck has taken his fall from favour with the manners of a gentleman, refusing to beg for a chance to redeem himself and instead simply going about his responsibilities with an absolute devotion. Cornelisz feels a quickening of his pulse as he anticipates the delight with which Zevanck will receive his instructions. For surely he has been chosen for the highest of honours.

'We are too many, are we not, David?' he asks, sincerely. 'Though we have reduced our number significantly we remain too many. We cannot sustain so many hungry mouths. We cannot have our strongest men falling sick while we waste resources upon those who have already begun to succumb to sickness.'

Zevanck flicks a glance at Gsbert, who lowers his eyes. Cornelisz knows that the men have already discussed what must come next. The sick, the crippled, the young – they linger in the surgeon's quarters, barely managing to swallow their daily rations and whimpering with pain and suffering as the agues and malarial convulsions torment them.

'Their suffering is to be brought to an end,' says Cornelisz, generously. 'They have endured enough.'

'The surgeon,' says Zevanck, his voice tremulous. 'He has already armed himself somehow. He has heard whispers that such an order may come. He shall not stand by while this is done, Captain General.'

'Then his sacrifice shall be remembered,' says Cornelisz, waving a glittering hand as if troubled by a buzzing fly. 'Try not to waste musket balls or powder. There are rocks aplenty to deliver the final blow.'

Zevanck nods, staring at the floor. Cornelisz sees him glance to the red cloak he was forced to give up following the botched massacre on Seal Island. He smiles benignly and nods his assent. Zevanck gathers up the garment and wraps it about himself, face full of pride at again being deemed a man of importance.

'The carpenters,' says Cornelisz, clicking his fingers as if he had forgotten some important piece of business. 'Egbert Roeloffsz and Warnar Dircx. I sense they have grown uncomfortable here upon Batavia's Graveyard. With their skills they would have no difficulty in crafting a vessel that could take them to the men on High Island. I fancy they have already begun their preparations for such a treacherous act. I would find myself considerably less troubled were their treachery no longer a problem to contend with.'

Zevanck receives the death sentence without a word. Looks upon the pile of swords near where Gsbert stands, excitedly waiting to be told whose deaths the day will bring. 'There are those among our number who have yet to prove themselves,' continues Jeronimus, thoughtfully. 'Permit those whose swords remain unblooded to carry out this task in my name. Allow them to prove their loyalty and value.'

'Yes, Captain General,' says Gsbert, who angles himself so he can see back through the tent flap to examine the gathered red-cloaks.

'Mattys has proven himself loyal, despite his earlier lack of discretion. He told me of some cacklers who may yet spread dissent,' continues Cornelisz. 'Men with the strength for gossip. I believe the time has come for us to transport them to another of the islands where they may search for food and water.'

'In truth?' asks Gsbert, surprised.

Cornelisz laughs, delighted. 'That is what the others shall be told, Gsbert. But Mattys may enjoy opportunity to see those sharks of whom he speaks so fondly. They need not reach the island. Have their bellies opened and their bodies thrown into the sea. And this evening, have Mattys come and describe it to me. I fancy he tells a colourful tale.'

Cornelisz suddenly feels an urge to look upon his kingdom. He moves forward with the suddenness of a striking scorpion and Gsbert stumbles backwards, half falling out of the tent. Cornelisz strides past him and takes his position a few paces away, on the highest point of the island. From here he can survey all that he rules. He feels the pack of red-cloaked men close around him but does not yet acknowledge them. Instead he stares down to where the predikant and his family are gathered, hunkered down in a little rock pool near the water's edge. The predikant is standing, reading from his gospel, while his wife and children claw the shellfish from the serrated rocks.

His eldest daughter, Judith, stops in her work for a moment and stands, one hand upon her hip, the other shielding her eyes from the bright sun. She gazes up at Cornelisz. He cannot hear what she says next but the harsh, salt-rimed gale carries with it the sound of laughter. A moment later, all the predikant's children are staring up at him. For a moment he sees himself as they view him. Sees himself puny and crook-backed, sickly and scarred; ridiculous in another man's finery. He hears his own growl, far back in his teeth, as a burning hatred for those who would mock him threatens to ignite.

He looks to his left. Coenraat lingers, desperate to be returned to favour. His mission was simple enough. He was despatched to Seal Island to bring back Lucretia, and to kill those who remained. He and Zevanck were clumsy in their execution of the task, just as they were when given the honour of journeying to the adjacent island and dealing with the provost and his gaggle of men, women and children. The provost and his family had made it aboard a yawl crafted from driftwood and salvage and had made their escape. It took Zevanck and Coenraat all their energy to catch up with the little skiff and demand it alter its course.

At gunpoint, the provost did as he was bid, journeying to where Cornelisz waited, waist-deep in the water. The provost demanded to know why he and his family had been accosted so violently. And then Cornelisz gave the word. All were massacred, hacked and bludgeoned to death with swords, pikes and the stocks of muskets. In the days that followed, Cornelisz found more and more sailors and soldiers joining his cause.

'Coenraat, I have a gift for you,' says Cornelisz, sweetly. 'The predikant's daughter. Judith. Does she please you?'

Coenraat opens his mouth once or twice like a dying fish. Glances at the short, broad-shouldered woman who plays with her brothers and sisters in the shallows. 'Yes, Captain General,' he says, sincerely. 'I am sure she would.'

'Then you are to be betrothed,' says Cornelisz, clapping him on the shoulder.

Coenraat splutters, unsure how to respond. 'Her father,' he says. 'He will not approve.'

Cornelisz smiles, pleased with the world and his place atop it. 'He shall have problems of his own soon enough. The wedding might at least lift him from his mourning.'

'Mourning?'

Cornelisz beckons Stonecutter. Beckons David Zevanck. 'It seems wrong that he should have so much, when so many have so little. I fear that he has been overburdened with responsibilities. Stonecutter. Trim his flock.'

Stonecutter looks down at the gathered family. Spits. Nods. 'And the predikant?'

Cornelisz waves a hand. 'Allow him to live. We shall need an officiant upon the happy day.'

Cornelisz is gratified that nobody speaks. To do so would taint a moment of true contentment.

34

It takes several hours for the survivor to sufficiently gather his wits to be questioned about the diabolical happenings upon the other islands. Otto is given the duty of attending to him; his manner gentle, his voice soft. He puts the young man back together as if repairing a scarecrow. Makes sure that his journey into wakefulness feels like a true deliverance from evil. He reveals his name to be Aris, an under-barber who had never been to sea before boarding the *Batavia*. He slowly reveals himself to be a slight, half-sighted young man of quiet dignity and some little education; well-mannered and polite despite his many tribulations.

He wins Otto's favour with his quiet courage, his stoicism in his approach to pain – biting his lip bloody as Otto softly pressed a white-hot knife blade to the deep wound upon his shoulder and watched the skin steam, bubble and bind. He managed pained thank yous as Otto drip-fed precious amber mouthfuls of brandy onto his swollen tongue. He maintained some semblance of dignity as he nibbled at the roasted carcass of the gaudily coloured bird that one of the French soldiers prepared for him, weeping with gratitude as the embarrassed mercenary pressed the gift into his bloodied hands.

The soldiers have almost lost patience by the time he is declared well enough to speak. Their day has been passed in a quiet buzz of anxiety; the men milling around the camp, casting sidelong glances at the distant smudge of Batavia's Graveyard, occasionally throwing a stone or a curse or hurling a fistful of sand into the sea. Only when Nicolaes gave the order did they begin to turn their nervous energy into something useful. They have passed the last few hours preparing for war: whittling driftwood and caulks into lethal-looking spikes, hammering nails into oars, attaching fists of jagged corals to twists of rope, binding twists of timber with twine and animal gut: succeeding in making slingshots and catapults.

Silence has slunk over the camp as stealthily as the darkness that now enfolds them. The men seem to have exhausted themselves with speculation and gossip. Each privately entertains a hope that the newcomer speaks false: that this is a ruse or a test and that the scores of men, women and children they left behind are still clinging to life.

It is a little after midnight when the survivor declares himself sufficiently revived to tell the men of High Island of the horrors committed in their absence. He emerges from Otto's shelter into a desolate, storm-lashed night; greeted by the low rumble of thunder, a table dragged across a stone floor. The rain comes a moment later, beating down with a ferocity that makes the few Papists cross themselves, and the others reach for their own private talismans. They clutch pebbles, shells, curious flakes of wood. One of the French mercenaries puts his faith in the skull of a dead bird, convinced it is a mystical totem that will ensure his survival until the rescue ship returns.

Otto guides the young man to the fireside, safe within the embrace of the little stone fort, protected by a flapping length of sailcloth strung across the low ramparts. Otto helps him into a little chair built of sackcloth and driftwood. He nods his gratitude, casting a blurry but appreciative glance over the little construction that these forty men have created with their rough hands. He sits and warms himself. Otto sits by his side, his manner subdued, his mouth downturned. He has already heard the newcomer's account of these past days. His hand shakes as he picks stones from the ground and tosses them, distractedly, into the fire.

Nicolaes squats down opposite the two men, taking his place at the head of the gaggle of men. He has resisted making enquiries while the new arrival has been too weak to talk. But now he seems a little recovered, Nicolaes has no intention of waiting until morning. He needs to know if his suspicions are founded. Needs to know why the sharks grow fat and the water froths pink and a malevolent spirit stalks his dreams.

'This is Aris,' says Otto, introducing him as if he were a new child joining the class. 'A brave man. He is grateful for your kindness and patience. I've told him he can expect the same even after he has explained himself to you all. Should I be proven wrong, I will take it hard.'

There are grumbles of approval from the gathered soldiers: a constellation of grubby, hollow-cheeked faces illuminated by the flickering fire. Aris looks to Hayes, who gives him an encouraging smile. He can be little more than twenty years old, yet there is a stone-grey tinge to his skin that ages him. Though he attempts to hold himself together, Nicolaes recognises the true fear in his eyes. This man has been witness to horrors that have crawled inside him, horrors that will never leave.

'You have been through much, my friend,' he says, kindly. Senses the great wall of tension from behind. He looks at Otto and winks. 'We are glad you have survived the ministrations of our poor excuse for a surgeon. You are clearly one who can endure any amount of torment.'

'Piss off,' jokes Otto, to a general chorus of laughter. 'Had you stitched him his skin would be so tight that his arse would be halfway up his back!'

Nicolaes gives a laugh, affecting the air of one who has found himself in many a similar predicament to this. He hears the rustle of the men settling down, lighting hand-carved pipes and enjoying precious pinches of tobacco, taking sips from the communal bottle of brandy as it is passed around. Aris, a little late, gives a titter of laughter, trying to join in with the general air of merriment. It is too much for him – tears spilling with the sudden release of emotion. Otto, at his side, puts a hand upon his shoulder. The soldiers look away, allowing the fragile, bloodied young man the chance to weep without rebuke.

'Tell them as you told me, Aris,' says Otto, soothingly. 'There is none here who will doubt your word.'

Nicolaes nods confirmation. Glances over the low wall to where he knows that tonight's sentries are following his newly issued commands. Any flicker of movement; any unusual sounds or glimpses of a vessel on the water, they are to raise Hell. They are no longer to view this island as part of the chain. High Island has become a fortress awaiting attack.

Aris steels himself. When he speaks, he addresses his

words to Nicolaes, occasionally raising his voice as the rain comes down harder and the thunder rolls over them like a tidal wave.

'We didn't know,' he says, shaking his head. 'Truly, you may doubt my word, but we did not know what was being done until it was too late to stop it.'

'We understand,' says Otto, still gentle. Nicolaes catches his eye. Gives a little shake of his head. He knows the lad needs to speak, and to speak in his own way.

Aris gazes past them, staring into a memory that causes his lip to tremble. 'The council had protected our interests, ensured we were all treated equally, that supplies were rationed and we all had a fair share. As soon as Cornelisz began to appoint his own men, all that changed. He began to assert his own will. His own men – the cadets and Stonecutter's group of soldiers – they began to get favourable treatment. The punishments for transgressions became harsher. And after you were despatched to find water, he did the same with scores more. Some forty souls were sent to Seal Island, a dozen more to the desolate rock we know as Traitors Island. He scattered us out so none of us truly knew what he intended. And then it began.'

He pauses, closing his eyes tight, against the butchery to which he was witness. Otto offers a kind word in his ear. Nicolaes holds himself still, listening to the thumping of his own heart and grinding his back teeth so hard that his jaw begins to throb.

'The first murder I knew of was the Englishman, John Pinten – his throat was slit as he lay in bed. Jan Hendricxsz and Allert Janssen – they were still newcomers to murder when they bled him out. They are his favoured executioners now. He has his Blood Council – men he trusts to kill without asking questions. Even as I recount this I find myself praying that it is naught but a feverish nightmare. But I know in my gut that these foul deeds occurred and that in my absence they happen still.'

Otto hands him a cup of water. Lets him use a precious mouthful to swill out his mouth. When he spits, he spits blood.

'They massacred the sick as they lay in their beds,' he whispers. 'Men whom I had cared for. Women and children whom I had bathed and whose wounds I had dressed and whom I had given my rations lest their likeness to corpses prompt the new council to end their lives. It was all for nothing. He was set upon their deaths from the moment he decided we were too many. None opposed him. Still I smell it – the blood that hung over the camp as if we were bedded down in a slaughterhouse – the flies that crawled upon their flesh before they were dragged to the water.'

'In the name of God,' whispers a Frieslander somewhere to Nicolaes's left. He hears the whisper of private prayers. Hears the sound of rising fury, fists smacked into open palms and lengths of hardened timber snapped in two.

'The killing of the sick emboldened him,' stammers Aris. 'Anybody who is not among his close circle of allies – all are at risk, though in those first days he at least made the pretence of acting with the authority of the island council. Passchier, the gunner; Jacop, our finest carpenter. He accused them of drinking wine from the stores. He sent his killers on a night like this, cold and squally, so the poor men did not hear the approach of his Blood Council. Hendricxsz led the cadets, bloodthirsty young bastards – Zevanck, van Os, Lucas Gillisz. And Cornelisz himself, clad in his finery, directing matters like a king. Zevanck bragged of the bloodshed that followed – slicing and stabbing and skewering those good men until the floor of their shelter was liquid with blood.'

Nicolaes turns to the soldiers behind him. Sees faces drained of colour, eyes wide in outrage and fear.

'Soon his men had a taste for it,' continues Aris, his voice trembling. 'By the time he had clothed them in red and made them swear their oaths there was no pretence any more. Their purpose was our deaths. His men swagger in their crimson cloaks, waving their weapons, toying with their treasures, revelling in the power they have over the merchants, the families – anybody who they suspect of being disloyal. He conducts sermons each dawn, telling his men that they are angels of fire, that they serve him as the saints who intercede with God. He claims there is no sin, that all acts of violence and lust and rage are acts of praise. I have never heard such heresy spoken. But truly there must be a demon within him. Some of the bodies were given proper burials but others were tossed to the great sharks or roasted upon the fire. He fed the roast flesh of a butchered cooper to a merchant who had failed to bow properly before him. Then he had Coenraat run him through with his pike.'

Nicolaes feels the bottle being passed to him. Takes a gulp. He realises he is shaking when the glass rattles against his teeth.

'The women,' he says, quietly. 'The families.'

Aris takes a deep, stuttering gulp of air. Otto puts a hand upon his, squeezing it softly. Looks to Nicolaes, his eyes flashing a warning.

'He has kept a handful for the common good,' he whispers. 'They are shared among his men. A couple are inviolate – the predikant's daughter is now the wife of his favoured counsellor, Coenraat.'

'The other?' asks Nicolaes, taking a stock from the fire and grinding it into the earth before him.

Aris looks to Otto then back to Nicolaes. 'The noblewoman upon whom his own sights are set – she is now displayed among his treasures as if she were a priceless statue.'

Nicolaes chews his cheek until he can taste blood. Controls himself so that his voice does not crack when he speaks. 'She lives?'

'I know of no woman who would not prefer death over such a life,' whispers Aris. 'But aye, her heart does beat.'

'Her life, Aris? Speak plain.'

Aris looks down at the floor. He seems ashamed to even speak of what he knows lest he be thought of as somehow complicit. 'Some nights he will invite those upon whom he looks fondly to come and look upon his treasures: his gold and jewels and ancient artefacts destined for the markets of the Indies. He insists she drape herself upon the pile, naked save the adornments he permits her. Should she refuse, she is passed to his men. If she wishes to eat, she must do as she is bid. He feeds her as if intent upon seduction, clothing her in fineries and having his chef craft the most exquisite delicacies for her from the supplies we keep for such special occasions. He is gentle in his manner, makes conversation as if they were in a dining room upon the Heerenstraat. But should she show displeasure at his company she is disrobed and thrown to his men. I do not know her but she was kind to the wives and children in those first days and I weep at the thought of what she endures.'

Nicolaes bares his teeth, drawing back his top lip. Were he a dog he would growl.

'Tell them of what you learned from the soldier whose throat was slit the day we left for the islands,' prompts Otto, glancing at Nicolaes. 'Of the mutiny.'

Aris nods, swallowing painfully. 'He and Jacobsz sought to seize the ship. He had already recruited the same men who serve him now. They were ever intent upon this – upon the deaths of all those who were surplus to their schemes. And Jacobsz left with the commandeur! Truly, how can we expect rescue when he who did this is at the helm of the vessel that could bring us aid?'

Nicolaes gets no opportunity to reply. From behind him, a French voice, full of disgust, rises above the howling of the gale.

'You spoke of the children. What of the families?'

Aris stares into the fire. At length, he nods. 'He makes killers of those he does not condemn to death. Men like the clerk, Deschamps. He said he would let him live if he killed one of the infants born aboard the ship. Deschamps sobbed as he carried out the task but carry it out he did. It gave Cornelisz a taste for it. I don't think any children remain.'

The men erupt in curses and blasphemies, damning the cowards who have carried out the devil's work in order to save their own skins. Nicolaes does not attempt quieten them. Everything they say is true. They deserve their rage.

'And you!' spits an older, broad-shouldered man soldier from Antwerp. Nicolaes cannot bring his name to mind. Just knows that some nights he weeps silently for the child born to his wife just a week before sailing, who was sick with fever when they left Texel. 'By what cowardice and treachery did you abandon your fellows? Who did you have to kill to be given chance to escape?'

All eyes turn on Aris, the mood of the gathered soldiers quickly turning.

'It is only through God's mercy that I am spared,' sobs Aris, wrapping his arms around his legs and staring into the flames. 'I know not what I did to cause my death sentence – I was simply roused from my tent and invited to stroll with Allert, the gunner. Within moments he had unsheathed a sword and was swinging it for my neck. It was fortune alone that I stumbled and the blade instead caught my shoulder. Somehow in the darkness I was able to flee. They searched for me but could not find where I hid, shivering and bleeding.

'I knew that by the dawn I would be done for and made my peace with the Almighty. I ran for the water. Only as I began to succumb to the cold did I glimpse the object that kept me afloat and which brought me here – an island that so many of us have come to think upon as a Promised Land. It took the last of my strength to haul the bodies of my fellows aboard – an action carried out in a state of near madness, as if some part of me believed that if I reached this land, this place, they might somehow be resurrected. Those who have tried to make their way here have been victim of especially cruel deaths. Cornelisz, for all that he has murdered us for sport, seems to want supplicants. He wants those he has abused to be grateful for any small act of mercy or kindness. I see jealousy in him when he curses your name. It is as if he is Lucifer, burning with indignation that Man still prays to the Lord.'

Nicolaes glances at the men around him. Their burst of aggression has already exhausted them. Nicolaes says nothing. Glares into the flames. For a moment he is reminded of a letter written in another life – the final testimony of his friend Dr Lambe. He had spoken of a leader clad in gold, a throne of skulls and kingdom of flame. He had read those words while on his way to meet Mrs Towerson, and then he had accepted a commission to kill and set right a grievous wrong. He thinks fleetingly of Jacob, half-dead in the shadows of Marshalsea Prison, appalled at his heresy for speaking so glibly about the wiles of Providence. He cannot help but wonder if all things are foretold – whether he is a pawn, a tool of destiny placed here to perform some task of greater significance than he could ever comprehend.

'The predikant,' he says at last. 'His family.'

Aris shakes his head. 'Stonecutter,' he explains. 'He and those whose swords were not yet bloodied in the captain general's name… they did as they were bid.'

'They were children,' stutters a voice nearby. 'Children of a godly man.'

Aris sags, his voice dropping low. 'Cornelisz invited the predikant and his daughter, Judith, to dine with him. In his absence, his family were all struck down. Sons, daughters, his good kind wife. Stonecutter struck and clubbed and stabbed them until no hearts were left beating. Then he came to where Cornelisz entertained the predikant and Judith. Wet with their blood, he presented Judith with a wedding gift – a necklace of their tongues. Cornelisz found it amusing. It was, he said, a suitable punishment for those who prayed to a false god.'

Nicolaes looks to Otto. His hands are white-knuckled around a sharp stone picked up from the hard ground. 'His youngest daughter sang in her cabin,' he says, quietly. 'She was no more than ten.'

'Her father, the predikant – he was forced to conduct Judith's marriage ceremony, to be witness to its consummation...'

'Please,' says one of the men to Nicolaes's rear. 'Please no more.'

'We were but sixty in number as I made my escape,' gasps Aris. 'More than a hundred are dead upon his orders. And still they talk of reducing it down to just those who will be needed to seize the rescue ship or whichever vessel is sighted. That is still their aim – to keep their wealth and take a vessel and commence a life of piracy.'

Nicolaes feels dizzy with the weight of it all. He is no stranger to death; has committed acts for which he expects to be barred from Heaven. But Cornelisz seems more devil than man. The evils done in his name are beyond anything of which Nicolaes can even conceive. He puts his hand down on the hard earth and hauls himself to his feet, the cold wind whipping at his skin, the light of the dying fire seeking out the hollows in his face. For a moment he thinks upon his uncle, Buckingham. Allows himself a moment's truth. He was never more than a useful implement. He was never more than a blade or a pistol ball or a shapely specimen who could be called upon to turn an enemy's head or reward an ally. He suddenly sees himself for what he is. Knows that, until now, he has never really mattered to anybody.

He turns wild eyes upon his men.

'They will come,' he says. 'These murderers. These monsters who serve the very devil. They will need to kill us all before they can make their escape.'

He looks out across the huddle of half-starved, rag-clothed men. Sees the urge for blood in every pair of eyes.

'You may have done bad things in your life,' he growls. 'May have drunk with the devil and bedded many a witch. You may have sold your souls for a few stuivers. But by God if there is any last whisper of decency within you then you will summon up your strength and make a vow this night. You vow vengeance. You vow defiance. You vow that you will give your every last drop of blood if it means that none of these men prosper from the evils done here. When they come, we are to be ready. When they come, we defend what we have. When they come, we prove ourselves soldiers. You follow orders, you do as you are bid, you listen to my commands. You be the best versions of yourselves. Do you understand me?'

The men give a lukewarm cheer, half swallowed by the rising gale.

Otto drags himself upright. So too does the French mercenary and the older man who weeps for his child, born in the infancy of the voyage and now dead at the hands of Stonecutter.

'He asked if you understand!' roars Otto, grabbing a flaming branch from the fire and thrusting it skyward. 'By God but this is a chance to do battle with the very devil!'

Now they stand. Now they roar. Now they grab their

own burning torches and wave them until the black sky is aflame with dancing sparks.

Nicolaes slinks into the darkness. Disappears into the night air as if slipping beneath ink-dark waves.

Only when he reaches the water and knows himself to be unobserved, does he permit himself to weep.

35

The voice is that of a drowning man: a desperate burbling clash of consonants; the high, fluted bleating of a goat. Cornelisz finds himself grinning, madly, as the words spill out of his flapping lips. He is sure it must be a language of sorts but the words mean nothing to him. He simply stands on the little hillock, his bare feet bleeding onto the bone-white coral, and allows the caress of the scorching sun to bring forth sounds from within him.

He hears the murmur of his follows behind him. Fancies that one or two cross themselves. Hears Zevanck growl an order that they cease any such heresy. Hears the whispers among his men.

'Tis sorcery!'

'He speaks as a demon...'

'He simply prays in another tongue...'

'He summons his strength. He understands that which we do not...'

Cornelisz notices his tongue fretting against his chin. It feels longer, as if he could simply let go of his mortal form and shed his human skin, could rise up like a basilisk with glowing eyes and long, venomous fangs. He has not eaten in several days but in truth he has never felt stronger. He is growing more powerful by the day. Each new death seems to increase his potency. Every time one of the merchants begs him for mercy he knows he comes closer to becoming what he was meant to be. He wishes Torrentius were witness to his transformation. Wishes the old pretender could see him here, naked but for red cape and golden chains, his cock jutting like a rapier, the scars upon his face glistening like quicksilver as bigger, stronger men look upon him in fear and awe.

He opens his eyes and stares straight into the sun. Absorbs the panorama of his kingdom. The wind still blows hard from the south but it is a scorched, stark day; the sun almost white as it reaches its zenith against the pale blue sky.

After a time, he realises he has stopped talking. The strange language is no longer bubbling from his lips. He tries to say an "amen", to give the performance some degree of familiarity. The word will not come. He feels a sudden pain in his throat; his tongue is too big. There is an unpleasant tickling sensation in his chest. He coughs and his mouth fills with the taste of metal. Spits blood upon the stone. The sight of it causes him a moment's concern. He knows himself to be more than a mortal man and yet the apothecary who lingers within him knows he is showing signs of decay. He examined himself in the full-length mirror when he awoke this morning and the sight had unsettled him. His bones protrude at his hips and shoulders, his features barely recognisable. His skin is drawn back over his cheekbones and there is something hawk-like about his nose. His fingers have the look of talons.

Zevanck had said nothing when Cornelisz ordered him

to file his long, brittle nails into points to better accentuate his transformation, though his hand had shaken as he ran the razor over his master's throat, scraping away the beard to expose his scale-speckled skin. The affliction seems much reduced. In places his flesh is the soft, pink skin of a newborn. Cornelisz had sat for more than an hour stroking his knuckles across his freshly shorn face. Then he had called Zevanck back to his tent and bid him shear his scalp. Zevanck, again, went about his task in a reverential silence.

Only when he saw the strange mottled birthmark upon his skull did Zevanck allow himself to exclaim. Cornelisz had almost forgotten that the disfiguration existed. He had laughed, delightedly, as he stared at the pattern with a hand-mirror. At length, the scaly configuration took upon a form. Viewed at the right angle, there was no mistaking that the port-wine staining upon his bare scalp looked like a serpent, coiled up and ready to strike.

Cornelisz realises he has stood idle long enough. He fears that the men are growing bored and disconsolate. There have been no deaths upon the island for the past five days and there is little to entertain those who wear the crimson cloaks. They have even stopped using the communal wives, too hot and listless to make the effort to bed the few remaining women.

He would order their deaths were it not for the quiet joy he experiences when he hears them whisper spiteful slander about Lucretia. They hold her in contempt for making a pact with the devil. They believe she has opened her legs for him in exchange for preferential treatment. Some even presume she connives with him about who to kill next. They believe her complicit in what happened to the predikant's family. Cornelisz does nothing to change their minds. If they believe him to have tupped the fairest of their number, he is happy to permit the lie.

In truth, she still denies him. She speaks little. Barely eats more than a morsel of food. Fouls herself where she lies. Sometimes she talks to her dead children or distant husband, her finger moving in the threads of the rug upon which she lies as if she were writing a journal. Cornelisz can watch her for hours at a time.

'Idle bastards.'

He hears the grumble from Stonecutter, a little way off to his left. Cornelisz does not respond immediately. There is no doubt that a hierarchy now exists between the members of his Blood Council. Stonecutter is now invaluable, promoted to his second-in-command. He was exemplary in the manner he led the executions of the predikant's family, emotionless, professional and utterly without mercy. He takes his orders from Cornelisz without uttering a word of dissent. He revels in his new title of lieutenant general – barking instructions to the young cadets who had outranked him when aboard ship. Coenraat, Zevanck and Wouter have raised no objections. They are next in command, outranked only by a god and his monster.

At length, he gives Stonecutter his attention. Marvels afresh at the huge, scarred man, scowling down towards the seafront where the predikant, half-mad with grief, delivers his trembling sermon to the sharks and the sea. Behind him are his killers, their red cloaks smeared with dried blood, their faces lean and burnt. He feels a surge of pride at having transformed such ordinary specimens into men of purpose. Jan Hendricxsz had been a jovial malingerer aboard the *Batavia*. He is now responsible for some twenty deaths. So too Gsbert, Mattys de Beer, Lenert van Os: they have done their duty and earned their place at his table – a murderous elite that will serve him well when they leave the island aboard whatever ship comes close enough to seize. He is sure they will continue to serve him well. He is less sure of the others. He fancies they murder only because the alternative is to become victims themselves.

'Somebody offends you, Stonecutter?' asks Cornelisz, benignly.

'That rabble of ungrateful bastards,' growls Stonecutter, nodding to the stick figures who lie upon the rock at the water's edge. 'They don't even have the strength to hide from him any more.'

Cornelisz follows his gaze. Sights young Jan Pelgrom, the cabin boy. He is not a true crimson cloak but his zeal for violence has made him useful to Cornelisz. He is still little more than a child but his first murder unleashed something primal within him. He scampers and whirls between the shelters, a knife clutched in one bloodied fist, begging for opportunity to do murder.

'They still fear him,' says Cornelisz. 'He still serves his purpose.'

'I don't want him aboard when we take the rescue ship. He's got the devil in him. Do you not hear him? He summons devils – demands demons to rise up and fight him.'

Cornelisz smiles, delighted at the hypocrisy. 'The high spirits of the young,' he says, wistfully. 'I wish more of our number had such energy.'

'He needs another chance to demonstrate how skilfully he wields the blade,' says Wouter, emerging from the throng of gathered men and taking his place beside his leader. Cornelisz flashes a look at the young soldier. He has proven himself a fine counsellor in recent days. He is good at keeping his temper and has a mind that Cornelisz has come to enjoy unravelling. He has had some schooling and is well liked by the men. He thinks before reacting. Cornelisz hopes to take the wet clay of such a man, and perhaps, in time, craft a son.

'You have a suggestion, Wouter?' he asks, his manner playful.

'The soldiers on High Island must now know of what occurs here. They will have noted the absent skiff. Should a ship come tomorrow they may seek to reach it before we do. They may, even now, be preparing for violence towards us. That damn fool Hayes – he may have some notion to come and retrieve those survivors we have not yet had opportunity to rid ourselves of. Would it not serve our purpose if they were so afraid of our wrath that even if the ocean was parted and a pathway laid, they would still remain where they are? Another display of might, a little more blood upon the sands, and even if Hayes comes, they will not look upon him for fear of retribution.'

Cornelisz feels a surge of pride. Truly, Wouter is a man of vision. 'Summon him, Stonecutter,' says Cornelisz, warmly. 'I enjoy the song in your voice.'

The big man does as instructed, roaring out a command with such ferocity that the last few seabirds on the island lift off from their roosts. The boy stops short. Looks upward, as if beckoned by God. Slowly he turns to look upon the highest point of the island and sees the men in red looking down at him. He half runs, half scurries to where the gathered red-cloaks form a half-circle about their leader. He seems more animal than boy, smeared in blood and filth, strange swirling symbols drawn in blood upon his face. Cornelisz considers the markings while the boy stares, wide-eyed, upon the maggoty pinkness of the captain general's newly shaved head and face. He glimpses the protuberance jutting between the folds of his cloak and gulps down a silly smile. Cornelisz realises that the swirls upon the boy's face are a mirror of his own, daubed there in blood as a sign of fidelity. The thought delights him.

The men are creating their own religions, their own tributes and rituals. He fancies that if he were to vanish now, the cult he has created would live on. Within a few centuries, the gospels written in his name would have elevated him to the status of Messiah.

'My sword, David,' says Cornelisz, quietly. Zevanck appears behind him, handing him the expensive weapon retrieved from the armoury during one of their sorties to the sinking ship. It is a fine piece with an intricately inlaid handle and a blade sharp enough to shave with.

'I have a use for you, Jan,' he says, indulgently. 'Here is my sword. The net-maker who lies there upon the shore and listens with one ear to the predikant's heresies – I fancy he has largely served his purpose but there is one function he may yet perform. My friend Stonecutter here – he does not believe that you have the strength to sever a man's head from his shoulders. Should I give you my sword, would you honour me in proving him wrong?'

The boy's eyes fill with happy tears. He moves forward as if to receive the sacrament. Reaches up for the blade and emits a low howl as it is snatched from his hand.

Cornelisz is surprised to see that Mattys, the broad-shouldered German mercenary, has snatched up the blade. 'Why favour the boy with such an honour when those who have served you better stand idle? Look at the little fellow – he is made of tattered rope! Should you want his head cleaved, allow me to do it as it should be done.'

Zevanck begins to protest that he, too, should be permitted the chance to shed blood. Cornelisz grins, indulgently, as his apostles bicker for his favour. Truly, the men have reached the peak of their adherence to his will. He fancies that there will never be a better chance to rid himself of those final few burdens that nag at him in the moments when his strength briefly fails. The soldiers led by Hayes are his primary concern. He is fast running out of supplies. Pelsaert may have somehow survived the journey to Batavia and be making his way back with a rescue vessel. And more than anything, he has not yet broken Lucretia. He has not spilled his seed into his Eve.

'Make a game of it.' Cornelisz smiles, licking his teeth and tasting blood 'Allow Jan to go first. Should the blade not cut through, one of you fine, strong gentlemen may finish the job. But make sure it is seen. Should anybody raise objection, slit their bellies and allow the sharks to feed. Consider it practice.'

The gathered red-cloaks nudge one another and move forward, sensing that more is to come. Cornelisz looks past them to his own splendid shelter. Pictures the slender body within, laid out among his treasures; her skin bloody from her last beating but defiance still flashing in her eyes. He is tired of waiting for to submit to him. He is a god. And a god does not seduce.

'The stars have aligned, my friends. Tomorrow we commune with the soldiers on High Island. We make a simple offer. Gold, coin, their own craft...'

There are protests from the other men. Though the water is running out and there is little food to share, they guard their share of the treasures as if it were enough to save their skins.

'Fear not,' says Cornelisz, warmly. 'It is a mere ruse. Without Hayes, I fancy they will follow whoever is willing to lead. Stonecutter, you and my finest killers are to make this offer. And as they consider it, you are to kill Hayes.'

A slow smile spreads across the lieutenant general's huge scarred face. 'And what if he's willing to take the offer?'

'I shall judge that,' he replies, simply.

'You mean to go?' asks Zevanck, concern in his voice.

'I fancy I can give Hayes what he wants and if he resists, it would please me to see his death. I shall insist upon it being exemplary – something that will stick in the minds of those who follow him.'

From the rocks, the cabin boy growls. He runs forward, trying to snatch the sword from Mattys, who holds it high and laughs as the boy grabs for it.

'All shall be well,' says Cornelisz, taking a deep breath as the high, iron reek of dried blood is carried towards him upon the salty air. 'Now, come with me, my friend. I have a purpose for you.'

Zevanck's face glows pink with pride as he feels Cornelisz link his arm through his own. He nods towards his shelter. 'I believe I am primed for fatherhood this day.'

Zevanck grins, delighted. 'You believe she will acquiesce?'

Cornelisz shakes his head. 'No, I fear her stubbornness

exceeds her sense. I must do that which you counselled several days ago.'

'You mean to take her?' enquires Zevanck. 'It's about time. I mean, she can't say you didn't do your best to woo her. She had every chance to make it sweet.'

Cornelisz nods. He is pleased the young man understands the complexities of women. 'Do you have rope?' he asks, politely.

'Oh yes.' Zevanck smiles. 'And a strong enough grip for those skinny ankles.'

Cornelisz does not even turn as the sounds of violence spill up from the main camp. Wonders, as he ducks under the tent flap and stares upon the half-dead thing that lies upon the Persian rug, whether the boy won the bet. He rather hopes so. He likes his spirit.

'My fair Lucretia,' he says, as she folds in upon herself and covers her head with her arms. 'You win, my dear. I cannot persuade you to give yourself to me.'

She stiffens. As he watches, a fly lands upon her bare skin. She does not have the strength to flick it away. It bites her. Feeds.

Cornelisz reaches out his arms. Zevanck disrobes him: two twists of tarred rope dangling from his wrists.

'Your husband would be proud of you,' he says, gently. 'You have not disgraced him.'

He moves towards her. Watches, dispassionately, as Zevanck sets about her with the lash.

Shakes his head, a little sad that it has come to this.

'I hope that is some comfort during what comes next.'

36

'Good Christ,' mutters Otto, squinting into the low sun and watching the two little boats emerge from the haze. 'Look at him.' He shakes his head. Spits onto the white rock. 'Look at all of them.'

Nicolaes rubs his jaw, flakes of skin coming away under his fingernails. He tried to shave himself this morning but found that his hand shook too much to control the blade. Otto offered to do it for him but Nicolaes had declined. He did not want the men thinking that he was putting himself above them; that anybody on the island should be considered subservient to anybody else. They are a company, a fraternity. He would rather appear before the demonic governor-general sporting a tattered pelt of beard than have the men think of him as anything other than the man he has been these past weeks.

'I feel a bit underdressed.' Otto laughs, pressing his thumb to his last remaining teeth and giving an incisor a wobble. He makes a great show of picking his nose and flicking away whatever he excavates from the darkness. 'There,' he says wiping his brow. 'That's better.'

Nicolaes gives a smile. Tugs at the cuffs of his shirt: reduced to tatters by the saltwater and sun. It hangs from his body in a way that makes him look like a drowned sailor caught in a net. He raises his hand and pats at the matted twist of hair he has wound up and pinned at the nape of his neck. Wonders, for an instant, what Buckingham would say were he to look upon him now.

'Hayes,' says Otto, pointedly. 'Wiebbe Hayes.' He repeats the name as if to remind Nicolaes who he is. 'Hayes, do you see…?'

Nicolaes grunts affirmation. He sees. Sees Jeronimus Cornelisz standing at the prow of the first vessel, dressed in enough finery to pass for a sultan. His cloak is blood-red against the washed-out grey of the sky and the black felt hat that crowns him is belted with strings of dazzling jewels: pearls, rubies, a fortune in golden coins, all drilled through the middle and strung on links of silver. Beneath his billowing cape he wears a silk shirt, black as ink, and a fine decorative cross-belt into which two flintlock pistols have been artfully placed. He sports an officer's rapier in a jewelled scabbard at his waist and his other hand rests upon the decorative head of a maplewood staff. He looks like the figurehead of a merchantman, a gaudily attired sculpture designed to demonstrate wealth and power.

Behind him, heaving at the oars, are his murderous elite: the men of his Blood Council. They, too, are clad in red, though their capes are stained and patchwork. Around them are the fins of the sharks; gliding through the iron waters, occasionally rising through the surf in a splash of grey belly and crow-black eyes; row after row of teeth catching the light as they ravenously await their next kill.

The lead boat comes closer, negotiating the rocks and shards of coral that jut from the frothing water in the little bay. The other boat hangs back beyond the reef. Nicolaes hears the men in the nearing boat, bellowing at one another, cursing the rocks, reaching out with staves to push themselves through the frothing waves. This close, Nicolaes can make out their features. Feels a chill creep into his bones as he thinks upon the crimes of these men; the lives taken, the abuses and cruelties perpetrated for no other purpose than greed.

'Christ, he looks like a maggot...'

Hayes tilts his head, trying to count the men. He fancies there are twenty men divided up between the two yawls. He knows that each will have musket and sword. Chews his cheek as he spies the two small cannons mounted on the rear boat. He wonders how many lives Cornelisz sacrificed in order to retrieve such weaponry from the sinking *Batavia*. He resists the urge to turn and look at his own command. He is one of forty able men, trained soldiers all, but the letter delivered last night by one of the French mercenaries had made it clear that Cornelisz would not come ashore if he saw more than Hayes and three of his men waiting at the water's edge.

The letter, written in the under-merchant's own hand, had been cordial in the extreme, insisting that any misunderstandings needed to be forgotten and that it suited both of their aims to conduct an amiable conversation about how to unify their forces. The Frenchman who brought the note from Batavia's Graveyard had acted as if he was doing Hayes and his men a huge favour. He spoke of the treasures that Cornelisz had safely recovered and the bountiful delights that came with loyalty. He spoke of the blood-soaked island as a place where birth and social status counted for nothing. This was, he claimed, a land of plenty, where a man could rise provided he was willing to serve the governor-general in all things. There had been, he claimed, some troublemakers who refused to acquiesce to this new order, but they had been dealt with. Now a glorious future lay ahead of his chosen men. Hayes, he swore, could be one of those apostles. He could be rich beyond measure and sit at the right hand of a born-again messiah.

Nicolaes had agreed to the terms outlined in the correspondence and then permitted the Frenchman to return to his master – resisting the overwhelming urge to beat him to death with a rock. Otto had cursed him for a fool. Why would he agree to meet the enemy while so unprotected? Why walk into the obvious trap set by this lying, conniving bastard? Nicolaes had been able to offer little explanation. He simply said that this was their one opportunity. If he could seize Cornelisz, his followers would be rudderless. Cornelisz was the evil weed taking root upon Batavia's Graveyard. It was his duty to pluck it out. Otto had grumbled for the rest of the evening – unhappy that Nicolaes's bravery placed him in this much danger. There was no way he was going to allow Nicolaes to face him without being at his side.

Nicolaes had not argued with him. He had permitted his soldiers to draw lots over who else would accompany him to the parlay. He is accompanied by two mercenaries: one German, one French. They each hold makeshift pikes – lengths of driftwood into which great iron nails have been hammered. Hayes is unarmed, as instructed. His clothes are rags; his boots worn down to tatty strips of leather. He has nowhere to conceal a weapon even if he had access to something that might even the odds.

'My friend,' shouts Cornelisz, from the vessel, waving regally. 'My full and faithful fellow, how it pains me to see you so reduced! Come now, let us forget our quarrels and embrace as equals!'

Otto leans in beside him, his beard tickling his cheek. 'Did he always talk like a cunt?'

Nicolaes nods. 'As far as I can recall.'

'You see who's with him?'

Nicolaes nods. Looks to his left, where the slope of the island conceals the little stone fortifications. He wishes they'd had more time. Wishes, above anything else, that there were somebody else to take the lead.

'Whatever happens, people will remember what you've done,' says Otto, his hand upon his arm. 'It's been an honour, Nicolaes.'

Nicolaes swallows, his throat sore. Says nothing. He watches as one of the big men seated behind Cornelisz leaps into the surf. Recognises the muscles and scars. Stonecutter. He sets his face in a grimace as he hauls the craft to shore, reaching up to take Cornelisz into his arms as if carrying a sleeping child. Carefully, reverently, he wades to higher ground and deposits Cornelisz onto the sand.

'He looks like a maggot,' echoes the Frenchman, gripping his pike. 'Un *asticot*.'

Half a dozen red-cloaks leap from the little yawl. They carry muskets. Swords. Clubs. The other vessel remains a bit further out to sea, the men dropping a makeshift anchor. They remain close enough to use their muskets, should they be required.

Cornelisz smooths himself down. Stares up to where the shabby band of soldiers are awaiting him. Removes his hat and bows, deeply. There are gasps of surprise from Otto and the two men at his side. His skin salmon-pink, Cornelisz's naked scalp sports a curiously mottled spray of shimmering scars. In the liquid light of the wind-blown dawn, his flesh takes on the appearance of glistening reptilian skin.

'No,' says Nicolaes, shaking his head. 'He looks like a snake.'

Cornelisz begins picking his way toward the quartet of raggedly dressed soldiers. Behind him, two of the red-cloaks are carrying offerings of peace. Clothing, blankets, shoes, wine; all of the items of comfort that were promised in his correspondence. Hayes stares past them. Looks at the faces of the men who follow the governor-general. Their countenances are set in bitter scowls, their eyes scanning the lip of the rise. They are ready for battle. Nicolaes tries to put names to faces but can see little he even recognises in the red-cloaked murderers. He picks out three young cadets, their faces now lean and lived-in after exposure to the elements; their eyes dulled by drink and endless death.

He sees one of the soldiers, a man with whom he and Otto had shared many a conversation upon the gun deck: a professional soldier from Utrecht. Looks past them to the other little boat. Spots another of the soldiers from the *Batavia*, quietly giving orders to the rabble of men. Recalls his name. Wouter, was it not? A clever gentleman from a good family brought low by bad investments. He had become a soldier because his family could not afford for him to take his place at university. He speaks good Latin, from what Nicolaes can recall about their brief interaction.

Crafted himself a little chess set from the wood of a broken wine barrel. Now he is understudy to the devil.

'My dear fellow,' says Cornelisz, slightly out of breath from the walk up the rocky rise. 'How it pains me to see you so dishevelled. You – the heroic knight who left to find water for our merry band. My I remember that goodly soul. Such a handsome and straight-backed soldier he could almost have been mistaken for a gentleman. Come, let me clothe you as befits a true Dutch hero. I have brought the best wines. Moreover, I have brought some glittering gifts that might demonstrate my obligation to putting our disagreements behind us.'

Nicolaes moves down the slope, picking his way towards the men in red. Glances left and right to where the scrub hems the highest point of the beach, bone-white grasses and smudges of moss clinging to the rocks that obscure the view beyond the edge of the beach. He stops a dozen paces away from Cornelisz. Keeps his features inscrutable as the little man in the blood-red cloak greets him with a wide smile and a further bow, the feather in his stolen hat touching the ground and a spray of golden coins raining down from the brim. He straightens up as if expecting a round of applause.

Nicolaes cannot even bring himself to give a nod. He just looks at him: sizes him up, tries to make sense of this silly little creature, this serpent in human flesh. He glances at his hands. They are white as sugar, still stained orange at the fingertips. Nicolaes feels a flicker of surprise that they are not gloved in blood. Glances again at his scarred, delicate face and tries to find the devil in him. Tries to comprehend how such a man has presided over countless murders and inveigled his way into the hearts of men who could break him over their knee.

'I see your men have pikes,' says Cornelisz, wagging his finger. 'I would be grateful if they laid them down.'

Nicolaes glances at the hilt of his sword. Looks past him to the array of weapons wielded by the red-cloaks. Cornelisz sees him staring. Flicks out his tongue, a viper tasting the air. Slides his sword from its scabbard and holds it upright, the light glinting off the blade.

'I was ever a poor fencer.' Cornelisz smiles, stabbing the blade into the soft sand and leaning upon the hilt. 'I'm told this is a fine blade but I have used it for little other than slicing the fine salted beef upon which I dine most evenings.'

Nicolaes looks him up and down. Looks at the angle in which he has positioned his feet. It is a fighting stance, angled to parry and slash. 'You are trained with sword, sir?' asks Nicolaes, and is glad that his voice does not tremble or the pain in his throat constrict his voice.

Cornelisz nods, half smiling as he considers some distant memory. 'I was a student of the great Giraldo Thibault in Amsterdam,' he says, aware of the ridiculousness of the boast. 'Alas, I cannot claim proficiency. I enjoyed the atmosphere more than the sport. I have always tired quickly and I will confide that it sometimes seemed as though his classes were more to do with mathematics and geometry than the art of sticking the pointy end into an opponent's guts.'

Nicolaes licks his lips. Concurs. 'I once fought a man who had studied with Thibault. Near impossible to land a blow. He had an answer to every strike.'

'Indeed,' says Cornelisz, scraping his sword against a

shard of rock. A shellfish has attached itself to the skull-shaped hunk of stone. Cornelisz gives its removal and execution his full attention, prising it off the rock with the tip of the priceless sword. He looks up, his interest in killing or devouring the morsel entirely gone. 'And yet you stand before me. You survived the duel?'

'Oh yes,' says Nicolaes, taking a deep breath of salty air. He catches the reek of unwashed skin. Of blood. Of the high vinegary tang of fish guts; the mildew and sawdust of rotting linens. 'He didn't anticipate the kick in the bollocks or the pistol ball in the brain.'

Cornelisz gives a laugh; a high-pitched titter that causes Otto, at Nicolaes's side, to emit a little laugh of his own.

'Still chuckling, are you?' growls Stonecutter, pushing through the throng and looking hard at Otto. He has a sword at his waist, stuffed into a belt fashioned from fine white hair. 'Thought I'd knocked that out of you months back.'

'I still laugh when something's funny,' says Otto, moving forward. He spits onto the rock, a tooth clattering bloodily away. 'I'm laughing now. Laughing as I look at you in your red cloak. Tell me, did somebody have to explain where to put your arms? Does your master here dress you in a morning the way a noblewoman clothes her favourite little lapdog?'

Stonecutter grins at the insult. Slowly, he turns his gaze on Nicolaes. 'Knew you were wrong from the off. I'd give a year's wages to know what you really are.'

'What I really am?' asks Nicolaes. 'I'm a soldier. Shipwrecked, just like the rest of you. And I'm a man trying to keep as many of us alive as I can.'

'You're no fucking soldier,' says Stonecutter. 'You're a spy. Knew it as soon as I looked at you. English, most likely, working for those bastards we dealt with in the Moluccas. I've fought plenty of men like you. Hurt them. Killed men of every flag you can name. Killed savages too. I tell you this, we all look the same after the light's been snuffed out. The natives I skewered on bamboo poles in Banda didn't look much different to those rich English merchants at Amboyna – not after a few days exposed to the flies and the birds and the sun. And you'll look the same soon, pretty-boy.'

Nicolaes breathes out, slowly. Remembers a crypt beneath an English church and a rich widow offering him a fortune to kill the men who tortured and killed her husband. Marvels, idly, at the twists and turns that life has thrown him in the months since; at the way Providence has deposited him here, upon an island at the edge of the world, within killing distance of her enemy.

'You are lost in a pleasant memory, perhaps?' asks the under-merchant, staring at him. 'Considering happier times? I swear, it does me good to know that a true hero like yourself can display such fortitude. I feared that you would think my offer of parlay a mere ruse. You are clearly a man of stout heart – eager to believe that your betters are ever true to their word. That, my good Hayes, is genuinely touching.'

Nicolaes drags his focus away from Stonecutter. Behind him, the red-cloaks are fanning out. When he looks back at Cornelisz, the little apothecary is staring at him with an intensity that causes his skin to pucker into gooseflesh. He can feel a sudden presence inside his skull, as if a spider were scuttling around within his mind.

'This is how you speak to men with whom you would make peace?' asks Nicolaes, the hairs on his arms rising; a feeling of cold, certain dread stealing over his flesh. His voice sounds ethereal, far away.

'Fine men,' whispers Cornelisz, his voice a sibilant whisper. 'Fine men. Men of vision. Men of purpose.'

Nicolaes shakes his head. Tilts it, as if trying to pour dirty water from his ear. He can feel something colonising him, burrowing deep; some tick or parasite intent upon worming into the very centre of his being.

'Imagine what you could be,' whispers Cornelisz, his voice arriving in the very centre of his head. 'Imagine the power.'

Nicolaes chews on his cheek until he can taste blood. 'Power?' he asks, and his voice seems to stick in his throat. He coughs, his mouth filling with blood, his eyes beginning to water. Fights it. Fights *him*. 'Tell me, Cornelisz – if I join you will I too be allowed the honour of murdering women and children? Will I too be permitted to hack down unarmed men; the sick, the dying, cripples in their beds? Will I forego my soul for a handful of coin and the chance to wait in line for my turn with a communal wife?'

Cornelisz lets a slow smile spread across his face. 'You have heard of the pleasures I provide for my men? I am sure they will gladly share with a fine fellow such as you...' He stops, abruptly, his piercing, pearlescent gaze flicking to Otto and back to Nicolaes. Grins, hugely, showing neat, pointed teeth. 'Or perhaps the female form is not to your taste? Rest assured, there is a cabin boy of not more than fourteen years who could do with having his wildness tamed. Should you wish it, my man Zevanck here will lash him down as I did the good Lucretia last night. My she was a sweet fit. Fought until the last, but still she succumbed. Do you not find that is true of so many? All that fight and it all ends the same way. I hope you can see the lesson I am trying to teach you.'

Nicolaes looks down at the rocks. He feels cold, suddenly. Cold and bone-tired. He is an unarmed man; hungry and in poor health. He has no blade. No pistol. He faces too many opponents. Who did he think he was trying to fool? He could prosper under Cornelisz. He could be a man of influence and power. He could be as splendid as Buckingham himself. Was that not his destiny? Had he not always sought to be the agent of an unassailable leader. Cornelisz could be his new Buckingham. He could retreat to the shadows and emerge only to do those jobs that serve his master's purpose. He thinks upon the lives he has taken. Remembers dead eyes and warm blood and those final, crimson-flecked breaths upon his cheeks.

He looks at Cornelisz. Sees the triumph in eyes that gleam black with malice. Feels the creature in his skull uncoil, unwind, set to strike…

'Nicolaes,' hisses Otto, nudging him in the back. 'Give the order. Give the fucking order…'

And Nicolaes sees Cornelisz for what he truly is. Feels the creature in his mind scream with frustration as he witnesses again the frail, ridiculous specimen who wields a stolen sword and stands in boots that are too big for him, crowned with a hat held up with his ears. Sees the creature that Cornelisz has tried so hard to disguise.

'Enough!' growls Stonecutter, throwing open his cloak. 'Kill him. Kill him now!'

Nicolaes sees Cornelisz raise his hands to his own throat and scuttle backwards in alarm as Stonecutter lunges forward and raises a huge bloodied cutlass. Sees it slash downwards towards his own exposed neck. Sees the men behind him unsheathe their own weapons and surge forward, teeth bared, blades dazzling in the low morning light.

Nicolaes slips beneath the blade. Reaches behind him and pulls the nail from the twist of matted ponytail. Slams his fist into Stonecutter's belly, the six-inch planking nail gripped between his fingers. Feels the gout of hot blood spurt over his fist as he pulls the nail free of the gaping wound and rams it again and again into the big man's scarred chest.

'Now!' roars Otto, and Nicolaes throws himself backwards, landing hard upon the coral. Two pikes whistle past him. Two of the cadets are thrown backwards by the force of the impact; the nails puncturing their flesh, splitting bone, skewering their hearts.

'David!' squeals Cornelisz, gathering up his sword and swinging it wildly. 'Coenraat!'

Otto stoops to gather the little slingshot tucked beneath the rock at his feet. Whirls it about his head and looses a needle-sharp stone. It strikes the Utrecht soldier in the very centre of his skull, taking him off his feet as though kicked by a horse. A rain of rocks begins to tumble from the high ground. The other mutineers stop in fright as they look upon their dead comrades: spears sticking out of their twitching, dying bodies. Cover their heads as rocks and nails and shards of coral spill down from the sky. They look to Cornelisz as he fights with the air, his hat slipping down over his eyes, stumbling in his too-big boots, shrieking commands at his dying disciples as they jerk like landed fish.

'Nicolaes, stay down!' bellows Otto, pushing him roughly to the ground as a great crash of cannon fire erupts from the other vessel. Nicolaes feels sand and stone and coral rain down upon him. Feels something warm and wet upon his exposed skin. Looks up, his hair in his eyes, to see the cadet called Gsbert torn completely in two, his torso a mince of twisted flesh and mashed bones, his head collapsing into the bloody hole as he disassembles into a gory collection of bloodied limbs.

'Fire!' shouts Nicolaes, hauling himself upright. 'Fire!'

The men above the little rise pull themselves to their feet. Two dozen men, skeletal and half-starved, swinging their morning stars, hurling their pikes, lashing out with the hand-built slingshots: stones searing through the air as swift and true as pistol balls. He hears the roar as the men whip the canvas cover from the little stone fort and raise the catapult. As tall as a man, its vibrating ropes emit a high, keening song as the gale plucks at its tautness before the basket is loosed: a collection of stones, of rocks, shards of coral and scavenged metal, all tumbling in a lethal hail upon the occupants of the other vessel – its crew leaping into the suddenly bloody water in a riot of screams and curses.

Soundlessly, sleek as nightfall, the sharks slip beneath the waves. The screams that follow are pained. Inhuman. Mercifully brief.

Nicolaes hauls himself up just as Cornelisz frees himself

of the cape and hat and pulls his flintlocks from his shirt. He hisses at Nicolaes, teeth bared, blood upon his tongue.

'Back! Get back! I'll fire. I'll do it! I will…'

Nicolaes walks towards him, eyes on his, refusing to show fear as the Governor-General of Batavia's Graveyard points the pistol at his chest. He bears down upon him like an angry father displeased with a wayward son. Watches the apothecary's hand shake. Sees his nose begin to run, his lip trembling, pinking fluid running from the open sores upon his face. Sees him glance left and right for help, glimpsing the bodies of his men. Sees him watch his empire crumble. Sees the pain of his loss grip at his features and the tears spill pitifully down his cheeks. Hears him scream, a howl of rage and grief and fear. He straightens his arm. Squeezes the trigger.

Nicolaes knocks the pistol aside, the shot thudding into the corpse of Coenraat van Huyssen. Grabs the squealing little man by the shirt front and drags him close.

'You are not a god, Jeronimus. You are not a messiah. You are barely even a man. You are nothing. Nothing at all.'

Nicolaes looks down. Feels the blade pricking at his ribs. Stares into the milky eyeball of the kicking, squirming under-merchant. Shakes his head and slaps him, lightly with the palm of his hand. 'You don't kill, Jeronimus,' he says, slapping him again with the back of his hand. 'You don't do your own murders. You haven't the strength to take a life unless you have your poisons.' He slaps him hard, watching blood run from his burst lip. 'Go on. Push it in me. Push it right in and take your revenge.'

Cornelisz writhes in his grasp. Nicolaes hears the clatter

as he drops the silver-hilted knife. Screws up his features in scorn and slams his fist into the weeping little man's stomach. He crumples to the ground, curled up in a ball, unintelligible mutterings spilling from his lips – curses and oaths and pleas. Nicolaes looks down at him. Sees the stain spreading across his expensive silken hose as he pisses himself in fright.

'You all right? Wiebbe – you all right?'

Nicolaes turns, startled. Sees Otto, his face flecked with a mist of blood. He holds Cornelisz's sword.

Nicolaes gives a nod. Turns to face the sea. The last of the red-cloaks is launching the little yawl, dragging up survivors from the smashed craft as the sharks feast in the crimson waters. He sees Wouter dragging himself aboard. Sees Stonecutter, his fist pushed into the ragged holes in his chest, hauling upon an oar, his body leaking blood with each beat of his heart.

'There! On the horizon! Nicolaes, look!'

The men upon the hill see it too. See the *Sardam*: a perfect silhouette where the sea meets the sky. They see the rescue ship, heading full sail for Batavia's Graveyard.

'By Christ, Nicolaes... they have men, muskets... if they get there first...'

Nicolaes turns and waves to the men on the lip of the rise. Feels his heart hammering in his chest as he beckons them down. Watches as half a dozen of his strongest men run forward, holding the stolen skiff above their heads and making for the water.

'Bind him,' instructs Nicolaes, gesturing to where Cornelisz crawls, making his way over the sharp rocks towards the water, smeared in the blood of his dead mutineers. 'Don't let the men kill him. I swear, I'll come back with help.'

The skiff splashes down into the shallows and Nicolaes runs into the ocean, the cold engulfing him, bloody water surging into his mouth. He feels something thud against him – rough flesh and muscle – and has to fight the urge to scream as he imagines himself torn in two by the feasting sharks. He trips, falls, glimpses a red sleeve wrapped about a hunk of half-chewed meat, and suddenly strong hands are pulling him aboard and thrusting an oar into his hands.

And then he is rowing for his life – each pull an act of desperation. They must reach the ship before the mutineers. They must warn the rescue ship that the remaining mutineers are armed and intent upon seizing the ship.

Nicolaes channels his every ounce of strength into hauling at the oars. Feels the surf spray upon his back. Hears a shriek from nearby as a huge, black-eyed shark rises from the grey waters and chomps down messily upon one of the floating dead.

'Pull,' he screams. 'Pull!'

Glances over his shoulder and sees that they are gaining – every stroke bringing them closer to Wouter and his gaggle of murderous followers.

'They're turning away,' screams one of the mercenaries, pulling so hard at the oars that his eyes seem to stand out on stalks. 'They're turning for the island!'

Nicolaes turns and sees that the mutineers have realised they cannot keep ahead of the swift little craft. They are turning away, heading back to the island, intent upon gathering their treasures and cutting the throats of anybody willing to tell what has happened these past weeks.

Nicolaes stops rowing. Turns and glares up at the prow of the mighty VOC ship. Looks upon the gentleman who stands at the rail, telescope to his eye, clad in a purple cloak and with a fine feather jutting from his tall black hat.

Looks upon their rescuer.

Looks upon Francisco Pelsaert.

'Hayes! Hayes! Hayes!'

Slaps upon his back, hands lose themselves in raucous celebration, Nicolaes de Pelgrom finally gives in to tears.

37

She sits at the writing desk like a puppet put away between performances. She is a marionette with cut strings. Her skin is pale as swan feathers; her eyes two dark, perfect coins. She is dressed in the fine pinkish dress gifted her by the commandeur but it is too big for the shape she has withered down to. She is a child dressed in adult garb.

Now and again she pats at her cap, making minute adjustments to herself: tucking away the strands of hair that always used to free themselves and twist into a question mark upon her fine, unlined brow. That there is now no hair to adjust does not stop her fingers from performing the familiar gesture. Her hair came away in clumps when Pelsaert's personal servant was sent to tend to her in the quarters where she was gently deposited by two stout, unspeaking sailors. He cleaned her with hot water, soap and the finest silk cloths. Dabbed unguents upon her sores and ran a cut-throat razor over the downy hair upon her skin, skirting the bruises and abrasions without a word. She did not fight him. Let herself be manipulated and operated like a figurine as he washed her skin and trimmed her nails and plaited her lank and matted hair.

She does not remember him leaving. She can taste meat

and spices and her belly is no longer growling with hunger but she has no memory of eating. Nor does she remember moving to this little chair and positioning herself at the writing desk. There is creamy writing paper laid out for her and a fine quill rests in an ornate ink pot, but as yet she has not written a word. She has nobody to write to.

Of all the excruciating torments she has suffered these past months, she focuses only on one cold and gnawing pain. Focuses on Boudewijn. She did not weep when Pelsaert shared the grim tidings in the little shelter on High Island where he tended to her recuperation in between overseeing the interrogations, teasing out the truth of a conspiracy and massacre unparalleled in its scale. He told her of her husband as gently as he could, shame-faced at having to heap further torment upon one who has suffered so much. Boudewijn was dead, he said, softly. He had been dead even before she left Amsterdam.

Her reaction was not tears. Indeed, she recalls a moment of unstoppable laughter bursting forth from her cut and swollen lips. Suddenly it all seemed so unceasingly ridiculous. She has written to a dead man these past months, has journeyed to the far end of the world to be reunited with a man who died of fever in the same week that their last living child had succumbed. The man to whom she reached out during her abasement and subjugation lies buried in a distant slave port. The letters he wrote her arrived at the Company headquarters a week after they left Texel.

She looks at the page again. Wonders whether it would be blasphemy to write a prayer when she has spent so many of these past days cursing God.

She hears footsteps outside the cabin. Hears raised voices

and a sudden peal of merriment: two men making fun of one another in the little lamp-lit corridor. She flinches at the sound. On the island, laughter was not a sound of happiness but a gleeful response to an opportunity to do violence. Her defilement was always conducted in front of a crowd of laughing, baying men. Each murder she witnessed was met with the snorts and full-throated chuckles of the Blood Council.

She wonders, quietly, whether she died upon Batavia's Graveyard. She feels more spectre than a living, breathing thing. It is only the pain that assures her she is still flesh and blood. The lashes upon her back would not heal. She was forced to endure stitches. She tore them during one of her night-time hallucinations and had to undergo ever more painful needlework at the clumsy fingers of the *Sardam*'s barber-surgeon. She feels as though her back is a tapestry – her skin stretched too tight over her bones.

She hears a creak at the door. Flinches. She hopes that it is Hayes. He has not been permitted to visit with her since they boarded the *Sardam*. He has been promoted to sergeant and is being feted by the crew as a true hero but he is still too lowly a rank to be permitted before the mast. She hears a rattly cough from beyond the door. Closes her eyes and steels herself before bidding him enter.

Commandeur Pelsaert is much reduced. He is still clad in the finery of a man of wealth and influence but the sickness that beset him aboard the *Batavia* worsened during the hellish voyage aboard the lifeboat. He shows some of the symptoms of malaria but Lucretia senses the apothecary's hand in his continuing ailments. She wonders what vials and potions the little serpent poured into the commandeur's wine those many nights. Wonders how long it will be before he succumbs to whatever poisons fester in his blood.

'Lucretia,' says Pelsaert, reaching out to steady himself on the doorframe. He looks every bit as ill as she does. Sweat greases his thin, sunken face and he wears his astrakhan cape like a sick old woman wrapped in a blanket. He does not wear his hat and his hair has lost much of its colour. He looks old and sick and weak.

'You are well, Francisco?' she asks, her voice not much more than a breath. 'It is done.'

He moves further into the room. Looks at the bed with a desperate longing. He seems too frail to stand.

'Please, Francisco. Please be seated.'

He staggers to the bed, gratefully. Produces a silk handkerchief and dabs at his brow. Closes his eyes for what seems like an age as he gathers his wits.

'The boy wept as we sailed away,' he says, his mouth dry. 'The other one, Wouter, the soldier. He took it for the kindness it was intended to be. The boy acted as he did throughout the trial. I cannot help but think I have done him a disservice in permitting him to live. The monster in that boy has long since devoured any trace of goodness.'

Lucretia readjusts herself upon the chair. Thinks, fleetingly, of the cabin boy. Pictures the feral creature who hunted men, women, children, all the while begging for a chance to slit throats and open bellies, crying out to devils and demons with whom he longed to do battle. He and Wouter have been spared the hangman's noose and instead been marooned upon some wild, unknown shore. They have been given brandy and a little bread and a few trinkets with which to barter among any natives they may encounter. Wouter had been grateful for the mercy until he learned that he was to be accompanied by the cabin boy.

'I fancy they will each kill the other before any savages stumble upon them,' mutters Pelsaert, half to himself. He looks up, hooded eyes filling with sadness as he looks upon Lucretia. He has been ceaseless in his apologies since her liberation. She has been gracious in her acceptance. And yet there is a gulf between them that will never be forded. He left her. He may not have known what Cornelisz was until he returned with the *Sardam*, but he did not take her with him in the longboat. He endured hardships of his own during those long weeks upon the sea, his life in the hands of the very man who had plotted his downfall. And yet Skipper Jacobsz achieved some semblance of redemption as he navigated the small craft to Batavia.

None of the men or women aboard were lost. Even the baby delivered aboard the *Batavia* still lived when they finally reached the fortress. That Jacobsz had steered them to a safe harbour did little to appease Pelsaert. When he reported to the governor-general about the wreck of the VOC's flagship, he made sure to relay the information that Zwaantie had whispered in his ear on those nights in the longboat. As her lover slept, she and Pelsaert warmed one another beneath his cloak. She told him of the planned mutiny. Told him that Jacobsz had deliberately hit the reef and had engineered the attack on Lucretia to incite mutiny among the men.

Jacobsz was dragged from his sick bed by VOC musketeers and hauled to the fortress dungeons. Pelsaert was given immediate command of the *Sardam* and ordered to return to the archipelago to retrieve whatever goods were still in the hold and any men who survived.

'I hear him still,' says Pelsaert, talking to the floor, his throat constricted. 'He meant to go on, Lucretia. Had we cut his bonds I swear he would have declared a fresh war upon all goodly men. I do not believe he ever sought to leave the islands. He had his kingdom and ruled it as he saw fit. It was his world without sin – a paradise for those with nothing in their hearts but black malice and greed.'

Lucretia suppresses a shudder as she thinks again of his weeping, scarred skin against hers. Shakes her head as her mind fills with recollections of that perfectly black eye, dead and passionless, inches from hers: Zevanck looking away out of sheer embarrassment as his Messiah rutted ineffectually between her legs; his member flopping flaccidly the moment she looked upon him. He wept when he finally mounted her. Sobbed against her like a scalded child. She hopes he saw her in his mind's eye as the rope tightened about his neck. Hopes her laughter rang in his ears as he dangled from the noose.

'We shall be in Batavia within the week,' says Pelsaert, cautiously. 'Time, I hope, for you to recover some of your strength. You will wish to be well recovered before embarking for the Provinces.'

Lucretia wrinkles her nose. Shrugs – an action she would never have imagined of herself upon the Heerenstraat. 'I have nowhere to go, Francisco. Besides, I do not wish to be pointed at in the street when word of my evil reaches Amsterdam.'

'Lucretia, there are none who believe…'

'They believe it, Francisco,' she snaps. 'You heard those

other women. Women whom I cared for, nursed, did my best to protect. They say I colluded with Cornelisz. That I was Eve to his Adam. That I gave myself to him willingly in order for better treatment. For luxuries and trinkets.' She screws up her eyes, refusing to let the tears fall. 'Perhaps I shall stay in Batavia for a time. They say it is a kingdom where somebody may begin again.'

Pelsaert stares again at the floor, his whole manner dejected. 'It is a place where a man may lose everything,' he says. 'Had you but seen the manner in which Governor-General Coen looked upon me! I had heard tales of his temper but I imagined myself about to be run through and my head mounted upon the castle walls! He has done much worse, Lucretia. Why even as I sought to regain my strength before returning to the *Batavia* he was ordering the execution of his own ward's lover and threatening to have her killed alongside him. Were it not for the apothecary I would declare him the worst man of my acquaintance.'

They sit in silence, each lost in their own thoughts.

'His hand was severed?' asks Lucretia, at last. 'I find it hard to imagine that he bled red.'

Pelsaert nods. 'There was a line of volunteers begging for opportunity to sever that wretched hand at the wrist. Among them were his own men. They all turned on him, at the last. All gave testimony that it was he who planned the mutiny, he who ordered the attack upon you. He who commanded the butchery of one hundred and sixty men, women and children.' He shakes his head, his eyes glazing over as he stares at nothing. A bead of sweat runs over his greasy cheek. Spills from his beard as he shakes his head. 'His last words were *"revenge, revenge"*,' he says, emotionlessly. 'As the noose went about his neck he cried out that there was no God but him. That these were his lands, he was the one true Messiah – that he had yet to complete his work and that all who wronged him would suffer an eternal torment. We sailed away before he breathed his last. None could watch.'

Lucretia nods. Smooths her dress. Looks again at the plain paper and black ink.

'Was it Hayes who took his hand?' she asks.

Pelsaert gives a little smile. 'He turned down the honour. Gave it to his friend, the cheerful young soldier whom I have elevated in the ranks. He did the deed without revelling in it. Took hammer and chisel to the apothecary's wrist and bandaged the stump without a word.'

'Did he scream?' asks Lucretia, fire flashing in her eyes. 'Did he beg for life?'

'Begged until he realised his entreaties were upon deaf ears. Then his vengeance spilled out like blood.'

'And his men?'

'We have executed the ringleaders on the island. There are some who have begged to be thrown upon the mercy of the governor-general in Batavia. I fancy they do not know the man. Their deaths will be brutal – even those who claim they only committed murder through fear of their own deaths.'

'And the predikant?'

Pelsaert looks away. 'His daughter is with child. Perhaps it can be a joyous event.'

Lucretia closes her eyes. If Pelsaert sees her rub her own slightly swollen belly, he does not show it.

They sit in silence for a time. Neither wants to leave

the cabin. Neither wants to let the world flood this small, manageable space.

'Zwaantie,' says Lucretia, at last. 'She is imprisoned alongside her lover?'

Pelsaert scratches his forehead. Grimaces as if in pain. 'She, too, was taken to the dungeons to be interrogated about the events aboard ship. I spoke up for her, as a good Christian should. Governor-General Coen had no such mercy.'

'She has been interrogated? Please, Francisco, tell me what part she played in these evil deeds. I fancy that I understand and then my senses are whipped away as I think upon some other explanation. Was she victim or villain?'

Pelsaert picks a hair from his cape. Looks way, embarrassed. 'She was not long a prisoner.'

Lucretia's eyes widen. 'She perished?'

'No,' he says, quietly. 'Her jailer was easily manipulated.'

'Speak plain, Francisco...'

'She escaped, Lucretia. I fancy now as I did from the very beginning, that girl was no maid. I fear she played her own game from the beginning.'

Lucretia glares at him. Sees the truth in his embarrassed little grin. She seduced him like she seduced every other man who could help her. Used what she had at her disposal. Made men weak with desire even as they believed her to be their plaything and sport.

'The treasures,' she asks, at last. 'You recovered sufficient to restore some standing?'

Pelsaert shrugs. All he believed of himself has been swept away. He fancies he is dying. Fancies that whatever comes next, history will remember him as the commander of a crew who mutinied, who abandoned his crew and passengers after a shipwreck, and who left his underling to commit scores of murders while establishing his own private kingdom. All he has left is his own sense of what is proper.

Painfully, he hauls himself to his feet. Apologises, once more, and leaves without another word.

Lucretia looks at the space he has occupied. Looks upon what he has left for her upon the silks.

The jewels glitter in the light of the candle. Rubies. Emeralds. Golden coins.

She closes her eyes and says a quiet, intimate prayer.

Picks up the quill.

Begins to write.

EPILOGUE

The Fortress of Batavia, Java

November 8, 1629

The heat hangs like damp linens, tangling the soldiers and sailors in its cloying folds. There is little breeze, even here, at the water's edge. The great mass of the towering fortress serves as a windbreak of sorts, blocking out any whisper of breeze that manages to slip past the vessels moored in the still, blue harbour. To the rear of the fortress is thick jungle: an oppressive, bristling shadow upon which the mighty VOC castle imperiously turns its back.

Nicolaes de Pelgrom loiters between a pile of stacked crates, enjoying the chaotic sounds of trade and struggle and life. He should already have slipped his way out of Batavia, but he cannot resist one last glance at his brothers in arms. He is dressed in civilian clothes; a comfortable linen shirt keeps him reasonably cool but his skin still chafes when he hoists his canvas bag upon his shoulder. He fancies his skin will forever be sensitive to light. Fancies, too, that the chill he picked up aboard the *Sardam* is creeping into his weakened bones. Although he perspires he trembles from time to time, shuddering as if something multi-legged and primal had stalked across his spine.

He leans his head against the crate, removing his simple cloth cap to wipe the grease from his brow. Watches the parade. The crowd assembled to greet the men of the *Sardam* and the *Batavia* seem unsure of how to react to this ragged stream of half-starved men. They seem tempted to hurl rocks, but the new governor-general had made it clear that this was to be a celebration of a true triumph. Pelsaert had recovered a fortune in treasures from the sunken flagship and had succeeded in crushing a rebellion led by his murderous underling. Pelsaert made sure that his own account of the past weeks was the only one that reached the eyes of the Company's senior men. He tarried at sea aboard the *Sardam*, dressing himself in his most exquisite finery, while exchanging correspondence with his own network of merchants and traders ashore.

It came as a surprise to learn that Governor-General Coen was dead, succumbing to fever only a matter of days after the *Sardam* left upon its rescue mission. He has been replaced by the even more formidable Jacques Specx. If nothing else, the new man is at least a pragmatist and has seen the wisdom in treating the mutiny, shipwreck and massacre as an opportunity for celebration – fixing it as such in the minds of the populous before the truth of the matter reaches the Gentlemen XVII.

Nicolaes looks up at the sound of a sudden cheer. Stares through a mesh of wicker baskets and coiled ropes; of bellowing cattle and stacked sails. Sees the prisoners being dragged ashore. Stonecutter still walks with a straight back, snarling at the men who line the quay. They are bakers, tailors, coopers, sailcloth-makers. Were it any ordinary day they would be doing a brisk trade with the men of any newly docked ship. Today they wave their arms and cheer the soldiers who put down an insurrection.

Nicolaes watches as a small man with dark hair picks up something from the dusty ground and hurls it at the roped-together men. Something hard strikes Stonecutter upon the brow and he bellows a challenge into the crowd. The nearest musketeer, splendid in his VOC finery, hits him in the jaw with the butt of his musket, to the sound of a great cheer from the men. He squints at those who gather him up. Recognises Salomon Deschamps, the officious little notary who served Pelsaert for almost a decade. He is a Company man, a true servant of the Provinces. And Jeronimus Cornelisz made him kill a child with his own hands to prove his fealty to the mutineers. Sentence has already been passed.

Those who begged to be given a chance to appear before the governor-general rather than die alongside Cornelisz have discovered that they chose the wrong option. Their executions will not be swift. Stonecutter, who survived the interrogations on the island for longer than any of the other men, is to be broken; his limbs smashed with mallets and threaded through the spokes of a cartwheel. His slow death will be observed by all within the fortress and his screams heard far out to sea. The Company will make an example of him.

Nicolaes spots a familiar face. Smiles, a little sadly. For

a time he imagined becoming Wiebbe Hayes. He enjoyed being hailed as a true swashbuckling hero and cannot help but feel a little proud at being twice promoted. He is now official, an ensign in the Army of the VOC. Were he to continue to wear the colours he would doubtless be given his pick of postings and all manner of handsome rewards. But he has lived enough lies. He is not Wiebbe Hayes. He is a man of low birth whom Providence has thrown like dice.

For a time, he would like to see who he becomes when he finally sheds the numerous skins of other men. Eventually, he fancies he will take passage back to Europe, but he is in no rush. He has no little sum of purloined silver in his coin purse and two handsome gold rings glitter on the fingers of his right hand. Even so, he has a bounty to collect. He put men in the ground for Mrs Towerson and though he killed neither the resurrected van Speult, or Governor-General Coen, or even the torturer of Amboyna, Stonecutter Pietersz, he fancies he has fulfilled his commission and would be within his rights to seek payment.

'He makes a fine figure, does he not, my handsome friend?'

The voice comes from behind him, low and sensual and earthy. He does not turn. Just smiles as he watches Otto file past, chin jutting forward, head back, musket upon his shoulder and a great beaming grin upon his face. Their goodbyes were tender; whispered assurances of friendship and promises to meet again. He feels a warm wave of fondness in his belly as he looks upon his friend. Knows, to his very bones, that Otto will never tell anybody where the hero of the *Batavia* disappeared to in the hours before the *Sardam* arrived at the docks.

'I understand that Governor-General Coen has succumbed to fever,' says Nicolaes, quietly.

He senses movement behind him. Smells perfume and arrack, sweat and sex. Feels Zwaantie appear at his side. She has eaten well these past weeks. Her skin has darkened and she suits native dress, her hair concealed beneath folds of fine soft cloth and her bare feet jutting from the hem of an elegant, multi-coloured dress. Her dark eyes sparkle as she gives him a little nod. He looks at her with his peripheral vision, checking her shapely outline for weapons. Spies the curved dagger in the sash that wraps around her waist.

'He didn't go gently,' says Zwaantie, with a little smile. 'Eyes bulging, tongue sticking out like invisible hands were pulling him inside out!' She makes a face, mimicking the final moments of the dying governor-general. 'It was Cornelisz's own vial that did for him. It kept Pelsaert just sick enough but a healthy dose, well, it can bring about the most excruciating of deaths. It seems foolish to employ a male food taster, does it not? Men in positions of authority seem so very malleable. Truly, men will do anything when their prick is in your hand – even turn a blind eye as a stranger serves their master his wine.'

Nicolaes turns his head. Looks upon the assassin who has been with him every step of the journey from Amsterdam. 'You've heard? What the apothecary did on the islands?'

Zwaantie purses her lips. 'I knew him for a bad man. I did not think him evil. Perhaps that is all evil is, eh? A word for the darkness that emerges when opportunity truly presents itself. Perhaps if it had not been for circumstance he would have lived an unremarkable life.'

Nicolaes gives her his full attention. 'Has she paid up yet?'

She nods. 'She's up there, somewhere. Watching from beneath a parasol, delighting in all this. Everybody she wants dead is dead, save for Stonecutter, and by Christ she'll enjoy watching him breathe his last.'

'And van Speult? Aboard the *Assendelft*? He was dead when I got there. All the wriggling I did to lose myself among the crew for long enough to reach his cabin and all for naught.'

'Nobody suspects a buxom little servant girl, Nicolaes,' she says, flashing her white teeth. 'I'll confess his death was not a pretty one. I swear I had his fat sweaty face twixt my thighs for an age before I felt him breathe his last.'

Nicolaes scratches at his face. He has shaven his beard into a neat triangle and pointed moustache, and is again looking like the man whom the Duke of Buckingham wielded like a blade. He can see Zwaantie admiring him, though he does not revel in her appreciation. She has beguiled every man she has needed to. Placed herself close to powerful and influential men and done whatever she has needed to in order to survive. She has taken the lives of all those responsible for the Amboyna outrage without ever arousing suspicion. She has done what Nicolaes de Pelgrom was sent to do, and done it far better than he could ever have imagined.

'You are Lady Towerson's other assassin, I presume,' he says, watching as Lucretia glides past upon a golden palanquin carried by four broad, bare-chested local men. 'Her safety net lest I fail?'

Zwaantie laughs, full-bodied and earthy. 'Oh Nicolaes,

no. You were the safety net, my friend. She had no doubts in my own ability to do that which was required but she required the assent of King Charles in order for the executions to proceed. Villiers secured that permission for her but asked a favour in return.'

Nicolaes rests against the crate. Feels the sweat upon his brow and the chill across his back. He has known Zwaantie as a charlatan since he first saw her at the dockside with Lucretia. Something about her manner had reminded him of his own skewed reflection. In her, he had seen a character that was all affectation and performance. Had seen himself. He knows already what she will tell him. Has known ever since Villiers sent him to that little church on the outskirts of London and sold him into the service of the grieving widow Towerson.

'He wanted rid of me? Wanted me out of the way?'

Zwaantie puts a warm palm upon his arm. Squeezes. Looks at him with brown eyes that seem full of genuine regret. 'Perhaps it was an order given out of love. He was the most hated man at court. He could tell the end was coming and wanted you well placed to prosper.'

Nicolaes looks away, watching the gannets circling in the blue sky. 'Perhaps,' he says.

Zwaantie cocks her head. 'You don't have to tell me, but was he really your uncle? Perhaps even your father?'

Nicolaes sighs. Shakes his head. 'They bedded a tavern-keeper's daughter in Leiden – I heard that story from the keeper of the almshouse where I was brought up. I know they left a locket as payment. I fancied they wouldn't remember the incident – just two young men rutting their way around Europe. I became the product of that encounter.

I think George saw through my lies as soon as I spoke them but he was impressed with my guile for trying to swindle my way into the good graces of a great English family. And he turned me into what I am.'

Zwaantie rests her head upon his shoulder, breathing out slowly. 'There'll be no more coin from the widow Towerson,' she says, sadly. 'It's been claimed.'

Nicolaes nods, his chin against the damp cloth around her crown. 'You deserve it,' he says, and means it.

'Lucretia,' she asks, after a moment's pause. 'I did not wish it. Not for a moment.'

Nicolaes does not speak. He senses she would like him to offer some word of forgiveness. Cannot find it in him.

'You are a gentle soul,' says Zwaantie, a smile in her voice. She gestures to the tail end of the procession. The predikant, sallow-faced and dead-eyed, bumbles along muttering to himself, his daughter clutching at his elbow. They flinch with every raised voice.

'Had I known…' begins Zwaantie, shaking her head. 'Had I thought him capable of such evil…'

'You would still have gone on the lifeboat,' finishes Nicolaes. 'We would all have gone on the lifeboat if we could.'

'You stayed. I saw you helping people down, shielding the women with your body as the waves crashed down. I saved my own skin and sucked the skipper's prick until he allowed me to accompany him here.'

Nicolaes smiles. 'You are very good at what you do, milady,' he says, with a little bow. 'Might I presume that Skipper Jacobsz has yet to work out who has shared his bed these many months?'

She rubs her jaw, remembering a harsh blow to the cheek that she cannot leave unavenged. 'He'll have a long time to work it out. He is to be put to the question. Interrogated over his part in the mutiny. Perhaps at the last he will realise that he was ever a pawn in the plans of wiser minds.'

'Men like Cornelisz?' asks Nicolaes, smiling as she moves against him.

'Women like me,' she whispers, and he feels her slip her hand into his.

They stay hidden among the chests and crates and coils of rope until the procession has gone by, until the final chants of 'Hayes, Hayes, Hayes!' have disappeared over the perfect blue water and away over the shimmering horizon.

Eventually, he knows he will have to let go of her hand.

Eventually, he will have to stop clutching her palm and breathing her in and feeling so damnably, giddily at peace.

Eventually, he is quite sure, he will tell himself it is folly to offer his sword and his services to this woman who has no need of him.

But, for now, there is no rush.

About the Author

DAVID MARK spent more than fifteen years as a journalist, including seven years as a crime reporter with the *Yorkshire Post*. His writing is heavily influenced by the court cases he covered: the defeatist and jaded police officers; the competent and incompetent investigators; the inertia of the justice system and the sheer raw grief of those touched by savagery and tragedy. He writes the McAvoy series, historical novels and psychological suspense thrillers. *Dark Winter* was selected for the Harrogate New Blood panel (where he was Reader in Residence) and was a Richard & Judy pick and a *Sunday Times* bestseller.

He has also written for the stage, for a Radio 4 drama (*A Marriage of Inconvenience*) and has contributed articles and reviews to several national and international publications. He is a regular performer at literary festivals and also teaches creative writing. David also starts to get all squirmy and self-conscious when he looks at stuff like this, so we'll leave it there.

@davidmarkwriter
www.davidmarkwriter.co.uk